BY ALAN DEAN FOSTER

The Black Hole
Cachalot
Dark Star
The Metrognome and Other Stories
Midworld
Nor Crystal Tears
Sentenced to Prism
Star Wars®: Splinter of the Mind's Eye
Star Trek® Logs One–Ten
Voyage to the City of the Dead
. . . Who Needs Enemies?
With Friends Like These . . .
Mad Amos
The Howling Stones
Parallelities
Quofum
Exceptions to Reality

THE ICERIGGER TRILOGY

Icerigger
Mission to Moulokin
The Deluge Drivers

THE ADVENTURES OF FLINX OF THE COMMONWEALTH

For Love of Mother-Not
The Tar-Aiym Krang
Orphan Star
The End of the Matter
Bloodhype
Flinx in Flux
Mid-Flinx
Flinx's Folly
Flinx Transcendent

THE DAMNED

Book One: A Call to Arms
Book Two: The False Mirror
Book Three: The Spoils of War

THE FOUNDING OF THE COMMONWEALTH

Phylogenesis
Dirge
Diuturnity's Dawn

FLINX TRANSCENDENT

FLINX
TRANSCENDENT

A PIP & FLINX ADVENTURE

ALAN DEAN FOSTER

BALLANTINE BOOKS • NEW YORK

Flinx Transcendent is a work of fiction. Names, characters, places, and incidents are the products of the author's imagination or are used fictitiously. Any resemblance to actual events, locales, or persons, living or dead, is entirely coincidental.

Published in the United States by Del Rey, an imprint of The Random House Publishing Group, a division of Random House, Inc., New York.

DEL REY is a registered trademark and the Del Rey colophon is a trademark of Random House, Inc.

LIBRARY OF CONGRESS CATALOGING-IN-PUBLICATION DATA
Foster, Alan Dean.
Flinx transcendent : a Pip and Flinx adventure / Alan Dean Foster.
p.   cm.
ISBN 978-0-345-49607-2 (alk. paper)
1. Humanx Commonwealth (Imaginary organization)—Fiction.
2. Flinx (Fictitious character)—Fiction.   3. Pip (Fictitious character : Foster)—Fiction.   I. Title.
PS3556.O756F575 2009
813'.54—dc22   2009006476

Printed in the United States of America on acid-free paper

www.delreybooks.com

2 4 6 8 9 7 5 3 1

FIRST EDITION

To the friends of Flinx and Pip, who have
waited patiently (okay, sometimes not so patiently)
for more than a third of a century to see him finally
get some closure. The three of us thank you.

ABU THE THIEF: *"You've got what you want. Now I'm going to get what I want."*

PRINCE AHMAD: *"What's that?"*

ABU: *"Some fun and adventure, at last!"*

—THE THIEF OF BAGHDAD, 1940

FLINX TRANSCENDENT

CHAPTER

1

Insofar as he knew, Flinx was the first unofficial, uninvited representative of his species to set foot on the AAnn homeworld of Blasusarr. Very few humans and even fewer thranx had ever been formally accredited to do so. Only the minimum number essential to facilitate those few diplomatic exchanges where electronic representations were insufficient and face-to-face conversation was demanded had ever been allowed actual physical access. The idea that a single human operating entirely on their own might somehow succeed in penetrating the elaborate and extensive defenses that redundantly englobed Blasusarr was sufficiently ludicrous to promulgate all by itself entirely new orders of cognitive absurdity. Everyone knew that no non-AAnn ship could so much as approach the outskirts of the homeworld system without being challenged—or blown to bits.

However, the AAnn scientists and engineers who had designed and built those impressive planetary defense systems had never envisioned a ship like the *Teacher*. But then, neither had anyone else.

The energetic and enthusiastic Ulru-Ujurrians, using all of their exponentially developing skills, imbued the entire body of Flinx's vessel with a chameleonic ability. The ship could so completely transform its appearance that one moment it could present the perfect likeness and detection signature of a private passenger craft, and the next that of a heavily armed military escort. Now settled in unobtrusive orbit around the AAnn homeworld, it displayed the convincing aspect of a minor clan AAnn cargo vessel. Furthermore, it was not the only persuasive transformation to have taken place in that vicinity. There was also the elaborate and difficult provisional makeover Flinx had devised for himself.

So accomplished was the result that he had been on Blasusarr for a local *teverravak,* or sixteen days, without drawing more than the occasional casual glance. Perfectly fashioned though it was, the simsuit that enveloped him completely would have been inadequate to sustain the ruse had he not been so knowledgeable in the ways of the quasi-reptilians among whom he moved. He knew how to emulate the loping AAnn gait, which involved bending slightly at the knees and invigorating each step with a slight hopping motion; was intimately familiar with their eloquent repertoire of communicative hand gestures; could eat their food (though the profoundly carnivorous diet was beginning to have adverse effects on his waistline); and, through the use of tiny but powerful integrated servos lodged in the suit's hindquarters, was even able to satisfactorily manipulate its integrated lightweight tail. Built-in nanoneuromatics operated the suit's double eyelids. Having to view the world through their slitted pupils somewhat restricted his peripheral vision, but the result was more than adequate. He saw everything that threatened to trip him.

Thus camouflaged and experienced, he passed freely if cautiously among his unknowing hosts, the loose spaces and the specially constructed sleeping pocket within the suit providing ample room for Pip to both rest and move about while retaining a certain amount of freedom.

Not even the operators of the subsurface transient burrow where Flinx had rented living space suspected that he was anything but a nye: a fully mature adult AAnn. Utilizing a mastery of his hosts' language that was rare among his kind, while keeping conversation to a minimum, he found himself accepted by his fellow burrow-dwellers as one of their own. He even took care to make appropriate use of the sand room in his quarters, remembering before departing each day to leave the suitably scaly impression of his simsuit on the heated surface.

Thankfully, the suit's thermosensitive cooling system was up to the task of coping with Blasusarr's demanding climate. The AAnn had evolved on a desert world. While Flinx normally would have had no trouble tolerating the dry forty-degree heat, any other kind of completely enclosed suit would have rendered it unbearable. Cocooned within its technologically advanced confines he stayed cool and reasonably comfortable, and could do most anything an AAnn could do without revealing his human identity. Eating, drinking, and voiding were the chief exceptions. He sustained his masquerade by making sure to perform such necessary functions only in private and under carefully controlled conditions.

The capital city of Blasusarr and therefore the entire AAnn empire, Krrassin was an immensely spread-out metropolis of long, low buildings punctuated only by the occasional unavoidable tower. While humans favored the view to be had from on high and the thranx chose where possible to cluster together belowground, the AAnn, having evolved from burrow-ambush predators, still preferred to live and work just below and just above the surface. The ideal AAnn dwelling was one partially subterranean but featuring long, narrow windows that provided a view exactly at ground level. In a city the size of Krrassin such panoramas were scarce and available only to the most privileged. Those forced to live high above the ground or deep below the surface had to make do with virtual visuals.

Having mastered their harsh environment, the majority of AAnn spent the bulk of their waking hours living and working within the vast interconnected warren that was the Great Burrow of Krrassin. Those who ventured outside on foot did so on external pedestrian walkways that, following tradition, crisscrossed the city in a succession of sweeping, concentric S-curves.

It was down one such gently curving avenue that Flinx presently found himself strolling. He kept to the extreme right or the left, avoiding the center path that was reserved for those citizens who wished to engage in ceremonial aggression; whether for purposes of social interaction, the striving for upward mobility that motivated all AAnn, or as a preliminary to deeper and more personal interrelationships that extended to but did not necessarily include procreation.

Sometimes several fights were in progress at the same time. It was not unusual for these to involve members of both sexes. Only rarely did they draw the attention of the preoccupied passersby who kept to the concord walks that flanked the contested middle walkway. The majority of these confrontational encounters were highly ritualized, though actual physical contact was common enough. By walking the center path and facing up to come what may, be it hostile, sexual, or social, combatants acquired status. Such status was recorded and cumulative. It was one very public way an individual AAnn could rise within the social order without being born into an aristocratic family. As he strove to blend ever deeper into AAnn society Flinx often scrutinized such confrontations with intense interest. It was good that he did.

Because on his eleventh day on Blasusarr the forcefully side-switching tail of a carelessly hurrying worker accidentally jostled Flinx off the left-hand walkway and straight onto the always contentious, ever challenging Middle Path.

Unlike the wide and winding pedestrian avenues that flanked it to left and right, the center core was not paved, unless one counted as pavement the expertly stylized and sterilized sand that had been imported to fill the gently meandering, slightly depressed four-meter-wide walkway. Flinx's clawed, sandal-shod AAnn "feet" slipped slightly in the soft sand as he fought to recover his footing. In the process they smeared the intricate whorls, ripples, and other imaginative patterns both traditional and contemporary that automated preprogrammed sand-grooming machinery incised anew every morning for the enjoyment and edification of passing nye. Recovering his balance as he straightened, he prepared to step back onto the right-side concourse.

Only to find his way blocked.

The lightly clad, iridescently scaled challenger was male, his stance unapologetically belligerent. Like any other nye one was likely to encounter on the Middle Path, he was looking for trouble. Were he not, he would have been striding along on the peaceful left or right walk and not in the sand-filled center. Flinx immediately tensed. At least his antagonist was not an aroused female looking to partner. The ingenious simsuit Flinx wore could replicate many aspects of AAnn physical behavior, but reptiloid intercourse was not one of them.

It was to be straightforward physical confrontation then. To what end and what degree he had yet to find out. Within the suit he could feel Pip's coils contracting around his shoulder as she sensed and responded to her master's heightened anxiety. Controlling his emotions, he did his best to calm her. Having to restrain her while he was engaged in combat was a complication he had learned how to deal with as a child. How difficult it was going to be on this particularly dangerous occasion depended largely on his adversary's intentions. With no status at risk Flinx was perfectly content to let his opponent triumph. The one thing he could *not* chance was damage to the concealing simsuit and subsequent revelation of his true identity. With luck and caution it would not come to that.

"Sspawn of Zithanitese," the big male hissed at him. The slur was accompanied by a gesture of third-degree contempt. Nothing too serious, Flinx decided as he analyzed the insult. It was too soon to relax, though. He had to respond appropriately and believably while ensuring that the confrontation did not escalate. He explored his considerable vocabulary of AAnn invective, seeking just the right balance between defiance and deference.

"Ssoured in the egg ssoundss ssuch," he retorted, upthrusting and bringing his simsuit-clad right arm around and down in a sweeping motion indicative of second-degree disrespect. It was an appropriately robust response, but not one so forceful as to invite the drawing of personal weaponry. As he swung his arm he was careful not to activate the sensors that would extend his simsuit's faux claws to the fullest.

Hissing scorn, tail switching from side to side in his excitement, the AAnn edged to his right. The attempt to get behind Flinx was blatant, executed deliberately and with no attempt at subtlety. His adversary wanted to prevail in the confrontation, Flinx saw, but not necessarily by having to pound his fellow citizen into the sand. Not that the AAnn would hesitate to do so if he thought it necessary.

Upon contact with the appropriate control, Flinx's servo-controlled false tail began to metronome in similar fashion, mimicking the back-and-forth swings of his opponent. That was about all the artificial appendage could do. If it came to an actual fight, the synthetic muscles that powered the fake extension were not strong enough to enable it to strike the challenger a serious blow. His antagonist's tail, Flinx knew, was considerably more flexible, and useful.

Parting his jaws, the AAnn flashed sharp teeth. Flinx responded in kind but could not open his mouth as wide lest its unnatural nature be revealed. Additionally, the limited exposure represented a ritual concession of sorts. His adversary promptly pounced on it.

"Your bite lackss sspirit. With ssuch ssmall biting one would sstarve. It would be a mercy to kill you before you die of hunger."

Though he badly wanted out of the confrontation, Flinx knew he could not concede so readily. To show such weakness would be to invite even greater insults—or worse, an actual beating. Under those circumstances he knew he would have no choice but to respond physically, though he might have difficulty restraining Pip from working her way clear of the simsuit in her eagerness to defend him.

"Otherss have tried. Otherss have died."

Bold words. The AAnn did not have to believe them, or try to test the truth of them. It was enough that the slightly awkward taller male sliding sideways across the sand had spoken them. Similar ritualized confrontations occurred by the thousands on the hundreds of identical Middle Paths that threaded their way through Krrassin, its suburbs, and across the length and breadth of Blasusarr. Their purpose was to provide a (usually) nonlethal means of regulating and fine-tuning status among energetic, upwardly mobile individuals, not to generate dozens of unproductive deaths.

Flinx could not fully display the simsuit's orthodontics, but he could at a touch of two sensors fully extend its synthesized claws. He did so now. But even as he revealed the simsuit's offensive bodyware he kept moving to his left and trying to circle around his opponent. How would the AAnn react? What degree of status did he seek to gain from the confrontation?

To Flinx's relief his adversary responded only with more words. Well-chosen words, to be sure, but far less dangerous than the headlong charge or scything hand swipe the simsuited human was preparing himself to counter.

"I do not resspond to sspittle with sslassh."

"Sso you ssay." Flinx reacted with acceptable neutrality.

The big male hissed once more and turned away. Without speaking another word he resumed striding down the Middle Path, looking for another fellow city dweller to confront. Flinx sensed his opponent's satisfaction. By being the one to state the initial challenge and subsequently forcing the other "AAnn" to choose between a fight or evading it, technically the nye had won the encounter. Flinx was more than happy to allow the combative male his triumph. The important thing was that actual combat had been avoided.

Busily making their way north and south along the properly paved flanking walkways, the rest of the pedestrian traffic had completely ignored the whole hissing, spitting, tooth-and-claw-displaying confrontation. As Flinx continued on his way, careful after his earlier unforeseen bump to hug the walls of low-lying buildings and avoid the Middle Path, he himself passed dozens of other, similar, Middle Walkway altercations. On one occasion he saw two females locked arm in arm, leg in leg, and tail in tail on the sand. Blood stained the intricately raked patterns on the ground beneath them. Along with his fellow preoccupied strollers, Flinx ignored the fight, which was far more serious than the one he had been involved in earlier. Such battles were routine.

In many ways this frequent daily physical conflict in search of standing and status was more honest than comparable confrontations among his own kind, he reflected as he strode along beneath the blistering sun. Which was more honest: gossiping and sniping about an enemy behind his back, or trying to rip the skin off said body part? The intended end was the same; only the cultural approach was different. Using both his eyes and his Talent he continued to investigate the AAnn who surrounded him.

Blasusarr. As dangerous a place in the galaxy as a representative of his species could find himself in. What he had already accomplished, by deliberately placing himself among humanxkind's mortal enemies and successfully surviving in their presence, was as far as he knew an unprecedented achievement.

When he had first voiced his intent to the *Teacher,* his ship had been appalled. It had objected strenuously. But it could not, even for what it believed to be his own good, go against its master's orders. So it had disguised itself appropriately, entered Imperial space, slipped into orbit around the AAnn homeworld, and deposited him via masked shuttle at a vast desert park outside the metropolis. Starting from there, the simsuit-clad Flinx had used his knowledge of AAnn language and culture to work his way into the city.

He had set himself the challenge partly because it was something no one else had ever done, partly because it was such an outrageous notion that no one had ever imagined trying it, and lastly because of what he had learned in the course of his previous sojourn on Gestalt: he no longer much cared what happened to him. If he survived his present enterprise, it was an accomplishment he could pass off with a shrug. If he failed, he would die, and that was no great loss either. Though it tried to argue him out of both the exploit and the depression that underlay it, the *Teacher* did not succeed. Now it drifted in veiled orbit, brooding and worrying about his day-to-day circumstances. It did not worry about itself, of course. Its intelligence was artificial, its worry programmed, its concern a function of a specific set of predetermined code.

Along with the *Teacher*'s shipmind, there were also certain active elements of the vessel's décor that worried about his health. They too were powerless to prevent him from embarking on what both their organic and inorganic minds were convinced was nothing less than a reckless jaunt.

Flinx's slide into increasingly irresponsible behavior had been accelerated enormously by what had happened to him and by what he had learned of his origins in the course of his recent visit to the frigid world of Gestalt. His lengthy, determined quest to find his father had ended in the revelation that such an individual did not and, in fact, never had existed. In discovering that half of his biological heritage consisted of nothing more than an impersonal concoction of designer proteins, artificially leveraged by indifferent scientists to produce a zygote that when matured would, they hoped, display certain interesting mental abilities, he had felt something fundamental drain out of him. He had been nothing more than a test, an experiment, one among many.

That the end result had turned out to be at once disappointing and far beyond anything its original Meliorare developers had envisioned was of no consolation to the experiment himself.

The discovery had left him more down on himself and on his species than at any time in his life. Well short of his thirtieth birthday, he had spent the preceding decade desperately trying to learn the truth about himself, only to wish now as he stalked the streets of alien Krrassin that he had never bothered to try. The search had led him to wondrous revelations and astounding adventures, to great friendships and an ever-strengthening love, but also to unsought, uncomfortable realizations about humankind and to a deepening personal malaise from which he seemed unable to extricate himself.

His unique empathic abilities had placed him in the position of potential savior of the galaxy. They had also rendered that potential savior increasingly indifferent to both his and its fate. Why should he trouble himself, if he was only the product of human experimentation and not humanity itself? He could live out the remainder of his natural life with Clarity Held. So could their children, should they have any. Though the threat to the Commonwealth and its galactic surrounds was advancing at increasing speed, he would be long dead before it began to affect the outermost star systems. Why risk his own life and happiness to save a species to which he belonged only through invention?

Could he even call himself human anymore?

Within the confines of the suit, Pip shifted uneasily in response to her master's troubled thoughts. While ever a comfort to him, her presence was also nonhuman. Empathetic but simplistic. Nor did he expect to find sympathy or understanding here, on the homeworld of the Commonwealth's most powerful adversary. He had come because it was a thing that had never been tried, and because he no longer deeply cared whether he lived or died. The time he had spent among the troubled youth of Visaria had given him a reason to stumble on. That brief flash of hope and inspiration had been more than negated by what he had learned about himself on Gestalt.

As he wound his way slowly up the winding curves of the paved pedestrian walkway, he found it numbing, if not exactly relaxing, to roam among intelligent but nonhuman sentients. When his still unpredictable, erratic Talent was functioning he was able to perceive their emotions. These were more consistently hostile, more inherently combative than those of his own kind. Yet they possessed a confidence and tranquility all their own, due not only to their alienness but to the culture in which they were grounded. Fight, argue, challenge—within this constant conflict lay a serenity that derived from consistency. It also inspired and drove each individual AAnn to always do their best, or else find themselves doomed to mediocrity. Humans possessed a similar drive, but one that was moderated by compassion.

What did it matter? What among either species, or among the thranx, or among any of the other intelligent species whose future was threatened by the Great Evil that was speeding toward the galaxy was worth the sacrifice of his own brief, transitory happiness? He thought of Clarity and Mother Mastiff, of Bran Tse-Mallory and Truzenzuzex. Surely those were examples of individuals worth saving. Because they happened to be his friends, or his love? Did anything else recommend them and link them?

Then it struck him.

Intelligence. Regardless of how he thought it was misused, in spite of how those who were fortunate enough to possess it frittered it away on trivial personal pursuits or feckless quarrels, that was the light that could not be allowed to go out. If the Great Evil was not confronted, if he did not do what little he could to help divert or defeat it, then he was ultimately as guilty as the billions he condemned. It had nothing to do with the confused delinquents of Visaria, or the slow-moving thinkers of Jast, or any other particular sentient species, humans included. It had to do with preserving the ability to *understand*. Trillions of stars and billions of years had culminated in a spark of comprehension here, a flash of awareness there. Experiment or not, he felt he was ethically bound, as an ancient Terran poet had once declared, to "Rage, rage, against the dying of the light." If that realization could be applied to an individual life, surely it was applicable to sentience as a whole. The shining clarity of his own intelligence, for example, was something that stood apart from the confusion of his origins.

A knife stabbed straight through his head, piercing the frontal lobe and shocking him all the way down to his toes. Subject to and unable to avoid the mental flare, poor Pip contracted spasmodically against his upper thigh.

All his deliberating, the best of his intentions and the worst of his indifference, continued to be held hostage to the horrific headaches that had increasingly plagued him as he grew and matured. Resist though he did the one that had just struck him, he still found himself unable to do little more than stagger into a public voiding slit cut from the inward-slanting jet-black wall of the nearest building. Leaning against the interior halfway between the street and the sanitizing receptor, his chest heaving as he sucked down short, trembling gasps, he fought to stay upright. If he let the agonizing pain overcome him and passed out, what-

ever decision he reached about the threat facing the galaxy or about anything else would be rendered moot. The most perfunctory medical
check would expose him for the impostor he was and see him sent off
under heavy guard to the nearest enforcement center. Fortunately, the
voiding slit was unoccupied when he stumbled into it.

It did not remain so for long.

Shorter than a male AAnn but wider of hip, the elegantly clad female who entered behind him started to turn away to allow the individual in front of her to finish his business unobserved. Taking a second
look at the slightly slumped male figure, she hesitated. His stance
showed he was improperly positioned to properly void. Instead, he appeared to be leaning against the enclosing, curving wall for support.
This insight instinctively suggested two possible courses of action. She
could attack him while he was physically weakened and potentially
gain status. Or she could demonstrate compassion, offer help, and perhaps gain the same. Much depended on how seriously he was incapacitated. If only a little, then a challenge would be worthwhile. If, however,
his condition was serious, then an assault on another nye who was not
in condition to fight back would cause her to lose merit.

Without having to turn to see her, Flinx sensed her confusion along
with her presence. Despite the pain coursing through his skull he concentrated on calming Pip. The last thing he needed was for the flying
snake to burst free from some unnatural opening in the simsuit to attack
a startled passerby. In response to his silent urgings, Pip remained
tightly wound around his right arm and made no move to defend him.

"*Pssannch.*" He fought to stand upright and move away from the
wall. "A falsse calling. The body playss trickss with digesstion. The
sstation is yourss." He managed to straighten. The invisible gnomes
mining for gold at the back of his skull continued their agonizing attempts at extraction.

Intensely bright slitted eyes stared into his own. One eyelid closed
briefly, then the second. "You look unwell, citizen."

Designed to accommodate one nye at a time, the voiding station
made a single privacy bend as it cut deeply into the wall. It was very
narrow and they were very close. He started to edge past her, remembering to finger the correct sensor so that his tail would not slap into her.

Were it to do so, the action could be interpreted as either a challenge or an invitation to classically violent AAnn cuddling—neither of which he wished to incite.

"A momentary pain. An old fighting injury, incurred againsst the bugss."

"Ahriinn!" She backed up, giving him as much room as possible to slide past. Soldiering was revered among the AAnn, with those who had seen action against their traditional enemies the thranx being held in the highest regard of all. "Iss there nothing I can do for you?"

Her words could have been an attempt to promote more intimate interaction. At the risk of appearing impolite, he fought back the pain in his head as he stepped toward the winding walkway beyond.

"I am mated," he gasped weakly in her direction.

"Sso am I," the female responded. "I freely abjure reproduction."

"No time," he muttered. *"Bachaanssk,* and in addition to that I am late for duty." With his left arm he executed a second-degree gesture of appreciation and stumbled out onto the street.

The throbbing that threatened to tear his head off his shoulders finally began to subside. Thankfully, the female did not pursue, choosing instead to make use of the hygienic facility that had given him temporary refuge. He could feel Pip relax slightly against his arm, responding in kind as his own concern eased.

It had been a near thing. He decided then and there he would take no more such risks. He had done enough, had won the hand he had played, had more than achieved the outrageous goals he had set for himself when he had first decided to embark on the attempt. Having survived a teverravak in the most closely guarded, sacrosanct part of the entire Empire, he would not push his luck any further. The gamble had been well taken, the time judiciously spent. It confirmed to him that irrespective of species, what ultimately mattered was that the glow of intelligence be preserved. That was what was worth fighting for, no matter which political or racial entity eventually came to dominate the galaxy. As a consequence he, Philip Lynx, would do his personal best to see that the ember of sentience continued to burn. No matter what *he* was, no matter how he or anyone else defined him, he saw that he remained one with that purpose.

Thus strengthened in resolve, he loped along until he found the public transport that had originally brought him to this part of the great city. Entering the small automated vehicle, he ignored his fellow passengers and turned to ease back into a support slot, taking care to ensure that his tail did not strike anyone nearby. Like the majority of his fellow travelers, save for the elderly or infirm, he disdained the use of the U-shaped fold-down seat, preferring to flaunt his health and fitness by standing for the duration of the journey. With one four-fingered hand he reached up and used a pointed claw to clean between several teeth. As it never became dirty, his perfectly rendered artificial dentition had no need of the attention, but the action helped him to blend in among the other passengers.

At individually selected stops various AAnn stepped on or off the nearly silent vehicle. It took some fifteen minutes for the high-speed urban transport to reach the densely developed, heavily populated inurb where Flinx had taken lodgings. No one looked in his direction when he exited the public vehicle.

As he strode slowly toward the building where he had lived for the past ten days, he reflected that he now knew more about the day-to-day workings of the Imperial capital than those Commonwealth specialists who were considered to be the most knowledgeable on the subject. That the sectors where he had spent his time were of no military importance whatsoever did not mitigate his achievement. Working his way into and through the city subsequent to his unsanctioned arrival he had chosen the present quarter as his base of operations specifically because it could be defined by its ordinariness. Going about their daily tasks while dealing with no more than the minimal number of socially acceptable face-to-face challenges, mid-level AAnn generally avoided their neighbors and kept scrupulously to themselves.

While there were no trees, native Blasusarrian desert landscaping spotted the inurb's pedestrian pathways and buildings with patches of green, brown, and a festering dark blue bushy growth that was endemic to the planet's largest continent. Additional shades and shapes were present in the form of public sculpture and structural adornment. Though coated or imbued with the muted tones favored by the natives, there was no lack of color. While individualistic artisans were held in low regard, when it came to communal aesthetics the AAnn were a dynamic and inventive species. Perhaps no human knew that better than Flinx, who alone among his kind had spent time among their artists.

Examples of high-quality collective work took the form of bas-reliefs and sculptures that erupted from the sides of sprawling, low-lying residential complexes. Some were solid and inert, while others were displayed as elaborate wave-and-sound projections. Scenes from AAnn history and selective popular entertainment were the most common. As he turned down the next-to-the-last pathway, which led to the entrance to his building, he found himself smiling, as always, at an imbedded wave projection that depicted charismatically brave AAnn warriors attacking and overwhelming a primitive redoubt full of quaking humans. From a stylistic standpoint, at least, it appeared that cheap propaganda transcended origin anywhere in the galaxy.

Everything he had brought with him on his soon-to-be-terminated unsanctioned excursion fit neatly into a single AAnn back-and-belly pack. The *Teacher* had experienced no difficulty in reproducing a flawless example of the straightforward baggage from examples contained in its extensive library. Not one of the AAnn Flinx had encountered since his arrival and infiltration had stopped him to question the source of his luggage. If they had, he would simply have identified it as the creation of one of the Empire's more distant colony worlds. Just as within the Commonwealth, expansion of colonization on a galactic scale allowed for a comforting degree of anonymity in product as well as person.

He would pick up his few belongings and begin to retrace his steps out of the city. A chartered automatic transport would take him to the remotest part of a nearby planetary park, a region of preserved and profound desolation little visited by those in whose interest it had been established. It was there he had been quietly dropped off by one of the *Teacher*'s masked shuttlecraft, and it was there that he would call and wait for pickup. He had survived his sojourn on the AAnn capital world and had learned a little more about himself. That and more would see him returning with fresh resolve to a previous decision now reinforced. He was once more certain of what he was going to do with the rest of his life. Rejuvenated and enlightened by the time spent on the AAnn homeworld, he was ready to leave.

Blasusarr's intense sun was setting, turning what could be seen of the horizon above the low buildings a fiery yellow and the undersides of outmatched clouds a deepening rust red. At this time of day few nye were out walking. The notion of a casual evening stroll was an exercise that appealed to very few of them. Even in the absence of pedestrian traffic he was careful to keep to the paved right-hand path and out of the winding sand-filled causeway that dominated the center of the street. It was not unknown for aggressive, hormone-driven AAnn to resort to a favored ploy of their primitive ancestors by burying themselves in the sand, there to wait until the time came to erupt and confront potential adversaries who would not have time to avoid the consequent challenge.

As he turned the last corner before his residence, he spared a glance for the woven sand sculpture that marked the intersection of multiple pathways. Held erect and in place by hand-sketched magnetic fields, the braided streams of multicolored sand and flecks of local gemstone were recycled in continuously shifting patterns; the fountain spewed stone instead of water. Sunset's blush turned the spout's sunward side to shards of stuttering rainbow.

Both the automated manager and live concierge of his building would be sorry to see him go. Not only had he paid for his stay in advance with his carefully counterfeited Imperial credit, he had freely rented the least desirable quarters in the entire structure: high up and on the shady side of the building. His view of the inevitable desert garden and exterior sand-filled relaxation area was from above: practically from overhead. From an AAnn point of view, his rooms were totally undesirable.

He did not expect to see the concierge when he checked out, nor was it necessary for him to do so. As an out-system visitor intent on commercial business, such personal interaction was not only unnecessary but an open invitation to spontaneous challenge. Flinx was confident that the somewhat elderly concierge was as eager as himself to avoid any gratuitous final farewells.

So he was more than a little surprised to see the elder nye, slightly stooped from his species' version of scoliosis, standing just outside the entrance to the building where he presented himself open to challenge by any casual passerby. Despite the AAnn's present choice of location and stance, Flinx saw right away that such a potential confrontation was unlikely.

Not when the concierge had half a dozen or so armed enforcers clustered closely around him.

CHAPTER

2

As far back as he could remember, Flinx had always had excellent reflexes. In Drallar, on Moth, they had helped to keep him always just out
of reach of the local police. Later, as he had traveled from one end of the
Commonwealth to the other, they had often been the difference between
life and death. A second or two slower, a second or three later under
threatening circumstances, and he might not be standing where he was
now.

In the rapidly fading light of evening a human might easily have
overlooked the approaching Flinx—but not an AAnn. The concierge
was old, but he was not blind. Before Flinx could react to the presence
of the enforcers and nip back out of sight, the Elder had spotted him.
Flinx turned and bolted, but not in time.

Had he been on a Commonwealth or a disputed world he quite
likely would have been dead. But on the Imperial homeworld the local
enforcers of Status and Order did not carry lethal weapons. Provided
proper etiquette was observed, social convention allowed for one citizen to slay another in the course of escalating one-on-one conflict, but
the same latitude was not granted to the authorities. The paralyzing neuronic bursts that flared in his direction were designed to incapacitate,
not to kill. Unfortunately, the similarity between human and AAnn

nervous systems was such that if one of the shots being fired in his direction did happen to hit home, it would most assuredly lay him out as flat and limp-tailed as any rightful resident of Krrassin.

Complicating his flight were Pip's attempts to work her way free of the confining suit so that she could go to his defense. If at all possible, he needed to continue to keep her existence a secret. Just because it appeared that he had been turned in to the city authorities did not mean they knew their quarry was a masquerading human. It was much more likely that the concierge or automated manager had discovered that the line of Imperial credit he had been using was forged. Or perhaps, despite the individualized burrow security he had employed to secure his quarters, one of the dwellings' maintenance workers had discovered something incriminating in his luggage. While minimal in number and inconspicuous in size, he *had* brought with him certain personal accoutrements whose origin could not be disguised. The presence among a visitor's effects of certain objects of non-AAnn manufacture would be sufficient in and of themselves to inspire a further investigation.

His mastery of the AAnn language might have enabled him to explain away the presence of the latter. But if the enforcers were there to pick him up for forgery, no amount of clever words would suffice to preserve his freedom. He would be hauled in for interrogation. Trapped within his clever cocoon, he would be able to keep his true identity confidential only until he was slipped under the first medical scanner. That was a risk he could not take—and so he ran. The loss of his personal effects did not trouble him. Regardless of value, inanimate objects could always be replaced.

He was a fast runner and in excellent condition. But the suit slowed him, having to keep a tight rein on Pip slowed him further, and the AAnn were accomplished runners in their own right. Free of the simsuit he might outrun them, at least over a distance. If he removed the suit, however, he might as well surrender now and save his wind. In the confines of the Imperial capital city an exposed human would not last out the night. Not only did the suit provide some measure of visual anonymity, it also masked his distinctive human scent.

He could hear them closing fast, hissing and shouting encouragement to one another. If he ducked into a park or building, they would act quickly to seal off the area, or else some resident was likely to point him out. There was one other option.

He stopped and turned to face them.

Half closing his eyes, Flinx called on his Talent as he strove to project. It was a technique he had used before, on everything from fellow humans to other sentients to lower orders of animals. As the weapons-wielding enforcers closed in on his unmoving shape he strained to cast fear in their direction, to coat their alien reptiloid minds with a thin but disquieting layer of alarm.

It was not working. Through his squint he could see that they were not slowing in their advance. Weapons aimed forward, tails snapping whiplike from side to side, they would be on him in seconds. So close had they drawn that they did not fire. They saw no reason to do so, since in less than a minute they would be able to throw down the citizen under suspicion and pin him to the ground.

Fear was a powerful emotion. It was one that required maximum exertion on his part to successfully deploy. But though this effort failed, he retained other options. Experience had taught him to always be ready to utilize a different approach. He could not render his foe fearful. Very well: he would try something else.

Not twenty meters from Flinx the first enforcer suddenly began to slow. Double eyelids blinking, she lowered her weapon to her side as she came to a gradual halt. Her tail stopped switching. A second enforcer drew up alongside her. Bemused, he found himself staring down at his own gun. One by one they were joined by the rest of the flashily uniformed patrol. Querulous phrases of soft bafflement were exchanged. Dropping down into the distinctive AAnn squat, one enforcer methodically began taking his weapon apart. Next to him his companion started to disrobe.

After considerable trial and error in the course of his frantic life Flinx had discovered that confusion was much easier to project than fear.

Turning, he resumed his flight. How long the mental projection he had laid upon his pursuers would last he did not know. He never knew. The time frame was as unpredictable as everything else about his Talent. It didn't matter. Their befuddlement need last only long enough for him to get away.

He knew he had made his escape when he was able to slow to a normal lope without any sign behind him of his pursuers. Moments later, he realized that same escape might be only temporary when he prepared to engage a transport, only to see that every nye in the hiring line in front of him was being required to present themselves before what was normally an inert, rarely used security scanner.

Edging off to one side while carefully staying out of the scanner's range and away from the AAnn lined up ahead of him, he debated how to proceed. Was the suddenly enhanced security only local, or had it been extended citywide? What should he do next? What *could* he do? The energized security measures meant that he was effectively marooned in Krrassin. It was much too far, and too dangerous, to try to walk to his preferred pickup point far out in the desert park.

It would be terribly ironic if his false alien identity proved to be his ultimate undoing. Designed and refined by the *Teacher* to such an extent that it was capable of deceiving native AAnn, it could not easily be altered by hand. Unlike with a human disguise, he could not effectively change its appearance by simply adding makeup or long hair. He could doff it entirely, of course, thereby eliminating all trace of the offworld credit thief whose identity he had adopted. Exposing himself as the only human in Krrassin, however, was unlikely to expand his freedom of movement.

Somehow he had to find a way to make his way back to the vast, unpopulated desert park that lay outside the boundaries of the capital without being arrested or having his true identity discovered. There one of the *Teacher*'s shuttles could touch down just long enough to pick him up. But even a perfectly disguised shuttle could hardly set down in the center of the sprawling city. If it could avoid detection and collision, there *was* room for it to do so at one of the four major shuttleports that served the metropolitan center of the Empire. The problem was that each of them lay almost as far outside the city limits as the much more amenable, less closely watched, and unpopulated recreation area.

As he was trying to decide the best course of action a pair of airborne scrutinizers coasted into view above the line of waiting automated transports. Equipped with paralysis weapons as well as surveillance gear, they could not only identify a wanted individual but knock him down and stand guard over him until organic representatives of the municipal authorities arrived. Surveying his surroundings, while trying to appear as indifferent to the security machines' arrival as the rest of the increasingly impatient transport customers, he started to retrace his steps. Once he had drifted back to the far end of the queue he veered to his right and allowed himself to be swept up by a cluster of kicking, biting, tail-snapping revelers out to enjoy an evening post-work. On any given evening few such groups were to be seen. While the AAnn were perfectly comfortable moving about at night, where and when possible they much preferred to take their relaxation in the heat of midday.

On a human-inhabited world, Flinx could have counted on being able to lose himself in a much bigger crowd. Here on broiling Blasusarr, the onset of night brought with it some relief from the heat of day but a consequent rise in individual visibility. While other AAnn were out and about, they did not gather in numbers adequate to fully occupy the attention of cruising security scanners and miscreant-seeking scrutinizers. If he did not soon get off the walking paths and out of sight, one or another of the relentless security devices was sure to spot him.

Renting new quarters in order to have a place to hide out was not an option. By now the appearance of his simsuit and all related formal identification would have been distributed throughout the city's closely integrated financial network. Any attempt to spend even a quarter-orbit of Imperial credit would immediately set off every alarm in the system. All he had going for him was that the authorities knew him only as Pahmiit ERRUJKJNN, an offworld traveler who was visiting Krrassin and Blasusarr on commercial business. They were still looking for a duplicitous fellow AAnn, not a masquerading human.

If it became known that a human resident of the Commonwealth was wandering the sandways of the capital unauthorized, the quasi-reptilian equivalent of all hell would break loose. He had to find a way to rendezvous with one of the *Teacher*'s shuttles before that happened.

He also needed nourishment, as did Pip. While the illusion of nyeness the simsuit projected was superb, the costume was not faultless. He could not maintain the illusion of being an AAnn while eating. In order to consume food he had to unseal and remove the reptilian head. This had been a simple matter when safe in the privacy of his rented quarters. Out on the street, it presented a much more difficult challenge.

The solution was to opt for a filling liquid meal; something that was not always easy to find on a world inhabited by highly evolved carnivores. Even so, locating a vendor would be the easy part. Paying for the food was where peril would enter into the equation. Any other human put in his position would have been at a loss as to how to proceed. Flinx, however, possessed one advantage the majority of his fellow primates did not.

He was an accomplished and experienced thief with a unique Talent.

Utilizing his ability to the same degree that he had on the pursuing enforcers, Flinx succeeded in confusing the operator of a small food shop into believing he had been paid in full for the flask of thick protein-rich soup Flinx accepted and tucked into his sidepack. The alien chowder would keep him fueled for a day or two, after which time he might well be forced to repeat the deception. Pip wouldn't like the strange-smelling gruel, but when she got hungry enough she would slurp it down just like her master. When it came to consumption of alien victuals, experience had taught Flinx that the prospect of imminent starvation was a wonderful motivator for the digestive system.

Later, as he was sipping the thick, meaty broth through the flask's integrated straw-spout, a different pair of hovering scrutinizers came drifting down the street where he was idling. Already more than a little deserted with the arrival of full darkness, the walkway on which he found himself offered little in the way of cover. Except for the food shop he had recently exploited, few other establishments were open. He needed to get away from public venues, and fast.

All the residential and commercial structures in his immediate vicinity were sealed for the night. Given time, he was confident he could defeat their integrated security systems. Time, however, was the one thing the implacable, fast-moving scrutinizers would not give him.

At the next intersection a large public transport paused to unload a trio of passengers. Operating at cross-angles to the curving pedestrian pathways, it traveled on a fixed preprogrammed path. Private transport would have been faster and safer, but now he had no choice. Breaking into a run, he sprint-loped in the transport's direction. Behind him, the scrutinizers had paused to perform bio-interrogation on a mated pair of puzzled pedestrians. Pivoting in midair, one casually turned its secondary scanner in Flinx's direction. Would it be able to identify him from a rear view?

He leaped through the open portal at the rear of the transport just before it started to close. The interior lighting was muted to suit AAnn visual tastes. Several of the half dozen or so passengers were resting in squatting position while the remainder stood erect. One Elder had to resort to the use of a fixed support brace that protruded from an interior wall. Lest they provoke an early evening challenge, none of his fellow riders looked in Flinx's direction. Not for the first time, he was glad of characteristic AAnn reticence in the presence of strangers. They tended to be much more cautious among themselves than when confronting his kind, or the thranx.

It was good that they exhibited disinterest or one of them might have been moved to comment on his awkward, ungainly stride. A soft warning stutter sounded from a concealed rooftop synth membrane and the transport accelerated smoothly. Flinx waited as long as he dared before turning ever so slightly to look back the way he had come. What he saw filled him with relief, if not exactly confidence. Behind the departing transport, the two scrutinizers were now interviewing the remaining nye who had stood between Flinx and the public conveyance itself. Had he remained on the walkway, he would have been next to have been interrogated. And he would not have been able to use his abilities to confuse patrolling machines as he had pursuing enforcers and weary food merchants.

Returning his attention to the center of the egg-shaped vehicle, he tilted his head back slightly and pretended to study the assorted glowing exhortations that formed a drifting nimbus within the concave ceiling. Two of the other passengers were doing likewise. There was no need to worry about his reactions as he perused the highly animated public notices. His AAnn visage masked the human expressions underneath.

He had hoped to find himself on a transport headed toward the outer rings of the metropolis, or at least parallel to where he had been staying. Instead, he was trapped on a vehicle headed toward the city center. He was accelerating into the very heart of the Imperial environs. There he was likely to find his every move subject to greater scrutiny than ever. As a lone human confronting the Empire, even his singular abilities might not be enough to enable him to escape detection and disclosure.

Well, he would worry about that tomorrow. One thing humans and

AAnn had in common was diurnality. Both species required a certain amount of nighttime rest. The problem of nourishment had been solved, if only temporarily. As for water, though the AAnn needed less of it to function effectively than did humans, Flinx felt from his experience of the city that it would not be difficult to come by. Since he could no longer safely rent a place to sleep, he would find some sheltered place near a pathway. The prospect of sleeping out in the open did not disturb him. He had done it often enough as a child on Moth.

As for the fact that he was about to do so on an entirely alien world, well, a dirty deserted alley was a dirty deserted alley irrespective of the species responsible for its aesthetics, design, and construction.

Upon exiting the public transport he found himself in a district dominated by large individual dwellings. On a human world they would have been called estates. That none of the structures within the individually fenced, carefully demarcated areas rose higher than a single story was an indication of their owners' wealth. It meant that the owners could afford to live in traditional fashion with the majority of their living space comfortably situated below the surface. Except for a few isolated plots of native growth, local landscaping consisted of artfully sculpted stone and sand. The dominant neighborhood aesthetic demanded that the extensive uninhabited, undeveloped regions of Blasusarr be replicated here deep within the capital city as faithfully as possible. In the center of Krrassin this could only be accomplished through means that were both artificial and costly.

Subdued radiance danced within the depths of the half-buried single-story structures. Without, lights were employed to indirectly illuminate expensive artificial pools and streams, miniature imitation buttes, and downsized mineral-stained synthetic escarpments. Some of the borders that separated wealthy neighbor from intransigent fellow resident were solid, some were ethereal, and others were as intangible as the electric current or light waves of which they were composed. Every aspect of the many habitats he slunk past, every individual feature and facet, proclaimed the power and position of their owners. He encountered no alleys here, dirty or otherwise.

Forcing an entrance into one of the protected private domains would be difficult for a wandering transient irrespective of species.

Those intending ill to the inhabitants would likely find themselves challenged by stringent security measures. As for Flinx, he was only searching for a quiet place to sleep away the night. If in so doing he also happened to chance upon a hiding place suitable for the longer term, he would happily lay claim to that as well. Safely inside the boundary of some scientist or noble or merchant's guarded sphere of influence, he would have a chance to catch his physical and mental breath safe from prying eyes both slitted and inorganic.

Had he not been experienced from an early age at breaking and entering he could not have penetrated the property he eventually chose without setting off some kind of alarm. That he was able to do so quietly and unobserved was a testament not only to his skills as an infiltrator but to a decade and a half of exploration that included the accumulation of a great deal of arcane knowledge about the AAnn and their Empire. The security measures he encountered and defeated one by one were alien in origin but, for him at least, perfectly comprehensible. Physics makes no exceptions for different species. The same general rules applied to security devices whether developed for use by humans, the thranx, the AAnn, the Quillp, or any of the other known sentient races with a fetish for privacy.

Once safely inside the property's fortified outer boundary and confident that his presence had not been detected, he went in search of more than just a square of ground on which to lay his head.

While similar in design and construction to the artificial desert environments that dominated the grounds of most of the neighboring estates, the one he had entered was distinguished by several especially garish motifs. The reds of the synthetic sandstone canyonets he found himself wandering through tended to be brighter, the yellows more sunshine than subdued, the naturally pale hues of orange and ivory embellished with scintillating flourishes of embedded quartz minerals. Even for the AAnn, this estate's simulated desert décor approached the tawdry. Not that the overwrought alien aesthetics caused him any suffering. He barely paid attention to them as he sought a place to conceal himself that was equally out of sight of both the main structure and the surrounding pathways.

As the night drew on, he finally found the perfect spot by nearly falling into it.

A pool on the protected property had been gouged from the earth. If its perfectly symmetrical oval shape had not been sufficient to identify it as artificial, the well-camouflaged conduits running its full length would have confirmed the observation. The clear water was stocked with native aquatic life-forms that had been genetically modified to emit varying hues of transgenic light. Not sufficient light to illuminate anyone standing at poolside, but enough to provoke admiring comments from casual bystanders. Flinx's reaction was doubtless different from that of the average visitor to the property: he found himself wondering if any of the multitude of gaudy swimmers were edible.

Despite the presence of so many small Blasusarrian swimmers, the water looked clean. Any chemical imprint was invisible. If the water was potable, that would render this particular bit of AAnn landscaping an even more inviting place to hide.

Selecting one of a dozen miniature side "canyons," he settled into one, stripped off his outer AAnn attire, and began methodically unsealing the simsuit. Despite its exceptional powers of renewal, it was still necessary from time to time to air the suit out and perform certain minimal maintenance procedures on the interior. These could not be done while the suit was still being occupied. Previously he had performed the requisite procedures while safe in his rented quarters. Deprived of his residence, he would have to do the work here.

Though it felt strange to find himself standing outside the simsuit in the open air of Blasusarr, he was not overly concerned. The night was advancing by the hour, he had not seen any movement from the vicinity of the property's main structure, and the extensive landscaping hid him from the view of anyone on the nearest public pathway. Robotic scrutinizers and patrolling enforcers would not enter the property of such an obviously important residence without good reason and first obtaining proper clearance.

By the time he had completed upkeep and maintenance on the suit it was very late indeed. The only sounds came from automatonic desert-dwellers that were nothing more than motile components of the landscaping itself. Were the swimmers in the pool likewise inorganic, or were they composed of flesh and assorted Blasusarrian bodily fluids? He could learn several things at once by slipping into the pool for a swim.

After so much time spent smothered in the confines of the simsuit, the feel of the cool water was almost unbearably refreshing against his bare skin. A creature of the air, Pip relaxed nearby on warm shotstone, content to occasionally swing her head around and sip from one of the two precision-engineered rivulets that fed the pool. Flinx floated naked on his back and gazed up at constellations that were as foreign as any an Earthly astronomer could imagine. In barely ten years he had seen many such sights, and had visited more than a few.

And if he and his friends did not find a way to stop something impossibly immense and inconceivably evil that was headed this way from behind those very same stars, in the not-so-far future those bright points of light would begin to be snuffed out one by one.

He let out a sigh. Arms spread wide, hands gently rowing, he pushed himself lazily across the pool. A perfect imitation of the real thing, the sculpted faux sandstone walls that surrounded him did a credible job of shutting out the alien world beyond. Eyes half closed, exhausted from the mental and physical strain of having to flee and avoid capture, he allowed himself to unwind in the cool, supportive liquid. Tomorrow he would devote himself to concocting a means for escaping the city and finding a place sufficiently desolate to accommodate a shuttle landing. Tomorrow he would ponder further the hostile universe and his exceptionally peculiar place within it. Tomorrow.

Tonight—tonight he would rest and allow himself to recuperate from the demands of the day. In the privacy of the extensive estate landscaping he could even see himself enjoying a full night's sleep.

So at ease did the refreshing pool, the private surrounds, the warm night, and his own fatigue put him that he failed to sense an approaching presence. Or perhaps his ever erratic Talent was simply not functioning at full efficiency. Whatever the reason, he continued to float nonchalantly in the midst of the comfortably cool basin unaware that he and Pip were no longer alone.

His serpentine companion, however, was not nearly so preoccupied with relaxation that she failed to notice the approaching intelligence. Raising her scaly head several centimeters off the ground, her eyes flicked in multiple directions as she sought its source. Folded against her sides, bright blue and pink wings twitched preparatory to unfurling. But instead of taking flight she slid into the water. With buoyant S-curves, she worked their way over to her master. Only when she slithered wet and slick onto his chest did Flinx fully open his eyes. Raising his head slightly from the water, he met her slitted gaze and grinned fondly.

"Lonely, Pip? Or just feel like a swim?"

By way of response the Alaspinian flying snake again lifted her head, this time shifting her attention toward his feet. Frowning slightly, Flinx backstroked a little faster as he peered into the darkness beyond the miniature artificial canyon. He heard nothing, saw nothing. But under the minidrag's prodding, he strove to reach out with the singular sense only he possessed.

Opening himself to greater surroundings, he abruptly and unexpectedly chanced across a third presence in addition to himself and Pip. It was alien, AAnn, and growing stronger every second. Startled by its unexpected proximity, he turned on his side and swam for the stone beach where he had left the simsuit. Dumped into the water by her master's turn, Pip swam swiftly and easily for the same shore.

Climbing out of the pool, intently searching the surrounding darkness, Flinx tried to dry himself as best he could. The AAnn-style backpack that was always attached to the simsuit contained all manner of useful gear and equipment brought from the *Teacher.* Ironically, what he needed at that moment was something as low-tech as a towel. Donning the simsuit while wet was certainly possible, but not very comfortable. He had no choice. Standing by the side of the pool in only his skin left him naked in more ways than one.

In any event, the presence his pet had alerted him to was dangerously close now and he had to move quickly. Making certain the simsuit was properly laid out and the tail deactivated, he picked it up by the ventral slit and began to insert his right leg. A considerably more complex piece of attire than, say, shorts and shirt, the simsuit required a good ten minutes to don correctly and another ten to verify that its multiple servo-controlled functions, from retractable claws to nictating ocular membranes, were functioning properly.

As it turned out he did not have ten minutes, much less the preferred twenty. He did not even have a couple. Rounding the far corner of the diminutive synthetic canyon the AAnn whose presence Flinx had sensed abruptly strode into view, outlined in the dim starlight. An instant later the unsuspecting nocturnal perambulator saw *him:* an unclothed human standing beside the pool gripping what in the shadows looked like nothing so much as the flayed skin of a fellow AAnn. To the late-night visitant the sight must have been a considerable shock.

Especially considering how young he was.

CHAPTER

3

That his nightly sojourns did not have formal familial approval made them all the more delicious. Wielding a wickedly curved traditional *bengk* carnage knife in one four-fingered hand, a convex *torgk* shield in the other, and a sharpened and embossed *pelgk* sheath over the last half meter of his slender tail, Kiijeem AVMd prowled the desert in search of the wily ssentoom. One had to be ever ready and alert on the trail of the ssentoom. Though not large, they were vicious little carnivores, boasting a pair of forward-facing tusks that could pierce personal protection and reach all the way to vital organs. Defiant and eager, Kiijeem wore not a single piece of body armor. He chose to hunt without it, confident in the knowledge that he was faster, stronger, and smarter than the wiliest representative of that dangerous and delectable species.

He could also hunt without armor secure in the knowledge that it had been a couple of hundred cycles since the last ssentoom had been killed anywhere within a dozen *corrls* of Krrassin's city limits. The fact that he was "hunting" on his family's property reduced the likelihood of such an encounter to practically nil. That knowledge did not prevent him, however, from enjoying the chase.

As usual, he had taken care to slip out of the residence unobserved. While such a late-night stroll would have been frowned upon by the adults, if he was caught it would have occasioned nothing stronger than a casual rebuke over the missed sleep time. What would have drawn more serious censure was his choice to go wandering around in the dark fully armed with traditional weapons. At his age, halfway between childhood and maturity, concerns would have been voiced over his competency to handle such lethal gear. Not that there was anything on the protected property capable of harming so much as a hopping infant, and the security fence kept intruders at bay, but fears would have been raised about the possibility of an accident.

It was to avoid just such tiresome lecturing from adult nye that he always kept his intentions secret. He had carried out his covert stalkings several times previously without having his activities discovered. Each successive successful excursion boosted his confidence in his ability to continue to do so. Each succeeding stalk increased his poise in the handling of weapons, his ability to negotiate obstacles in the dark, and his growing physical prowess.

Besides that, they were fun.

A hint of movement caught his eye. He froze, dropping immediately into the preliminary attack crouch all AAnn learned from the time they were old enough to stop hopping and start running. With the bengk held low and ready to thrust and the torgk positioned in front of his chest, he advanced slowly on his quarry. Knees bent, tail cocked and ready to snap to left or right, he silently shadowed his prey.

There it was, just in front of him. Its back was to him and its eyes and attention elsewhere. Clutching the haft of the bengk steadfastly, Kiijeem contracted his powerful thigh muscles, hissed softly in expectation, and leaped.

The bengk descended. There was no cry from the victim. The point of the curved blade pierced its carapace directly behind the skull. Caught entirely by surprise, the hard-shelled bhrossod barely had time to utter a short, sharp, soft *unkk*. It was still alive when Kiijeem raised the pinioned creature aloft on the point of his blade. It was about half the length of the knife, possessed no biting parts, and continued to kick spasmodically with all ten legs. Eventually these stopped convulsing and grew still. Placing the dead animal back on the ground, Kiijeem used one clawed, sandal-shod foot to push the dead vermin off the

blade. While it was a long way from dispatching the fierce and dangerous ssentoom, at least it was a kill.

In his mind's eye he imagined it was a thranx, hereditary foe of the
Empire, all slashing foot-hands and drooling mouthparts. His slashing
bengk had smashed through the hard protective chitin over its spine.
Now its ichorous bodily fluids were draining away harmlessly into the
absorptive, cleansing sands of Blasusarr. Wiping his bengk clean
against the leg of his body suit, Kiijeem resumed his search for the ever-
elusive ssentoom. Surely there was one to be found in this wild and
empty reach of uninhabited desert! Doubtless crouched at the very back
of its burrow, cowering in fear from the knowledge that the greatest traditional hunter of all the AAnn was close on its trail.

More movement, this time off to his left, caught his attention. Could
it be a ssentoom? The brief flash of motion certainly suggested something considerably larger and more active than the harmless and unlucky bhrossod. For an instant Kiijeem, self-anointed mighty hunter
that he was, hesitated. Nothing so large ought to have been able to slip
past the property's security perimeter. Was part of the barrier down
along with its attendant warning electronics? If so, it might be time to
call a premature halt to his nighttime stalking and alert an adult. What if
some addled ambler had found a hole in the fence and come looking for
loot, challenge, or trouble of an unspecified nature? Kiijeem might hunt
ssentoom in the middle of the morning, but he was not sure he was
ready to challenge a trouble-seeking adult.

What was this? he chided himself. Was he not Kiijeem AVMd,
fourth of a titled litter, progeny of a noble family? Were the weapons he
carried nothing more than decoration; a boost to an ailing confidence, a
sop to a frail ego? Why should he, who hunted the deadly ssentoom (if
only in his imagination), fear a trespassing citizen? One who was probably mentally deficient or unstable or both? Steeling himself he pressed
on, secure in the likelihood that he would have the element of surprise
on his side, the justification of an affronted property owner in reserve,
and the knowledge that come what may he was a very fast runner.

He had detected the movement on the far shore of the west pool, the
one that was home to his family's prized collection of rare southern
temperate river water-dwellers. Was the intruder a common thief?

Would someone intent on pilfering small aquatic animals embark on such an activity heavily armed? It seemed superfluous. With that comforting thought in mind Kiijeem continued his advance.

In keeping with the aesthetics of the high-priced landscaper, the tailored terrain grew more rugged as he approached the pool. Moonlight outlined a figure standing there. Raising the bengk, Kiijeem started forward. As the outlines of the figure grew more defined, he began to slow. In a reflex gesture reflecting his utter astonishment, his tongue slid out of his mouth to hang down the right side of his jaw. The only sound he emitted was a soft metallic *tap* as his tail muscles relaxed and the sheathed tip slumped to the ground. He halted.

He could not believe what he was seeing.

Standing before him was a bipedal being he recognized instantly from the standardized component of his formal studies. It was much, much taller than he would have expected. Perhaps an unusual example of its kind. It was slender but well muscled and, just as the relevant imagery had taught him, completely tailless. It was one thing to learn in studies that a tall biped could stand upright without a tail and not fall over, quite another to see the phenomenon in person. While the eyes that were staring back at him were somewhat flattened in their orbits, the pupils were impossibly round.

Something far smaller and much more colorful was hovering in the air nearby. An alien flying creature, it resembled Kiijeem far more closely than it did its owner. A pet of some kind, or symbiote. The young nye did not recognize the Alaspinian flying snake, having never encountered Alaspin or minidrags in his studies. The tall biped he knew well, however. It was a human. An ally of the thranx, a cofounding race of the hated Commonwealth, and therefore also an implacable enemy. A mixture of fear, loathing, and revulsion churned through the AAnn's digestive organs. The creature's most distinctive defining characteristic was far more obvious in the flesh than it had ever been in the course of his studies.

It looked so . . . so *soft.*

The pulpy flesh had no covering. No scales, as would be natural. No chitin, as did the thranx and many other creatures. Virtually no fur. Even in the poor light Kiijeem thought he could actually see the blood flowing beneath the ridiculously gauzy, easily damaged skin. Why, a well-aimed rock could tear it! The sheath-point that presently covered Kiijeem's tail could pierce such a fragile creature straight through from front to back. Except . . .

This was a *human,* and one thing his studies had emphasized when discussing the softskins was that they were not nearly as fragile as they looked. And what about the dead, eviscerated AAnn the creature was holding?

No, the limp object was not a dead AAnn, he saw as he peered harder. While it looked exactly like the flayed skin of a nye, the interior was lined not with dripping blood vessels and torn muscle but with a smooth material whose origin was clearly synthetic. Woven into the fabric, for such he decided it had to be, were a multitude of embedded sensors and advanced instrumentation. It was something like a costume, then. Somehow Kiijeem did not think the human had brought it with him so he could inconspicuously attend a clan function. Which led to the obvious question of just what he *was* doing with it (by now Kiijeem was certain the creature standing before him was a male of the disgusting species) and what he was doing here. On Blasusarr. In Krrassin. On Kiijeem's family property, at night, by the west pool.

Notwithstanding the rarity of the specimens that dwelled in the pool, Kiijeem doubted this representative of an adversarial species had come all this way and gone to all this trouble simply to steal an assortment of native water-dwellers.

All this flashed through his mind even as he was simultaneously trying to decide whether to challenge or run. The revolting elasticity and apparent vulnerability of its body aside, the human was a good deal taller and heavier than the startled adolescent. While Kiijeem could not see any weaponry, that did not mean the intruder was unarmed. In fact, as an interloper in the capital city it was unlikely he would have come here unequipped to defend himself. There was also the matter of the attendant flying creature, which might possess abilities that posed a danger in themselves.

Mighty hunter though he was, at that moment Kiijeem found himself yearning for the gently warmed sand that filled the sleeping area in his private quarters. The main residence was uncomfortably far away.

The two stood staring at one another, the distance between them too close for comfort but sufficient to allow a moment's contemplation in lieu of the need to take immediate action. Had the situation been reversed, had a human of Kiijeem's age encountered a mature AAnn in similar circumstances on Earth, the human's conditioning would have told him to run. An AAnn, however, was made of sterner stuff. Or was the more foolishly obstinate. Letting out a long, deep hiss (as deep as he could manage, anyway) Kiijeem took several deliberate steps forward, raised the bengk above his hairless head, and assumed the posture of one issuing a formal challenge. His studied pose was highlighted by complementary traditional gesturing. Maybe he hoped this would frighten the human into flight. If so, he was disappointed.

Stepping out of the simsuit skin and laying it down carefully on the smooth rock, the tall intruder cocked his head slightly to one side and continued to stare silently back at his blustering young challenger. Was the creature deaf, or dumb, or both? an anxious Kiijeem wondered as he gripped the bengk a little tighter. Was it even now preparing some kind of unimaginable, unthinkable alien response? The youth's legs did not shake—he was too well trained for that. But thoughts of whirling about, casting his play-weaponry aside, and racing like mad for the safety of the main residence began to loom ever more prominently in his thoughts.

Time passed and still the human made no threatening gestures. What was it thinking? How could it be so confident and controlled standing there naked and unprotected? What threat, what unknown danger, Kiijeem wondered wildly, was he overlooking?

In reality, nothing that another human would have detected. Or any other sentient, for that matter. The young AAnn had no way of knowing that Flinx had already sized up his youthful challenger and found the threat he posed wanting. Kiijeem's roiling uncertainty and hesitation were as plain for Flinx to perceive as if the AAnn had announced them himself.

They were all laid out for the singular human to read, in the young nye's emotions.

What to do with this frightened but potentially dangerous adolescent? Flinx found himself wondering. Though he had no weapons himself, he felt that his experience would allow him to easily disarm the youth in any hand-to-tail combat. Alternatively, Flinx could summon up fear and Pip would kill the AAnn in an instant. Neither of those options appealed to him. Though undeniably scared, the young AAnn was also courageous enough to put forward the standard fighting challenge of his kind. Flinx didn't want to hurt him. In all the time he had spent on Bla-susarr he had managed to avoid injuring a single resident. He did not want to start here, now, with this spirited but inexperienced youth. By the same token he could hardly let the young male attack him or run off to seek help. What to do, how to respond?

The most important thing was to keep the youngster from raising any kind of alarm. Having been challenged, Flinx decided that for the moment at least, the best thing to do was play along. Projecting an emotion onto the youngster, if the mental effort succeeded, might calm him down—or it might send him screaming off into the night. Panicky screams were something to be avoided.

Holding the fingers of his right hand together, Flinx passed the inner edge against his throat, then used both hands to perform a second-degree gesture of martial acknowledgment that perfectly complemented the youth's preliminary gesticulations.

"I am called Flinx, of no family known to you, and I accept your challenge." He indicated Pip, hovering threateningly nearby. "My companion will not interfere. Initiate as you will." So saying, he dropped into as close an approximation of the traditional AAnn fighting crouch as his lanky human physiognomy would allow. Accepting a challenge while naked and unarmed would have seemed foolhardy to another AAnn—or another human. His helpless appearance notwithstanding, Flinx was far from defenseless.

If Kiijeem had been startled and confused before, he was now baffled beyond reason. That did not prevent him from responding appropriately.

"I am called Kiijeem, Fourth-born of the Family AVM, and it iss I who issuess thiss challenge." Double eyelids blinked in surprise as he realized that the human had not only responded in the approved manner to the initial challenge, but had done so in perfect, only slightly accented speech.

Why would a human master the AAnn language? Self-evidently this was no diplomat, wandering about unannounced on family property with some kind of AAnn costume-covering in hand. Was he a thief?

Surely there was nothing worth taking from the family residence that justified the risk of making a clandestine landing on Blasusarr. What then was the creature's motivation?

A spy. Of all possibilities he could imagine, that was the one that made the most sense to young Kiijeem. Except—a spy would logically attempt to infiltrate a military base, or some important scientific establishment, or at the very least a key commercial enterprise. One would not go to the trouble of sneaking onto the secured property of a wealthy and respected but by no means crucially important capital city family. The more Kiijeem mulled the situation, the further it shifted from the menacing to the farcical.

Had his parents hired a clever actor to don a human simsuit while carrying around an empty AAnn skin? Was this an attempt by them, or other of his relatives, or of his study friends, to frighten him? Perhaps to dissuade him from his nocturnal rambles? Or had he offended someone his own age and thereby unknowingly set into motion what was nothing more than an elaborate prank? It would certainly explain the tall figure's linguistic fluency and familiarity with AAnn custom if it was nothing more than another of his own kind. Perhaps a professional hireling walking on flexstilts. Heedless of the individual who had just responded to his challenge, Kiijeem looked around intently. Searching the surrounding darkness, he found only silence. If anyone was looking on and watching, he could not see them. Nor could he hear any eager breathing or hissing laughter.

Well, *chissann,* there was one way to find out. Having issued a challenge and subsequently had it accepted, he could not back away now without sacrificing what little adult status he had managed to acquire. If this *was* some kind of cunning subterfuge and those who had organized it were watching from hiding, the worst thing he could do was turn and run. Aside from the loss of all-important status, the humiliation would stick to him for years.

"Prepare to defend yoursself," he hissed in the sharpest tone he could muster. Holding the torgk close against his chest, he raised the curved bengk high over his head, kicked off his quick-release sandals, and initiated a ceremonial advance. As he did so, he could not keep from noticing the human-shape's external ears. He stared at his in-

scrutable opponent. What purpose did all that extraneous flesh and liga-
mentation serve? He shook himself. He had made a start to a fight. A
fight in which he, at least, was wielding weapons that were anything but
childish. If someone was playing a trick on him, if this was a game, a
few quick swipes of the bengk ought to expose it swiftly enough.

Shifting into the formal posture AAnn employed for hand-to-hand
combat, Flinx took a half step backward and lowered his clawless hands.
His adversary was young and probably inexperienced, but there was
nothing juvenile about the blade he was gripping, about the killing point
that tipped the end of the sheath that covered his tail, or about the sharp
claws on his feet. Serious injury and even death could come at Flinx
from any one of several different directions. He did not want to hurt the
youth—but neither could he coddle the young AAnn at the risk of damage to himself.

Seeing that Pip was watching him and not his approaching attacker,
Flinx made sure to keep his thoughts calm. There was no real danger
here, he told himself. Everything was manageable. He faced nothing
more dangerous than a little strenuous exercise. The nighttime visitor
was not an enemy. Perceiving his thoughts, the deadly flying snake
slowed her wing beats and settled back to the ground. Flinx relaxed.
Feeding off her master's relaxation, the minidrag's mind was eased that
much more. Still, she did not fold her wings flat against her sides, and
she stayed alert.

Kiijeem continued to advance one stealthy step at a time. His un-
shod claws scraped rock, seeking the most secure foothold. If this *was*
a game, the hypothesized unseen players were not ready to call it off.
Was he actually going to have to bleed the tall figure confronting him?
And what was it doing with its arms and hands? Why had it positioned
itself with one leg in advance of the other, instead of side by side to gain
the most height when leaping and kicking out?

It did not matter. If constrained within a clever costume, whoever
had been hired or otherwise engaged to frighten him would find their
movements correspondingly restricted. The realization was reassuring.
Letting out a swelling battle hiss, his tail whipping behind him, Kiijeem
AVMd charged across the painstakingly sculpted, slightly sloping sandstone that enclosed the artificial pool.

Overlooked by the onrushing reptilian figure and reassured by her master's muted emotions, Pip lay half dozing on the slice of rock where she had decided to rest and ignored them both.

At a chosen distance from his target, Kiijeem gave free rein to his powerful leg muscles and leaped. Though not yet fully mature he was strong for his age and the beneficiary of good martial training. As he started to descend toward his taller target, he cocked his legs and prepared to kick out, keeping bengk and tail in reserve. Still the shape before him did not move; merely continued to track him with its peculiar round eyes. Choosing the optimum moment, Kiijeem kicked. Still uncertain as to the seriousness of the challenge, he elected to strike for the chest instead of the head. If he was fighting an actor constrained by a costume, he did not want to mutilate or kill.

He need not have worried. As his legs shot forward in the direction of his opponent he expected it to try a blocking maneuver or to retreat. Instead, the tall shape ducked and threw itself *forward*. Exhibiting a suppleness that reflected the flexibility of a truly soft body, it tucked into a ball and rolled. As Kiijeem dropped farther and tried to adjust the striking angle of his double kick, the human figure thrust out and upward with both legs. Kiijeem flicked his tail downward, but he was not quite fast enough. Before the tail's sheathed point could strike home, both of his opponent's feet made contact between the base of the AAnn's tail and his legs.

The swift kick in the behind sent Kiijeem sprawling unceremoniously on the rocks. His landing was as undignified as it was unanticipated. Fortunately for him, the claws on human feet were stunted and harmless. Momentarily stunned, he recovered in time to see the human shape standing once more erect on both legs, still somehow managing to maintain itself upright in the absence of a counterbalancing tail. Expecting an attack, Kiijeem scrambled frantically to regain his footing. Lying on the ground, he was vulnerable.

The figure did not attack. Instead, it stood breathing easily while staring back at him. The fingers on both fleshy hands curled inward against the palms: a sign of inoffensiveness. Truly, Kiijeem decided, this was the most peculiar deception in which he had ever participated. His opponent ought to have rushed him when he was down. What kind of game was being played here? Was his adversary showing deliberate disdain for Kiijeem's fighting skills? But if that was the case, why was the tall shape not making the appropriate accompanying gestures of contempt? Rising to his feet, Kiijeem dropped back into a fighting crouch.

"I intend you no injury, I wish you no harm," the figure declared in its barely accented AAnn.

"Sspawn of sswamp," Kiijeem hissed. "I will take your tail!" As he charged a second time it struck him how futile the threat must sound. His opponent had no tail. Unless, Kiijeem reminded himself, it was coiled and bound inside the base of the human suit to further the illusion.

Maybe this was some kind of test, he told himself as he rushed forward, bengk at the ready. If so, he would not be found wanting.

Let it not be said that he failed to learn from experience. This time he did not jump. Instead, at the last instant he dropped into a slide, legs thrust out in front of him, intending to take his foe's feet out from underneath. No unarmored human could have duplicated that swift slide on unforgiving rock without sacrificing plenty of skin. The young AAnn's scaly hide protected him from any scrapes or cuts. To distract his opponent Kiijeem threw his torgk upward, straight at the figure's face. This left him free to strike out with the bengk at whatever portion of his rival's anatomy came within reach.

None did. The figure simply jumped straight up into the air. One downward-sweeping arm batted the flying torgk aside. Digging in with his claws, Kiijeem stopped his slide directly beneath the falling human shape. Bengk and tail upraised, he waited for his opponent to simply fall on the point of blade or sheath. His intent was still only to wound and not to kill. Lying on the nearby sandstone, a suddenly concerned Pip raised her head to eye the ongoing combat.

As the figure fell toward him it twisted in midair. Demonstrating un-AAnn-like flexibility at the thigh, one leg swung out and around to hook the upthrust tail and half coil around it, trapping it and rendering it harmless. At the same time an arm snapped downward to knock aside the hand holding the bengk. The fingers of the other hand spread wide.

The air whooshed out of Kiijeem as the heavy body landed on top of him. His tail was hooked and trapped, the hand holding the bengk was pinned to one side, and his adversary's other hand . . .

The other soft but powerful hand was gripping his throat.

Only the fact that those clutching fingers were clawless kept Kiijeem from giving in completely to panic. The blunt keratin at the tips of those five (why five and not the normal four? he wondered) could do him no harm. But the fingers themselves—how strong were they?

He was utterly helpless, Kiijeem realized. His legs were free, but the heavy body lying atop his pinned form prevented him from flexing enough to make contact with his clawed feet. He struggled to kick free, to no avail. What if his opponent chose to tighten further those choking fingers? Kiijeem considered yelping for help, but if this was a test, or a masquerade, it would only magnify the humiliation of his defeat. At the hands of an unarmed opponent, no less.

He waited for his enemy to increase the pressure on his throat. He waited for him to claim the right to inflict a ceremonial injury. He waited for a rush of hissing laughter from hidden, unseen mouths. What happened next unnerved him completely.

The tall, lanky figure released the grip on his throat, carefully straightened the leg that had locked itself around Kiijeem's tail, rose, and stepped back to look down at him. Lying on the ground, Kiijeem let the fingers clutching the bengk loosen as he stared dazedly up at his opponent.

"I attacked with weaponss. You have the right to claim damage." He waited stoically. As the tailless shape came slowly toward him he closed his eyes and tensed.

A soft, pulpy hand made contact with his own right one. Five digits wrapped around his four. Not to break, not to dislocate, but to pull. The strength in those spongy fingers was as surprising as the figure's agility. As they helped him upright, Kiijeem could detect nothing of artifice about the gesture. Breathing hard, he stared up at his infuriatingly phlegmatic opponent.

"You inflict no injury." Even an actor, he knew, would leap at the opportunity to acquire that germane bit of status, if only as a bonus in addition to whatever payment he had been promised. Kiijeem looked around. The night was still calm, the exclusive residential neighborhood still quiet. No shapes emerged from the darkness to laugh, to chide, or to admonish him. His lower jaw dropped to reveal sharp teeth, and his tongue lay flat and numb against his palate.

"It's a human thing," Flinx told him, careful not to show any teeth of his own as he smiled back.

"You . . . ," Kiijeem searched for appropriate words. "You really *are* a human."

"Truly," Flinx replied, this time without even a trace of an offworld accent.

"How can thiss be? How can *you* be?" Aware that he was still gripping the bengk, Kiijeem realized that the figure standing before him was within easy stabbing range. The tip of his tail twitched, instinctive preparation for whipping around and striking. The appendage seemed oddly heavy. Looking around, he saw that something had attached itself to the very tip.

The small flying creature had wrapped its coils around the end. Staring at the brightly colored blue and pink creature, Kiijeem took in the slitted eyes, the scaly body, and reflected that it was the one he would have been comfortable conversing with. Alas, while the winged thing was somewhat perceptive it was just as obviously not sentient.

"If I cannot be," Flinx replied gently as he took a seat on the sandstone and crossed his long legs, "then who are you talking to?"

"I wass being literal, not solipssisstic." Kiijeem squatted down into a resting crouch. After a moment's indecision he laid the bengk aside. But not out of reach. That would have been foolish. And un-AAnn-like. "What I meant wass that you, a human, should not be on Blasussarr." Double eyelids blinked in succession. "You are not an operative attached to the Commonwealth diplomatic corpss?"

"No." Flinx chuckled. "They would be as upset to learn that I'm here as would your own officials."

"Then what *are* you doing here?" a genuinely curious Kiijeem inquired. "To my knowledge, no human hass ever managed ssuch a thing."

"I'm here because," Flinx explained thoughtfully, "to my knowledge, 'no human has ever managed such a thing.'" He looked away from the now intensely interested young nye, toward the night sky. "I seem to have a propensity for doing things none of my kind have done before. My own ship thinks I'm crazy."

Two revelations to ponder in one short phrase, Kiijeem decided.

"I'm crazy" and "My own ship thinks." He determined now was not the time or place to probe more deeply into either claim.

"You are lying. There cannot be a human sship near Blasussarr. Any incoming vessel not intercepted in the outer reachess of the home ssysstem would be obliterated long before it could enter into orbit."

Flinx did not smile. "Technological advances exist that the Empire knows nothing about. Or for that matter, the Commonwealth. My ship is not your typical voyager through space-plus. And I am not your usual human."

"I would not know. I have never encountered a ssoftsskin before. Only in sstudiess. Never in the flessh." Aware that the weight had left his tail, he looked on as the colorful flying creature buzzed over to land on its master's shoulder.

"Disappointed?" Flinx asked him. "Afraid?" He already sensed that the young nye was afraid of him, but he was curious to see how the youth would respond to a direct query.

"A little, truly," Kiijeem replied with admirable honesty. "You are not going to kill me." It was not a question. Had the human intended murder, he would already have carried it out.

"No. You are not my enemy." Drawing his knees up to his chest, Flinx clasped his arms around them. As dawn began to threaten, the coldest part of the night probed harder at his exposed flesh.

"The Empire and the Commonwealth have been enemiess for a long time." As he spoke, Kiijeem tried to note all the details of the soft-skin's alien anatomy. In many ways the sight was laughable; in others, fascinating.

"I am not the Commonwealth," Flinx told him somberly. "And you, I hope, are not the Empire. I know your name, and you know mine. By the sand that shelters life, I would beg your friendship."

None of this was proceeding as Kiijeem had expected. First the human had physically upended him and now it was unsettling him mentally as well. As the victor in their combat the softskin was in a position to *demand* friendship. There was no need for him to beseech it. But that was just what he was doing. Gratuitously and without being asked, he had given back to Kiijeem the share of status that the nye had lost in the course of the fight. It was a generous gift.

But—could he respond? Whoever heard of an AAnn granting

friendship to a human? One might as well offer it to a rabid thranx. Yet given the circumstances of their meeting, how could he refuse? More beguilingly, Kiijeem was not sure he *wanted* to refuse.

Though he sensed the ambivalence in the young AAnn's emotions, Flinx did not try to intervene, either verbally or with his Talent. It was important that, whatever decision this youth came to, he reach it on his own. Only in that way would it last. Flinx was optimistic. Given his youth, Kiijeem might not yet have acquired the visceral hatred of humans that was prevalent among his kind. Noninterference in the young nye's decision was, on Flinx's part, something of a gamble. He smiled inwardly. He had gambled similarly on one or two occasions in the past, and he was still here.

His assessment paid off. Turning his head to one side, Kiijeem exposed his throat. At the same time, he reached out toward the human, the claws on his hand fully retracted. Across the distance that separated them, Flinx mimicked the clutching gesture flawlessly.

"Sso you are telling me," a now far more at ease Kiijeem began as he lowered his arm, "that you have ssomehow penetrated all Imperial planetary and ssysstem defenssess ssolely in the sservice of a perssonal interesst?"

Flinx nodded, then thought to add the appropriate AAnn gesture of third-degree reassurance. "That's one reason. There is another." Turning slightly to his left, he glanced at the eastern sky. It was starting to lighten. "Not enough time for complete explanations now, I'm afraid. You and I have struck concordance. I'm not sure others of your kind would be so accommodating if they were aware of my presence here." He turned back to his young host. "Also, the city authorities are looking for me."

Kiijeem looked startled. "They know there iss a ssoftsskin in Krrassin?"

Flinx smiled. "No. They're looking for a nye who has made use of illicit exchange." He indicated his neatly laid-out simsuit. "Not only have I passed illegally among your kind, I've passed illegal funds."

"Sso that iss what you are doing here, on the property of my family." Kiijeem's emotions had run the gamut all the way from fear to delight. "You are a fugitive twice over: as a ssoftsskin without portfolio and as a common criminal."

Flinx shrugged. "Anymore it seems like I'm always doing things in multiples." He indicated an artificial rock overhang, the area it sheltered hidden from both the low-lying main residence and the street. "Can I stay awhile, and if I do will you keep my presence here a secret?"

"Are we not now friendss in combat, ssoftsskin?" Straightening out of his crouch, Kiijeem approached as Flinx rose to his feet. Turning his head to one side, the young AAnn exposed his throat. Flinx gripped it lightly, withdrew his hand, and turned his own head. Had he not been able to perceive the nye's emotions, he would never have taken such a chance. Young as he was, Kiijeem still had claws sharp enough to rip out a human throat.

The AAnn touched him appropriately and then stepped back. "You may sstay. Can you eat normal food?" Flinx gestured assent, though without the typical tail embellishment. Even in the absence of the accompanying gesture, Kiijeem understood. "You musst hide during the day. Tonight I will bring you ssomething to eat. Thiss area of the compound iss maintained and groomed by automatics. They are unssophisssticated and eassily avoided." He studied the tall human. "Tonight you will answwer my quesstionss. I have many."

"I have a few of my own," Flinx replied. The possibilities presented by this unexpected new relationship were unspooling in his mind. In seeking a quiet place to hide for the night, he might have found a good deal more.

If Flinx handled it right, young Kiijeem AVMd might just be his way safely out of the capital city of Krrassin and off the homeworld of the predatory AAnn.

CHAPTER

4

Hidden away within an artificial landscape on private property deep in the capital city on the homeworld of humanxkind's most implacable enemies, Flinx took pleasure in a surprisingly relaxing sleep. While the sandstone crevice in which he had sequestered himself for the night was hard and unyielding, the simsuit on which he was lying provided some padding. As for Pip, she obtained all the heat she needed for a good night's rest by simply coiling up next to her recumbent master.

The sun woke Flinx with enough force to remind him that he needed the simsuit as much to prevent sunstroke and sunburn as to fool the AAnn. Following a long draught of suit-treated water suctioned from the pool complemented by a measured sip from his liquid food supplies, he emerged from the crevice to examine his surroundings in daylight.

Not more than two meters high, the section of the main residence that protruded above ground level was clearly visible across the sculpted terrain. From a distance it was impossible to estimate the true size of the low-lying habitation. Given the extent of the surrounding fenced property and its location within the capital's boundaries, Flinx speculated that it would be considerable. Kiijeem's extended family was clearly very well off and the brevity of the young AAnn's surname further confirmed its status.

He crouched back under cover when a private transport rose from an underground garage. Humming softly, it accelerated parallel to his location. The vehicle paused at the fence line only long enough to satisfy Security before exiting onto the nearest passway and rising toward the distant domes and squat edifices that marked the center of the city. Half an hour later an entirely different transport appeared and entered the property. It did not head for the subterranean garage. Instead, it disgorged its trio of passengers outside and aboveground. The visitors then entered the underground complex by means of a down-sloping rampway. Friends or workers, Flinx theorized, having no means of determining the newcomers' status. Reaching out toward them, he found that their emotions were flat and uninformative.

Not so those of the single figure that drew near his hiding place an hour later. Alien feelings rose and dipped in a combustible mix of anticipation, exhilaration, and uncertainty. Flinx sensed Kiijeem's approach well before he actually saw the young nye. All sentients, he had long ago discovered, broadcast their own distinctive emotive signature. He could recognize these as easily as a dog could identify animals by smell. At least, he could when his always unpredictable, irritatingly erratic Talent was functioning, as it was now.

He considered donning the simsuit in preparation for the impending meeting, then decided against it. There was no reason for him to do so as long as he was careful to keep out of the direct glare of Blasusarr's star. True, he would be more comfortable inside the self-regulating, temperature-controlled suit, but why waste the power when he could cool off just as easily with a simple dip in the pool? So he stayed in the shadows and waited for Kiijeem to find him.

The youthful AAnn did so eagerly, greeting him with a far more casual gesture than he had employed in the course of their previous encounter. "You are ressted for hunting?" he inquired energetically.

"Rested to kill," Flinx replied politely and in kind. They were neither going to hunt nor kill anything except time, he knew, but many revered AAnn traditions dated to a time when Kiijeem's ancestors had stalked prey in packs across the wide hot stretches of Blasusarr's unforgiving deserts and plateaus. As man and AAnn looked on, Pip decided to pursue one of the nearby pool's many aquatic life-forms.

"Your companion takess well to water," Kiijeem commented. "I have read that it iss much the ssame with your sspeciess."

Unlike the thranx, who had a disconcerting tendency to sink instead of float and as a consequence possessed (with a few daredevil exceptions) a visceral fear of water, the AAnn could swim. Not as efficiently as humans, but with the aid of their tails they could manage reasonably well. Flinx decided to postpone any demonstration. While the emotions the young AAnn was disseminating confirmed that his current amity was genuine, he was still no boon teenage acquaintance. The relationship between them could change at any moment, Flinx knew. The same instinctive wariness that had sustained him and kept him alive since childhood had taught him that when and where possible it was always best to keep one's abilities a secret from a potential foe, no matter how unlikely the prospect of conflict might seem at the moment.

So he did not offer to demonstrate the human ability to swim by going for a dip. Instead, he indicated the lumpy package that hung from a strap over Kiijeem's left shoulder.

"Food and drink, as I promissed." Setting the fabric container down, the young nye proceeded to unseal it. Some of the contents he passed to Flinx while keeping the rest for himself.

The tidily prepared cubes and slabs had the look, smell, consistency, and taste of various kinds of meat. Flinx knew they had been grown in vast protein factories. Only a specialist could have told them from actual animal flesh. Dining on the latter had long since been a privilege reserved for those AAnn who had access to significant income. Kiijeem's family might be rich enough to afford real meat, but not to the point of allowing one of their offspring access to it for a casual midday meal.

Flinx dug into the alien offering with gusto. AAnn food was better than liquid supplements, which was all that his suit could supply. Having been forced to survive on it many times in the course of the preceding couple of weeks, his system welcomed the change. Small doses of the metabolic supplements he swallowed every morning allowed him to assimilate even the most exotic components of local fare without damage to his stomach or intestines.

Kiijeem looked on in amazement as the tall human downed cube after cube of local food. "Your teeth are flat and few are pointed. How can they prepare ssomething like *kolipk* for digesstion?"

In between chews, Flinx pulled back his lips to reveal his teeth to his host. It was a physical feat the stiff-jawed AAnn could not duplicate. Kiijeem flinched at the sight.

"See?" Flinx told him as he relaxed his mouth. "The front teeth are incisors. Flat, but designed for cutting. All AAnn teeth are like daggers, short and sharp. Those of my kind are more diverse. Some are like slicing blades, a few are like daggers, and most are evolved for grinding. Remember that we are omnivores and consume plant matter as well." He resumed eating.

Kiijeem performed a second-degree gesture of amazement. "Fasscinating. It is almosst as if the evolutionary process wass unssure which direction your biology sshould take."

"We often wonder about such things ourselves." He gestured at a dark purple slab of protein. "Pass me another piece of that seared *hilthopk*, will you?" The youth complied.

"How do you come to know sso much about our wayss, our food, our language?" Kiijeem asked him. "According to my sstudiess, humanss and AAnn rarely encounter one another except in the coursse of formalizing diplomatic or commercial exchangess." He hesitated before adding, "And in battle."

Flinx let it slide. "I suppose you could say that I am a rare kind of human. I have a particular reason for being interested in all species. Including those with whom the Commonwealth government does not always get along. As a consequence I've spent an unusual amount of time in the company of other sentients—including your own kind. Most recently on a world called Jast."

"Jasst," Kiijeem repeated. "I have heard of it. It hass not been prominent in my sstudiess."

"It's not an Imperial world," Flinx informed him. "It's independent, though inclining more to the Imperial orbit than that of the Commonwealth. There are many of your kind working there." Recent memories came flooding back. "I spent some time there. More than I anticipated. A lot of it was among artists of your species."

Kiijeem's reaction was reflexive. "*Pfssaact!* Some artisstss are important in their way. Indusstrial dessignerss, for example. But mosst are weak and little more than a burden on ssociety. Art sshould be an adjunct to a true life. Thosse who choosse to do nothing but art are little more than parassitess. Humanx ssociety, if I remember correctly, viewss thiss differently." Reinforced by gesture and emotion, the implication in the youth's tone was that humans and thranx were both debased species because they chose to honor full-time artists and viewed creative endeavors as an acceptable way of spending one's entire existence.

Sidestepping a characteristic AAnn invitation to argument, Flinx elaborated. "I think you might feel differently about this particular group of artists. For one thing, they chose to live apart from the rest of AAnn society. Your kind are especially gregarious, and such self-enforced isolation on an alien world represents a considerable sacrifice for them."

"Fleeing and hiding by any other name . . ." Unpersuaded, Kiijeem blew dismissively through the nostrils located at the end of his short snout.

"I was badly injured and they took me in," Flinx continued. "My own kind did not; the dominant Jastian sentients, the Vssey, did not. Only this group of AAnn artisans freely offered me shelter and succor. They could just as easily have finished me off and made a meal of my remains." He met the youth's slitted gaze without blinking. "Most members of your species would have done exactly that. At least one of them tried. But not the members of this Tier." He leaned back against a stone slab that was being warmed by the heat of day.

"I'd lost my memory. My time among the members of this Tier helped me regain it. They treated me as one of their own. One in particular . . ." His voice trailed away.

Though what little he knew of the remarkably flexible and expressive human face had been learned only in the past day or so, Kiijeem thought he detected suggestions of emotions not formerly encountered. The sudden fall-off of the human's voice and deliberate noncompletion of a whole thought also seemed to point to previously unencountered ambiguity. Curious as to the cause, he pressed his visitor for further explanation.

"You did not finissh the narrative. You were sspeaking, I believe, of an individual nye."

Flinx eyed his young host sharply. "You're a perceptive one, Kiijeem."

The AAnn responded with a gesture indicting first-degree concurrence. "In ssocial groupss I am often ssingled out for approbation of my sskillss at obsservation."

"Truly," Flinx conceded. "The female's name was Chraluuc. Like all of the Tier to which she belonged, she was an artist. She was charged, I suspect originally against her will, with looking after my amnesiac self. We became friends. Good friends. More than most, she wished me to be a bridge between human and AAnn."

"What happened to her?" Kiijeem was much intrigued. In all his studies he had never encountered an instance of a personal, as opposed to the occasional professional, closeness between a human and one of his own kind.

"The same thing that happens to all of us." Flinx spoke softly, remembering. "She died. Too soon." He eyed the young AAnn. Round eyes peered deeply into slitted pupils. "I've spent much of my life not doing that."

Kiijeem was momentarily confused. "Not doing what?"

"Dying." Straining to see past the landscaping off to his right, Flinx peered in the direction of the main residence. "I wouldn't want that to happen to you."

"Not to worry on that sscore." To emphasize his confidence, the crouching AAnn smacked the ground twice with his tail. "Sshould sserious conflict arisse between uss, I can alwayss turn you in to the authoritiess."

It was a characteristic AAnn trait, Flinx knew well, to be direct to the point of tactlessness.

"Truly you could," he admitted dryly. "But it is my hope that you and I might foster a friendship similar to the one I formed on Jast."

"Time will reveal," Kiijeem told his guest, as straightforward as ever. "For the moment I sstill find you far too interessting to ssacrifice." Underlying his enthusiasm, the tip of his tail kept flicking from side to side. And according to his emotions, Flinx sensed a suggestion of thrill. No doubt from the danger inherent in being so intimate with one of his species' traditional adversaries.

Fine, Flinx decided. Keep the youngster interested, keep him involved, and he will be far less inclined to reveal his visitor's presence.

Kiijeem's inquisitiveness was as unbounded as his boldness. Adjusting his stance and settling into an ever-lower crouch while utilizing his tail for balance, he used his long, narrow, flexible tongue to clean the outer membrane of first one eye and then the other.

"Tell me about humankind. I know more of the thranx becausse my people have had longer contact with them. But where humanss are concerned, the information available iss less extenssive. I have sseen how you eat. How can you chew with your jawss insside your sskull? As you walk, don't thosse protruding external earss catch on thingss? You sstand perfectly sstraight: how do your kneess handle the consstant pressure?" Leaning to one side, he tried to see behind his guest. "And by the Great Egg, I cannot fathom how your kind can sstand upright, much less run, in the abssence of a tail to provide sstability."

"Well, to a large extent that has to do with how our internal ears are made," Flinx began.

In the days that followed he educated his young host not only in the particulars of human physiology, but in the art, music, theater, science, and sociology of his species, as well as the history of the Commonwealth. Hailing from a culture in which aggressive behavior was prized, expected, and rewarded, Kiijeem took a special interest in Flinx's description of pre-Amalgamation intra-human wars.

"Thesse taless of your once planet-bound sspeciess are very different from thosse of the dissgusstingly placid thranx, and do not ssound sso very different from what I have learned of my own kind and itss drive to make the leap out into intersstellar sspace. Though I am sstill young and have no experience of ssuch thingss, it sseemss to me that your kind and mine may have more in common than you do with the repellent hardsshellss. Yet you are alliess with them and not with uss."

Flinx had to smile. "Are you sure you're not preparing for a career in the Imperial diplomatic corps?"

"I have not yet chossen a life pace," Kiijeem confessed. A slight pressure on the end of his spine caused him to look down and back. Having coiled around his tail, Pip was playing with the twitching tip.

"She likes you," Flinx told his host. "You should be flattered. She usually doesn't take quickly to strangers."

Kiijeem turned back to the human. While the absence of a tail had many disadvantages, there was one clear benefit. The softskin could sit on any surface, in any position, without the risk of damage to the smallest of his vertebrae.

"Her epidermiss iss very ssimilar to that of my kind. I feel that sshe ssenssess a kinsship."

"I'm sure that she does," Flinx agreed. *But if you try to hurt me, superficial similarities notwithstanding, she'll kill you without a second's hesitation.* He did not voice the caution. Despite his deepening camaraderie with the young AAnn, there was nothing to be gained by filling him in on every little detail.

It was getting late. Or rather, early. Soon the sun would be up. Kiijeem straightened his body, rising up out of his resting crouch, his tail stiffening behind him. "Thesse passt dayss and the captivating time I have sspent in your company have enabled me to come to a decission."

Flinx tensed slightly, readying himself for whatever might come. "Truly, it is always constructive when one comes to a decision."

Both optical membranes were withdrawn as the youth looked over at him. "My decission iss—that I am not afraid of you any longer."

Flinx relaxed. "That's a good decision to come to." Extending an arm, he indicated the landscaped surroundings where he had spent the past week in comparative safety and comfort. "For my part, I have to point out that as agreeable as our meetings and conversations have been, we both know they can't continue forever. I've already spent more time here than I intended—and that has been because of you. I'm not complaining, mind—knowledge has been passed in both directions. But now . . ." Using both hands he executed a first-degree gesture of urgency. "Now I am truly compelled to move onward because of matters that lie beyond my control. It's time for me to leave."

Kiijeem eyed his guest speculatively. "You are expected ssomewhere elsse? You do not sstrike me as the type of individual who fretss over a missed appointment."

"The appointment I have to keep," Flinx replied solemnly, "involves the future of your kind as well as mine. As well as everyone's." How to describe his situation to this youthful representative of another species? How to convey even a hint of the seriousness, the weight, the overwhelming burden that life and circumstance had placed on his shoulders? Should he even try? If he tried, would his explanation make any sense? And if it did, what were the chances of it being believed? Better to keep his reasoning nonspecific and ill-defined.

"All I can tell you, Kiijeem, is that for the sake of the Commonwealth *and* the Empire, I *must* be allowed to return to my ship."

His host considered. His response, when it was finally forthcoming, was not encouraging. "I have been able to keep you ssafe here becausse my family iss highly resspected, elevated in sstatuss, and dwellss on property that iss professionally ssecured." A clawed hand gestured toward the distant, night-shadowed fence line. "But once you are beyond the family boundariess you will once again rissk attracting the notice of Imperial Ssecurity and find yoursself ssubject to public ssearching."

Flinx gestured over at his now thoroughly aired-out simsuit. "I passed secretly and safely among you for a full teverravak. I can do so again. I only need to keep my identity a secret long enough to get out of the city. I've prearranged a location with my ship. It's situated well outside the city, in a locality infrequently visited by locals. A place where a fast-moving shuttle can touch down just long enough to make an unauthorized pickup. By the time its vector has been detected and analyzed by Planetary Security, I'll be back on board my vessel and safely on my way outsystem."

"A heartening sscenario," Kiijeem conceded, "but one I mysself conssider unlikely. While one of my age knowss but little of how Planetary Ssecurity workss, I *do* know that likenessess of your ssimulated sself have been widely dissperssed and viewed on all formss of general media for the passt sseveral dayss." He indicated the rock crevice where Flinx had been storing the carefully folded simsuit. "The appearance of your AAnn perssona at any time would quickly trigger an active ressponsse." Using a clawed hand to trace a diagram in the air, the youth made a sign indicative of supplementary third-degree mirth.

"The narration accompanying thesse portrayalss of your dissguissed sself hass often verged on the pretentiouss. The continued inability of the authoriticess to trace the origin of 'the myssteriouss forger and accomplisshed currency thief,' as you have been desscribed, hass provided a perssisstent albeit minor sstory line for the sseriouss media."

Kiijeem expelled a series of rising hisses that constituted laughter among his kind. "I cannot imagine the hyssterical reaction that would enssue if they had any idea what you really are."

Flinx mulled his young friend's observations. "I think I still might be able to slip out of the city, especially if I travel at night. But I can't argue the fundamentals of this with you, Kiijeem. If my AAnn image has indeed been disseminated widely among the general public, any movement on my part is going to entail a real risk." He studied the young nye thoughtfully. "You could smuggle me out in a vehicle."

"I would have to produce a ssuitable explanation as to why I would need the private usse of a family transsport." The youth did not immediately reject the idea. "The vehicle'ss progress would be tracked. If your dessired landing location iss as remote as you ssuggesst, quesstionss would be raissed as to what I wass doing there." Vertical violet pupils met Flinx's steady gaze. "Given ssuch aid you might indeed make your esscape, ssoftsskin. But I would be left behind to deal with the awkward queriess that would inevitably follow. If your true identity wass ssubssequently learned, ssuch a revelation could mean not only the end of my prosspectss but of my life. And worsse sstill, immensse loss of sstatuss to my family." He hesitated. "But if you believe it iss the only way . . ."

"No," Flinx told him bluntly. "I won't chance it on that basis, Kiijeem. I've spent much of the past couple of years trying to decide if my own kind is worth the sacrifice of my own future and happiness. If I were to ask you to risk yours, I could never justify preserving my own." He punctuated his decision with a first-degree gesture signifying concordance.

"Sstrange." His age notwithstanding, Kiijeem turned unexpectedly philosophical. "I offer to take ssuch a rissk for you, and your ressponsse iss to refusse it becausse it would imperil me. If thiss were to be known, you would gain sstatuss among my kind."

Flinx muttered a reply. "I already suffer from more status than I'd like to have, thanks."

Kiijeem was not sure he understood this response. He felt he was incapable of grasping the proper context. In any case, he did not push for a more extensive explanation. It was enough to realize that the soft-skin would not put him at risk even in order to advance his own ends. It confirmed what Kiijeem had come to believe: this was not the human of his studies. No matter how hostile or threatening the others of his species might be, it was clear that there was sufficient individual variance to allow for one whose thoughts and actions were, in their slightly twisted way, almost nyelike.

"I'll have to try and get back to the pickup point the same way I left it," Flinx was telling him. "By making use of public transportation." Looking to his left, he eyed the folded simsuit where it lay waiting in its crevice. "I can't modify the face—the suit material was formed in a single piece. But maybe I can disguise it somehow. At least enough to prevent immediate identification by roving automatics." A small smile played at the corners of his mouth. "A pity your kind doesn't wear hats."

Kiijeem patiently indicated fourth-degree ignorance. "What iss a 'hat'?"

Flinx passed a hand over his red hair. "An item of clothing designed to cover the head."

"Why would one want to cover one's head?"

"Well, for one thing, to keep the sun off."

"Why would you want to keep the ssun off your head?" Instead of being enlightened, Kiijeem found himself more confused than ever.

Flinx sighed as Pip glided down to land softly in his lap. Absently, he stroked the back of her head and upper body as she curled up against him. "My kind can suffer if the head is exposed to too much sun."

"What a sstrange concept." Every time the softskin said something, Kiijeem learned something new about this alien species. "We welcome the ssun on our headss."

"It's really not the sun I need to block, but my bogus reptilian visage." From a distance Flinx continued to study the folds of his disguise. "What I *need* is the AAnn equivalent of a chameleon suit. Even if you could get hold of one for me, I probably couldn't make it fit right." He chewed worriedly on his lower lip. "There has to be *some* way to hide my face."

Kiijeem had a thought. "Perhapss if your face wass bandaged up, as if you had been in a sseriouss accident."

Flinx considered the notion for several moments before finally shaking his head. Kiijeem had come to learn that among softskins, this odd side-to-side motion was a simplistic indication of negativity.

"Good thought," Flinx told his young friend. "Your kind are sufficiently private so that no one would be likely to pry about the cause of the bandaging. But what about one of your publicans, those who are employed by the state to aid citizens in distress? I can't have a solicitous health professional inquiring about my 'condition,' no matter how caring their intentions. All it would take is for one specialist to have a close look at my simsuit and my subterfuge would be exposed."

"That iss sso." Kiijeem slumped. "I had not thought of that."

"We'll think of something," Flinx assured his young friend. "What we have to do is come up with a list of possibilities and winnow them down to the least inauspicious."

As an assessment of available options intended to save his life, it was a conclusion decidedly lacking in optimism.

CHAPTER

5

Vunkiil BNCCRSQ did not very much like her job. For one thing, the work was too easy, too repetitive. Without challenge there was little room in which to acquire status and therefore few opportunities for advancement. She longed for a crisis that would allow her to demonstrate her exceptional competency. One serious enough to allow her to reap the formal name of BNCCRS. Alas, it seemed that the "Qucent" of her family name was likely to be attached to her until her scales dulled in hue and her claws grew blunt and old.

What attracted her attention that afternoon did not exactly qualify as a crisis, but it was at least curious enough to entice her away from her tiresome regular duties.

In her position in the station as one of a dozen monitors of traffic in orbit above Blasusarr's largest continent, it was her task to keep track of a certain number of vessels both coming and going that had been assigned to her watch. Over the past several days one had drawn just a little more notice than most. Not because it had done anything unusual, not because its visual or electronic signature was in any way out of the ordinary, but simply because it had done precisely that—nothing. Not merely nothing unusual, but nothing at all. That was in and of itself—unusual.

Vessels did not arrive in orbit around the homeworld for no reason.

Interstellar travel was always difficult, dangerous, and expensive. It was not undertaken for a lark. As with any action taken by the AAnn and their allies, reason and purpose underlay every activity. Yet in all the time it had been in quiet, standard orbit around Blasusarr since arriving from outsystem, this particular minor commercial vessel had distinguished itself by doing nothing. While doing nothing did not exactly constitute a hazard, the complete lack of action and response was sufficiently out of the ordinary to finally invite her attention.

She might well be making a fool of herself for following up on the observation, she knew. There could be any number of perfectly rational explanations for the vessel's continued inaction. She debated with herself for one more day before deciding that the prudent course of action would be to find a colleague to concur with her opinion. The reason she delayed was that if additional action was taken on her recommendation she would be the one to garner all the blame, but if anything positive resulted, she would have to share the credit with her defender. After wrestling with the conundrum for part of yet another morning, she finally decided there was no way she could plausibly proceed without at least one corroborator. She found herself turning to Arubaat DJJKWWE, the monitor who was stationed next to her.

"I have a requesst: run a sstock ssafeguard on the vessel occupying thesse coordinatess." Without waiting for a response she reallocated the relevant information to his station. Tail tip barely flicking the floor behind his seat, he complied without looking over at her.

"A class twenty-four cargo craft, with minimal if any passenger-carrying capability," he reported with becoming swiftness. "Onboard life ssupport appearss to be active. When queried, it resspondss appropriately."

"But alwayss electronically." She leaned slightly though not provocatively in his direction. She wanted confirmation, not a fight. "I have been querying the craft for sseveral dayss now and have yet to receive a ssingle vissual of any member of the crew."

Her colleague's dismissal was unapologetically sarcastic. "Perhaps the crew iss sshy. They need only resspond appropriately to formal queriess. Nothing requiress that they sshow themsselvess." The third-degree gesture of apathy he flipped in her direction matched his tone. "For thiss you interrupt my own sscanning?"

"In the time that I have been monitoring them," she replied frostily, "they have done nothing but acknowledge presscribed ssignalss. They have initiated no application for landing, forwarded no requesst for cusstomss clearance, ressponded uninteresstedly to repeated offerss to clear cargo. Do you not find thiss odd? Or possibly you think they have come all thiss way ssolely to drift in orbit around the homeworld and admire itss landsscape?"

Reluctantly, Arubaat found himself somewhat drawn to his colleague's disquiet. "They have not yet requessted permission to ssend down a sshuttle, or to validate their bussiness here?"

"Nothing," she told him firmly. "All codess and queriess are answered with a promptness that iss only undersscored by their lack of detail."

"Not likely a ssecretive thranx warsship, then. What elsse can it be?" Returning his attention to his own station, the now intrigued Arubaat sent skyward a series of electronic requests. They were answered without delay—and without a hint of elaboration. His carefully formatted queries had generated the minimum response required to satisfy regulations. The automated files were completely satisfied.

He, however, was not. At least, not entirely. Much as he hated to admit it, his coworker and natural work-rival might be on to something. How could he make the most of her apparent insight to benefit himself? Much depended on what she wanted to do next, on how she wanted to proceed. So he asked her. After first formally registering his own interest in the matter, of course.

Distastefully but not unexpectedly, she recorded his official acknowledgment of support before elaborating. "The sship'ss crew musst have ssome agenda in mind, whether commercial or otherwisse. It iss incumbent upon uss"—and she took care to emphasize the "uss"—"as Imperial monitorss to find out what it iss. There alsso existstss the possibility that thosse aboard have ssuffered a collective injury either to themsselvess or to their communicationss facilitiess. Or they may be ssuffering under adversse circumsstances we cannot envission—becausse they can do nothing more than ressppond automatically and electronically to our inquiriess."

Arubaat withheld comment until the female had concluded her review of the situation. "What do you proposse?"

Taking the necessary risk, Vunkiil plunged ahead. "A formal investigation. I would conssider mysself remiss in my dutiess were I to ssuggesst anything less. A crewed orbital monitor needss to approach the vessel in quesstion and examine it with more than jusst insstrumentss."

Her colleague made a second-degree gesture of concurrence. "I will ssecond your recommendation—bassed ssolely, of coursse, on your assessment of the ssituation."

"Of coursse," she responded flatly. It would have been unrealistic to expect anything less from a fellow and equally ambitious nye. Arubaat was taking steps to cover his tail in the event the time-consuming and costly inspection revealed nothing out of the ordinary.

Too late for second thoughts, she told herself. The bones had been thrown. While she still felt confident she had made the right decision in requesting the detailed check, her convictions would have been greatly reinforced if only she could have come up with a better rationale for the continuing silence of the mysterious craft's peculiarly nonresponsive crew.

One reason that never occurred to her was that the vessel in question might not have a crew.

Kiijeem had hardly retired for the remainder of the night, slipping quietly back to his quarters in the main residence, when the integrated communit inside the hood of Flinx's simsuit sang softly for attention. Inconspicuous as it was, the sound was so unexpected that a startled Flinx looked around in momentary shock before settling on the source.

It was the *Teacher* calling. It had to be. There was nothing and no one else within a hundred parsecs that had access to that special frequency or the means to address him. The call itself told him immediately that something was wrong. While on the surface of another world *he* contacted the *ship*. It did not, would not, try to contact him unless something had gone amiss.

Hurrying over to the suit, he picked it up and positioned it so that the internal receptor was close to the side of his head. Though the *Teacher* could bend frequencies as efficiently as a child could snap elastic bands, it was still important to keep all such clandestine communications as brief as possible to avoid any chance they might be traced and tracked.

"I'm here," he declared simply.

"I wish you were here," the *Teacher* replied. "I am currently undergoing examination by a small orbital patrol vessel of the type favored by the AAnn. I am certain that this is because both my programmed and extemporaneous responses to all ground-based inquiries as to purpose and intent have been purely abstract."

"Can you be certain of this?" a suddenly tense Flinx asked.

"I am being asked to present a member of my 'crew' to respond to these queries in person. I have managed to gain a delay by claiming that a general illness is present among the 'crew' and that a suitable presentation will be made available to the immigration and transit authorities within a two-day. They have accepted this explanation but are persistent with their uncomfortably close observations. While my present facade was fashioned to its usual meticulous standards, there are details that will not stand up to any actual attempt at boarding."

This was bad, Flinx knew. Very bad. If the *Teacher*'s exterior was discovered to be false, his ship would draw an immediate response that was likely to be as overwhelming as it was unwelcome. If the *Teacher* was determined to be of Commonwealth origin, not even its advanced design, technology, and capabilities would be sufficient to allow it to escape safely outsystem. Even if it did manage to flee successfully, in the process it would be forced to leave at least one important component of itself behind.

Him.

"I'm assuming you've evaluated potential lines of response to this probe," he murmured toward the pickup.

"I have." The *Teacher*'s prompt response was encouraging. "I could easily destroy the inspecting vessel. However, the reaction this would provoke would likely prove disadvantageous to your presence here."

Same old *Teacher*, Flinx told himself. As thoroughgoing a master of understatement as an artificial intelligence could possibly be.

"Let's assume we discard that option as unworkable," he replied dryly. "What else have you got?"

"I will generate a lengthy and detailed rationale for having to hastily depart outsystem. One that conforms to and is suitable for all the pertinent AAnn procedures in my database. My calculation is that this will engender some minor irritation at the lowest levels of the relevant bureaucracies. It should quickly be forgotten. After a short but suitable interval spent undetectably in space-plus during which time I will completely revamp and rechameleonize my external appearance, I will return. For several days at least, a newly arrived, completely different ship occupying a completely different orbit should not arouse similar discomfiting suspicions among those still searching for my previous incarnation. Several days constitute ample time in which to pin-plunge a shuttle, recover you from the surface, and disappear safely back into space-plus."

Flinx considered. The ship's suggestion was typically comprehensive and well thought out. There was only one flaw he could find in the proposal.

"That means I'll be stuck here. Until you can reconfigure and return."

"Until I can reconfigure and return, yes." There was a pause, then, "To attempt anything more forward and direct while I am under such close observation would be to put both of us unnecessarily at serious risk."

The *Teacher* was not arguing on its own behalf, Flinx knew. It would do exactly as it was instructed. If he ordered it to make an attempt to pick him up on the grounds of the Imperial Palace itself, it would comply. And in all likelihood be vaporized in the process.

"How much time will you need?" he murmured. "To depart out-system, enter space-plus, jump back, reconfigure, and return?"

"Certain components of the course of action you state are not immediately quantifiable. Given the variability of the conditions involved I would rather not venture specifics. Say, no less than a few days, no more than a couple of local teverravaks."

A single teverravak was sixteen Blasusarrian days, Flinx knew. Even with Kiijeem's help, could he continue to avoid the attention of the authorities for that long? Or even continue to avoid coming to the notice of members of the young AAnn's extended family? Only the day before he had nearly been discovered by a pair of distant relations who had been walking the family property. Fortunately they had been more interested in finding a place to complete a secluded mating than in searching the crannies and crevices of the landscaped pool where he was hiding.

He really had no choice, he realized. The mounting risk to the *Teacher* had to be addressed immediately. He took a deep breath as a concerned Pip stirred to wakefulness nearby.

"Initiate the program described at your preferred speed," he whispered into the pickup. "Carry out the necessary measures as fast as you can—without compromise. I understand that we risk disaster if you make an attempt to return before modification is properly completed. The new camouflage has to be at least as effective as your present disguise."

"I concur absolutely." Did the ship sound relieved? Flinx wondered. "I will exert maximum effort, Flinx, and resume contact as soon as is safe. Until then, you must preserve yourself and all your functions without recourse to my facilities."

"You can count on that," he muttered fervently. There was no need to say good-bye, farewell, or anything else. All that needed to be said had been said.

Setting the simsuit aside, he lay down on the cool sandstone. His gaze wandered upward to focus on the unfamiliar stars. Somewhere up there the *Teacher* would be formulating excuses to satisfy increasingly inquisitive AAnn administrators of both the organic and electronic variety. Shortly thereafter his ship would head outsystem, whereupon it would make the jump to the safety and anonymity of space-plus as soon as was feasible.

At which point, he reflected, he would be well and truly alone on an alien and hostile world.

Not entirely alone, he reminded himself as an attentive Pip pushed up against him. And not entirely hostile, either. Overhead, something native that sported a long tail and membranous wings passed between him and a waning moon. Young Kiijeem was not hostile. Aggressively curious, perhaps, but not hostile. Still, he was a nye, he was AAnn, and the youth of any sentient species could be fickle in its own idiosyncratic way. What if one afternoon his host decided that he had learned as much as he could from his secretive human visitor? What if fear of discovery made him decide to turn Flinx over to the authorities? Would he not gain considerable status from doing so? How far, and for how long, could Flinx continue to trust him?

Among his own species there were those comparable in age to Kiijeem who would happily turn him in for monetary reward. Flinx had recently met several examples of them on Visaria. Could he reasonably expect the youthful representative of an entirely different species, an antagonistic one at that, to exhibit a greater degree of altruism?

There was no avoiding the reality: his present situation was terribly fragile. So be it: he would have to find a way to strengthen it. If the one young nye with whom he had established a relationship was tentative, then he must somehow find a way to engage with others made of sterner stuff. But how to make contact with other AAnn, preferably adults, who would not reflexively turn him over to Krrassin Security? How could he tell whom to trust? Even assuming that his Talent remained functional, reading their emotions could only reveal how a sentient was feeling at a particular moment. He had no way of predicting how a prospective friend might feel about him the next day, or even the next hour.

He had filled the eager Kiijeem with knowledge, and the young nye had appeared to thrive on the flow of information. Dare he entrust similar knowledge and his true identity to some adult? The *Teacher* could not help him now. He needed local allies. AAnn with access to greater resources than Kiijeem could command. To acquire such while simultaneously avoiding incarceration and accompanying unpleasant interrogation presented him with by far the most difficult undertaking he had contemplated since setting down on Blasusarr.

Among the several constants that transcended species there was one he knew from his study of and time spent among the AAnn that he could count on. Power invariably attracts additional power. To acquire the kind of freedom of movement he sought, he needed clout of a kind the admirably candid Kiijeem self-admittedly could not muster.

Perhaps, Flinx told himself, his young friend knew someone who could.

It had rained earlier in the evening. For an industrialized capital city the air of Krrassin was unusually clean. No doubt extra effort was made to ensure that the atmosphere of the Imperial capital reflected its importance. Even so, a certain amount of pollution was unavoidable. The rain had cleared that away, so that the alien atmosphere smelled fresh and clean.

Sucking down positive ions, Flinx felt physically buoyant but mentally hesitant. The food Kiijeem had smuggled out that afternoon for his guest's late-night meal was not only edible but delicious, further adding to Flinx's sense of well-being. As carnivorous at heart as the AAnn, Pip had gorged herself on one particular sausage-like victual. Now her usually aerodynamic shape flaunted an unmistakable bulge in the region of her lower-middle, just behind her last wing-rib.

The attentive Kiijeem had settled into his customary listening crouch nearby. He always chose the same spot between Flinx and the distant residence so that if anyone approached unexpectedly from the buildings the young AAnn would block their view of the softskin.

"Tell me ssomething exciting tonight, Flinx-friend. Enlighten me with ssomething new."

Kiijeem made virtually the same request every evening, and Flinx had been happy to respond accordingly. He would do so again on this night—though on this occasion to a degree his youthful host could not possibly imagine. But first . . .

"I have to ask you a question, Kiijeem AVMd." At Flinx's uncommon use of the AAnn's full family name, Kiijeem tensed slightly. Ceasing its usual flicking back and forth, his tail stiffened into a balancing rod held straight out behind him. Both nictating membranes retracted, allowing the single moon overhead to shine more brightly than ever in his reptilian eyes.

"Ssomething iss wrong?" The young AAnn's tone reflected his uncertainty.

"The question first." Flinx exhaled slowly as he stared hard at the scaly biped. "Have you given any thought to terminating our contact and turning me over to the authorities in expectation of the status it would gain you?"

Kiijeem paused. His four-fingered right hand swayed slowly back and forth, a clear indication of distress. Confused, he could not decide on the proper gesture to employ to express his feelings. He did not need to. Flinx perceived them as clearly as if the youth was writing them down. Taken by surprise and feeling cornered by Flinx's unexpected question, the youngster was struggling to formulate a suitable reply. Finally he looked over at the silent, waiting human.

"Of coursse I have. But I have, demonsstrably, not acted on it."

An honest answer. It was what Flinx had hoped for. For Kiijeem to have declared that he had never experienced such thoughts would have been for him to deny his very self. The assertion of one lie would have led Flinx to suspect the existence of others. If not completely reassured, he felt that he could at least proceed with a certain degree of confidence that he was hearing the truth. He continued the penetrating line of questioning.

"Have you thought of killing me?"

"Truly." Kiijeem's tone remained muted, but his emotions were boiling. "How could I not wonder what you would tasste like?"

"I am told by other AAnn with whom I've spoken that the flavor lies somewhere between fresh *ilathk* and salted *cuurconn.*"

Finally gaining control of his troubled fingers, Kiijeem hastened to gesture second-degree bewilderment accentuated by third-degree curiosity. "I do not undersstand why you purssue thiss jarring line of quesstioning."

"I need to be sure of your mind-set regarding me before I tell you what I have to say next." Glancing out of the corner of his left eye he saw that the seriously overfed Pip was in no condition to come to his aid if the conversation should take an unpleasant turn. He had already lost the support of the *Teacher* for the time being. Now it appeared that the same was true of his childhood companion as well. However proceedings developed, he was going to have to deal with them on his own.

Well, it wouldn't be the first time.

"I'm going to have to remain here on Blasusarr and in Krrassin for longer than I anticipated."

Kiijeem relaxed visibly. Sinking lower into his crouch, his tail resumed its normal healthy side-to-side switching. "I feared you were going to ssay that you had to depart. I cannot tell you how deeply I have come to value thesse nocturnal exchangess. I feel that I learn more in a night here than in a teverravak'ss worth of formal daytime sstudiess."

Flinx was flattered, but that did not alter what he had to tell his enthusiastic and impressionable young host. "I'm glad I've been able to further your education." With a start he realized, not for the first time, the uncannily perceptive rationale that lay behind the name the Ulru-Ujurrians had given to the ship they had constructed for him.

"But I don't feel that I can stay in this spot much longer. I was almost discovered yesterday."

"Yess, you sspoke to me of the near encounter." With hand and tail Kiijeem gestured back through the night in the direction of the residence. "The incident wass atypical. Thiss iss not a favored part of the family compound for freeloping. It liess too far from the main buildingss."

"Nevertheless," Flinx went on, "I feel that I have to move. As I said and for reasons you don't need to know, I can't leave Blasusarr yet. Maybe not for a number of days. It's looking more and more like I might have more trouble than I originally anticipated in departing without being detected." Rising from where he had been sitting, he walked over to his host and squatted before him. This lowered him to eye level with the crouching youth.

"You've been a good friend, Kiijeem. Twice-truly. But if I'm going to be certain of leaving your world without being captured or shot down in the attempt, I feel—I fear—that I'm going to need the assistance of someone with more status than yourself."

The young AAnn digested the softskin's words. A comparable, characteristically brash human youth might have taken offense at the implication underlying Flinx's words. An analytical young thranx would have readily agreed with the conclusion. A Largessian would not have cared one way or the other. Flinx was taking a risk describing his situation so candidly to his host. But if Kiijeem had not revealed the human's presence to the authorities by now, there was a good chance he would continue to keep it a secret despite his guest's just-confessed vulnerability.

Flinx ardently hoped he was reading the young nye's emotions correctly.

He was, but Kiijeem was not so ready to agree to the roundabout request that he give up exclusive access to his remarkable visitor.

"You have been forthright with me, Flinx-friend. Sso you will not take exception or raisse a challenge if I am likewisse with you."

Flinx sat back, stretching out his legs as he relaxed from the squat. "Go ahead. It's to be expected you'd have questions."

No less bold and direct for their youth, slitted pupils eyed him piercingly. "If you are going to leave, why sshould I not reveal your exisstence to the authoritiess and garner the sstatuss to be gained from ssuch a revelation?"

At this Pip raised her head and upper body to stare at the suddenly cool AAnn. At the moment, given her heavy burden of undigested food, it was all that she could do.

"I have become your friend." Flinx stared unblinkingly back. "You have said so on more than one occasion."

"There iss an old ssaying among my kind that you may know. 'Where sstatuss sstandss tall, friendsship fallss.' "

Flinx tensed. He still felt that, if necessary, he could kill this intelligent young predator with his bare hands. "Do you adhere to that saying?"

"Truly I do," Kiijeem replied candidly, "except—in thiss particular insstance. You are my friend. I have declared it to be sso. I will help you—but I would like to know *why* I sshould do sso. I need to know thiss not for mysself. Friendsship iss reasson enough to jusstify it on my part. But if I am to help you in ssecuring the assisstance of one greater than mysself, before doing sso that individual will demand a rationale ssuperior to jusst knowing that you are my friend."

Though he was less than pleased with the AAnn's rejoinder, Flinx certainly understood it. He responded with a first-degree gesture of comprehension. "I appreciate the need you express, and I will provide such a rationale—to whomever you place me in contact with."

Kiijeem persisted. "I would sshare it."

His guest looked away. "With the best will in the world, Kiijeem, I say that such knowledge as I would share should not be for you."

The AAnn's tail tip arced straight up behind his back. "You think me lacking the capacity to comprehend?"

Unexpectedly, Flinx found himself torn. Why should he care whether he spared his youthful host the revelation he intended to reserve for an older, wiser AAnn mind? Ideally a Class-A mind—except that he knew of only one such intellect. Himself. Was it just that he believed from experience that a more mature nye would be better able to deal with the revelations? No, there was no reason to spare the vulnerable, unworldly Kiijeem from the kernel of furtive knowledge that was so much a part of Flinx. No reason whatsoever—except that he was a friend and Flinx did not want to risk damaging him.

"It's not a matter of comprehension," he tried to explain. "It's a question of—maturity isn't the right term. All I can tell you is that in order to wholly persuade one of your kind with sufficiently high status to maintain my anonymity while helping me, they have to *experience* what I know."

The explanation caught Kiijeem off guard. "How can they do that?"

"The experiencing is part of the explanation." Uncomfortable at what he found himself confessing, Flinx found himself shifting his position edgily on the warm rock.

"I inssisst on knowing thiss rationale for mysself," a frustrated Kiijeem persisted. "I *demand* to know it!" Straightening out of his crouch, he raised both clawed hands defensively in front of him and took a step backward. "Tell me or otherwisse I will divulge your pressence here."

Flinx sighed heavily. Over the course of the past several years it was debatable whether he had become a greater danger to his enemies or to his friends.

"Let's do this," he ventured hopefully. "I'll tell you the facts behind the rationale. If you still insist on the actual experience then—we'll see."

He was offering a compromise. Recognizing it, Kiijeem considered before replying. His tail tip relaxed and slumped groundward. "I am alwayss willing to lissten to the prologue that precedess the play."

"Good." In the hope that words alone would be enough to convince his youthful host, Flinx settled down to explain the looming peril that had become the driving force behind not only his life but that of his closest acquaintances. He knew all too well what sharing the full experience could do to a delicate mind. If Clarity Held had been with him, he suspected she could have explained the quandary far more effectively to the uncompromisingly curious young AAnn, and in such a way that he might drop his insistence on sharing it as hurriedly as he would a drop of Pip's poison. Because for better or worse, to both her enlightenment and detriment, Clarity had been obliged to share that experience.

Flinx settled himself a little closer to his alert, bright-eyed young host.

"You may very well not believe much of what I'm about to tell you. . . ."

CHAPTER
6

How many times over the past years had he been forced to relive the multiple terrifying encounters? The memories themselves were foul and fetid, the sour taste of something spoiled lingering on the brain. The information he was about to share with the young nye was infinitely more troubling. How should he proceed? How safely and reassuringly to convey the certain information that extinction on a galactic scale was coming this way—without actually showing it to him?

"I have the ability to—sense certain things, Kiijeem. And what I can't sense, others have shown me." There, he thought. Even Maybeso could approve of wording that simple and straightforward. "Over the years I've been made aware of an impending threat. A threat that includes not only you and I, but both of our respective civilizations and, in fact, the entire galaxy. Not just cultures and species, but the planets they live on and the stars they circle."

Kiijeem looked properly staggered, started to fashion a gesture of fourth-degree incredulity, thought better of it, and kept still. His continued silence, Flinx decided, commended him.

"I said that there was much you wouldn't believe."

The young AAnn's tail was barely moving. "Continue, *pssakk*. If nothing elsse, you ssurely have my attention. Your verity I can pass judgment on later."

Flinx nodded, then shifted his attention deliberately skyward. "You don't need to know how I was made aware of this threat. It was first crystallized for me some ten Commonwealth years ago. I've had to live with the knowledge of what it is, and of what I am, ever since."

Kiijeem pondered the human's words. "What could be a threat to an entire galaxy, except perhapss a colliding galaxy? Unless my ssimple asstronomical sstudiess have been sseverely remiss, that iss ssomething not in the offing."

"There is something else," Flinx informed him gravely. "Something more, much more. A something of which very, very few humans and thranx are aware. Though the effort seems futile they—we—are fumbling about trying to find some way, any way, that this threat might be confronted." He lowered his gaze back to his youthful host.

"I cannot describe it any other way other than to say that this menacing phenomenon is composed of pure evil. I realize such a depiction smacks more of philosophy than physics, but having tried on repeated occasions to describe it to others, that is the impression I am always left with subsequent to encountering it. It is coming this way, toward our galaxy, in the wake of a region human astronomers have for centuries called the Great Emptiness, and their thranx counterparts the Great Void. The object, the phenomenon, the deformation of standard physics—whatever you want to call it—is about three hundred million light-years wide and occupies a total volume of space some hundred million megaparsecs in extent."

Kiijeem had ceased moving as his gifted but adolescent mind struggled to grasp such impossible dimensions. Having been forced to deal with the inconceivable for so many years, Flinx could only sympathize with him. Trying to comprehend such scale was enough to give any sentient a headache.

"In place of this phenomenon, nothing else exists. Where it passes, everything except a few streamers of free hydrogen disappears. I'm told it may violate the law of the conservation of energy. If it keeps coming this way, continues on its present path, it could conceivably obliterate the entire galaxy. Commonwealth, Empire—everything vanishes."

"What—*jezzantt*—what doess it look like?" Kiijeem's voice had grown even softer than usual. "You ssaid you are aware of it, that you have knowledge of what it iss."

"I don't know what it looks like. I can only describe the feeling I get when I am mentally in its vicinity." Flinx found himself remembering, and did not want to. "Its actual physical appearance, insofar as it has one, is blocked from our view by an immense gravitational lens of dark matter. Or maybe the lens is part of the phenomenon. The scientists with whom I have been sharing my knowledge are among the most accomplished to be found anywhere in the Commonwealth, but this is something beyond their ken. Beyond anyone's, they feel."

Kiijeem struggled to grasp the incomprehensible. "If they cannot undersstand it or desscribe thiss menace, how can they, or you, or anyone, envissage a meanss for combating it?"

"There are other sciences involved besides those of the Commonwealth." Leaning forward, Flinx traced the outline of a familiar alien pyramid in the dust that covered the sandstone. "Nontraditional physics and the discoveries of prehumanx species. An ancient but still functioning potential weapon." He sat back. "All of them little more than negligible hopes, to my way of thinking. But my friends are more optimistic, and they're more knowledgeable and more experienced than I am. And I've given my word that I'll try and help."

"You?" Though still undecided whether to believe any or all of the incredible story the softskin had just told him, Kiijeem found himself eyeing his guest in a new light. "You are but one human. An exceptionally bold and interessting example, truly, but one only. If I were to give credence to your tale, which iss more fantasstical even than the ssemiliterate ravingss of the great talltale twirler Vuusskandd L himsself, the lasst thing I would imagine iss that a ssingle individual could have any influence at all on a threat of ssuch magnitude."

Flinx gazed back into the penetrating, forward-facing alien eyes. "Then we are in complete agreement. Because I think exactly the same thing. But there are those who believe otherwise. My friends and"—he dropped his gaze—"others. Some others I can identify, some who still remain a mystery to me. They come to me in dreams. Unbidden, and sometimes when I'm awake."

Kiijeem considered. "Iss it permitted to me to ssimultaneoussly believe your sstory and doubt your ssanity?"

"Once again, we are in agreement. Believe me, there are many times when I've doubted it myself. Even so, I find myself doing my best to honor the trust that those I know and respect have placed in me. It's about all I have left. That, and the knowledge, the surety, that this extragalactic threat to all of us is very real and not just a figment of a pained imagination. Of my imagination."

"Granting for the moment and for the purpossess of disscussion the reality of what you sspeak—what can you do, Flinx? What could anyone do?"

"I am not anyone," Flinx replied more sharply than he intended. "I would give everything I have and everything I own to be just 'anyone.' For the chance to live nothing more complex and burdensome than a normal softskin life. But I'm not. I'm different. Forces I don't understand and can't even identify agree with minds that sometimes make no sense that I am some kind of fulcrum, nexus, key, on which the sole slim chance of stopping this peril rests. It's not a responsibility I want. I didn't seek it and I'd do anything to be rid of it."

A throbbing had begun at the back of his head, an all-too-familiar pounding: one of his headaches starting up. He had to bring this discussion to an end before it incapacitated him. Or worse, caused him to perhaps project involuntarily and dangerously onto his young AAnn friend.

"That's it," he finished tersely. "That's why I have to be assured of safe passage off Blasusarr before I can risk trying to leave. That's why you have to help me make contact with someone powerful enough to ensure my safety. Because if I'm killed trying to depart, forces neither you nor I can comprehend believe that it will be the end of any chance or opportunity to save the galaxy in which we live. The catastrophe probably won't strike until long after we're both dead, but strike it will."

"You assk me to accept a great deal, Flinx-friend." Kiijeem made a gesture of first-degree uncertainty. "Thingss very highly educated adult nye would dissmiss as madness and delirium."

"You haven't acquired their prejudices," Flinx countered.

The youth contemplated his choices. "What if I sstill inssisst on ssharing thiss 'experience' of which you sspeak?"

Flinx closed his eyes, then opened them more slowly. "I told you that if you insisted, then we'd see. I can do what you request. I'm not sure you'd survive. Your mind is not fully developed and, more importantly, not like mine." *Nobody's mind is like mine,* he knew, but there was nothing to be gained from further pursuing that line of reasoning

with Kiijeem. "Your mind is—I don't want to say 'immature.' It's fragile. Susceptible. Your experience of this existence is limited, your
knowledge of worlds beyond confined to academics. Though we're not
so very dissimilar in chronological age, I've spent most of my life doing
nothing but *having* experiences. Intellectually, emotionally, and in
many other ways I've become calloused." Leaning forward suddenly, he
reached out and took Kiijeem's right hand in his own. The swiftness of
the softskin's act took the young AAnn by surprise.

"I don't want to hurt you, Kiijeem. I need your help. I would sacrifice my tail to gain it, if I had one. But I don't want to see you broken.
I've seen it happen to others who got—who got too close to me and to
what I know."

How would the youth respond to such a plea? Flinx wondered anxiously. Among his own kind such language could easily be interpreted
as a sign of weakness, of a lack of resolve and determination. The appeal was a very human thing to do. At the same time Flinx was being
coolly calculating. If he shared all that he could with the youngster and
the experience left the young AAnn comatose or dead, he would also be
of no further use.

Kiijeem remained dubious. On the other hand, the softskin had
been, insofar as Kiijeem had been able to tell, truthful and forthright in
all that they had discussed between them. If the human was lying, in the
end it would be worse for him than it would be for Kiijeem himself. The
human must know that. Therefore, everything he had just chronicled
was either an elaborate suicidal lie or . . .

Or he was telling the truth, preposterous as it seemed.

Kiijeem felt a tightening in his throat. The entire galaxy under
threat of destruction. Perhaps not in time to imperil himself, but possibly his descendants, his extended family. The Imperial realm at risk.
Or—nothing at all. Quite likely what he was hearing was little more
than the imaginative ravings of a demented softskin.

There was one thing he could not bring himself to dispute. In the
course of his life it was apparent that this Flinx had been compelled to
make some difficult decisions. The human was brave or foolhardy or
both. Which begged the question.

What then was Kiijeem AVMd?

One more time he allowed his eyes to meet the unnaturally round ones of his visitor. He thought he saw something there. Or perhaps his imagination was also far-reaching.

"I think I know jusst the nye who can help."

Kiijeem was not permitted to travel outside the family compound after a certain hour lest he find himself challenged by an older youth—or worse, an adult urgently in search of status. That meant they would have to cross part of the city in the daytime. The dense crowds among which they would find themselves would help to shield Flinx from the attention of security monitors, but the same concerns that had prevented him from trying to reach his desert touchdown site on his own still applied. Before they could go anywhere, they somehow had to change his appearance.

"The simsuit that allows me to pass as one of your kind is not malleable," Flinx explained the following day. He held up the sophisticated skin so that his young host could marvel at the detail. "It allows me to do many things: simulate tail movement, flex claws, even operate both eye membranes. But I can't alter its appearance."

"Truly, you have ssaid sso before." Turning, Kiijeem reached back and dug around in the depths of the container that he used for hiding the rations that he had been smuggling out to his guest. "That iss why I have brought thiss."

Kiijeem unfolded a square of plain brown, gauzy material. The lower edge was hemmed with a strip of heavier, darker brown that was almost bronze in color. Eyeing it dubiously, Flinx was not impressed.

"What am I supposed to do with that?" he wondered aloud. "Put it over my head?"

"Exactly." Kiijeem held it out to the human. "It iss transslucent enough to ssee through, breathess well, and will completely massk your featuress from patrolling ssecurity perssonnel as well as automatic sscannerss."

Taking the synthetic material, Flinx eyed it suspiciously. It weighed very little. "Won't I look silly walking around with this over my head?"

"Not ssilly." Kiijeem corrected him somberly. "Pathetic."

"Pathe . . .?" Flinx set the material aside. Pip immediately commenced an investigation of the intriguing soft folds. "Why? What does

the wearing of this signify? Come to think of it, I don't remember seeing it on any other nye."

"Not all who are allowed to wear the *ijkk* choosse to do sso,"
Kiijeem explained. "You ssee the metallic hem? The ijkk itsself ssigni-
fiess a dessire for privacy. The color of the metal band indicatess that the
wearer iss impotent."

Flinx nearly smiled. "I mean no offense, Kiijeem, but I didn't know
you were mature enough to be familiar with the concept."

"Mature enough, ssoftsskin, to kill you if you continue to mock me."

"Truly." Flinx readily conceded the point even as he repressed a diffident smile. "Please accept my groveling contrition." For good measure
he added a second-degree gesture of apology.

Kiijeem was appropriately mollified. "No one will challenge the
wearer of an ijkk that iss thussly hemmed. Indeed, painss will be taken
to avoid you. Obsscured within, you may draw more attention than you
are accusstomed to receiving from my sspeciess, but it will only be of
the sstaring kind. Unless we happen to encounter a physsician who happenss to sspecialize in the treatment of ssuch biological dissorderss, no
one iss likely to sspeak to you. Nor will you be challenged. The sstatuss
of anyone who dared to do sso would immediately be diminisshed, not
enlarged."

On a human world a widow could obtain privacy by wearing a full
head covering in black, Flinx knew. Here, the wearing of the brown,
bronze-trimmed, veiling fabric signified a death of a different kind. No
wonder Kiijeem had confidence in the simple disguise. To the ever-
aggressive AAnn the loss of reproductive capability would be second
only to death itself. Seeing one of their own so publicly garbed they
would feel only pity and would go out of their way to respect the
wretched nye's lamentable condition.

Turning away from where Pip was slinking through the depths of
the lightweight accessory, Flinx leaned slightly to his right for a better
view of the distant, sunken main residence. "How will you get free to
escort me? I doubt I could find your friends on my own."

"Truly alsso, Flinx-friend. Additionally, a more perssonal introduction iss necessary if your appearance iss not to sspread panic and confus-
sion. It iss important, I think, that I perssonally explain your pressence

here lesst fright and alarm enssue. To address your concern: desspite my resstrictive sstudiess, I am permitted ssome sself-time. I have not in quite ssome time vissited in persson the friendss of whom I sspeak. We communicate electronically. Iss it not the ssame with my age counterpartss among your kind?"

"Depends on the individual. I never did much electronic communicating myself." *Or communicating of any kind,* he added silently. "I'm more the listening than the talking type. I like to know how individuals—feel."

"You will feel confident, I think, once we are outsside my ressidence compound and back among ssmall packss of my people." Reaching down, he picked up the ijkk. As she slithered to one side, Pip raised her iridescent emerald-hued head and hissed at him. Kiijeem had no idea how fortunate he was that she did not perceive him as an enemy.

The young AAnn looked on in absorbed fascination as Flinx began the slow process of donning the simsuit. The interior lining was essentially one large spray-woven sensor. Picking up the slightest twitches of his muscles, ligaments, and tendons as well as the movements of his bones, millions of minuscule sensor points instantly transferred that information to the artificial counterparts that lined the interior of the suit. While Flinx moved like a human, the suit's interwoven computational system logics automatically transcribed the actions into the correspondingly appropriate movements for an adult nye. Fed to the suit's silent servos and other integrated systems, it allowed the wearer to simulate the physicality of an AAnn to a degree no actor could equal.

Slipping into her built-in internal pouch, Pip folded her wings tightly against her sides, curled up, and went to sleep against her master. While there was room for her to move around inside the simsuit without sacrificing its believability, unless something roiled Flinx's emotions she was quite content to rest and do as little as possible.

Only after the suit's ventral self-seal melded itself invisibly into its scaly milieu and the ocular pickups activated was the illusion complete. Turning to face his young host, Flinx spread his arms, at ease as the suit's sensors and servos were instructed by the integral woven computer to force his limbs into the AAnn gesture that best approximated his physical intent. The artifice was uncanny. Kiijeem's unmitigated astonishment at the comprehensiveness of the consequent masquerade did not surprise Flinx. He had been fooling far more perceptive and mature nye for many days now.

"Truly I ssee," the youth hissed softly, "and yet it iss sstill hard to accept. I know you are within. I ssaw you don the array mysself. Yet the russe iss sso complete that I think if I ssaw you on a city path I would not be able to ssingle you out from among the horde."

"I should hope not," Flinx told him. "If anyone does, then you won't have to worry about how your friends will react to me." Crouching down by the side of the pool, he settled into the conventional AAnn posture for drinking from an open body of water and proceeded to sip lightly. He was not particularly thirsty: his suit provided for such needs. But he was especially proud of the way the suit's faux tongue worked and wanted to show off, just a bit, for his young friend.

"*Crssagg*—amazing," Kiijeem murmured as he looked on. When Flinx finally straightened, the youth was holding his visitor's AAnn garb out to him—along with the ijkk. "Dress yoursself. Do not put on the ijkk until we are well outsside the ressidence. We do not want to attract attention from the housse."

Flinx indicated his understanding as he slipped back into the unprepossessing AAnn vest, kilt, and sandals he had worn since he had first donned the simsuit. Deftly manipulating the suit's clawed fingers, he secured the ubiquitous AAnn travel pouch around his waist. Clutching the lightweight head covering in one taloned hand, he followed Kiijeem as his host led the way out of the desert landscaping that had served as Flinx's sanctuary for the last several days.

Off to their left the main residence lay baking under the glare of Blasusarr's relentless star. As they made progress Flinx could see the rooflines of other expensive sunken residences; dull, natural, or gleaming according to their owners' tastes. Avoiding the main gate through which non-aircar vehicles entered, Kiijeem led him to a small, older side portal in the artificial stone barrier. The youth activated an interrupt in the photonic alarm system, the two of them stepped through, and for the first time in many days Flinx found himself once more striding along a pedestrian pathway.

Hardly any nye were out in the middle of the morning in the exclusive quarter, but crowds increased as they loped easily toward the nearest commercial area. From there Kiijeem led the way onto a public transport and proceeded to enter the necessary individualized programming. A private vehicle, they both knew, might draw personal attention. Public transport was slower, but it was safer to take the extra time in a vehicle filled with other passengers and thereby limit the opportunities for detection.

While the ijkk Flinx wore loosely over his head drew the occasional curious, even kindhearted glance, the only real danger arose from Kiijeem's irrepressible nervousness. While Flinx had no difficulty relaxing in his resting crouch near the rear of the transport, Kiijeem exhibited the air of one who at any moment was expecting a formal challenge from one of Krrassin's grand champion fighters. Only after the back of the vehicle had emptied out a little did Flinx lean toward his young companion.

"No one suspects us, no one senses me." The simsuit's voice box added an appropriate artificial rasp to his otherwise fluent command of the language. "Will you relax? You're attracting far more attention than I am." Coiled in her pouch against his left side, Pip squirmed slightly as she sensed her master's tension. "Do I have to pin your tail against a wall to keep it from snapping?"

"Truly, you are right." Kiijeem made an effort to calm down. His tail tip stopped banging against the transport's inner wall, though it did not stop twitching entirely. "I ssupposse we could even sspeak loud enough to be overheard without raissing any undue alarm."

"Of coursse we can." Flinx was at his reassuring best. "I conversed with many nye before I met you. None ever suspected my identity. You can even call me by my real name."

Kiijeem considered. "Yess—Fflinxx *could* be an AAnn name. An unussual one, but it hass the right ssoundingss."

"Anybody asks, just tell 'em I'm from the sticks." Flinx was enjoying the view out the sweeping transparent wall of the transport as it soared eastward several meters above the manicured sands below.

"The *what?*" Kiijeem was confused by a term that did not translate well.

Flinx elaborated. "I'm from offworld. Some small, out-of-the-way Imperial planet with a reputation for backwardness."

"*Ahpessx,*" his friend responded understandingly, adding a third-degree gesture indicative of quiet glee. "I know jusst the world. We will identify you as a vissiting agriculturalisst from Quepht-nuum. That fact by itsself will be enough to excusse any errorss you may make, verbal or otherwisse." Kiijeem seemed pleased with the label he had assigned to his companion, while Flinx saw neither reason nor need to dispute it. He was not in the least ashamed to find himself designated the AAnn equivalent of an Imperial hick.

They were on the transport for what seemed an eternity. The interior was sealed and, of course, not air-conditioned. If not for his simsuit's ability to evaporate his mammalian sweat, recycle it as drinking water, and otherwise keep him cool and his body temperature stable, Flinx knew he would have fainted from heatstroke hours ago.

As the transport hummed eastward, picking up and disgorging passengers along the way, it occurred to Flinx that he could make an excuse for them to disembark. Once out of sight, he could kill Kiijeem easily. That would lose him the potentially useful contacts he sought, but would also allow him to find another hiding place in a completely different part of the city. Perhaps a location where he could safely hide out long enough to await the return of the reconfigured *Teacher*. That would mean he would not need the help of Kiijeem's more powerful friends.

Of course if he did such a thing, carried out such a disgraceful act, it would only prove that he was no more worth saving from the menace that lay behind the Great Emptiness than the other humans and assorted sentients he had been quick to disparage on previous occasions. Besides, he liked Kiijeem, even though he was quite aware that should the right opportunity present itself the young nye would swallow his dismay at the loss of his offworld acquaintance and happily sample the softskin's flesh. While such instinctive behavior might repel the average human or thranx, in Flinx's wide-ranging experience it did not disqualify Kiijeem's entire species from the prospect of salvation.

Anyhow, the entire galaxy was at stake. In order to save the benign species, he had to save them all.

Only two other passengers remained by the time the transport entered a part of the capital city's western residential zone. Marked by steep-sided hills and lengthy escarpments, so perfectly rendered were these geological features that he needed Kiijeem to confirm the artificiality of their nature.

So this was how the upper levels of AAnn society managed to enjoy sweeping views from their dwellings while still remaining largely underground, he reflected as the transport turned silently down a winding accessway. If the ground where you choose to live is flat, construct your residence and then build an obligatory mountain around it. Even to his undiscerning human eye, the amount of effort and expense that had to have gone into each individual dwelling in order to make it look as though it had been excavated from natural rock must have been considerable. There was even one estate that was "buried" entirely in a row of artfully sculpted barchan dunes. Characteristic longitudinal windows gleamed from the slip faces of sand that never shifted no matter how strong were the winds that blew against them. Clearly, the AAnn who could afford to live in this district must hold positions of considerable importance within the Imperial hierarchy. In response to his query, Kiijeem confirmed as much.

"Truly only the mosst important nye dwell here, outsside of the Imperial family itsself." He motioned second-degree self-importance. The verbal equivalent in a human would have been called boasting.

"Like my friendss."

Flinx regarded his guide from behind imitation AAnn eyes. "Your friends hold positions of such importance? Within the government?"

Kiijeem looked away and his tail drooped slightly. "*Fssabb,* not exactly. It would be more correct to ssay they are the offsspring of thosse who actually hold ssuch possitionss."

Great, Flinx thought as he studied the extensive, expensive surroundings. Additional juveniles to deal with. Not that it mattered, if they could provide the safeguarding he needed.

The transport slowed to a halt outside a picture-perfect replica of a small sand-swept butte that was complete down to fossils of extinct Blasusarrian life-forms that were embedded prominently in one layer of sedimentary "rock." The complete structure was a good three stories high and gave no indication of how far the dwelling continued belowground. As the vehicle touched ground Flinx hopped off behind his escort, his simsuit's simulated leg muscles handling the shock of the short jump in faithful imitation of an adult AAnn.

Unlike at the AVM residence of Kiijeem's family, here there was no fence. No visible fence, anyway. Pausing atop what looked like a vacant patch of desert soil, Kiijeem waited for the sensors beneath his feet to respond to his presence. While not expecting the kind of sophisticated internal scanning devices that might be present at an official checkpoint, Flinx nonetheless took care to stand just to the right of the dedicated clearing.

"We are being made known," Kiijeem informed him helpfully. "I will sspeak to my friendss. When lasst I contacted them they were home alone, engrossed in their daily sstudiess."

"*Will* they make time for us?" Flinx continued to marvel at the beauty and perfection of the multiple layers of artificial stone.

Kiijeem made a gesture of second-degree assurance. "They are among my oldesst group-companionss. I have told them to expect mysself and a friend." His tail slapped reflexively at the ground. "I think I am going to enjoy thiss."

Why wouldn't you? Flinx mused. *It's not your skin at stake if they lose control, panic, and decide to turn me in.*

Popping out of a camouflaged burrow, a diminutive automaton in the shape of a local *jarlt* approached them, stood up on its hind legs, and trilled musically before disappearing back into its hole.

"We are announced." Kiijeem started toward the high, slightly overhung sandstone wall in which windows that had been treated to match the color of their surroundings were clearly visible. "Dwelling ssecurity hass been muted accordingly. Pleasse accompany me. And remain at my sside. For an adult to trail behind ssomeone of my age would look ssusspiciouss. My friendss are ssuppossed to be alone, the adultss in ressidence away at work—but we sshould sstill take care."

"Don't worry." Flinx lengthened his stride until he was walking parallel to his guide. "I've spent my whole life taking care."

The hall they entered bespoke the wealth of the residence's extended family. Two stories high, opposing walls of simulated sandstone flaunted patterns composed of embedded synthetic gems. Water flowed down one wall; a singing, soulful reminder of a time when such scarce fluid meant life itself to the primitive ancestors of the modern AAnn.

"Try it," Kiijeem urged him, seeing his visitor staring at the cascade.

Flinx did not hesitate. Nothing in the emotions emanating from the young nye suggested treachery. Utilizing his simsuit's mouth and servo-driven tongue, he sipped at the edge of the artificial cataract. Mildly acidic, the cool flow agitated his taste buds with overtones of meat and mango. The liquid that formed the decorative waterfall came flavored.

Sunshine poured in from overhead via a lengthy polarized skylight. In the absence of freestanding furniture, here and there the fake sandstone had been warped to form places to sit or to crouch in comfort. A shallow sand pit provided ample room for relaxing or fighting.

His attention was drawn away from the décor by movement near the rear of the entry hall. Not one but two young nye were bounding toward them. Healthy, active, and well attired, they appeared to be of about the same age as Kiijeem, though both were slightly larger. The female wore a selection of metal bands around her tail that extended from its base to its end. Neither was as big as the simsuited Flinx.

"Your friend iss tall," declared the male as he halted before them. As he spoke, his sister was exchanging the traditional throat grab with Kiijeem. "A sshame he musst wear the ijkk."

So used had he become to the head covering that Flinx had forgotten its presence—and its meaning. Without waiting for approval from Kiijeem, he doffed it and shoved the crumpled fabric into his waist pouch. His new hosts regarded him with interest.

"Where are you from?" the female asked as the male exchanged greetings with Flinx's escort. "Kiijeem ssayss you are from offworld. Truly, I do not recognize your pouch dessign and the remainder of your apparel iss nondesscript." For an AAnn her voice was unusually liquid, Flinx decided. No doubt an occasion for sympathy among the more normal raspy-voiced members of her social group.

"I will reveal all truths in good time," Flinx informed her.

The two youths exchanged gestures and a glance. "You certainly sspeak like an offworlder," the male acknowledged. "But I forget my mannerss. I am Eiipul IXb and this is my ssisster, Eiipul IXc." He gestured pridefully but without condescension. "We are the sscionss of Lord Eiipul IX."

Eiipul. It was a name Flinx thought he recognized from his manifold studies. Something to do with the history of Amalgamation times, though he could not place the precise reference. The partial recollection only served to further confirm Kiijeem's assurance that his friends did indeed have access to the kind of clout Flinx would need to ensure his safe departure from Blasusarr.

"I am Flinx," he replied simply.

The female gestured confusion. "No family name?" She eyed her brother uncertainly.

"Perhapss all the resst of hiss entire family iss dead," Eiipul IXb opined clumsily. "Or possibly the name hass been withdrawn, or iss being reconssidered." He looked up at Flinx. "Doess your name lacking have anything to do with your wearing of the ijkk?"

"Inssenssitive, inssenssitive," Kiijeem chided his friend. "But you will undersstand ssoon. Have I not promissed you the ssurprisse of all ssurprissess?"

"Truly yess," responded the female eagerly. "It musst be a great ssecret for you to assk that it not be revealed to a parent." Turning, she gestured simultaneously with hand and tail. "Come to the commonss and tell all—I cannot wait!"

The commons was the central room of the extended dwelling; a large circular chamber from which hallways radiated outward to other parts of the residential compound like spokes from a wheel. Like the entryway it was also an impressive two stories high, capped by a dome of spun multihued quartz that added another half story to the overall height. The enclosing curving walls were fashioned of synthesized copper minerals, mostly turquoise and azurite flecked with splotches of less-familiar cupric ores. The lighting was appropriately subdued, while the fine-grained pink sand that filled the central depression had been imported from a famous quarry in the center of the southern continent. Ten percent of the carefully coiffured sand was composed of natural colored carbon crystals, Kiijeem informed him. Truly, Flinx realized, the extended family of Lord Eiipul IX was a wealthy one indeed.

Settling themselves into comfortable crouches on the sand at an equitable distance from their guests, the two youngsters let their forearms dangle down between their bent front legs and regarded their guests expectantly. Taking care to remain well out of informal striking range, Kiijeem explained their purpose in coming and the need for continuing secrecy.

"My friend Flinx hass been hiding with me for a number of dayss now, but my family ressidence iss not conducive to maintain hiss anonymity among uss. He requiress a place where none will ssearch for him, and alsso requiress assisstance in departing Krrassin unobsserved."

"How sstimulating!" Eiipul IXc made a gesture indicative of second-degree excitement as she contemplated the tall visitor in this new light. "You are a criminal."

"Not exactly," Flinx replied honestly.

Her brother tilted his head slightly to one side as he considered Kiijeem's companion. "Then why the need for all thiss continuing ssecrecy? Why musst you leave Blasussarr unobsserved?"

Flinx turned to Kiijeem, not wanting to do anything that might upset his young friend. Kiijeem gestured third-degree indifference coupled with overtones suggesting he would not be responsible for whatever happened from now on. Deciding there was nothing to be gained from postponing the unavoidable, Flinx reached up and began fingering the hidden seals of his simsuit. When he was finished he reached up and pushed under his protruding reptilian chin.

It was a good thing there was no one else in the residence. Both young Eiipuls began to shriek like steam engines as their well-mannered visitor's head started to come off.

CHAPTER

7

To their credit and despite their initial horror, neither covered their eyes. Even young AAnn were made of stern stuff. But the high-pitched whistle-hiss that constituted an AAnn scream echoed around the commons chamber for the better part of a minute as Flinx continued to peel off the simsuit. Yawning widely and flicking her tongue to taste her new surroundings, Pip emerged from the collapsing internal resting pocket to slither up Flinx's left arm and onto his shoulder and neck. Her appearance prompted fresh hissing from the already seriously shocked Eiipul siblings.

It was the sister who first connected the appearance of hairless, scaleless human flesh with something she had previously seen only in studies.

"By the Pregnant Pouch of Passhawntt—a ssoftsskin! A *live* ssoftsskin!" Simultaneously fascinated and repelled, she favored the disrobing Flinx with a stare not unlike that a human might employ while eyeing the emergence of a botfly larva from the meat of his thigh. Her brother was no less revoltingly captivated—until it occurred to him that he and his sister were crouching there witness to this revelation while wholly weaponless. Rising abruptly, he moved quickly toward a cabinet built into the blue wall. Divining his intent, Kiijeem hurried to intercept him.

"There iss no need to panic." Kiijeem indicated the now unashamedly unsuited Flinx. "He iss a friend."

"That?" One clawed hand paused halfway to the weapons locker, Eiipul IXb stood awestruck and appalled. "Kijeem-friend, it iss a *ssoftsskin*. A human. A citizen of the desspissed Commonwealth! It iss friend to *thranx*."

"Thiss one iss different," Kiijeem reassured him. "Hiss reassonss for coming here among uss make little ssensse to me." He looked over at the silently standing Flinx. "They would make even less ssensse, I think, to hiss own kind."

"Then why iss he here?" Eiipul IXc gaped at the amazing apparition that had appeared in the hub of her home. *"How* iss he here? And what iss that more normal-looking ssmall coiled thing that hass wrapped itsself around hiss neck and arm?"

"I'm going to tell you everything." Squatting down, Flinx settled into a close approximation of an AAnn resting crouch. Without the aid of the simsuit he could not maintain the posture for very long: his leg muscles were differently arranged. But he thought the familiar stance would help to reassure his edgy hosts.

"You sspeak naturally," the female observed in wonderment. "Though your voice iss even more sslippery than mine."

"I told you he wass different." Kiijeem was thoroughly enjoying the unsettling effect Flinx's unmasking had had on his friends. AAnn loved surprise and shock, even when it was coupled with fear. "Truly, the sstory he hass to tell iss beyond remarkable. I am not ssure I believe all of it mysself. But I believe enough of it to have brought him here, to sseek the help of the Family Eiipul."

Cautiously, the brother settled himself into a crouch on the other side of the circle, as far away from the intrusive human as could be considered polite. His civility was instinctive and not prompted by a sudden acceptance of anything the softskin or Kiijeem had said. The weapons cabinet remained close at hand. The young female started to join him, then impulsively started across the sand.

"Ssisster," he began, alarmed, "conssider your posssition!"

"That iss jusst what I am doing," she replied as she approached to within an arm's length of the crouching Flinx. She extended a clawed hand. Though at ease, he tracked her movements intently. One flick of her clawed hands could shred his face or tear out his throat. On his shoulder, Pip tensed slightly.

"May I," she began hesitantly, "may I—touch you, Flinx-guesst?"

"Go ahead," he told her without wavering.

Her left hand rose and reached toward him. The claws retracted and the tips of her fingers made contact with his right shoulder. They drew slowly down his chest as far as his stomach before withdrawing. Gesturing gratitude mixed with muted delight, she stepped backward, her tail swaying slowly from side to side. It took him a moment to identify the meaning of the unusual hissing that accompanied her retreat.

She was giggling. It was, to the best of his knowledge, not a common mode of expression among the AAnn.

"They *are* ssoft." She settled back down alongside her uneasy brother. "Like a blood pudding." Her attention shifted back to the improbable visitor. "I am ssurprissed you do not ssimply collapsse and ssplassh out all over the floor, like a big greasy puddle."

In his life Flinx had been compared to many things, but never before to a big greasy puddle. He was not offended; he had been called far worse.

Her brother had recovered the emblematic AAnn bravado that had been momentarily wiped away by the revelation of Flinx's true appearance. "Friendsship extendss only sso far." He glanced pointedly in Kiijeem's direction before turning back to the human. Had the situation been reversed, Flinx knew, Kiijeem would have said and done exactly the same as his friend. "Why sshould we not report your pressence here to the appropriate authoritiess, much less put at rissk our possition both within and without the family in order to assisst you in leaving our world ssecretly?"

"I assure you that I have found mysself wondering the ssame." Kiijeem turned to his guest. "You musst explain to them, Flinx-friend. You musst tell them everything that you told me."

"I know," Flinx murmured ruefully.

Despite his disinclination to do so, he proceeded to do just that.

The exquisite commons room could be solemn or joyous according to the desires of its occupants. After Flinx had finished it was dead silent for long minutes. Having already heard the tale in its entirety, Kiijeem was quiet and composed. In contrast, the emotions of the twins reflected confusion and uncertainty. That was to be expected, Flinx knew. He awaited the inevitable questions.

The first query came from Eiipul IXc and was a compliment to her maturity. "If we had appeared before you on your homeworld, emerged from ssynthetic human sskinss, and told ssuch a sstory, how would you react?"

Flinx had to smile. "I'd be suspicious and skeptical. I'd also think that if I needed to fabricate a falsehood in order to get me safely off the planet, I would invent something a lot less grandiose. No need to claim the fate of the galaxy is at stake, much less that I'm the key to maybe saving it. I would look at anyone telling such a tale and think that he was either the biggest liar in the history of interspecies relations, completely insane—or that if there was even a nub of truth to what he was saying, he might deserve to be taken seriously."

Eiipul IXb's response was swift. "Truly, I find mysself tending to credit the firsst ssuppossition."

"I am ssimilarly inclined," his sister added, albeit not quite as quickly.

Kiijeem stepped forward. "Flinx ssayss that he can impart a sshared experience that will confirm everything he hass claimed."

"Sso then." The disbelieving brother studied his friend. "You have sshared thiss 'experience'?"

Lowering his eyes, Kiijeem gestured second-degree self-effacement. "I regret to ssay that I have not. I have repeatedly requessted to do sso, but Flinx inssisstss that I am not ssufficiently developed mentally and that to partake of it could be sserioussly damaging to me."

The sister scrutinized the tall human. "How convenient. You claim evidence but declare that itss revelation would be injuriouss to thosse dessirouss of it. You pressent our friend with a possible lie the ssize of the ssouthern continent and then proceed to inssult him when he re-quesstss proof. I sshould sshoot you mysself."

Pip's head came up to focus on the young AAnn and Flinx hastened to calm the minidrag. "No insult was meant or intended. If I did not value Kiijeem as a friend, I would not be so hesitant to share this expe-rience with him. I've had occasion to do so with another who was close to me, a very mature human whose affection I value more highly than you do Kiijeem's friendship, and it was a near thing that no lasting damage resulted." He stared hard at her. "I don't want anything bad to happen to Kiijeem—nor do I want anything bad to happen to either of you. The kind of conclusive confirmation I have to offer will be hazardous enough for a mature member of your kind to experience. That is if, as Kiijeem believes, you can recommend one you think resilient enough to deal with it."

"I sstill think you are a sspy desserving of interrogation and possible execution," the brother stated straightforwardly. Flinx stiffened. If necessary, he was prepared to make his escape and flee the residence. The twin youths knew even less of his fighting abilities than did Kiijeem. Flinx was confident that if necessary he and Pip could deal with all three of them. It was the last thing he wanted to do—but as always, he was prepared to do it.

"But," the brother continued, "the ressolution to this puzzle iss truly quite ssimple. We will introduce you to precissely the kind of mature, powerful nye whosse assisstance you require and leave the decission concerning what to do with you up to him." He glanced at his sister, who gestured first-degree concurrence. "Tonight, when thiss individual will have time and you can be pressented to him, we will learn truly how much veracity there iss to the bizarrely extraordinary tale you have related. If you are telling truth, then it will be up to him to decide how to resspond. If you are nothing more than the clever fabricator of an elaborate falssehood, then we three here will acquire sstatuss for having identified you and turned you in." Brother and sister turned their attention to the watchful Kiijeem.

Unmindful of what Flinx might think or how the human might react, the remaining young AAnn responded without hesitation. "That iss a ssumming-up with which I can willingly concur."

The three of them waited for the softskin's response. While not wholly reassuring, they found it surprisingly worthy.

"If I were one of you," Flinx told them simply, "I would do no less."

It was not the first time Flinx had been inside an AAnn structure, but it was the first time he had been inside a private residence. That it was not a typical dwelling complex he knew from what Kiijeem had already told him of the wealth and standing of the Eiipul extended family. In point of fact, his young friend's predescription was unnecessary. Even someone utterly unfamiliar with AAnn culture would have been able to recognize the family's affluence from a casual stroll through the rooms.

The design of the central commons was followed throughout the complex: walls and ceilings soared in curves and waves that employed a minimum of straight lines. Light poured in from above instead of through side windows. Technological enhancements were artfully concealed within walls, floors, and ceilings. Poured floors were fashioned of welded sand, pebbled glass, and other natural desert materials. The hallways and portals that separated individual chambers tended to be high and narrow.

The cumulative effect was akin to walking through a series of small slot canyons of the kind common to water-eroded desert terrain on Earth—or Moth. As he trailed his young hosts through the complex, Flinx was reminded of the time he had found himself relying on the guidance of an elderly prospector named Knigta Yakus to help him survive an entirely different kind of journey on his own homeworld.

As they showed off their residence (and by inference the lofty status of their extended family), with the typical AAnn pride that an unknowing human would have considered excessive braggadocio, Flinx felt that his new hosts were growing more and more comfortable with his simsuited presence. That changed when a muted musical squawking echoed through the recreation room where they were currently relaxing.

From where he was lying in a pool of heated sand, Eiipul IXb whipped around to stand bolt upright. Both ocular membranes fully retracted, he stared wide-eyed at an image that had appeared off to one side. Flinx needed no special visual equipment to grasp the meaning of the three-dimensional projection. It showed a trio of adults entering the complex via the main entrance.

"Quickly!" the brother hissed, gesturing toward Flinx and Kiijeem with one clawed hand. "The matriarch and companion coussinss have returned home early. We musst hide you until tonight."

"Why?" wondered Kiijeem even as he hurried along in his friends' wake. "Flinx-friend'ss fanciful facade fooled all of uss. Why sshould it not deceive your matriarch as well?"

"Well it might—but that iss not a chance my brother and I dessire to take," the sister retorted as they rushed hurriedly down a corridor. "A rissk not taken iss one whosse conssequencess need not be contemplated."

Flinx was not happy when the corridor became a steep ramp that descended one and possibly two levels underground. While neither claustrophobic nor fearful of subterranean realms, he didn't like it when he found himself confined to a place with no apparent escape route. Sealed with his thoughts in the dimly-lit storage room where his hosts left him, he felt trapped. It hardly improved his mood or his confidence when Kiijeem chose to depart along with the Eiipul siblings.

He was left with only Pip for companionship. Unlike her master she had no compunction about exploring the multitude of storage containers that surrounded them. The one advantage to his enforced isolation was that it gave him the opportunity to unseal the simsuit's headpiece. The touch of dry, fresh air on his face, the chance to respirate without having to suck air in through filters, was invigorating. He felt he was relatively safe in exposing himself. Kiijeem's friends would not have chosen the storage room for a softskin's hiding place if they felt it was likely to see any traffic.

Imprecisely, he could sense alien emotions overhead. They were mixed now. More aggressive, more challenging, than those that would have been generated by a comparable gathering of humans. Though he did not know the young Eiipuls well enough yet to unequivocally differentiate their feelings from the group of recently arrived adult females, he was able to easily pick Kiijeem's out of the considerable emotional haze. As always, it was strange to be able to perceive the emotions of other sentients while at the same time being unable to hear or understand a single word of what they were saying.

"What if the ssoftsskin iss lying?" While the family matriarch held domestic court at the far end of the eating chamber, Eiipul IXc challenged her brother and her friend with an anxious whisper.

Kiijeem looked up from his drink, confident that the newly arrived adult nye were too far away to overhear. "I believe he iss telling the truth."

"We know what you believe," Eiipul IXb responded with becoming curtness. "Your 'belief' iss inssufficient to abrogate the prosspect."

His friend set his drink aside, which was the proper reaction when challenged. "Are you thinking of divulging his pressence to the authoritiess?"

"I do not know what to think to do, Kiijeem." With a slightly dulled claw the brother picked nervously at the lower edge of his chin. "My insstinctive inclination iss to think all hiss talk of some vasst myssteriouss threat to the entire galaxy iss nothing but the ravingss of an adverssary who hass ssucccumbed to madness. Hiss inssisstence that he iss ssomehow essential to confronting ssuch a colossal danger makess even less ssensse."

"Yet in hiss actionss and hiss wordss he appearss entirely rational and normal. For a human," his sister added hastily. "Which leadss to the inevitable corollary: what if he iss not mad? What if he sspeakss truth truly, as Kiijeem apparently believess?"

"I do not know, I do not know." Pried loose by the constantly probing claw, a dislodged snout scale now hung loose and unflattering from Eiipul IXb's chin.

"Well, fssankk—we will learn the truth tonight." His sister tried to reassure her sibling while at the same time maintaining a superior argumentative position. "If a loss of sstatuss, or worsse, iss to follow, it will not be uss who ssufferss firsst, hardesst, or longesst from an error in judgment."

She did not have to look in Kiijeem's direction for him to know who she meant.

Seated in the farthest corner of the dark storeroom, his knees drawn up to his chest, Flinx looked on in silence as Pip happily slithered over and around one container after the other, staring, sniffing, sampling. Though she employed all her senses in the course of her exploration, the minidrag was having a hard time divining the contents of the securely sealed shapes. Her indifferent master did no better. The sundry AAnn containers and complex labels held no meaning for him and little interest.

He had of his own free will placed himself in a difficult, dangerous position. By now the *Teacher* was likely safely outsystem, speeding through space-plus in a fixed arc that would bring her reconfigured profile back to Blasusarr on a different angle of approach. His ship could not help him even in a dire emergency. He still had Pip, of course. And his own singular Talent, which had the disconcerting habit of deserting him when he most needed to make use of it.

He sighed. He would manage. Hadn't he always? But it felt strange. He was used to taking care of himself and not having to rely on the goodwill of others—much less the goodwill of a trio of unpredictable young aliens whose government was dedicated to everlasting Imperial expansion at the expense of the Commonwealth and of his kind.

Looking to his left, he imagined that Clarity Held was sitting there next to him. And was glad that she was not. At least she was safe, back on New Riviera and under the protection of Bran Tse-Mallory and Truzenzuzex. In the absence of any friend save a small, empathetic flying snake he found himself drifting into depression. He did his best to displace it with anticipation.

Time passed slowly in the underground storage chamber. The interminable hours spent isolated in the gloom and silence would have driven the average human to distraction. Flinx was not average. And not, he reminded himself, strictly human. Not according to the disquieting discoveries he had only just made on Gestalt. Reflecting on that did nothing to lighten his mood.

His melancholy was interrupted, if not exactly relieved, by a change in the emotional atmosphere high above him. The tide of alien sensations that had ebbed back and forth all late afternoon and long into what he assumed must be evening began to fade until only the emotive signatures of the three youths remained. Yet despite their apparent return to isolation, none of them came down the rampway to escort him back upstairs or even to check in on him. Unable to take the risk of ascending on his own, he was reduced to helpless waiting and silent speculation.

Then a new emotional presence made itself known. Or rather, burst onto his consciousness. Not only was it more focused and resolute than any he had previously discerned in the residence, it was by far the most powerful he had perceived since first arriving on Blasusarr. Without question, a distinctive presence had entered the dwelling.

Shortly thereafter, Kiijeem and Eiipul IXc appeared in the doorway to the storage chamber, and he found himself ascending to confront it.

No one said anything, no words were spoken, as they retraced the ramp route back to ground level and continued on to the upper levels of the artificial butte that formed the core of the residential compound.

Flinx wanted to ask questions but, mindful of the earnestness that now enveloped his young friends, kept silent. He had the feeling that very soon he could ask anything he wanted.

They led him into a single chamber that occupied the entire top level of the dwelling. Long, narrow windows wound their way through the simulated rock walls like small streams that had been turned on their sides. Outside, night had settled over the city. Peering through a half-meter-high vein of weaving transparency Flinx saw that there was still just enough light to enable him to perceive some of the surrounding neighborhood. Stretching to some hills on the horizon, the replication of empty Blasusarrian desert was astonishing in its authenticity. Only the lights that gleamed from within apparently solid cliffs and crags hinted that they were in fact hollow structures and not natural formations.

A voice rasped from the far end of the room. Rising from the resting stool on which he had been sitting, a solidly built nye rose to confront the arrivals. Formal but undeniably fond greetings were exchanged. At Kiijeem's urging Flinx was then thrust forward. His young friend's emotions had taken a decidedly atypical turn.

He was openly frightened.

Within the simsuit Pip was stirring against her master. She, too, sensed the threat posed by the emotionally forceful individual they were confronting.

Flinx's Talent had already provided the answer to one question: on the basis of his emotional depth alone, here was an AAnn with enough potential muscle to push through and secure the safe passage off Blasusarr that Flinx required. Whether he could be convinced to do so would require more than just portentous words on Flinx's part. He became aware that Eiipul IXc was speaking.

"Flinx, make now an acquaintance with Lord Eiipul IX—our patriarch."

There was an admirable lack of condescension in the noble AAnn's response as he carried out the familiar formal exchange of throat-grasping with his tall guest. "You are a good friend of Kiijeem AVMd as well as my offspring, I am told."

"Truly," Flinx replied. Despite mentally preparing himself, he was more taken aback than he had expected. Of all the AAnn he had encountered in person over the years, here was by far the most striking personality. The nye's piercing gaze, powerful grip, forceful emotions, and unusually broad physique marked him as physically as well as mentally exceptional among his kind. An individual, Flinx warned himself, not to be played. With this scion of a noble family only honesty would succeed. Which was fine. Honesty was all Flinx had to give.

Lord Eiipul indicated the twins. "I am informed that you have ssomething to reveal to me that I will find of esspecial interesst. I await your pressentation."

Nothing to be gained by hesitation, Flinx told himself. Without further delay he began to unseal the simsuit.

Lord Eiipul's reaction was instructive. As Flinx began to slip out of the suit and reveal his human self, the AAnn maintained his preternatural poise emotionally as well as physically. He did not call out, did not run, did not reach for a concealed weapon. Just stood and stared, taking in the astonishing disclosure with a coolness that suggested he encountered such radical metamorphoses every day. His otherwise faultless deportment betrayed only the slightest hint of concern. Most humans confronted with a similar revelation would by now have run screaming, or at least exhibited the first signs of shock.

When Flinx eventually stepped out of the last of the suit to stand naked and exposed in all his humanness, Lord Eiipul looked him carefully up and down, thought a moment, and then turned to his female issue.

"Iss thiss the creature'ss true form, or iss there another AAnn insside a human ssuit?"

If not for the deadly seriousness of the situation, Flinx would have felt free to laugh. Not only was this nye mentally strong, the unexpected appearance of an alien softskin in his own dwelling had not cost him his sense of humor.

"I am entirely human." Flinx took a step toward the master of the residence while taking care to keep out of slashing range of those mature talons and tail. "If you require it, further proof of species can be provided."

Lord Eiipul gestured third-degree understanding coupled with second-degree contempt. "That will not be required. I have encountered humanss before. In the brief time you have been sspeaking your sstink hass ssufficiently impinged upon the appropriate receptorss." His nostrils flared meaningfully as he turned to eye his uneasy, expectant off-spring and their friend.

"You were correct. I do find thiss dissplay of interesst. Later we will find out how you arranged it." Raising the curved drinking utensil he was holding, he turned back to Flinx. "Before I have you killed," he said casually, "I need to know sseveral thingss, ssoftsskin. How you came to be on Blasussarr, how you managed to find your way into my home, and how you ssucceeded in convincing the mosst favored among my brood to find you worthy of not being sslaughtered on ssight."

"I'm a likable kind of guy," Flinx told him as Pip's head rose from his shoulder to lock on the adult AAnn. Lord Eiipul noticed the movement. He did not acknowledge the minidrag's sudden attention, but neither did he ignore it.

"Your masstery of a modesst tongue doess you jusstice," his host declared. "It will not ssave your life, but I confess I find it a remarkable disstraction. How come you by ssuch fluency in a language mosst of your kind desspisse and the majority cannot manage?"

"I come by it honestly," Flinx told him. "By study, through life experience, and as one of your own."

Eiipul IXc leaned close to her brother. "Our ssuppossitionss were correct—the creature *iss* mad."

Kiijeem looked on in dismay. This was not going as he had hoped. Had he been wrong to believe the softskin? If the human did not do something dramatic in the next minute or two, Lord Eiipul would terminate the confrontation—and likely the softskin as well, with consequences to his increasingly uneasy progeny and their worried friend that would be far from pleasant.

"I had not thought my perceptive abilitiess sso diminisshed with age." With slow deliberation the senior AAnn set his half-full drinking vessel aside. It immediately attached itself to a nearby freestanding clasper. His eyes never left the tall visitor.

"You look like a ssoftsskin, you sstink like a ssoftsskin, and desspite your esstimable command of our language, you sspeak with the oiliness of a ssoftsskin." As one scaly palm drifted above the other Flinx could make out the nano-instrumentation that had been etched into the nye's wrist scales. Lord Eiipul had no need to pick up a weapon—one had been embedded in the back of his left hand. "Correct me if I assume too much, but I pressume that you will alsso die like a human. But not before you have provided ssatissfactory ansswerss to the quesstionss I earlier possed."

Without hesitation Flinx advanced until he was standing within striking range. The reduced distance between them did not go unnoticed by Lord Eiipul IX.

"My formal name is Philip Lynx." He glanced over at the increasingly anxious Kiijeem and the two Eiipul siblings. "I am more commonly known as Flinx." Executing a flawless gesture demanding of first-degree respect, he added yet one more name.

"I am also called, and have been authoritatively recorded as, Flinx LLVVRXX—of the Tier Ssaiinn."

CHAPTER

8

Talon-tipped fingers continued to hover above the muscular back of a hand that had been etched with lethal instrumentation. One set of nictating membranes flickered as Lord Eiipul blinked back at the uncannily self-possessed visitor.

"How do you, human, come to have knowledge of that noted Tier of eclectic artissanss? And how do you come by a name that, while common, reekss of validity?" Off to one side, his offspring were gaping at the mammal in their midst.

As for Kiijeem, he stood astounded and indignant in equal measure. The softskin had revealed much to him, but in all their nightly sessions together it had never once made known this naming. A *true* naming. He was hurt by the omission. Of course, in withholding the information until confronted by an adult he considered to be his equal, the visitor was only doing what an AAnn of equivalent status would have done. This realization caused Kiijeem to view his human friend in still another new light. Without question his guest had told him a great deal.

How much had he withheld?

"The name was given to me," Flinx explained, "when I was adopted into their Tier by the applicable family. This occurred not long ago on a world that lies between the Empire and the Commonwealth. A neutral world called Jast."

"I know of it," Lord Eiipul acknowledged. "Jusst as I know of the Ssaiinn. Your claim iss—quite asstounding."

Eiipul IXb stepped forward, his tone deferential. "We had no idea! The creature deceivess uss! Until thiss very moment we did not . . ."

"Lock your teeth!" Lord Eiipul hissed sharply. The young male retreated immediately and lapsed into silence. "Have ssome resspect for your ssuperior." Turning back to Flinx, his tone was solemn. "Your remarkable assertion sstandss unverified. What iss undeniable iss that you are a remarkable sspecimen of your kind, in wayss that are sstill to be learned. Along with how you ssucceeded in coming to Krrassin. Would I be correct in assuming that the informality and ssurprisse attendant on thiss particular encounter leadss me to believe that your pressence on Blasussarr iss not authorized by your government?"

"Wherever I find myself, I authorize my own presence," Flinx informed his host quietly. "Since nobody else seems to want to do so."

"Ah, *chizzent.* With every word you sspeak you mark yoursself as different from the resst of your kind. Will you drink with me before you die?"

Wary but willing, Flinx moved closer. "I'll drink with you even in the absence of death."

Careful not to strike the human with his tail as he turned, Lord Eiipul led Flinx to the far end of the room. Kiijeem and the twins followed at a distance. The tapering terminus of the top floor was dominated by a curving transparent wall many meters in height. It wrapped around the narrowing end of the artificial butte like a port on a small ship. Through the sweeping transparency Flinx could make out other costly residences illuminated by their internal lights and the glow of a moon.

Calling forth two fresh containers of liquid from a concealed dispenser, Lord Eiipul took one metal cone and passed the other to his guest. Flinx had no trouble using it properly. He had been drinking from similar utensils ever since he had arrived in Krrassin.

"Sso—you are a member of a Tier and of a family. I have never before heard of or encountered ssuch a contradiction, not even in the fanciess of playwrightss."

Flinx lowered the cold container from his lips. "I believe I may be the first of my kind to be so honored."

That penetrating, experienced gaze fixed him in its predatory sights. "You conssider it an honor, then?"

Flinx further astounded his host by making the correct gesture to signify first-degree assent. "I consider it an honor to be accounted a member of any family, of any species, that would have me as a member of its Tier."

"And are you an artisst? Iss that how you gained thiss remarkable admission?"

"I can draw, a little. I can do many things, a little. In a time of serious personal need, the Ssaiinn showed me great compassion."

Lord Eiipul executed a gesture indicative of second-degree incredulity. "All artisstss are by definition more than a little unssound in their reassoning. A Tier of artissanss . . . ," he hissed softly to himself. "If one sshiftss one'ss mind away from normal reassoning, I ssupposse there iss a certain sskewed ssensse to ssuch a thing." Raising his drinking utensil, he saluted the visitor. "Iss that why you have worked to evade every imaginable ssecurity meassure and put your life at grave rissk to come here to the capital of the Empire? To practisse ssome bizarre variant of human-AAnn 'art'?"

In a way, the Lord nye was perhaps not so very far wrong, a startled Flinx found himself thinking. He plunged onward with his explanation.

"Lord Eiipul, there exists a threat to the entire galaxy: Empire and Commonwealth and all else alike. Thus far its existence and extent are known to only a very few humans and thranx." He indicated the staring, fascinated, and more than slightly awed trio of younger AAnn. "Now, because of my presence and my need, your progeny and their friend know of it. Any hope of countering this threat and saving all that exists seems to somehow center on me. This is not a responsibility I have sought and no one wishes it were otherwise more than I.

"As to why I came here—well, I did so because it's something that hasn't been done by any of my kind. Not like this, alone and uninvited. I wanted to see what typical AAnn life and society was like for myself, without an official escort. Now that I've done that, I believe more than ever that your kind are as much worth saving as my own."

"How magnanimouss of you." Lord Eiipul added an appropriate

gesture of second-degree sarcasm. "How noble. No doubt we sshould be eternally grateful for your generouss approval."

"I speak solely as a friend and mean no disrespect." Flinx took a deep breath and tried to gaze as deeply into the noble AAnn's eyes as possible. "As to the danger of which I speak, I can if necessary offer incontrovertible proof of its existence."

"Can you truly?" was Lord Eiipul's diffident reply. "You have chartss sshowing the location of thiss 'threat'? Sstatissticss attessting to itss sstrength? Imagess, meassurementss, relevant equationss?"

"No," Flinx admitted. "At least, not enough to convince you, or the scientists you would call upon to analyze such records. Such things are extremely limited in content anyway."

"Then," his host quietly demanded to know, "how do you expect mysself, or my more credulouss offsspring, or any other half-mature repressentative of my kind to believe a ssingle iota of what you are babbling?"

Flinx did not hesitate. "I think I can show you for yourself."

For the first time since Flinx had revealed himself as a stealth soft-skin, Lord Eiipul's emotions suggested a hint of uncertainty.

"*Sshow* it to me? How do you proposse to accomplissh ssuch? With what kind of insstrumentss?"

"No instruments." Flinx spoke softly, matter-of-factly. He had already laid claim to the extraordinary. It was but a small leap to lay claim to the impossible. "I have the ability to 'go' to the place from where the threat arises. It still lies behind a region of space impenetrable to nearly all instrumentation. Over the years I have projected myself there or found myself projected there by—others. On occasion others have in this fashion shared the experience of contact with me. I have—a certain Talent." He looked past the quietly incredulous nye to the three staring youths.

"Kiijeem AVMd asked me to share this experience with him. I turned him down. Just as I turned down your own disbelieving offspring. The threat, the danger, the cosmic specter that I have come to call the Great Evil, is not something for an immature mind to touch upon." He returned his attention to his host. "There is risk involved. Each time I do this I never know if I myself will survive the experience."

For the second time that evening, Lord Eiipul IX set his drink aside.

"You are a bold and beguiling member of your unfortunately benighted sspeciess, which hass the regrettable quality of having amalgamated with the detessted thranx. You will prove a fit and interessting ssubject for official interrogation and probable dissection, under which circum-sstancess I am ssure you will acquit yoursself admirably." His right hand moved toward the instrumentation embedded in his left wrist.

Flinx's right hand shot forward to grasp his host's left wrist and simultaneously block the mechanism that would summon aid. Each of the twins let out a warning hiss and dropped into a fighting crouch while a seriously flustered Kiijeem debated how he, as a guest, ought to proceed. Almost as soon as Flinx's fingers closed around the nye's forearm, Lord Eiipul twisted and spun. Flinx's grasp was cast off as the nye's tail swung around like a whip. It cracked through the air where the human's face had been an instant before.

Seconds later they stood confronting each other: Eiipul in the time-honored fighting pose of his kind, Flinx bent at the knees with his left leg in front of his body and his right slightly behind. Off to one side the three younger AAnn stood ready to attack, waiting for a sign from the one adult in their midst.

"I demand the right of challenge!" Flinx declared, adding the appropriate first-degree gesture. "As a member of a recognized Tier and honorable family, that right is mine to claim."

Breathing easily in and out, Lord Eiipul studied the incongruous presence confronting him in his own home. "Thiss iss not the sstreet, ssoftsskin. We are not sstrollerss on the central walkway, well met halfway between profession and home. I losse no sstatuss by refussing your challenge and turning you over to the appropriate authority."

Flinx smiled thinly. "Only in your own eyes." He nodded in the direction of the three youths. "And in those of your offspring, of course."

Eiipul found himself concurrently amused, impressed, and taken aback by this unexpected rejoinder. "You know more of our wayss than jusst how to sspeak them, sslug-thinker. Who could have imagined it? A ssoftsskin as ssly as he iss ssmart." Flinx saw toned muscles tense beneath shining scales, sensed the rise in ancient predatory feelings that had yet to be bred out of the space-going pseudo-reptilian species, and watched as the senior AAnn kicked off his finely made sandals one by one. "Look to your loinss, human!"

"And you to yours!" Flinx readied himself as his opponent's powerful thigh muscles contracted and the nye sprang at him, crossing the space between them in a single leap.

Their intent laid bare by their emotions, Eiipul IXb and IXc each took a step forward. Their purpose was to aid their parent and end the fight as quickly as possible. Before they could even approach the two adult combatants they found themselves confronting something small, winged, and bright of body and wing. The minidrag hovered in the air before them, its jaws parted. Hesitating, brother and sister contemplated the flying creature. In their culture, a wide-open mouth was always to be considered a threat. What danger the alien organism posed to them they did not know. It was as foreign to their experience as the softskin currently skirmishing with their patriarch. But they had been taught well.

When you are confronted by something that is much smaller than you yet obviously unafraid despite the disparity in size, it suggests two things. Either the being in question is bluffing—or it is not. There is usually only one way to find out where the truth lies.

Holding their ground and facing something entirely outside their experience, it appeared that in this particular instance neither brother nor sister was inclined to test which reality was the correct one.

Flinx found himself unable to guess Lord Eiipul's age. Not that it mattered. The noble was fast, perceptive, and a master of AAnn fighting techniques. His high-velocity attack employed frequent high kicks featuring extended claws, slashing hands, vicious snaps of tooth-laden jaws, and that ever-present dangerously whipping tail. At least the latter was not equipped with an armored point, as Kiijeem's had been when Flinx had originally encountered his young host.

He could have tried projecting on his adversary. A touch of fear, a hint of uncertainty, a soupçon of indecision: any of these would have slowed the tornado of teeth, claws, and tail that Lord Eiipul had become. But in order to properly engage his Talent, Flinx needed a hiatus of at least a few seconds in order to concentrate. Eiipul did not grant him that much of a lull. The AAnn just kept coming; slashing, cutting, kicking, and biting in an attempt to bring his opponent down. A human with no experience of AAnn fighting techniques would have already buckled, lacerated and torn.

Flinx was not so straightforward an opponent. Using hands and feet he was able to block thrusting claws before they could cut and tear. Employing his greater height, he was able to fend off his foe's repeated attempts to fasten strong jaws on arm or leg. He did not strike out himself, made no attempt to cripple or immobilize his enemy. It was Eiipul's help he sought, not his death. If he could just continue to hold his attacker off, his youth and greater stamina ought to slow the contest to a point where he could simply tackle an exhausted Eiipul and hold his opponent down until he conceded.

Lord Eiipul IX was no fool. He knew when he was being toyed with. Instead of making him think, this only enraged him further. The human, a *softskin,* was *condescending* to him! In hand-to-hand combat! It was scarcely to be believed. He redoubled his efforts. But regardless of the attacking combination he employed, each time he struck, the softskin somehow managed to deflect his most forceful effort. Truly, the human was taller, and truly, he had the advantage of youth, but Eiipul felt that his long experience should have more than countered both of these factors. Instead he found every thrust shunted aside, every kick blocked, every bite clamping down only on empty air. His legs were starting to grow heavy—he could not kick as high and as often as in earlier days. His breathing was coming in longer, deeper gasps. And his tail threatened to become an appendage useful for little more than maintaining balance. It was no longer the sound barrier–breaking weapon of yore.

In addition to mounting fatigue, he was also beginning to feel the first inklings of fear.

He did not show it, of course. Not only his opponent but his offspring were watching. *Why didn't the softskin strike back?* Several times Eiipul realized that a failed attack had exposed him to a potentially ruinous riposte by the human. And each time, his surprisingly agile opponent had simply waited for Eiipul to recover and attack again.

Even though it was a strategy that had already failed several times, he decided to go low and try to take his taller opponent's legs out from under him. Once again he feinted with both hands, one after the other, bit down with his jaws, and whirled. His tail whipped around, extending his reach beyond his feet.

Too slow, he realized immediately. Far too slow. The softskin could easily step back out of range. Or worse, leap forward. A move like that would put him on Eiipul's back.

That was exactly what happened. Dimly, he heard the escalating hisses of dismay from his progeny and their damnable friend Kiijeem. Though slim, the human was heavier than Eiipul expected. The alien weight forced him to the floor. He flailed with his tail but struck nothing; the softskin was too high on his back. One fleshy but muscular arm went under Eiipul's chin, forcing his jaws closed, up, and back. The other limb—long, limber, and deceptively soft—pulled the noble's right arm behind his back. Pressure was applied. Despite himself, Eiipul let out a hiss of pain. There was enough weight behind that grip to break the bone.

The human continued to pull—and abruptly rolled over onto his own back. A disoriented Eiipul found himself dragged on top, albeit with his arm still pinned. His tail was free now to strike downward against the human's legs. Incongruously round pupils peered up into his own.

"I yield, noble Eiipul! I am defeated. I cast mysself upon your mercy."

What softskin twaddle was this? a bewildered Eiipul found himself wondering. The alien grip on his right arm was still unyielding. The human had been in complete control, in a position to end the fight however he saw fit. Instead, he had chosen to roll over onto his back and surrender. It made no sense, absolutely no sense.

As little sense, in fact, as the softskin's mad, lunatic tale about an undetectable threat to the entire galaxy and his individual involvement in some fantastic attempt to deal with it.

Voices drew his attention. Unexpectedly released from their anguish by the surprising turn of events, his offspring were shouting wildly at him.

"Throat!" his daughter was screaming. "Tear out hiss throat!"

"Legss!" Eiipul IXb was hissing from the top of his larynx. "Dissembowel before it can risse!" Standing beside him, a thoughtful Kiijeem remained silent. Less personally involved in the preceding combat, only he among the trio of younglings suspected what had actually occurred.

Opening his mouth, Lord Eiipul revealed teeth that were far more sharklike than mammalian. Slowly, he lowered his gaping jaws toward Flinx. Off to the side Pip fluttered uncertainly.

When that compilation of razor-sharp dentition had dropped very close to the human's face, Eiipul hissed in an angry whisper, "Why are you doing thiss?"

"Doing what?" With both his hands occupied the human could not gesture any degree of guile, but Eiipul divined it nonetheless.

"Allowing me a triumph. I could not touch you and wass clearly tiring. You patronize me, ssoftsskin!"

Flinx smiled tightly even as he wondered if the AAnn noble was familiar enough with humankind to recognize the significance of the expression. "No—truly, no. I submit for the same reasons I challenged. To obtain your help—and because your offspring are looking on. While I feel no hesitation to do you injury, I would not have you lose status before them and their friend."

Ignoring the imploring from his progeny to finish the fight, Eiipul drew back slightly. "Truly, you are the mosst AAnn of ssoftsskinss I have ever encountered or heard tell of. Your adoptive Tier sshould be proud. I would hear more of how you came to be one of them."

Flinx's smile widened ever so slightly. "That may prove difficult if you rip my throat out or disembowel me."

"Truly that would inconvenience converssation." Raising his voice, he straightened atop the prone human and glared over at his offspring. His tail whipped victoriously back and forth behind him, clearing Flinx's legs by barely a centimeter.

"The ssoftsskin hass proven himsself a worthy adverssary! On behalf of our family and our ancesstorss I have generoussly decided to grant him leniency. You will oblige me in thiss matter and upon hiss releasse make no covert movess to sstrike him." Once again putting his jaws close to the human's face, he whispered a second time. "I musst assk you to releasse my right arm lesst my declaration ssmell of facetiousness." Flinx promptly complied, and then allowed Eiipul to "help" the vanquished human to his feet.

"Most impressive is your fighting, most impressive is your character, honored nye," Flinx murmured humbly. "I owe you my life."

Though expressively challenged due to their stiff, scaly epidermis, the looks on the faces of Eiipul's offspring as they gazed admiringly at their victorious parent were probably worth a good quarter-jump in family status—at least in their young eyes. Significantly, Kiijeem's expression was considerably less rapt—but he said nothing.

It was always useful, Flinx knew, when one could, to demonstrate to any AAnn, even a youth, the efficacy of diplomacy over force.

"There sstill remainss the matter of what to do with you, ssoft-sskin." Eiipul studied his tall visitor contemplatively. The anger and antagonism that had been simmering within him previously had largely faded away, Flinx perceived. The AAnn's emotions were more under control—and reflective of his continuing confusion. "I am sstill inclined to deliver you to the proper authoritiess, except . . ."

"Except . . . ," Flinx prompted him, adding a second-degree genuflection of appreciation.

"Thiss inssane sstory of yourss. I know of many ssentientss, AAnn and otherwisse, who found themsselvess driven to death by their delussionss. But you sstrike me as rational as well as intelligent. Your tale and your actionss sseem to me to be sstrongly at oddss with one another. You believe in thiss delussion of yourss sso deeply that you are willing to die to further propound it?"

"Such is the choice that life and circumstance have forced upon me," Flinx replied coolly.

His host hissed softly. "If you are lying, or delussional as are sso many of your kind, or if thiss iss ssome kind of conjurer trick, be assured that I will learn the truth. And then I will ssee to it that you are dealt with more harsshly than otherwisse would be the casse." His tone hardened. "Your unprecedented affiliation with a Tier family notwiths-standing."

Flinx had anticipated and prepared for just such a response. "It won't matter. If what I will try to show you fails to eventuate—and there is never any guarantee of success—then you can have me taken away and killed and the galaxy and everything in it goes to hell anyway. So in the long run, it doesn't matter."

His host gestured third-degree accord. "All fatalisstss are at peace with themsselvess until the knife beginss to cut. Then reality takess over." He shifted his stance, relaxing his legs. "What do I have to do to participate in thiss 'experience' you proposse to sshare? Nothing requiring elaborate or extenssive planning, I hope. I disslike the wassting of time. Not even a ssoftsskin sshould be late for hiss own demisse."

"That's something I'm always prepared for," Flinx admitted, "though I admit to being receptive to regular postponements." Looking around, he searched for something soft. A hard species that had evolved in a tough environment, the AAnn did not go in for plush pillows and thick rugs. Settling on a small depression filled with ornamental colored sand, he walked over and lay down. It was as unyielding as the rest of the floor, but at least it was warmed from beneath. Responding to a gesture from her master, Pip darted away from where she had continued to confront the three young nye and rejoined him, settling down to coil herself contentedly on his chest. He regretted that he was about to unsettle her emotions. Hopefully they would become no less agitated than his own.

Realizing that he was as comfortable as he was going to get, he looked up and over at the increasingly bemused Lord Eiipul IX.

"We are ready to begin, noble nye. Or at least to try. Do you have anything that will help you sleep?"

It was always the same. It was always slightly different. Different and the same. It was always horrifying.

When he regained consciousness he was drenched in sweat. At least, he reflected, by letting himself drift and be drawn mentally outward toward the distant reaches of the universe while he was naked he did not come back to reality encased in cold, wet clothes. Forcing open his eyes, he immediately looked downward in the direction of the slight weight on his chest. Eyes open, Pip was struggling to uncoil her body and unfurl her wings. She did not sweat, but he could sense her distress. As a more primitive empath, she shared his feelings without knowing exactly what he felt. This time she seemed in an unusual rush to regain her strength.

Possibly it had something to do with the weapons Eiipul IXb and IXc were aiming in his direction.

Kiijeem stood behind them. At the moment, his own emotions were badly muddled. While looking askance at his friends, he was eyeing the rapidly reviving Flinx with the usual expectation and uncertainty—but this time there was also an unmistakable trace of the innate aggression he had radiated when he had first encountered the visiting human.

Something was wrong, Flinx realized. Pip was perceiving it as well, which explained why she was fighting harder than usual to recover from the experience. She was in a hurry to get airborne so that she could protect him. Reaching down, he put a hand around her body, pinning her wings against her sides as he exuded feelings of tranquility and reassurance. She relaxed a little, but not completely. It was evident she did not altogether buy the contrived calm he was struggling to impart.

He was not sure that he did, either.

"What have you done to our patriarch?" Eiipul IXc hissed threateningly as she kept the pistol she was holding pointed directly at the center of Flinx's torso.

"Nothing more or less than what I said that I would try to do." In the absence of specifics he spoke as calmly as he could while facing the weapon. "Which was to attempt to provide incontrovertible proof of my story. I think that I did that. I *felt* that I did that, though in the state of stasis that is entered it's difficult to be certain of anything."

"Be certain of thiss," her brother growled at him. "If the damage perssissstss, the next sstate you enter will be that of extinction."

As soon as he felt enough of his strength had returned, Flinx sat up. "Damage?" A coldness began to creep up his spine. What had he done? "I don't understand."

Without lowering their weapons, the twins stepped back. "Look upon the Lord Eiipul, and you will." The pistol jerked in the brother's hand. "Try to flee and you will die, along with your gaudy pet."

Still holding tightly to Pip, Flinx locked eyes with the minidrag before depositing her gently onto his right shoulder. Under the circumstances he was having a difficult time sustaining the emotional illusion that all was well and everything was fine. Her gaze kept darting from him to the Eiipul offspring and back again. He struggled to contain her with his feelings even as his own were seriously conflicted.

Lord Eiipul IX lay on a horizontal resting platform nearby, where his offspring and Kiijeem had moved him. The nye was lying on his right side (AAnn did not lie on their backs), eyes wide open, nictating membranes retracted, staring into the distance. Bending toward him under the watchful, seething glares of his progeny, Flinx waved one hand slowly back and forth over his host's face. The eyes did not respond. The AAnn was breathing slowly and steadily, but he did not react to any of Flinx's physical stimuli nor indicate in any other fashion that he was still alive. Though no expert on AAnn physiology, Flinx felt fairly confident in voicing a diagnosis.

"Lord Eiipul is in shock."

"Truly," growled his daughter. "Tell uss ssomething we know not. Tell uss how to bring him back."

"I'd try some energizing medications," Flinx told her. "Anything organic and benign that's likely to give the nervous system a jolt and . . ."

"We have already done thuss." With his free hand Eiipul IXb pointed to a nearby spiral table. A small air injection device rested on the polished stone. Glancing at the attached opaque clip, Flinx had no way of telling whether it was full or empty. "Hiss body twitchess in ressponsse to sspecific sstimulantss, but otherwisse there iss no reaction. Sshouting ssimilarly provokess no ressponsse."

His mind, Flinx mused. It was his mind. The AAnn's consciousness was adrift. Eiipul had not come back all the way. Clarity had survived the shared experience of a glancing contact with the Great Evil without suffering any permanent physical or mental side effects. Had he misjudged the mature nye's capacity for coping with the same kind of contact? Was the makeup of the AAnn psyche so different that it could not survive a similar encounter?

Once more he looked down at the immobilized nye. Flinx felt he was rapidly running out of time. Traditionally impatient by nature, the younger Eiipuls would not wait forever before shooting to cripple him and then calling for assistance.

If he could not reach the benumbed AAnn physically or through eye contact, Flinx realized, then he would have to try to do so emotively.

Closing his eyes, he reached out. He had done this under pressure before. The present circumstances were no more or less threatening than a number of similar situations he had been forced to cope with.

At first he encountered nothing. Emotionally Lord Eiipul was a blank, an empty vessel devoid of feeling. Probing the alien emotive void, Flinx grew more and more apprehensive. If the paralysis extended this deeply, Lord Eiipul might truly be gone, his mind locked in permanent retreat.

There—something. A hint of awareness, cowering in the distance, enveloped in fear and anxiety. He reached toward it, projecting the most serene and soothing feelings he could muster. What he touched was not human. It was thoroughly AAnn. Certain sentiments, however, or at least variants thereof, are common to the majority of sentient species.

Dread and loathing, for example.

Lord Eiipul IX was the descendant of a long line of noble nye whose ancestry could be traced back to single-planetary origins. He was highly intelligent, a trained fighter, skilled in the arts of war, politics, economics, and status rivalry. Decades of intense competition within the fierce upper strata of AAnn society had left him scarred but never bowed. There was nothing in the Empire, the Commonwealth, or the unknown dark galactic reaches framing both that he found intimidating. Gently, expertly, with skill born of years of ever-increasing experience, Flinx massaged and worked to repair the AAnn's tattered emotions.

Lord Eiipul woke up screaming.

CHAPTER

9

Nothing they had experienced in their young lives prepared Eiipul's off-spring or Kiijeem for that reaction. The brother dropped his pistol while his sister, stumbling backward until she pressed up against the nearest wall, just did manage to keep a shaky grip on hers. To his credit Kiijeem held his ground. Or perhaps he was simply unable to move. Frozen to the spot, he stared at the resting platform on which the noble, the es-timable, the most venerable Lord Eiipul IX was twitching and tossing and shrieking like a newborn that had been cast into a fire. AAnn, espe-cially those in their prime, did not react like this. No matter the circum-stances, regardless of pain or suffering, they forever held fast to a legacy of stoicism that bordered on the fanatical.

Confronted with the unexpectedly violent reaction, Flinx did the only thing he could think of: bending over and reaching down, he wrapped both arms around the possessed nye and held him tightly as he tried to still the convulsions. While Pip slithered crazily around his neck and shoulders, he pulled the AAnn as close to him as he dared. Madly flailing claws slashed at his bare chest. Wincing from the pain, turning his head to one side to protect his eyes and face, Flinx ignored the cuts and lacerations as he concentrated on projecting feelings of reassurance, comfort, and support onto the sufferer. Uncertain how to react, desperately wanting to help but afraid to interfere, the three younger AAnn remained as they were and just stared.

Slowly, agonizingly, little by emotive little, Flinx brought Lord Eiipul IX back. Back to reality, back to himself. The AAnn's turbulent emotions calmed, the terror that had inundated him receded. An outer eyelid flickered, then the inner. His mind began to clear and his gaze to focus. Unhelpfully, the first thing they saw was the naked alien specter of Flinx hovering over him.

Instinctively, a four-fingered, claw-tipped hand rose and pushed. Releasing his hold with his left arm, Flinx quickly slid his right out from beneath the AAnn's back and moved away. Blood from the nye's unconscious, automatic clawing oozed down the tall human's bare chest and belly to mix with the perspiration that always lingered from the debilitating mental journey.

Tentatively, Eiipul IXc stepped forward to peer down at the patriarch. "Honored ssire, we have been sso truly truly vexed! We have sseen you alive yet dead. We did not know what to do, how to help." Her gaze rose to the wounded softskin bleeding silently nearby. "We wanted to kill the vissitor—but at the ssame time we were afraid to kill it."

Grimacing, Lord Eiipul raised himself to a sitting position. His unusually rapid breathing was the only remaining indication that he had undergone an experience out of the ordinary. That, and the dark red liquid trickling from his mouth. His jaws had been clenched tightly enough to bleed.

He did not answer his offspring, did not respond to her declaration. Swinging his legs and tail off the platform, he placed his sandaled feet on the floor, stood motionless long enough to be confident of his balance, and then started toward the watching Flinx. On the third step he stumbled and nearly fell. Alarmed, the twins broke in his direction, but he waved them off. Using his tail for balance, he resumed his slow advance on the softskin.

Halting within arm's reach, Eiipul turned his head to the left and exposed his throat. Within the room, no one breathed. When Flinx continued to hesitate, the noble reached out, took the human's right hand, and placed it against his unprotected neck.

"You cannot kill me," he declared solemnly, "becausse I have jusst died."

As he observed the tableau, Kiijeem found himself remembering. Remembering how insistent he had been that the softskin allow him to share in the hazily described experience. How the human had refused and how angry he, Kiijeem AVMd, had become. He tried to swallow, only to discover that all the moisture had fled from his throat.

Flinx lowered his arm, allowing the AAnn to turn his head back to him once again. "I'm sorry. When words failed, I didn't know any other way to convince you." Turning, he walked over to the sweeping window. Inclining his head, he bent slightly at the waist in order to look up at the night sky.

"It keeps speeding up. The phenomenon that's coming this way. I and my friends—the few Commonwealth scientists who are also aware of it—thought it would be hundreds of years before the danger it poses would become imminent." Straightening as he reached up to caress Pip, he turned to look back at his host. "Each time I reach out to encounter it I'm less certain of that time frame. If it keeps on accelerating it's conceivable it might burst out of the Great Emptiness and begin to affect the outer reaches of the galaxy as soon as in our lifetimes."

"Sshannt, ssoftsskin. There iss no need for additional emphassiss. I will not doubt your word again." Pivoting slightly, he finally addressed his offspring. "Sstand and breathe. I am alive, I am well, but I am changed. As would be anyone who had been obliged to sshare what I have jusst sshared." He looked back at Flinx. "I do not know how you did what you jusst did, human. Manifesstly, you are different. The how and why of that I leave to cleverer, more sspecialized mindss than mine. For now I will content mysself with that which I know. With what I have—experienced. I know it wass not an illusion. Would that it had been. You have accomplisshed what you intended, human. I believe your sstory."

For the first time that evening, Flinx allowed himself to unwind slightly. "Then you agree to hide me until my ship can return to pick me up, and will help me travel to the pickup site unobserved?"

Lord Eiipul regarded the softskin standing before him. "No."

Flinx could not hide his surprise. The AAnn's emotions belied his response. Something was being left unsaid. "I don't understand."

"As you have all too clearly sshown," Eiipul replied, "thiss danger iss one that threatenss all civilizationss, all living thingss. It iss not,

sshould not, be the province of óne sspeciess—far less a ssingle repressentative of that sspeciess. You bear a burden I would not sshare for
the chance to be chossen Emperor.

"The Empire and the Commonwealth sstand at oddss yet pressently
hold to an uneassy peace. It iss plain to me that all ssuch conflict musst
be put asside lesst an unforesseen incident, an unpredictable encounter,
might interfere with your effortss to try and counter thiss . . . thiss . . ."

Eloquent as Lord Eiipul was, he could not find the words to describe what he had just experienced. It was likely he did not wish to. Describing would require remembering. "While it iss unlikely you will be
given overt assisstance, it musst be made certain that you are permitted
to proceed with the assurance that no facet of the Empire will in any
way interfere with your effortss."

This was getting out of hand, Flinx saw. All he wanted was help in
getting off Blasusarr safely and unobtrusively. But Lord Eiipul would
not be denied.

"I ssee only one way to achieve ssuch assurance, for good and for a
certainty." He was watching the softskin closely. "What I jusst ssurvived. What you jusst sshowed to me. Can you—can you sshare it with
more than one individual at a time?"

"I don't know," Flinx answered honestly. "I myself have previously
shared the contact with multiple minds, but they accompanied me unbidden, and they weren't human."

"All to the good." Lord Eiipul sounded encouraged. "Neither am I.
Neither are thosse with whom I wissh you to sshare sso that they too
may be convinced, and sso that the Empire will do what it can to facilitate your effortss to ssave uss all."

Unable to stand by in silence any longer, Eiipul IXc stepped forward. "Honored parent, are you ssuggessting that the horror you jusst
ssurvived be sshared with other nye?"

"It iss the only way," he told her with atypical gentleness. "I mysself would not accept the ssoftsskin'ss wordss by themsselvess. I had to
be sshown. I had to *experience*. It would be the ssame with any otherss.
They would not accept jusst an explanation any more than did I. Only
by experiencing will they believe." He turned back to the waiting Flinx.

"I will take the preparatory sstepss. At the appropriate moment, I
will make the necessary introduction." He gestured to where Flinx's

simsuit was neatly laid out on a polished section of floor. "I fear that for one more time, at leasst, you musst employ your ingeniouss dissguisse."

Flinx took a deep breath. It was evident from his emotions as well as from his words that Lord Eiipul was not going to be dissuaded from the course of action he had chosen. On the positive side, Flinx had to admit that it would be very useful in the furtherance of his activities if the representatives of the AAnn Empire, wherever and whenever he might happen to encounter them, had been specifically instructed to give a certain tall young human freedom to proceed wherever and however he wished.

"All right," he replied resignedly. "If you think it's that necessary. With whom do you want me to share? Mates of yours? Other family members?" He mulled other possibilities. "Representatives of the military?"

Lord Eiipul gestured first-degree inclusiveness underscored with pure unconditionality. "As the threat you sshowed to me iss the greatesst that can be imagined, sso therefore musst the greatesst be exposssed to it. I sshall assume the necessary rissk."

Flinx was instantly on guard. "What risk?"

The AAnn met his gaze unflinchingly. "I will make arrangementss sso that you can sshare your experience of thiss galaxy-wide threat with the Imperial Gathering and with the Emperor himsself."

Startled hisses rose from his offspring. "Honored ssire, no!" Eiipul IXb rushed his parent, followed closely by his sister. Flinx noted that Kiijeem held back. This was a family matter. No matter what opinion he might hold, no matter what insight he felt he could bring to the discussion, the twins' friend would remain aloof from the debate. If the outcome went well, he stood to benefit. If it ended in disaster, he could claim noninvolvement. No wonder the strongest emotion Flinx read from his young friend was satisfaction. The feelings currently being broadcast by the two Eiipul progeny constituted another emotive state entirely.

They were frightened, as well as indignant.

"Conssider, my lord," his daughter was pleading, "that if the unprecedented confrontation you proposse sshould fail, it could mean the end of your career."

"Not only your career." Her brother was politely irate. "The family

Eiipul itsself could be ruined. Everything that our ancesstorss have built, our illusstriouss family hisstory, our sstanding within the Empire—all could be ssacrificed on the altar of a hassty decission. We could losse everything—even our name."

Their patriarch was silent. For a moment Flinx thought the fretful twins might have persuaded Lord Eiipul to change his mind. But as it turned out he was only gathering his thoughts.

"If you had come into contact with the ssame monsstroussness as did I, you would underssstand," he informed his offspring gravely. "You would hassten to my ssupport and not think to challenge it. But you sstood outsside the dire. For thiss I am grateful. For thiss *you* sshould be grateful. Revel in your continued ignorance and be glad our vissitor hass chossen not to convey to you the full force of hiss knowledge." Off to one side, Kiijeem eyed Flinx meaningfully as Lord Eiipul turned back to the softskin.

"You musst do as I ssuggesst." The noble's tail flicked sharply to the right. "Otherwisse, I will not help you."

There it was. Whatever happened from now on, Flinx could consider himself absolved. The decision had been forced on him. Decision, and opportunity. Still . . .

"I don't know if I can do what you request, Lord Eiipul. I've never tried, at least not intentionally, to share the experience with more than one other sentient at a time."

"You sshared with me." From the dispenser at his side the AAnn noble drew forth a fresh libation. "You will find the Emperor an admirable entity, and there are many in the Gathering who are wiser and more knowledgeable than mysself. None, I think, will be immune to the importance of what you musst reveal to them."

"Speaking of immunity," Flinx reminded his host, "there is danger involved. You now know that."

"Better than I would wissh to," Eiipul admitted. "Yet all knowledge concealss within it danger to a greater or lesser degree." He gestured third-degree amusement. "If it did not, governmentss would not be sso anxiouss to regulate it." Coming closer, he lowered his voice.

"I give you, Flinx of the Commonwealth, Flinx LLVVRXX of the Tier Ssaiinn, a chance to interact with the ssupreme leaderss of the

Empire. It iss an opportunity no human hass ever been offered before. Not the head of your government, not the Lasst Ressort of your United Church, not the mosst eminent among your sscientissts, not the resspected leaderss of your military. You musst sshow my own kind what iss at sstake." He stepped back. "Only then will you be assured of a ssafe departure from thiss world, and the chance to carry on your essential work."

Flinx found himself pondering what was at once an offer and a command. If he refused Eiipul's request, his options would be seriously limited. If he agreed, and could bring it off, there could be ancillary benefits. Thinking back to his time on Jast among the Tier of Ssaiinn inevitably led him to fond remembrances of one exceptional AAnn: the female, Chraluuc, who had looked after and taken a special interest in him. She had wanted him to be a bridge between humans and her kind. Here was an opportunity to do so on a scale neither of them could ever have foreseen.

Of course, if he failed in the effort not only would humans and AAnn not be drawn closer together, but he could quite easily end up dead.

He refocused his attention on the noble nye waiting in front of him. His emotions elevated but under control, Eiipul awaited his answer.

"If you can really get me that kind of audience," Flinx sighed, "I'll try to do what you ask. I'll try as I've never tried before."

"Excellent, my illicit friend! I will sstart work immediately." Eiipul gestured to his left. "Meanwhile, you are my guesst. We will enssconce you in a part of the ressidence that iss clossed to vissitorss, even to family. There you can resst and recover your sstrength. You will need it all, I think," he concluded solemnly.

"Honored ssire," his daughter protested. "Thiss iss madness! If the ssoftsskin iss found out, if it becomess known we are harboring a human illegally arrived on Blasussarr, that will be the end of our family sstatuss as ssurely as if all of uss perisshed at the human'ss handss!"

"Then," Lord Eiipul told his protesting offspring firmly, "it will behoove you and your brother and your friend to enssure that that eventuality doess not come to pass. *Azzissn*?"

Taking a respectful step backward, she dropped her eyes and mumbled reluctantly, "Azzissn." In this unhappy acquiescence she was joined by her brother and also by the attentive Kiijeem.

"It iss decided." Turning back to his unforeseen guest, Lord Eiipul started to extend a welcoming tail tip. Remembering that his visitor was conspicuously deficient in that department, the noble quickly substituted a proffered hand instead. Four scaly fingers gripped five decidedly softer ones.

"Now then, can you eat proper food?"

"I find most AAnn cuisine quite agreeable, as does my companion." Flinx added a slight nod in the direction of the minidrag riding comfortably on his left shoulder. "Though after a while a steady regimen of meat and its synthetic derivatives does become tiresome."

His host responded with a visible shudder. "I undersstand. I am familiar with the human diet. At leasst you are not thranx. We will try to sscrounge ssome 'edible' plant matter sso you can vary your intake. Meanwhile, I would have you tell me everything you can about thiss horror that sspeedss toward uss and threatenss all of exisstence." He sucked in a deep, whistling breath. "Though I have but infinitessimally ssenssed it for mysself, I would sstill know more. If there iss more to know." Taking Flinx's hand, he led the taller human toward a lift. His offspring and their friend trailed obediently behind.

"Well," Flinx began, "it's manifestly the largest life-form that's ever been identified—if it can be called a life-form in the usual sense."

Lord Eiipul gestured second-degree ignorance. "The universse iss far too vasst to be comprehended by beingss as inssignificant as oursselvess. We can look, we can sspeculate, we can even meassure, but we cannot comprehend. Who can ssay but that there may exisst larger entitiess sstill, perhapss even thosse capable of feeding on such an immenssity as threatenss uss now?"

Struggling to imagine something vast enough to threaten the Great Evil that was racing toward the outskirts of the Milky Way, Flinx found that he agreed unhesitatingly with his host. Nothing "living" could be as large as the Great Evil, yet it patently existed. Why could there not exist something greater still? The attempt to envision anything so immense simply overwhelmed the rudimentary network of neurons that comprised an ordinary mind. Even mathematics was overwhelmed. At such times it helped enormously to have an anchor, a grounding. Something solid and real and true to hold on to.

It was at such times that he invariably thought of Clarity Held.

They settled Flinx in a small storage area, aboveground and safely away from passing eyes both AAnn and electronic. Unlike the large subterranean chamber where he had previously been hidden, this one had lights, a heated sand sleeping basin, access to AAnn entertainment, even a window. Lord Eiipul assured Flinx that the likelihood of him being discovered was virtually nil. In the absence of a direct reference or reason, Krrassin Security would never stoop to quizzing the members of an important family about a possible sighting of an offworlder wanted for something as insignificant as credit forgery.

Time proved that the noble Eiipul knew whereof he spoke. Visitors and members of the extended family came and went without coming anywhere near Flinx's isolated chamber. Safe and secure, he was able at last to rest and relax.

The only interruptions to his daily routine arrived in the form of the still wary Eiipul offspring. When not occupied with daily studies, tasks, or family business, they joined Kiijeem in frequenting the softskin's hideaway, peppering him with questions about everything from daily life in the reviled Commonwealth to the nature of the colorful scaled flying creature that was the human's constant companion. Flinx answered them all readily. Ignorance breeds hatred, while conversely, education slays ignorance. Knowledge, he knew from a lifetime of personal experience, is a more effective weapon than a gun. As Truzenzuzex had once pointed out, it's hard to convince an enemy of the rightness of your cause while you're blowing his head off.

He would have been happy to stay in the storeroom awaiting the return of the reconfigured *Teacher*. Such a simplistic solution to his situation was not to be, however. Converted to a greater reality by what Flinx had shared with him, Lord Eiipul was convinced the attempt had to be made to sway the entire Imperial Gathering. If it could be done, a reluctant Flinx knew, it would be a milestone not only in the history of the Empire but in AAnn-human relations as well.

And all he had wanted to do was spend a few days on Blasusarr to prove to himself that *that* could be done. Was he fated, he wondered, to never be allowed to do anything small and simple?

When the day arrived to escort Flinx into the very heart of Krrassin there was no need to hide him. Sealed securely in his simsuit he was such the figure of an ordinary AAnn that the twins found themselves once more taken aback by the perfection of the illusion. Once his guest had again donned the eye-averting ijkk, Lord Eiipul accompanied him out into the characteristically harsh Blasusarrian light of early morning. The integrated polarizing lenses that camouflaged Flinx's eyes immediately darkened to protect his more sensitive human retinas. He felt his eyes watering anyway. He had not stepped outside since entering the Eiipul compound.

He remembered to fold his tail as Eiipul preceded him into the private family vehicle. The interior was far more luxurious than that of the various public transports he had ridden in the course of his stay on Blasusarr. Rare woods and lustrous concaves of tactile glass lined the walls. Powerfully rhythmic AAnn music, all drums and bells and atonal electronics, emanated discreetly from an unseen source.

As the automated craft rose, rotated, and smoothly accelerated through a waiting gap in the residence's security barrier, Flinx stared out the tinted canopy at the surrounding synthetic desert. After a while, the expensive pseudo-canyons and faux buttes gave way to more utilitarian structures of poured and molded walls and domes. These prosaic edifices jumped through no aesthetic hoops in expensive attempts to disguise their function.

Though traveling at maximum altitude on a level reserved for VIPs, the AAnn aircar still had to negotiate a bevy of traffic. This was Krrassin, after all. The capital, the economic and military hub, the heart of the AAnn interstellar Empire. The homeworld of the Commonwealth's most dynamic and cunning adversaries.

Flinx felt no anxiety, experienced no discomfort at this knowledge. Having never felt quite at home anywhere, not even on Moth, he was therefore equally at ease everywhere in the galaxy. Vagabond and chameleon that he was, home was wherever he happened to be at the moment.

That realization did not entirely squelch the rising trepidation he felt as the nearly silent vehicle drew within sight of the central administrative compound. Here decisions were made that affected not only Krrassin, but Blasusarr and all the worlds of the Empire. The lives, the futures of billions of intelligent beings ebbed and flowed according to judgments rendered within the complex by a hundred or so of the most noble AAnn. Actual choices and preferences were discussed, debated, fought over, and finally voted upon within a single structure known as The Eye of the Nye.

That impressive mass now loomed directly ahead. Analogous constructions on Earth consisted of clusters of needle-like towers or immense domes. On Hivehom, several substantial artificial caverns had been deftly hollowed out of the ground to serve the needs of the greater hive.

In contrast to both, The Eye of the Nye took the form of a single immense rock several square kilometers in extent. Rust red in hue, it had been skillfully shot through with ornamental streaks of azure and silver. In keeping with the traditions of those it had been built to accommodate, it was only five stories high. As always and especially in this sacrosanct place, the AAnn had built outward and not upward. If tradition held true throughout, Flinx knew, the hall would have an internal configuration like an iceberg, with the preponderance of its extensive chambers and corridors situated belowground.

Matte-flat in the morning sun, the red roof was perfectly level and utterly unadorned; devoid of antennae, signs, drifting decorations, spires, or any kind of architectural fillip. In contrast, the building's streaks of silver and slashes of bright blue exploded against his retinas.

He was going in there. Essentially alone, to try to influence an entire alien polity. One that would regard him, as Lord Eiipul originally had, with ingrained suspicion or worse. The *Teacher* was right: surely he was mentally unbalanced. Pip stirred uneasily against his side in the suit's internal pouch. He struggled to prepare himself mentally. Maybe it was better if he *was* a little crazy.

Madness is always the best armor against reality.

It was also a cheap out. He knew he wasn't mad. Retreating into psychosis would have been easy, especially in light of all that he knew and had experienced. Holding on to sanity was always the more difficult course for any sentient being.

The true immensity of the structure did not really hit home until the aircar cleared Security and proceeded deeper into the complex. The Great Hall was a city unto itself, frantic with activity and invested with purpose. Other vehicles darted in all directions, usually at a greater velocity than their own. When his host ordered the transport to turn down a narrower corridor, they found themselves traveling among a swarm of workers riding personalized vehicles.

After what seemed like half an hour they arrived at a parking area. As they disembarked, Eiipul told Flinx it was safe to remove the ijkk and leave it behind.

"No one will be looking for a common criminal in here," he explained confidently. "The kind of antisocial figure repressented by your falsse AAnn identity would never make it passt the firsst ssecurity checkpoint."

Taking extra care with his servo-assisted AAnn gait, Flinx loped alongside Lord Eiipul as they made their way through crowds of busy, intent AAnn. Focused on their individual tasks, hardly any of the workers glanced in the direction of the two nye. Flinx was unusually tall for an AAnn, but not to the point of drawing impolite (and potentially challenge-triggering) stares. The only interruptions came from the occasional passerby who would pause long enough to salute the status of the important noble who was Flinx's host and guide.

The final corridor they entered was different from any that had preceded it. Longer than most and devoid of doorways or branching passages, it had been machined from a single tube of some pale golden-brown metal. It reminded Flinx of translucent bronze. The hordes of workers had thinned here as well. Only a few AAnn strode the impressive span. Though their voices were kept to a respectful hiss, they still echoed off the flawless, seamless curved walls and ceiling.

"We are very closse now." Flinx noted that in this place even Lord Eiipul had lowered his voice. "Make no eye contact with anyone we meet, resspond to no queriess. As my guesst, you are protected from challenge within The Eye. But I am not omnipotent. Even my influence hass itss limitss."

Flinx gestured third-degree understanding. It was enough. Ahead, the light was growing brighter. The tunnel corridor was opening out into a larger space. How much larger he could not imagine until he and his host entered the chamber at the end of the bronze-colored corridor. He did not gasp for breath: in his short life he had seen far too much to be overawed by a mere room. But while he was not overawed, he was certainly impressed.

He had stood in chambers with higher ceilings. The core of a far-away structure that housed a certain ancient weapon/musical instrument, for example, rose to a greater peak. He had wandered through more extensive artificial voids, such as the interior of an ancient construct that appeared from the outside to be a methane dwarf but was in reality an unimaginably massive alien starship. But he had never before entered into one that was at once so expansive, so alien, and so beautiful.

The AAnn artisans who comprised the Tier of Ssaiinn would have approved, he decided as he admired his surroundings. For all he knew, some of them might have contributed to the decoration.

The inner sanctum known as The Eye of the Nye ran almost the entire width of the building. A full five stories high, it was crowned by an immense shallow dome of synthetic quartz that had been treated to change color at predetermined intervals. One moment it was a deep, rich amethyst purple, the next a golden citrine yellow, then transparent as crystal, followed by a tinting of sapphire blue, after which it appeared shot through with simulated rutile—the material of which the dome was composed progressively traversing every color of the visible spectrum.

Mammoth metallic bas-reliefs moving slowly across the walls depicted the history of the AAnn, from the race's humble beginnings as small nomadic bands struggling to survive the harsh landscape of Blasusarr, to the great internecine wars of unification finally won by Keisscha the Firsst, to the rapid rise of technology and the eventual expansion of the Empire to other worlds. Gaps in this hovering history were filled with dazzling knife-edge mosaics fashioned of gemstones and rare metals. Formed from a single continuous viscous pour of bonding chemicals infused with tons of finely ground synthetic corundum, the artfully sculpted floor glistened as if paved with a trillion trillion minuscule jewels.

In addition to the traditional spiral glowlamps, natural light pouring in through the immense dome provided not only plenty of illumination but additional heat. Without the simsuit's integral climate control, heat-stroke would have felled Flinx an hour ago.

Hovering in sharp contrast to the long-established and time-honored conventional ornamentation, contemporary no-nonsense AAnn infolos drifted everywhere. Their presence constituted an exorbitant waste of energy whose purpose was not only to supply information but to celebrate the importance of The Eye and those who were allowed to work therein. As he and his host made their way forward through the cavernous chamber, Flinx saw numerous nye gathered around one or more of the highly responsive migratory knowledge-base projections. Many of the most important decisions involving the course of the Empire were hotly debated in front of those infolos, Eiipul informed him, with the results to be voted on later.

Though the discussions were frequently loud and seemingly hostile, Flinx knew that such voluble acrimony was characteristic of the AAnn. Surprisingly, physical confrontations seemed to be lacking. When queried about this, Lord Eiipul responded with a gesture of second-degree amusement. The highly knowledgeable human was apparently ignorant of something that was a well-known fact to every AAnn.

"Challengess are forbidden in The Eye of the Nye. With sso much high sstatuss at sstake, if confrontationss were allowed here they would take up too much of the time essential to actually making crucial decissionss." Extending one arm in a broad, sweeping gesture, he indicated the vast, crowded, noisy space in which they stood. "For the ssake of the Empire, argumentss made in here can only be contessted with verbal violence."

Flinx started to nod, caught himself just in time, and responded instead with the appropriate gesture. "What happens when disagreements unresolved inside find their way outside?"

"On ssuch occassionss," his guide informed him matter-of-factly, "it iss not uncommon for vacanciess to appear in the body politic. Thiss iss not a problem. For every noble or technocrat who perisshess in a challenge, ten eagerly await to take their place."

Flinx was hardly surprised by the noble's explanation. "I'd always heard that AAnn affairs of state were a bloody business."

Eiipul took no umbrage at his guest's remark. "Toughness iss forged in conflict. I mysself have taken and ssurvived many physsical as well as verbal blowss, and have prevailed in as many combatss as de-batess." Holding up his left arm and turning sideways, he showed Flinx a depression that ran lengthwise from elbow to shoulder. "You mark where musscle and connective tissue iss missing and was not resstored? The result of a ssomewhat heated disspute involving continental eco-nomicss." He lowered the permanently scarred arm.

Flinx was at once appalled and impressed. Personally, he could not recall having read or heard of an instance where a human economist had resolved a disagreement with a fellow academician by ripping out the other's tendons and ligaments. Clearly, Lord Eiipul regarded the disfig-urement as a mark of honor. AAnn medical science was more than ad-vanced enough for him to have had the muscle repaired or restored, had he so desired.

The great expanse of The Eye had a practical as well as ceremonial purpose. Its extent and the specific design of the highly embellished walls served to mute the volume of ongoing AAnn political delibera-tions. Apparently there was no such thing as a quiet debate among the AAnn. Flinx felt that the sometimes petty bickering he overheard as he loped onward alongside Eiipul was unworthy of the grand surround-ings. Nevertheless, in the course of all the ancillary hissing and scream-ing it seemed that necessary decisions were eventually arrived at, consensus was periodically reached, and the resultant resolutions were set down to form new policy throughout the Empire. Though each noble was first and foremost out to advance the cause of him or herself and their extended families, it was clear that the raucous alien process still managed the work of successfully governing the Empire.

Reflecting on how closely the system reminded him of certain less savory aspects of human political discourse, Flinx found himself won-dering not for the first time how the soft-spoken, conciliatory thranx had ever succeeded in establishing a functional political union with his own far more fractious species.

At the touch of a clawed hand on the forearm of his suit, he leaned to his left, the better to hear his guide's whispered hiss.

"Ssay nothing. Leave everything to me. You do not know the proper protocolss. We musst work our way through the cusstomary Sspiral that Sswirlss. Within it you encounter a politeness that exisstss nowhere elsse in Krrassin, or for that matter anywhere the length and breadth of the Empire. As I have told you, we will not face challenge in the traditional ssensse. Here all battless are fought with wordss and phrassess, with gessturess and eye contact. It iss a ssign of resspect."

"Respect?" Flinx murmured in response. "Respect for what?"

"For the eminence of the Emperor, of coursse." Raising a hand, Eiipul gestured toward the center of the crowd immediately in front of them. It was composed of stylish AAnn strolling in an ever-tightening spiral. "He iss there, at the nexuss. The loci of Empire. We musst reach him. It will not be a ssimple matter."

Flinx had already surmised as much. Making personal contact with a head of government was never easy. Ignoring the sporadic interrogatories that were lobbed in his direction, Flinx kept his jaws shut and stayed close to Eiipul, marveling as his host demonstrated exquisite skill with both language and gesticulation. With proficiency born of long experience the AAnn noble replied to, deflected, or disregarded each and every query that came his way, including those that were intended for his tall companion. In this manner they worked their way deeper and deeper into the eddying throng of nobles, bureaucrats, and advisers.

It was amazing to see so many commanding, combative AAnn functioning in such close quarters with nary a knife or claw being unleashed. Occasionally Flinx was nudged sharply by a passing nye or accidentally found himself bumping up against a crowding individual he could not avoid. Out on the street any of these contacts would have been sufficient reason for the offended to initiate personal combat. Here in The Eye of the Nye, at the hub of Empire, an atypical civility governed everything that was said, gestured, or done.

"There!" Raising one hand, Eiipul pointed with two of his four fingers. A modest open space loomed not far ahead of them, a circle of deference. Leaning against a resting post at its center, an elderly nye crouched low. Unpretentious, functional, and formal, his garb suggested nothing about his identity or his station. His attire contrasted powerfully with the far more costly, elegant apparel of those who swirled around him. At the moment he was conversing with a high-level government functionary from offworld. The latter's gestures were filled with fawning, while his tone dripped supplication. Both nye were flanked by two discreetly armed guards nearly as tall as Flinx.

"*Jirasst,* human! Before uss sstandss the Beloved, the Wisse, the

Clear-thinking and Ssharp-of-wit, Highesst Prince-of-the-Circle Nav-vur W, Emperor of all the AAnn." Breathy reverence was absent from Lord Eiipul's voice. In its place there was a wealth of genuine respect. "In hiss persson iss embodied all the hisstory of my kind and all itss hopess for a bountiful and prossperouss future. We sstand here at the heart of the Empire." Once more he glanced over at Flinx, his voice low. "No human hass ever sstood sso near to the Imperial Pressence. What-ever happenss from now on, whatever your fate, know that you are the recipient of a ssingular honor."

"I don't feel honored," Flinx replied in his usual self-possessed tone. "I feel hot and itchy. No matter how hard it tries to keep me com-fortable and how much I work with the interior lining, some part of this simsuit always grates."

Lord Eiipul gestured second-degree exasperation. "Truly, you are an unclassifiable example of your ssad, ill-fated sspeciess. Desspite having sshared the dreadful experience you promised and having thereby become convinced of the truth of your outrageouss assertionss, a part of me sstill findss you to be afflicted with a deep and dissturbing madness."

"That makes two of us," Flinx told him.

Eiipul looked up sharply. "Thiss iss not the time or place to tell me ssuch a thing."

Flinx had to smile. Recognizing the expression as one that had no proper AAnn analog, the simsuit's programming and mouth-servos did not try to reproduce it.

"I'm waxing sarcastic." He hastened to reassure his already nervous host. "Madness would be too easy an excuse for my actions and some of the things I've done in my life. Repeated excursions into idiosyn-crasy and the inexplicable sometimes mark me as eccentric but—I'm not mad. It would be too painless an excuse."

His host relaxed—slightly. "Pleasse remember if you would, *trazzakk,* that more than jusst your expendable ssoftsskin life iss at sstake here."

"That's true," Flinx agreed. "The lives of everyone are at stake here." Able to see over the heads of the majority of swarming, deliber-ating AAnn, he strained for a better view of the Emperor. "How do we present ourselves?"

A much-relieved Eiipul was able to turn thoughtful again. "We are very near, truly. From here on we musst take our time and proceed with caution. Every etiquette musst be obsserved. Converssations cannot be ignored." He nodded forward. "As iss normal, otherss will try to engage uss in debate with an eye toward denying uss access. Attemptss will be made to divert uss from our preferred coursse. I will do my besst to facilitate our final approach, employing all of my sskillss at missdirection and evassion. With time and patience we will be able to . . ." He broke off to gape at the visitor. *"What are you doing?"*

"Saving time," Flinx told him calmly. "Mother Mastiff always did scold me about never having any patience."

In the center of The Eye of the Nye, within shouting range of the greatly beloved and most exalted Emperor Navvur W and surrounded by hundreds of the most eminent representatives of the AAnn Empire, any one of whom would be eager to acquire immediate status by tearing a presumptuous softskin to pieces, Flinx systematically began to disrobe. . . .

CHAPTER

10

While it was a certainty that in the course of its belligerent history and aggressive expansion the Empire of the AAnn had suffered shocks greater and more debilitating, surely none were more intimate than the one that rippled through the great hall called The Eye of the Nye on that fine third-season morning. A horrified Lord Eiipul IX edged away from Flinx, though he was all too aware that no matter what he did, in such close confines and subject to such intense scrutiny he did not have time or distance to edge far enough away. Halting in his retreat, eyes flashing, he drew himself up to his full height. He had cast in his lot with this softskin no matter what the creature did and no matter how outrageous its behavior.

Flinx's straightforward strip accomplished its intended purpose. As he exposed himself he quickly drew the attention of every double-lidded eye within range of his naked, incontestably human form. It required barely a moment longer for his presence to become known to every one of the hundreds of notable nye circulating in the chamber, as his image was flashed to every individual's personal information device.

Emerging from the resting pouch of the collapsing simsuit, Pip unfurled her brilliantly hued wings and took to the air of The Eye, relieved as always to be free of the confines of the simsuit. The presence below of hundreds of gesticulating, pointing, shouting AAnn disturbed her not in the least. As long as her master evinced no concern she was quite content, and the vast interior space of The Eye presented agreeable opportunities for soaring.

Though they were among the most honored and accomplished soldiers in the Imperial military, it still took the two tall AAnn flanking the Emperor more than a moment to draw their weapons. The idea that a human might suddenly appear unannounced in the midst of the Spiral at the center of The Eye was analogous to an AAnn abruptly materializing next to the President of the Commonwealth while he was enjoying breakfast with his family. As something that could not be imagined, the reality was difficult for even the most well trained to accept.

The impossibility went a long way toward explaining the absence of alarm. Since such a thing patently could not be, there had to be an alternative explanation. A clever prank of some kind, concocted by political allies to amuse the Emperor, or perhaps a test of a spectacularly convincing new projection device. Even those who found themselves standing close to the startling manifestation found themselves doubting its authenticity. In fact, of all those within striking distance of the revealed Flinx, only one exhibited any bona fide agitation. Lord Eiipul continued to stare at his guest in disbelief even as he struggled to decide what he could possibly do next.

Flinx saved him the trouble.

Naked, Flinx started toward the Emperor as Pip circled self-assuredly overhead. Rousing themselves, it occurred to both highly honored bodyguards that perhaps it might be a good idea to place themselves between the apparition and the Emperor, even if what they were confronting was nothing more than an ingenious projection. Coming to a halt, the projection proceeded to speak. Its clear, perfectly comprehensible speech only served to further underlie its unreality.

"My name is Flinx LLVVRXX. Though a softskin, I am a full member of the Tier of Ssaiinn. To my knowledge, I am the only human to have been so honored." The Emperor Navvur W, he saw, was looking straight at him. The Imperial physique might be worn, but those dark blue eyes were not. They were penetrating. "I am not a holo, a tactile field, a simulation, or a mechanism. I am very real. I come to you without the knowledge of my government or my kind to share with you a danger that threatens all living beings, including every citizen of the Empire." He gestured to his nearby and presently paralyzed host. "I would spare you this knowledge, but my friend insists it must be made known to all in order to ensure my safe departure from Blasusarr and the continuation of my search for a possible means of dealing with this threat."

At this explanation a great many eyes turned as one to focus on Lord Eiipul, who was not at all thankful for the massed attention. Hissing began to rise around him and around the softskin, a swelling sizzle like the foreshadowing of a thousand geysers about to erupt. Raising one hand sharply, Navvur W gestured for third-degree silence. Immediately, the dangerously escalating outrage ceased. The increasingly irate and angry glares, Flinx noted, remained locked on him and his host. In addition to the two honor guards, others nearby had also drawn weapons.

"A mosst imaginative disscoursse," the Emperor murmured into the ensuing silence. "But then, your kind iss known for itss flightss of imagination. It iss to be expected that one sso brazen would think large. 'A danger that threatenss all living beingss'? Truly, I would expect no modessty from one who hass accomplisshed what you have done." His attention flicked briefly in the direction of Flinx's host. "Albeit with an as yet to be determined modicum of outsside help."

Under that unblinking Imperial gaze, Lord Eiipul seemed to shrink in upon himself.

Fearlessly approaching Flinx, the Emperor stepped between his anxious bodyguards. Murmurs of concern rose from the inner circle of advisers and nobles. A second time the Emperor gestured, and for a second time the center of The Eye was still.

"Can none of you ssee that the creature iss more than weaponless?" Navvur W looked back at Flinx. "Truly, ssoftsskin, what iss your purposse in coming to a place where none of your kind have sstood before? Iss it to kill me?" Stressed hisses rose from the assembled. The Emperor ignored them.

"I am no assassin." Flinx stared down at the unruffled reptilian figure standing curiously before him. "I spoke the truth." As he raised an arm to gesture, several dozen weapons drew down on his torso.

The Emperor irritably motioned them off. "*Crissandd.* If it wanted to kill me, the attempt would have been made sseveral time-partss ago.

The time for murder hass already passed." Muzzles and other lethal focal points were lowered. Navvur W turned back to the visitor.

"You will leave thiss chamber alive, but not thiss building. You know that, do you not? Bravery iss no guarantee of ssurvival. But before you die, quesstionss will be assked—and ansswered." He started to turn away. "Thiss hass been a more interessting diverssion than mosst. Now it iss a matter for the Ssecurity Sservicess. I have a full sschedule today and I have already wassted too much time on thiss fasscinating but otherwisse irrelevant alien intrussion."

As well as the two bodyguards, other armed AAnn started to surge forward. By simply springing toward Flinx, Lord Eiipul caused the closing crowd to pause. He knew the hiatus would not last and that he had to speak fast.

"Venerable Navvur! I am Lord Eiipul IX. It iss true I have abetted thiss intruding ssoftsskin. Know that he sspeakss the truth when he ssayss that he did not wissh to come here. He doess not wissh to sshare the reality of the danger to which he referss unless he iss given no choice. He sspeakss truly when he ssayss that I inssissted on it." Turning a slow circle, his tail clearing the space behind him, Eiipul addressed himself to the tense assembly.

"Many of you know me. I am no wild thinker prone to flightss of fancy or mental aberrationss. Wild as it iss, I have come to believe thiss ssoftsskin'ss tale." Throwing an arm skyward, he made an unmistakably powerful gesture indicative of first-degree peril. "There *iss* a danger out there, beyond the Empire, beyond the edge of thiss galaxy, that possess a threat to all living thingss. It cannot be sstopped by warsshipss. It cannot be sstopped by any conventional meanss." He indicated the silent figure of Flinx.

"Thiss ssoftsskin ssayss that he iss a key to the only possibility of countering thiss threat."

"Not only a ssoftsskin prophet, but a mad one!" someone in the crowd shouted. Hissing laughter followed the remark.

"No prophet," Flinx responded quietly. "A little different from others of my kind, yes, but no prophet. Believe me, no one in the galaxy wishes it were otherwise more than myself."

"He doess not look very much like a ssavior," another onlooker commented. "To me, he lookss like meat."

Pausing, the Emperor turned back. "Very much sso. Lord Eiipul, by your actionss today you have already forfeited your possition, your sstatuss, and the previoussly highly regarded hisstory of your formerly noble family. I do, however, believe you when you ssay that you are not addled. What could possibly have possessed you to do thiss thing on behalf of a ssingle intruding ssoftsskin?"

Breathing hard, Eiipul confronted the Imperial presence. "Becausse, venerable Navvur, he sshowed it to me."

The Emperor gestured second-degree bemusement. "He sshowed you a threat to the entire galaxy? Tell me, Lord Eiipul, where iss thiss threat, that he could reveal it to you? Outsside the city, perhapss? Ssomewhere on the Quassquin Plain?"

Flinx stepped forward before his host could reply. "The threat comes from behind a region known as the Great Emptiness, an area of sky blocked by an immense gravitational lens that is impenetrable to the usual array of astronomical instruments."

"*Assikk,*" the Emperor murmured. "It iss invissible to telesscopess, to deep-sspace ssenssorss, to magnifying insstrumentation of all kindss—but, asstonisshingly, not to you." He glanced disdainfully at the anxious Eiipul. "And evidently, not to certain sselected oness."

"I can show it to you, too," Flinx responded without hesitation. "That is, not *show,* exactly. It's far too big to show, or to try and comprehend visually. What I can offer is more in the nature of a shared experiencing. I didn't lie to Lord Eiipul about it and I won't lie to you. The sharing can be dangerous. Not every sentient can handle the experience."

For a second time, Navvur W gestured amusement. "You will forgive me if I decline your generouss offer, ssoftsskin. There iss only one of me and I wass not raissed up to thiss ssupreme possition to wasste irreplaceable time ssharing 'experiencess' with crazed ssoftsskins, however bold they may be. I have little enough time each day in which to disscuss important experiencess with my own advisserss." He started to turn away again, his tail barely in motion.

"I am ssure, however, that ranking memberss of the Ssecurity Sservicess will find your ramblingss entertaining—at leasst for a little while. They will, I fear, be far more interessted in how you as a repressentative of your sspeciess ssucceeded in arriving ssafely here on

Blasussarr without attracting their attention than in any of your enter-taining but less ssenssible ramblingss. I will mysself be interessted in the ressultss of thosse engagementss. I ssusspect your revelationss may ressult in damage to more than a few careerss." With a soft hiss, he turned back to his resting post.

"Remove the creature. Keep me apprissed of any worthwhile find-ingss that may ressult from itss interrogation. Lord Eiipul I will deal with later. He iss desserving of a little time to get hiss family affairss in order."

Swallowed up as bodyguards and a handful of close retainers and advisers closed in around him, the Emperor disappeared. Soldiers and nobles immediately pressed forward to contain Flinx and his increas-ingly panicky host. Weapons were raised and aimed in Pip's direction. Uncertain which of the numerous targets below to deal with first, she flew higher and waited for some kind of indication from her master as to how she should respond.

Flinx found himself reflecting sadly that there was no time. Never enough time to do anything the way he preferred to do it. It didn't seem to matter which sentient he was trying to connect with: a member of his own kind, thranx, AAnn, representatives of other species. Individual minds were always so impatient, individual bodies unable to wait.

A plethora of clawed hands reached for him. He knew he had one chance. It was not the first time in his life he had only had one chance. On that proverbial one chance had frequently hinged his hopes of ac-complishing wildly different things.

Facing the place where the Emperor had been surrounded by his protectors, Flinx closed his eyes and focused. Like it or not, the casually dismissive leader of the Empire was going to see what Flinx had seen, experience what he had experienced. Flinx concentrated as hard as he ever had, intent on transporting the mind of that one supremely power-ful representative of AAnn-kind along with him on the difficult and dangerous mental journey he had made so many times before. He felt himself slipping, slipping, away from his surroundings, away from the noise and the eyes and the reaching alien hands. It was happening again. Even there in The Eye of the Nye it was happening. He anticipated it, he foresaw it, he expected it.

What he did not expect was taking along all of them. . . .

■ ■ ■

So many stars, brilliant and blinding. So many nebulae, vast and diffuse. Above all, so much space, stark and infinite and so very, very black.

No nestling greenness accompanied his outward reaching this time. The profound and reassuring deep warmth was also absent, as was the coldly calculating presence of a certain incredibly ancient weapon. He no longer needed their help. Having several times previously been boosted outward, he could now cast his inner self to that terrible, distant place without external assistance. Knowing where and what it was that he sought, he flung his awake-asleep consciousness toward it.

Each time he suffered to make the contact it became more familiar, the process of state-of-mind journeying more clear-cut. Each time it changed him a little, not only physically but mentally. An unavoidable corollary of his unique mind and extraordinary nervous system, he was certain. The Meliorares who had made him would no doubt have been pleased. He wished he could have met them all, known them all. So he could have killed them all. He wished, as he had on many occasions, that he had never been born. Of course, if that had been the case then it was likely that his mother would not have been paid. For her services.

The intergalactic abyss, Bran Tse-Mallory would have told him, was a poor place for a pity party. Whimper if you want, but save civilization first. Not because it's your duty, not because you'll be a hero, but because it's the right thing to do. In the abrogation of rightness only anarchy wins.

Blackness and stars he sensed rather than saw—and a presence. No, Flinx corrected himself. A multiplicity of presences. Navvur W, Emperor of all the AAnn, was there, just as Flinx had intended. So too was the small, affectionate, familiar mind-shape of Pip. What he had not intended and could not entirely account for was the presence of dozens of other nonhuman species. In projecting powerfully enough to drag the essence of the Emperor along with him, he had inadvertently also brought along a hundred of Navvur's closest advisers. Each time he used his Talent, he reflected bemusedly, it strengthened a little more. He could only hope it would not strengthen to the point of killing him.

The scene in The Eye, he mused, must be one of complete chaos. He could only hope that no one would panic and shoot down his physical body. Should that happen, his inner self might be lost forever in the frightful nether regions of interstellar space.

No time to ruminate on that now. His thoughts and those he had brought with him had been projected elsewhere. To the edge of the galaxy and beyond. Distance was not a state of mind: mind was a state of distance. At least it was to the intentionally garbled and cunningly re-assembled DNA of Philip Lynx.

Dragging the minds of the Emperor and his advisers along with him, Flinx felt his thought-self burst through the space occupied by the obstructing gravitational lens. Explosive stars and radiant nebulae vanished. They had been swallowed up, consumed, obliterated by something so immense it could only be described as a series of dark equations. Where previously the gloom had been pierced by points and swaths of light, now there was only darkness. An utter absence of luminosity.

But not of presence.

As on previous occasions a thin tendril of hesitant perception reached out to scarcely skim the outermost reaches of the onrushing Evil. The feeblest touch, the slightest contact, was all that was necessary to convey the colossal malignancy of the force that was rushing toward the galaxy—and, he sensed, continuing to accelerate. Flinx knew it, recognized it, was far more familiar with it than he had ever wanted to become.

The incalculable foulness was new to the quintessence of the Emperor Navvur W, however. Equally, it was something never experienced and not imaginable by the essences of his hundred advisers. Among them all only one diminutive spark of consciousness proved able to cope with the assault on the senses. Flinx recognized the thought-self of Lord Eiipul. Along with everyone else who had been standing adjacent to the Emperor when Flinx had projected, he too had been wrenched outward by the force of the human's metaphysical dislocation.

In consequence of barely perceiving the outermost edge of the onrushing Evil that lay behind the Great Emptiness, a host of silent, terrified screams momentarily filled a minuscule portion of the endless extragalactic desolation. Like saplings caught in a hurricane, individual specks of sanity began to fragment and splinter. It would do no good to confirm his thesis to a congregation of the hopelessly insane, Flinx realized. He began to pull away, to recoil. Away from a supraphysical malignancy too vast to be comprehended, too excessively loathsome to be understood.

Cognizance fled from that place of interstellar horror, the diversity of confused and confined nonhuman minds drawn and shepherded away by one that was more than human. Fled and retreated back to a region of welcoming warm stars, of planets swarming with life, of respiration and intimation and meditation. A hundred and two minds withdrew all the way back to just one of those star systems, to a single world as blissfully unknowing as all the others of the unspeakable fate awaiting it. Back to one moderately spacious chamber inside one building within the boundaries of one city. Not all of them, alas, returned whole.

It was a risk a reluctant Flinx had been forced to take.

Opening his eyes, he stopped swaying and once more took stock of his surroundings. His physical self was intact. He had not been shot. As near as he could determine, he had not been touched. The slight weight on his left shoulder was that of an Alaspinian minidrag. Glancing down, he saw that Pip was exhausted but otherwise unchanged by the experience they had just shared. Turning his attention to the milling throng of larger, more sentient reptilian shapes that surrounded him, he found himself confronting a far greater range of consequences.

Pandemonium reigned in the great chamber of The Eye of the Nye. To his right, the Emperor Navvur W was struggling to stand upright. In this he was aided by a frightened bevy of newly arrived technicians. Grim-faced medical personnel worked their way through the shocked, confused crowd, attending to the unconscious, the gibbering, the sobbing, and those whose thought-selves had returned only in part. Close to the naked human, a dazed but otherwise coherent Lord Eiipul stood staring fixedly in the direction of the Emperor.

"The venerable Navvur appearss to have ssurvived the encounter," Flinx's host commented coolly. Sharp eyes turned to study the bewildered crowd. "Not sso all of my dissbelieving brethren."

Observing the newly arrived medical forces at work, Flinx could only concur. "I meant to convey only the Emperor with me. Sometimes—no, make that many times—I don't know what my Talent is going to do or how it's going to react to the demands I place on it." His mouth tightened. "I've damaged some of those here. I've damaged people before. I never mean to. Unless they're trying to hurt me, and even then I try to minimize the effects."

Lord Eiipul turned sharply on the softskin. "'Minimize the effectss'? What 'effectss'? The effectss of what? Can you do more than jusst sshare thiss dreadful and dangeroussly enlightening experience, Flinx LLVVRXX? Iss there more to you and your capabilitiess than you have told?"

Turning quickly away, Flinx started toward where Navvur W was showing signs of rapid recovery. "Hadn't we better be sure we stay close to the Emperor lest some of his destabilized and more assertive bodyguards decide to resolve matters on their own initiative?" Keen to further change the subject, he indicated some of the less speedy-to-recover nobles receiving medical attention. "Assuming we're not killed, won't you benefit from the unintended damage that the experience has inflicted on some of your rivals?"

Distracted by the notion, Eiipul scrutinized the surrounding circle of badly battered AAnn nobility, then looked back up at the human. "Truly you comprehend our cusstomss in wayss I would never have thought possible for a ssoftsskin."

Flinx shrugged, aware that the meaning behind the shoulder-lifting gesture might be lost on his host. "Since I feel comfortable everywhere and at home nowhere, I've had to learn to empathize with every species' customs."

It was not the response Eiipul had been expecting. He felt an unexpected and entirely deviant surge of sympathy for the human. "I ssensse that you are obliged to deal not only with demonic forcess on the outsskirtss of the galaxy but alsso within yoursself."

Flinx started to nod, remembered to gesture second-degree concurrence. "There are times when I don't know which troubles me more." He resumed advancing toward the rapidly improving Emperor.

By the time the two of them had approached to within speaking distance of Navvur, the ruler of all the AAnn had recovered to the point where he took note of their presence. Bodyguards, this time with weapons drawn, moved to intercept the noble and the softskin. Unmistakably shaken by the experience he had just undergone but with his innate perspicacity unimpaired, Navvur W gestured his sentinels aside.

Stopping just out of arm and tail reach, Flinx stared placidly back at the Emperor of all the AAnn. As it often did at the most inopportune moments, his inborn sarcasm chose that moment to reassert itself. "*Tssant,* venerable Navvur. Did you find my ramblings entertaining?"

To his credit, the Emperor ignored the gibe. As he had stated earlier, he had little time to waste. "What jusst happened here, and how did you do it?"

Flinx sighed. "I did what I promised I would do. I showed you the threat of which I spoke. That's all I can do. How I did so doesn't matter. What matters is your response. Are you going to believe me or are you going to kill me?" He paused only a moment. "It really doesn't matter, because in the long run if I'm not allowed the opportunity to try and find a way of stopping what's coming, everyone and everything is going to die anyway."

"You sspeak too much of death," Navvur hissed softly in reply. "Sspeak to me of life."

"Let me go. Let me rendezvous with my ship."

The Emperor hesitated. "You will return to the Commonwealth, sspeak of your experiencess here, and tell them we are weak."

Flinx gestured first-degree demurral. "I will return, yes, but only to pursue a defense against what you just experienced. I have little interest whatsoever in the unending historical squabbles that divide the Empire and the Commonwealth."

"Ah." Navvur looked pleased. "You guard firsst of all your own interesstss. How very like a nye. In that event, why sshould you care what happenss to anyone elsse, far less everyone elsse?"

Flinx looked away. "There are those I do care about. Friends. A certain member of my species of the other gender in particular. We will not be impacted by what is coming this way, but our grandchildren might be."

The Emperor of the AAnn gestured first-degree comprehension underscored by second-degree bemusement. "Ssoftsskinss," was all he hissed, as if that explained everything.

Lowering his gaze, Flinx did not blink as he focused on the slitted pupils of the venerated AAnn standing opposite. "*Do you believe me? Do you believe what you experienced?*"

Navvur turned to judge those around him. The usual spiral of eager supplicants and prattling advisers currently resembled a scene after a battle. Medical personnel were everywhere. After studying the sight for a long minute he turned back. Not to Flinx, but to the AAnn noble standing beside him.

"Lord Eiipul IX, you believed the expossition of thiss ssoftsskin from the beginning. How doess what we all jusst experienced differ from what you went through before?"

"It wass very much identical, essteemed Navvur. The only difference I am aware of iss that thiss time I had more company."

The Emperor gestured absently to himself. "Confirmation of intergalactic horrorss unimaginable iss not ssomething to be wisshed for, but at the ssame time cannot be denied. Truth iss truth." He turned back to the silently waiting Flinx. "By the ssand that sshelterss life, ssoftsskin, and againsst all logic, I find that I musst believe you." His tone hardened, the hissed consonants emerging sharper and more biting than ever. "Woe unto you and your kind if thiss iss ultimately determined to be ssome ssort of clever diverssion from the verity of exisstence. You musst know that as ssoon as thiss ssession iss dissolved, a full account of everything that hass transspired will be passed on to the Imperial asstronomical council. The mosst advanced insstrumentss will be sset to ssearching that portion of the heavenss you have ssingled out for attention. What they find there may determine the fate of many, whosse collective future hass now become your ressponssibility."

Flinx responded without hesitation. "Nothing would please me more, venerable Navvur, than for your scientists to deep-scan that section of the heavens and find nothing more than the most dull and boring extension of normality."

"*Krazzumk,*" the Emperor grunted. "You threaten apocalypsse yet assk for little."

For the second time that morning, Flinx shrugged diffidently. "I ask only to be allowed to go."

Navvur considered. "I know what I experienced, I know what I felt, I know what I ssenssed in place of sseeing. What I do not know iss how one ssmall and inssignificant being ssuch as yoursself, remarkable though you may be, can possibly think you can ssuccessfully confront and combat a menace greater in extent than entire clussterss of sstarss."

How much should he explain? Flinx found himself wondering. How much *could* he explain? "I hope . . . ," he began. "I hope to have—help."

The Emperor let out an ascending hiss. "It would have to be help on a cossmic sscale to deal with ssuch a cossmic peril. *My* hope would be to die long before thiss phenomenon—if it iss as real as it appearss— reachess the outsskirtss of our galaxy." Bright piercing eyes searched Flinx's own. "You appear to me to ssuffer from a debilitating affliction common among your kind, Flinx LLVVRXX of the Ssaiinn. You are an incorrigible optimisst."

"If I was not," Flinx told him, "I suppose I would have given myself up for lost a long, long time ago."

Was that a reptilian twinkle in the Emperor's eye? "You 'ssup-posse'?"

"I said I was optimistic." Reaching up, Flinx stroked the back of Pip's neck.

"Mysself," Navvur replied thoughtfully, "I find optimissm to be a mental sstate inconducive to ssurvival. That doess not mean it sshould not be encouraged. One thing iss ssurely rightful: if what you sshared jusst now with me and mine iss veritable, then as you ssay it truly will not matter if you live or die." He made a gesture that pronounced first-degree judgment. "Accordingly, I have decided to let you li—"

He was interrupted by a screaming noble, hands and claws extended and teeth bared, who made a sudden leap straight for the human's throat.

CHAPTER

11

The violent, unexpected onslaught triggered several synchronous responses. Although the attack was clearly aimed at the softskin in their midst, Navvur's bodyguards took no chances. Weapons were leveled as they rushed to fill the space between the assailant and the Emperor. High overhead Pip took immediate note of the sudden upsurge in her master's emotions, folded her wings to her sides, and dropped like a stone toward the hurtling AAnn. At the last instant she spread both brightly hued membranes and rocketed off to one side. Startled nobles and advisers ducked or flinched as she shot past just over their heads. She broke off the counterattack because Flinx empathically urged her to do so. Another party had already intervened on his behalf.

Launching himself forward, Lord Eiipul IX smacked into the side of the bounding assailant and sent both of them crashing to the glittering floor of The Eye. His interception of the assault was not the end of it. Tail flailing, the enraged noble who had launched the attack promptly turned his ire on his fellow nye.

Wanting to intervene but unsure of the proper protocol for doing so, Flinx could only stand by and watch as Eiipul took up the fight on behalf of his guest. He himself had fought AAnn before, had observed AAnn battling humans and thranx, had even seen them fighting one another—

but never in traditional combat devoid of weapons. A small space cleared for the combatants as spectators backed up to give them room. No one else offered to intercede. Nor did Flinx feel that he could do so either in the absence of any word or sign from the attentive Emperor.

He tried to envision the heads of two major companies or great trading families engaging in hand-to-hand combat on the floor of the Earth's center of government, with representatives from other worlds quietly looking on. AAnn custom ran old and deep, he reflected somberly.

Neither fighter was young. Both were experienced. Tails switching robustly from side to side, teeth bared, clawed hands upraised, they circled one another as each searched for an opening, an advantage, a misstep on the part of his opponent.

"Kwarranssk," Eiipul hissed, "did you not sshare the experience of the menace? Are you blind to the danger that threatenss uss all?"

"It iss all nothing more than a sscheming trick of the ssoftsskin'ss!" The attacker was adamant. "Why do you intervene on itss behalf?"

"Did you not hear the pronouncement of the venerable Navvur?" Eiipul's powerful leg muscles were taut, ready to launch him at his adversary any second. His opponent was no less prepared.

"Even one sso gifted as the revered Navvur may be fooled," the attacker growled. "No ssentient iss immune to clever deception." Eyes full of fury flicked in Flinx's direction. "The ssoftsskin sseekss only to make hiss esscape by meanss of a clever ssubterfuge." Peering at the surrounding, encircling crowd, the frothing noble beseeched his peers.

"We know nothing of what thiss intruder hass learned of Blasussarr, of our sstrengthss and weaknessess here! To let him go free without further ressearching the truth of hiss assertionss iss worsse than foolissh." Returning his full attention to the attentive Eiipul, he concluded, "To harbor ssuch a sspy consstitutess treasson!" Then he launched himself.

Tails flailing, teeth and claws flashing, they slammed together in the space that had been cleared for them. The ritual clash differed little from those Flinx had encountered every day on the central sand-paved walkways of Krrassin. What was different this time was that far more than status was at stake. Talons slashed at eyes, teeth snapped at arteries, and mini-sonic booms echoed as tails snapped at exposed faces.

The razored claws of Eiipul's opponent ripped scales loose, goug-
ing bloody gashes in his flanks. Ignoring the lacerations, Eiipul sought
a firmer, deadlier grip. Closing around his rival's throat, the noble's
jaws clamped shut. Blood fountained, staining both combatants and the
beautiful floor.

An utterly barbaric and uncivilized exhibition, humans of comparable age and standing would have declared while turning away in revulsion. Until one of them was forced into a similar situation, Flinx knew.
He had seen too much, experienced too much, to be lulled as were so
many of his "civilized" species into thinking otherwise. Given the right
circumstances and motivation, any pair of suitably antagonistic humans
would quickly find themselves reduced to a similarly primordial style of
combat. The only difference between them and the thrashing, grappling
AAnn was a lack of sharp teeth, claws, and tail.

It was all over in a couple of minutes. Tail whipping slowly from
side to side as he wiped at his bloodstained jaws, Lord Eiipul rose and
stepped back. Blood gushing from the torn arteries in his opponent's
neck began to pool on the gem-encrusted floor. Pushing their way to
the front, a pair of medical techs bent over the gravely injured attacker.
Only advanced technology allowed them to stanch the bleeding in time
to save the nye's life. Breathing hard, Eiipul expressed his gratitude
to them.

"Better that one doess not die," he explained to Flinx as his seriously wounded adversary was hustled away through the crowd. "Were
he to do sso it would mean a sseriouss feud between hiss family and
mine." Eyes afire with the aftermath of bloodlust, he looked back at
Flinx. "That ssuch a demisse sshould happen over a ssoftsskin would
make ssuch a feud all the worsse. Far better that it hass been avoided."

"I'm thankful, too," Flinx admitted as Pip settled back onto his
shoulder. "I don't want anyone to die on account of me." He nodded in
the direction taken by the wounded nye and the attending techs. "Not
him, and not you. I'm sure he, too, is responsible for the upkeep and development of an unknown number of offspring."

As Eiipul opened his mouth to respond, they were interrupted.
Flanked by his guards, Navvur W had rejoined them. This time his attention was focused on Flinx's host and not the invasive human.

"Your family hass alwayss produced ssuperior warriorss. It wass a fair fight, and one not initiated by you."

A deferential Eiipul sheathed his claws, stilled the switching of his tail, and executed an especially elegant gesture of first-degree subservience. "Venerable Navvur honorss me."

"Venerable Navvur iss alwayss judiciouss when addressing thosse with blood on their face," the Emperor replied dryly. Raising a cloth-covered forearm, Eiipul resumed cleaning his snout and jaws. Though he proceeded conscientiously, he did not hurry the process.

The Emperor turned back to Flinx. "You are without doubt the mosst interessting sspecimen of your kind I have ever encountered. In comparisson, your accredited diplomatic repressentativess are dull and dry, while the human prissonerss I have sseen undergoing interrogation are belligerent and foolissh. I would have you sstay awhile longer, Flinx LLVVRXX of the Tier Ssaiinn."

Flinx gestured first-degree regret. "You speak of a dialogue I think I would enjoy myself, Excellence. But I cannot turn or delay from the responsibility that weighs on me. Having experienced the cause, I know you will understand."

"Truly," the Emperor grudgingly acknowledged. "And as it threatenss uss all, I am left to wonder why you have not sshared the devasstatingly enlightening experience of ssome momentss ago with repressentativess of your own government and people. Or *have* you done sso, in a manner sso ssecretive and cautiouss that Imperial Intelligence remainss unaware of it?" Eyes that missed nothing bored into Flinx's own. "Or wass the unfortunate Baron HJNN, the Long Fang who hass jusst left uss unwalking, correct in ssaying that the event wass nothing more than a well-crafted russe dessigned to ssecure your freedom and that, insstead of sstanding here converssing with you, I sshould be doubting the evidence of my own ssenssess?" .

Other nobles and advisers had crowded around close. Even Eiipul, who had leaped to Flinx's defense, looked momentarily uncertain. Flinx was not surprised. Certain realities are harder to accept than the most outrageous fantasies. Especially the discomfiting ones.

"Everything you went through was real and true," he insisted. "Nothing was manipulated for effect. The menace was, and is, exactly as you experienced it. I also spoke the truth when I said that those who know of it among my own kind are still few." Studying the scaly faces surrounding him he absently gestured third-degree reassurance. "As many of the AAnn are now aware of its existence and extent as are thranx and humans. As to your question about why I have not shared this knowledge with more of my own kind . . ."

He suddenly found himself wishing he was somewhere, anywhere, else. That he did not have to explain himself yet again, to still another cluster of sentients standing in judgment of him and his motives. And yet again, he had no choice.

"There are within the Commonwealth humans who want to kill me. There are in the government those who want to arrest me. And there are those in the United Church who want to question me. Given the state of affairs surrounding my person, you'll understand when I say I can only reveal myself and what I know to a chosen few."

"And what, *tssaak,* do *you* want out of all thiss?" the Emperor of all the AAnn asked him sagely.

"The same thing I've wanted all my life," Flinx told him. "To be left alone."

"Yet your conviction that ssomehow you are vital to any attempt to counter thiss oncoming peril meanss that you cannot be left alone. But at the ssame time you cannot assk for all the help you would wissh becausse thosse whosse assisstance you might sseek would be interessted in other detailss of your 'sstate of affairss,' as you put it." Navvur W gestured second-degree empathy. "What a dreadful disscord musst be your life!"

Flinx felt obliged to protest. "There are good moments."

It sounded weak even to him.

"You do not ssay 'good dayss.'" Navvur had not been chosen supreme leader of his kind because he lacked insight. "There iss much that our resspective sspeciess do not have in common, but I believe an appreciation of irony iss sshared by both. From what you tell me, it would appear that you are ssafer here, at thiss moment, ssurrounded by ssworn enemiess of your government, than you would be on many of your own worldss." Teeth that were still sharp flashed in jaws that could still bite. "You may be the only ssoftsskin within hundredss of parssecss who iss ssafe from being sslain at the firsst opportunity."

Flinx was not startled by the Emperor's observation, but neither had he expected it. "I don't feel safe anywhere. It may be my destiny to never feel safe anywhere."

One of the shaken nobles who had suffered and survived Flinx's shared experience spoke up. "Doess it pleasse you to know that you have made many of *uss* feel far less ssafe?"

Flinx looked over at her. "I don't like frightening people. That was not my intent." He looked at Lord Eiipul, then back at the Emperor. "You forced my hand."

"To our benefit, or to our detriment." A pensive Navvur gestured second-degree disquiet. "I wonder."

"I only share the truth," Flinx mumbled unhappily.

"Truly," hissed several thoughtful onlookers.

"So—what is your decision, honored Navvur? What are you going to do with me?" Standing alone, Flinx waited.

In addition to a single set of round eyes, a sizable number of reptilian ones were focused on Navvur W. The Emperor appeared to be meditating. But it was only for show. He had already decided how to deal with this exceptionally curious softskin who laid claim to a Tier name, hissed eloquently the true tongue, and had demonstrated the ability to foresee an apocalypse—or merely frighten. Aware of his audience, he gathered his Imperial self.

"Either you are an honesst mutation of a mosst unique ssort—or you are the cleveresst conjurer in the sspiral arm. One thing I have decided you are not iss a sspy. You talk far too much to be a deviouss agent of your or any other government. You have sshared or sshammed a wonder. My heart tellss me it doess not exisst. My head—my head fearss that it may.

"Only becausse of that ssmall and implaussible possibility I have decided to sspare your life."

Animated hissing rose from the circle of AAnn that surrounded the softskin and the Emperor. Some of it voiced accord, some hostility, some was simply supportive of whatever choice their Emperor chose to make. Among the congregation of attentive nye, Lord Eiipul IX looked relieved most of all.

"Thank you, venerable Navvur." Flinx's gratitude was heartfelt. "If it turns out that I'm able to do something, it will preserve the AAnn as unreservedly as it does my own kind."

The Emperor spoke without looking at the tall human. "I have the feeling thosse of uss currently alive will never know whether you ssucceed or fail."

"I will find a way to let you know," Flinx was surprised to hear himself replying.

Navvur looked up anew. "You truly believe the reality of what you have sshown, don't you? If it iss sso, then you will need all the help you can get." A hand gestured at the closely packed crowd of nobles and advisers. "I fear that we cannot assisst you directly in your effort. But it iss perhapss possible to improve the climate in which you apply yourrself.

"As ssomeone of your wide-ranging knowledge iss doubtless aware, though no active sstate of warfare pressently exisstss between the Empire and the Commonwealth, with sso many pointss of tangency and expanssion, minor unofficial dissputess frequently arisse."

Flinx gestured third-degree comprehension, even though he knew that the "minor unofficial disputes" the Emperor was referring to were usually the result of AAnn probing and aggression as the minions of the Empire worked to continuously test the limits of Commonwealth tolerance.

"I will composse and have issued a command," Navvur continued, "ordering that all ssuch dissputess are to be rigoroussly avoided for"— he considered briefly—"a period of one Commonwealth year from the date of your departure from Blasussarr. Thiss will enssure that any exertionss on your behalf that might take place in border regionss are not interrupted or thwarted by one of the petty missunderssstandingss that sseem to plague the relationsship between your government and an Empire that sseeks only peace."

Sure it does, Flinx mused while prudently withholding comment. Anything he could say was likely to be counterproductive, and this was neither the time nor place to discuss the complex issue of ongoing hostility between their respective species. It appeared that his humble efforts to achieve little more than safe passage off Blasusarr for himself and Pip had unintentionally accomplished rather more; what amounted to a year's worth of interstellar peace between the Empire and the Commonwealth. It was not the first time his labors had produced an unexpected result.

Irony, he reflected, was the spice of circumstance.

"Thiss directive will not be publicized." Turning a slow circle, Navvur gazed warningly at his subjects, meeting the eyes of as many as he possibly could. "No word of it iss to pass beyond The Eye. Were it to become widely known, sspecific ssoftsskinss and particular nye might try to take advantage of it." When he completed his formal pirouette he was once again facing Flinx.

"I can pledge you no more than a year of peace between our peo-pless. Any attempt to extend it for a longer period of time would be to deny our very sselvess—and place even my possition in jeopardy." He gestured second-degree resignation. "Thosse not privy to the experi-ence you sshared would not undersstand."

"I know," Flinx told him. "I realize the difficulty." The majority of humans and virtually no thranx would not have empathized with the Emperor's position—but Flinx did. Here was another chameleon like himself, he mused. An individual for whom change was a constant, who could never relax if he expected to survive. In addition to belonging to separate sentient species, however, they were clearly marked by one other key difference.

He doubted the Emperor Navvur W spent part of every day worry-ing about his sanity.

Over the course of the following ten days spent waiting for the return from space-plus of the reconfigured *Teacher,* he saw and experienced more of AAnn society and culture than specialized xenologists who had spent years studying and trying to understand the belligerent, danger-ous, expansionist civilization that had long been in conflict with the Commonwealth. This despite the fact that his expanded circle of hosts did their best to keep his presence in Krrassin a secret from the local population. While there was no potential problem in allowing resident AAnn a glimpse of a visiting human, paradoxically the Emperor and his inner circle were cognizant of Flinx's desire to keep his presence on Blasusarr hidden from his own kind. So to prevent word from reaching the staff of the one official, accredited Commonwealth mission in the capital, Flinx's excursions were conducted in secrecy and with him wearing his simsuit.

Those among the Imperial advisers with an inclination to engineering who had a chance to examine him close-up were fascinated by the intricate camouflaging ensemble. Flinx readily identified with their interest, having himself on prior occasions been forced to deal with AAnn who had disguised themselves as humans. His mastery of their language and the revelation that he was an officially adopted member of a recognized Tier only increased his curiosity value. Though he continued to move about Krrassin and its vicinity undercover, he found that he had become something of a minor celebrity among those assigned to escort him.

All the more reason, he felt, to take his leave as soon as possible. But with no means of contacting the *Teacher* while it was making its way back to the Blasusarrian system from deep space, he could only wait, be thankful he was still alive, and do his best to satisfy the curiosity of his hosts while hiding his true identity, abilities, and resources from as many as possible.

As promised, several Blasusarrian ten-days passed before the communit built into his suit signaled for attention. It was not necessary for him to check the signal's origin. Only one offworld individual knew his location, and it was not organic.

"I have successfully entered orbit in the new guise of a private research vessel from Orakkum." Though anxiety was not an emotion programmed into the *Teacher*'s manifold speech patterns, Flinx chose to believe that he could hear a smidgen of concern in the message. "Please acknowledge if you have survived."

"Survived and thrived, I think—much to my own surprise."

"I understand survived," the ship responded promptly, "and am joyed to receive the information. In the context of the circumstances that mandated my hasty departure, I do not comprehend 'thrived.'"

Alone in the comfortable and well-secured first-floor room that had been provided by the government for the duration of his stay, Flinx was able to speak freely. He had discovered that he enjoyed lying on his back in the basin of heated sand that was a favored means of relaxation among the AAnn. It reminded him of the picture-perfect beaches on Nur.

"You know how sometimes I enter into seemingly simple situations and they blow up out of all proportion?" he began.

"Not you, Flinx. I have never observed that happening to you."

The ship's exterior might have been reconfigured during its hiatus in space-plus in order to fool Planetary Security, Flinx mused, but its integrated sarcasm remained unchanged.

"Several incidents of significance have occurred in your absence." Head turned slightly to the right, he addressed the communit pickup inside the head of the suit, neatly shucked nearby. "The bad thing is that many more AAnn have become aware of my presence here. The good thing is that I have been able to turn that to my advantage."

"I cannot conceive," the *Teacher* responded, "of how your presence on Blasusarr becoming known to additional AAnn could in any way become advantageous."

"A few months ago, neither could I," he replied. "I'll explain it all when I'm back on board." Sitting up on the sand, Flinx let the heated grains trickle through his bare toes.

"When should I send down a shuttle?"

Flinx looked around his chamber. Normally spare and utilitarian, it was filled with gifts from AAnn acquaintances and admirers. Dominating the display was a glistening, vitreous sculpture that was a present from Lord Eiipul IX himself and his extended family. Unexpectedly, Flinx found his eyes growing moist. Chraluuc of the Ssaiinn should have been there with him.

"That won't be necessary. Provide your coordinates. It would be impolite not to offer my hosts the opportunity to supply the necessary extra-atmospheric transportation."

"Your 'hosts' . . . ?" The shipmind contemplated possible interpretations of this seemingly contradictory designation. "You are not confined or under duress and are speaking freely?"

"Analyze my speech and decide for yourself."

As a matter of security, the *Teacher* had already done so. "It is clear that a most remarkable turn of events has taken place in my absence. Not the first time something like it has occurred."

Flinx shrugged, though there was no one present to see it. "It's how I was raised, ship. To adapt to difficult circumstances."

"I suppose I should not be surprised. I will provide the coordinates. When should I expect your arrival?"

"As soon as my hosts can arrange it. I'll alert you." Unexpectedly, he heard himself asking, "Everything is all right with you? Have you been seeing to the maintenance of the plants in the lounge?"

"My physical condition is excellent. Your decorative vegetation appears to be flourishing. Some of the oldest required trimming. In contrast, certain more recent arrivals exhibit what appears to be a kind of internal biological restraint that keeps them from overgrowing. No doubt a xenobotanist would find such cytological self-discipline of more than passing interest."

"Maybe I'll do some research myself once I'm back aboard," Flinx commented absently.

Rising from the sand, he stood motionless while blowers gently removed adhering granules from his back and lower body. Whereas the virtually moisture-free particles slid neatly off the slick scales of the AAnn, the therapeutic grains tended to stick to his sweaty mammalian epidermis. Bending over, he brushed at his legs to hasten the process. Nearby, Pip's head emerged from where she had contentedly buried herself in the depths of the heated basin.

"Get out of there. We're leaving," he murmured.

Leaving for work, he told himself. Leaving for destiny, whatever it now had in store for him. His immediate future, at least, was determined. That in itself was something of a change for him. Once back on board the *Teacher* he knew he could look forward to weeks and probably months of continuing to search for a single alien mechanism that could by now be anywhere in the Blight—or even beyond it. Not a needle in a haystack, but an atom in the needle in the haystack. Yet again the prospect of locating the wandering Tar-Aiym weapons platform struck him as hopeless. But he had promised his friends and mentors that he would try.

As he prepared to use the local communicator to contact his hosts and inform them of his intent to depart, it occurred to him that the search might not seem quite so hopeless if he had help.

His departure from Blasusarr was quietly momentous. As the first softskin to cement actual friendship as opposed to formal alliance with the Imperial government, he was eligible for a suitably honorific send-off. Instead, with the disappointed consent of his hosts, he departed in a small, unprepossessing military shuttle. The unaware crew was surprised to see so many important personages present to exchange farewells with a single tall but otherwise ordinary-appearing nye. Tentative inquiries as to the traveler's identity were met with an official response that was notable only for its lack of actual information. The crew did not press the matter. The solitary traveler was left to himself, and the crew went about the business of preparing for liftoff with the efficiency for which the AAnn military was noted.

"Farewell." Lord Eiipul IX exchanged final throat-grabs with the softskin in the simsuit. "I rissked a great deal on your behalf. I am glad I have nothing to regret. In fact, *grissanb,* my family'ss sstatuss iss sstrengthened becausse of it."

"I'm pleased." Stroking the side of his suit over the concealed resting pouch within, Flinx calmed Pip. She always seemed to know when they were about to leave for somewhere new.

Partings were concluded with other AAnn he had met. Last of all was young Kiijeem. His female parent was in the small group, her tongue flicking proudly.

"You have brought status to your family," Flinx told him.

"Truly." Slitted pupils regarded Flinx's own as the young nye's tail switched smoothly back and forth. "For ssomeone I sshould have killed on ssight, you have proven to be a usseful acquaintance."

"Keep that thought." Flinx smiled, careful not to show his teeth. "The useful part, not the bit about killing."

Kiijeem's responsive gesticulation was a sign of third-degree poise. "I am AAnn. I can never put killing from my mind."

Flinx gestured understanding. "Then try to concentrate it where it will do more good than harm." He turned to start up the ramp that led into the waiting shuttle.

The leathery tip of a tail touched his spine. Looking around, he saw that Kiijeem remained reluctant to step back and rejoin the crowd of onlookers.

"Will I ever see you again, Flinx LLVVRXX of the Tier Ssaiinn? Will I ever be able once more to crouch and conversse with you about peopless and worldss beyond my ken, that I will only be able to learn of and vissit in the form of your kind and knowing desscriptionss?"

The AAnn being very fond of protocol and formalities, Flinx had anticipated that the ritual surrounding his departure would be somewhat prolonged. He had expected to be impatient. He had expected to be tired. He had even expected to be bored.

He had not expected to be touched.

Flanking the entrance to the military shuttle, one of the soldiers who had been observing the ceremony let out a hiss of uncertainty as she noted the actions of the older and young nye on the ramp below. Their vacillation seemed a waste of time and energy. It made no sense to her. She glanced across at her colleague.

"I know that we were warned that there might be ssome asspectss to thiss particular leave-taking that could be perceived as out of the ordinary—but for what possible reasson could the passenger and the youth be gripping each other'ss handss like that?"

Tired from standing, the other soldier gestured third-degree lack of interest. "Who knowss? Perhapss they are preparing to fight."

As the AAnn shuttle decelerated in preparation for rendezvousing with what appeared to be an unusually ill-equipped Imperial scientific re-search vessel, Flinx found himself gazing in admiration at a ship he did not recognize. In the course of its stealthy sojourn in space-plus the *Teacher* had completely revamped its exterior. Gone was the battered and slightly disreputable epidermis of an interworld cargo craft. In its place was an exterior adroit enough to fool the occupants of any Impe-rial craft. Once safely back within the boundaries of the Common-wealth, the ship would revert to a more mundane human-designed configuration. But until it passed beyond the borders of the Empire, it would continue to cleave to its latest nonhuman schematic.

A speedy, formal farewell to the commander of the shuttle, a trans-fer to a receiving lock equally disguised, and Flinx found himself back in the familiar, comforting surrounds of his ship. Outside, lit by the ac-tinic glow of desert-swathed Blasusarr, the AAnn shuttle was pulling away. Once at a safe distance it ignited its main drive and dropped swiftly toward the world below. A world that he had experienced and come to know perhaps better than any other member of his species.

The accumulation of arcane knowledge and esoteric experiences was a habit he had no desire to break, he mused as he made his way through the familiar corridors.

"Welcome back." The shipmind greeted him as he emerged into the command center. His favorite cold drink was waiting for him on one arm of the pilot's chair. He took the drink but did not sit down, preferring to sip as he stood and stared out the curved, sweeping port. Beyond, Blasusarr gleamed in the light of its star. He had gone where few humans had gone before him and had done so in a manner previously unimaginable. His achievement far exceeded anything he had dared hope for when he had arrived weeks ago. Not only was he leaving the Imperial homeworld in one piece, he was departing having made new friendships, having acquired new knowledge, and having secured (even if only for a year) a peace treaty between AAnn and humanxkind.

Not bad for a few weeks' furtive and highly illegal stopover, he reflected.

"It's good to be back. Did you miss me?"

"I was naturally concerned for your well-being," the ship replied equably. "The question implies application of an emotion to which I am not mathematically privy." There was a slight, probably programmed pause. "I do admit to wanting to know how you went from being flushed and chased from hiding to returning via an AAnn Imperial military shuttlecraft. I feel this perceptible contradiction constitutes a deficiency in my database that is seriously demanding of redress."

Sighing deeply, Flinx turned from the port and slumped down in the chair. "I'll fill you in on all the details in the course of our journey. Prepare departure."

"Should I take up again the previous vector?" was the prompt query. "So that we may continue with the prior search? Which, I am compelled to point out, has suffered recently from your detour and a delay that can only be described as grievous."

"I know, I know," Flinx muttered irritably. "I swear, you're like an old mother hen sometimes!"

"An important function of my programming, though in no wise avian. You yourself have repeatedly remarked on its importance."

"I know that, too." Flinx chugged the rest of his drink, deliberately chilling his mouth and throat. The headache that was coalescing at the back of his skull had nothing to do with the temperature of the liquid he was imbibing. "First Jast, then Visaria, then Gestalt, and now here." Not for the first time he wished for a face he could look into, talk to, evaluate. But there was only the interior of the ship, with its molded walls and silent, compliant instrumentation. From the time he had accepted the ship from its builders, the Ulru-Ujurrians, he had refused to assign it a visible avatar.

He saw enough faces in his dreams.

"I've learned something from each of those visits to each of those worlds, ship. And the one thing I've decided is that I can't go on with this search by myself. I've got to have help. Support. And not just moral support of the kind offered by Bran and Tru. I don't think I can go on with this alone."

"You are the only one who might establish contact with the wandering Tar-Aiym weapons platform that is the object of the search." The ship's tone was simultaneously cool, unforgiving, and sympathetic. "What kind of help could you possibly need? Or find useful?"

"I'm trying to clarify." Wrestling with words and concepts, Flinx struggled to explain himself to a machine. "It's just—it's too much for one person. It's too much for me anymore." Looking up he found himself staring, in lieu of a face, at one of the several visual pickups that lined the room. "Maybe, at heart, that's the real reason I've kept off going back into the Blight."

The ship lapsed into silence. When it felt that enough time had passed and the stillness had endured long enough, it inquired just as if there had been no discussion preceding its request, "Vector?"

Without hesitation this time, Flinx supplied one.

The *Teacher* did not delay in reacting. "You gainsay your own words. You contradict your own emotions. You do not seek the indicated destination in search of help. You have another motive. Reasons that have nothing to do with the critical search on which we are embarked." Programming aside, the ship's tone was unabashedly accusatory.

"I understand your reaction, but you're wrong," Flinx insisted. "Or half wrong. Yes, I have an ulterior motive for wanting to go there. But it's also where I hope to find help. The kind of help I most need. Once we're safely back in space-plus I'll fill you in on the details and try to make you understand. I know it's not an easy concept for a machine to grasp."

"I already understand," the shipmind grumbled. "You can parse all you want, but it will take some effort on your part to convince me that I have left anything out of my judgment. A detour is still a detour."

That was all the *Teacher* had to say on the subject. Despite Flinx's demurral it knew enough about humans to follow his reasoning.

Just as it knew enough to recognize an equivocation when it heard one. . . .

CHAPTER

12

Not only was Clarity Held all wrapped up in her work, she was all worked up in her wrap. Whereas her irritation and impatience were on open display, the half-body bandage that extended from neck to waist and covered much of her torso was not. It would have taken a knowledgeable physician to spot the extensions and connectors where they emerged from the opening of the sleeveless tanning top.

Though much of the injury she had suffered in the fight to try to leave Nur with Flinx had long since healed, the bandage ensured that the skin on her back would redevelop without scars. Certainly it was more comfortable than the spray of synthetic chitin the Eint Truzenzuzex had initially used to stanch the bleeding and save her life. It was only days later, while she was recovering from surgery, that the thranx philosoph and his human companion, the sociologist-soldier Bran Tse-Mallory, decided she was recovered enough to be told that Flinx had left to continue the search for the wandering Tar-Aiym weapons platform without her.

"We wanted to go with him, too," Tse-Mallory explained, "but he insisted we stay behind to look after you. We've done that."

And done it well, she knew. The nihilists of the Order of Null who wanted Flinx dead and had attacked them at the shuttleport had not shown themselves in his absence. So under the watchful eyes of the two senior Commonwealth scientists, one human and the other thranx, she was allowed to recuperate in peace.

Her spleen had been badly lacerated in the attack. Bioengineers had grown her a new one. Her lungs had been punctured. They had been stitched. Several veins had been shredded. The organosynth tubing that had replaced them was indistinguishable from the originals save for their vivid turquoise hue, which none could see unless she was opened up. Her blond hair had been burned away from the back of her neck to the top of her head. That, at least, had regrown all by itself.

Her irritation stemmed from the presence of minuscule specks of shrapnel, some of which even after a year were still lodged deep in her body. Sometimes difficult to detect, they were gradually working their way up and outward. Only a week ago a physician had squeezed a small bump just below her left clavicle and popped out a shard of sharp plexalloy.

"It's safer this way than utilizing repetitive probes or surgery," he told her apologetically. "Given a little time and a little help, it's amazing how well the body does at healing itself. Better when and where possible to let Nature make the repairs in her own good time."

Which was all well and fine, she muttered by way of reply, if you were not the one who had to deal with the continual itching and stinging as microscopic fragments of bone, metal, plastic, glass, and other insoluble invaders slowly worked their way to the surface of your epidermis.

Not only did the bandage help her flesh to heal, it also monitored her condition. If a piece of shrapnel migrated too close to a large blood vessel or internal organ, the sensors imprinted into the bandage would raise an alarm and pinpoint the location. Other sensors sent regular reports to her wrist or home communit, which then passed the information along to the local hospital.

At least she had been able to work, if not to go home. Her doctors insisted she remain at the facility for another couple of weeks. At that time the bandage would be removed. Though it was less of an imposition than a silk scarf, she would be glad to be rid of it.

This being Nur/New Riviera, the facility was more of a medical resort than a hospital. Located on the shore of one of the northern hemisphere's extensive, exquisite lakes, it offered all the comforts of a first-class lodge. From her room or outside on the beach she was able to communicate with the company she worked for in the capital city of Sphene. Her superiors at Ulricam had been genuinely concerned for her health and supportive of her efforts to maintain a daily work schedule. It helped that Tse-Mallory and Truzenzuzex had been able to suppress the literal details surrounding her injury. Insofar as her bosses knew, after seeing off a friend at the shuttleport she had been seriously injured in a subsequent skimmer accident.

The friend in question was in reality much more than that, and she had not seen him off. One moment the battle to reach Flinx's shuttlecraft had been raging in full fury, with weaponry erupting all around them. A bright flash had wiped out consciousness, vision, and sound. The next thing she remembered was waking up in the hospital, dazed, immobilized, swathed in protein bandages, hooked up to an assortment of imposing and intimidating instrumentation, and in spite of a sufficiency of numbing pharmaceuticals and soothing radiation, in considerable pain. That the only face looking down at her at that moment happened to be hard-shelled, antennaed, and boasting large compound eyes was not completely reassuring.

Flinx would be back, Truzenzuzex had assured her when she was coherent enough to understand. Between the need to find the wandering Tar-Aiym weapons platform and escape the attentions of the murderous Order of Null, it would have been foolish as well as counterproductive for him to linger on Nur. Hard as it had been for him to leave her, he had given in to the greater need and resumed his journey and search. But not before extracting promises from Truzenzuzex and Tse-Mallory to stay behind and look after her. This they had done while at the same time managing to continue their own research into the looming menace.

They were, doubtless, pursuing it right now, she told herself as she adjusted the trim on the sunfoil. Her right shoulder ached as the wind rippled the featherweight material. It did not matter that her doctors insisted that by now she should feel no pain in that area of her body. *Physicians be damned,* she thought. When she exerted too much pressure, it *hurt.*

Hurt almost as much as Flinx's absence. She pushed him out of her mind. It had been many months now since she had regained consciousness in the surgical ward in Sphene, only to learn of his departure. Yes, his need to flee without her had been forced on him by circumstances beyond their control. But this ongoing business of seeing her beloved only once every couple of years or so was beginning to grow old.

She shook her head even as she fought with the phototaxic craft's simplified control bar. Billowing sheets of light-sensitive material gathered energy that lifted the slim bar of reinforced aerogel out of the water. Sitting on the single seat, her legs pointed forward down the length of the craft, she shot eastward at high speed. With a shake of her head, half a dozen tightly bound blond braids trailed out behind her. Shaved into the hair on the left side of her head was the outline of a Terran scorpion, while the right side displayed an ancient swear word sheared in runic. One image pictorial, one written, both shouting a very personal kind of defiance at the universe.

She squinted ahead. Time to turn back. Clouds on the horizon hinted at the impending onset of bad weather. Of course, as a general rule, "bad weather" for the temperate reaches of paradisiacal Nur meant nothing worse than a steady, tepid rain. Still, that would not be the best time to be out sunfoiling, especially on a lake as big as Sintram. Rain would not harm her body bandage, but its sensors would report the drop in surface temperature and consequent stress on her body, just as they were doing right now. Taking a deep breath, she twisted her arms and brought the sunfoil around sharply. The triple sails adjusted accordingly, and a minute later she was shooting back toward the shore in the direction of the recuperation facility.

Momentarily taken aback by the sudden shift of direction, a brilliant pink and blue winged shape had to bank sharply and hurry to catch up. Wrapping a coil around the topsail, Scrap promptly buckled its upper half.

"Get *off* there!" Clarity waved crossly up at the uncomprehending minidrag. There was no danger, even if the flying snake collapsed the entire sail, but its loss would slow the rider's return.

Riding the curling bow wave of the sunfoil's three-centimeter-wide keel, native harru repeatedly broke the surface, their multiple horizontal fins giving them enough lift occasionally to take to the air.

Abandoning his momentary perch atop the sail, whose shape rebounded nicely, a diving Scrap snapped up a harru in his jaws, spun gracefully in midair, and dumped the squirming, eel-like water-dweller in Clarity's lap. Squealing involuntarily, she flailed at the flapping, convulsing creature until it slid back into the water.

"Just don't *help,* okay?" Patting her lap, she directed the minidrag to land there. It refused, preferring soaring to soaking.

Tambrogh Barryn was waiting for her at the dock. He was in love with her, she knew. So was Mandrassa, her chief physician, and at least half a dozen others at the convalescence complex. To each and every one she was polite, she smiled, she engaged in courteous conversation; and she brushed them all off. They could not understand why. Exceedingly attractive, well educated, with an enviable career, and unmated, she evinced none of the psychological signs of someone obsessed with personal privacy or captivated by the prospect of permanent solitude. On a social basis she mixed freely and enjoyably with the other patients as well as with those responsible for her treatment.

For a while, rumors persisted that she might be the tacit cohort of the tall, powerfully built scientist who called in regularly to check on her progress. It seemed unlikely. Not only was the untalkative visitor significantly older, no one ever observed them engaged in any physical intimacy beyond an occasional affectionate hug of the kind a brother might give to a sister. The frequent concomitant presence of an equally mature thranx during such visits further seemed to belie any deeper relationship.

Then why, patients and medical personnel and service attendants alike wondered as they continued to ponder her situation, did she continue to refuse any measure of social interaction beyond the purely civil? When frustrated would-be suitors finally inquired directly, she inevitably responded that she already had a swain. The ongoing nonappearance of this mysterious individual only further whetted the curiosity of the perpetually hopeful.

She let Barryn help her collapse the sunfoil and stow it in its locker. As they worked he admired the play of her muscles beneath the translucent bandage that covered most of her upper body. It would be coming off next week, she had told him. He shared her anticipation. Maybe some of her importunate inhibitions would disappear along with the bandage.

His gaze rose beyond her to take in the lake's flat horizon. "Rain coming."

"I think so, too," she agreed, "so I thought I'd better come back. Not that I couldn't have handled it." Genuinely violent storms on New Riviera were confined to the polar regions; it was a world with a climate more benign than any humankind had yet to discover. "Anyway, I was getting hungry." Reaching up, she stroked the back of the minidrag that rode on her neck and shoulder.

More than one potential courtier had been put off by the faithful presence of the flying snake. Its species hailed from a world called Alaspin, she told Barryn when he had first inquired about the minidrag. She further explained that they shared a deep empathetic relationship. One that the flying snake itself had initiated. The vividly colored minidrag was a constant companion, friend, and protector.

"Protector?" he responded dubiously. "It's barely as long as my arm."

"He's not a constrictor," she told him while caressing the sinuous shape. "His kind spits poison from a special mouth-throat sac. Not only is it an incredibly powerful neurotoxin, it's also highly caustic. On a very primitive level, individuals of the species are true empaths. He can sense my emotions and react to them."

Upon being enlightened as to the flying snake's capabilities, it was no wonder that so many of her would-be suitors neglected to ask for a second date. Tambrogh Barryn was not so easily intimidated. He thought the exceptional patient more than worth pursuing, even at the risk of disturbing her unusual pet. Mindful of the depth of his feelings toward her, he had no fear of the minidrag detecting and responding to them—assuming there was more to the business of it being an empathetic telepath than just a clever attempt on her part to deflect unwanted attention. A check of the Nur Shell came up with very little information on the world of Alaspin and next to nothing on the reptilian creature she said had come from there.

Much more than the ever-present minidrag, which after all was nothing more than an odd pet, he was displeased by the unremitting attention that was lavished on her by the peculiar pair of visitors, who came all too frequently. His associates at the complex seemed a little afraid of the large old man and his thranx companion. Barryn could not understand why. The man was big, but also old, while the thranx was merely small and old. Just because they doted on Clarity, he pointed out to his friends, did not mean they would interfere should she choose to enter into a relationship. As to the perpetually absent paramour of whom she sometimes spoke, that entity might be as much an invention as the flying snake's toxicity, with both intended for the same purpose:

to ward off unwanted attention. He should be glad of both minidrag and make-believe suitor, he knew. Otherwise the interest that would have been shown to Clarity Held would have been insufferable, and the competition for her attention far more congested.

"Can I buy you lunch?" He did not try to take her arm as they strode inland and up the slight slope that led away from the dock. Having seen her shrug off physical approaches from others he knew better than to force the issue.

She smiled up at him. Despite what others said, he chose to take every smile as an encouragement. "You know that between insurance through Ulricam and aid from friends my stay here is fully paid for. Including meals."

He made light of her rejection. "So you'd deny me the pleasure of paying for it twice? If I pay, you can have two desserts."

·This time she laughed. Even better than a smile, he mused. The portents were promising. Perhaps later, under cover of the storm clouds and the warm rain that would come with them, he might make bold enough to try to share more than a dessert.

"You're very sweet, Tam."

"Hey, who else but a sweet guy would offer a woman two desserts?"

Even as he said it, a voice in his head was telling him to shut up. He was big and strong and words had never been his forte—as he had just proved. That had never caused him any trouble with women, however. They never seemed to catch on to the fact that his frequent silences arose not from a sensitive desire to listen to what they had to say but from an inability to put coherent sentences together. This manifest intellectual deficiency seemed to perturb them not at all. They could talk all they wanted to and he would sit in silence. And when they chose not to talk, they could stare at his chiseled features unaware of the silly grins that parasitized their features.

For reasons he could not fathom, this time-tested methodology had failed to make an impression on Clarity Held. It was almost as if she *wanted* to have an intelligent conversation, wanted him to talk. He did his best to comply. Usually he did better than "Who else but a sweet guy would offer a woman two desserts." He knew he had to progress, even if the strain made his head hurt.

Pick a subject she enjoys talking about, he thought. *Even if you couldn't care less about it. That always works.*

"So—tell me more about this guy you're engaged to."

"We're not engaged," she replied quickly. That surprised him. It also, of course, did not displease him. "Our relationship goes deeper than that. We don't have to have a formal engagement. We have—shared experiences."

A safely enigmatic retort, he decided. Could mean anything or nothing. Or it could be another evasion, like the scientific gibberish about the flying creature's venomous capabilities.

"I can't figure it out, Clarity. If you're so tight with this guy, how come nobody ever sees you with him?"

She shook her head and her tight blond braids flew from side to side, sending the last adhering droplets of lake water flying. They were halfway to the nearest building, climbing the walkway that split a lawn of cultured, ankle-high catharia. Thumb-sized beurre flowers of azure and gold sprang from the three-sided flanks of tapering blue-green stems.

"He has to travel a lot."

"On business? What is he, based in Sphene?"

This generated a broad smile. What had he said, Barryn wondered, that was so amusing?

"Not exactly," she murmured casually. "His work takes him a little farther afield than that."

Barryn persisted. "The southern continent? He still ought to be able to make it up here to see you once in a while while you're convalescing. If he really cared for you, that is."

At that, the flying snake lifted its head from her shoulder to stare fixedly at him. Could it have sensed something? True telepaths were only tall tales—the empathetic kind as much as any other.

"His work is difficult and very demanding," she told him, not smiling now. "There's a lot of stress. The kind of stress no one can imagine."

Barryn took mild offense. "I work with seriously hurt people. That involves a lot of stress, too, you know."

"I know, Tam. You're a good person and you work hard." Reaching out, she gently patted his right arm. He would have accounted it a small triumph had he been able to escape the feeling that she was patronizing him. The prospect of killing lunch notwithstanding, he decided the time had come for directness.

"Look, you know how much I like you, Clarity. What is it about this guy, who can never find the time to visit you when you're hurt? Why can't you just shake him? Is he better looking than me? Smarter, richer? What? I at least deserve to know what I'm up against."

She stopped, staring out across the lake whose hues so often mirrored what she was feeling. "Philip and I go back years, Tam. We've been through a lot together. More than I can explain." Turning back to him, she met his gaze with a look that was at once compassionate and unyielding. "If you want me to be specific, yes: he's richer than you and smarter than you. None of which matters. Nothing matters except what's inside him. I've been lucky enough to have been allowed to see that. I've been damned to have been allowed to see that. You know how people sometimes say they feel like they have the weight of the world on their shoulders? Well, Philip has the weight of the whole galaxy on his."

Barryn was taken aback. How did one respond to something so outrageous? If it was a testament of undying love, it was the most outlandish one he had ever heard.

"But," she finished with a sigh as she resumed walking, "you can still take me to lunch. I won't deny that I don't get lonely sometimes, even with Bran and Tru's regular visits."

"The old guy and the bug?"

Her smile returned. He was glad to see it, though the words that accompanied its resurgence left him feeling, for a second time, that she just might be patronizing him.

"Maybe one day there'll be a chance for you to meet and talk to them. I think you'd be surprised. They also have a tendency to get around. . . ."

Barryn felt that he was making progress. Slow progress, to be sure, but moving in the right direction. Though the occasional condescension she displayed toward him was offensive, he chose to ignore it. If she wanted to feel superior, as long as it advanced their relationship he was perfectly willing to let her. Given time, he was confident that would change. While not the brightest guy in the world, or even the brightest at the medical complex, he knew he was not stupid.

It was a routinely beautiful morning. They were lying side by side on the beach, relaxing atop cooling air lounges. From time to time he felt free to admire her out of the corner of a shaded eye. With the body bandage now gone she was more beautiful than ever. And her joy at its removal had only increased his determination to forge a liaison.

Then, and for no discernible reason, that damned cold-eyed pet of hers suddenly went nuts.

One minute it was lying at her feet, a coil of somnolent iridescent color. The next, both he and Clarity were jolted from their dozing by a loud retort. What sounded like a large piece of canvas cracking in the wind was the snap of a pair of pleated wings opening wide. Sitting up, Barryn gaped at the flying snake as it shot skyward. He had watched it take to the air many times before, but never so explosively.

Clarity was no less bewildered. "Scrap—get back here!" The minidrag didn't hear her. It was already rocketing inland, heading straight for the heart of the medical complex. *"Scrap!"* She looked for support to the man now sitting up on the lounge beside her. Her bewilderment was plain. "I've only seen him react like this once before, and that was a long time ago."

As always, Barryn refused to refer to the vicious flying creature as a "he."

"Maybe it senses a threat. You've told me that it responds to your feelings." Rising from the lounge, he moved to sit down beside her. When he slipped a comforting arm around her now fully healed shoulders, she did not pull away. "Are you feeling threatened?"

"No," she muttered restively. "I feel fine." She was staring in the direction of the complex. "I can't see him anymore. It's not like him to fly out of sight." She started to stand. "I'd better go look for him. If Scrap's sensing a threat where none really exists, he could frighten some people. It's happened before."

I can't imagine why. Barryn kept his sarcasm to himself. Why would anyone get upset to suddenly find a venomous airborne alien reptiloid darting in front of their face? He couldn't care less about the minidrag or why it had abruptly gone shooting off inland. His real concern, his real interest, lay with Clarity. Anyone else confronted by the flying snake would have to deal with it themselves.

"Just stay here and relax." He squeezed her bare shoulder a little tighter. "I'm sure your pet will be right back as soon as it determines you're not in any danger. In any event, *I'm* here."

She didn't bite on that, but he refused to let it discourage him. If luck was really with him, the flying snake might never come back. As in any large medical complex, there was a security team. Maybe one of them would shoot the little monster.

"Oh."

Clarity did not shout the exclamation. Her voice remained level and controlled. But the strangest expression came over her face as she sat there beside him. It was one he had not encountered previously and did not recognize. Slipping free of his reassuring, mildly possessive grasp, she rose and started toward the complex.

"Clarity? Clarity, love?" he called after her in confusion. She appeared not to hear him.

Peering in the direction she was walking, he expected to see the flying snake returning to its master. But there was no sign of the minidrag. Meanwhile, ahead of her a single figure had detached itself from the crowd of convalescents, medical personnel, and visitors. It was walking toward her, and she was advancing toward it. Tambrogh Barryn's gaze narrowed.

Though he did not recognize the stranger, Barryn could not escape the certainty that the other man's arrival did not bode well for his hopes regarding Clarity.

Upslope, Flinx halted. She looked exactly as he remembered her. No, he corrected himself quickly. She looked much better than he remembered, because the last time he had seen her she had been enveloped in a halo of sweat and blood, her torso ravaged from behind. Looking at her now, that horrific image finally began to recede into memory. The medtechs and their instrumentation had done their job well. She had been restored to him. Her beauty, her movement, her form intact and unmarred.

Also her full neuromuscular functionality, as evinced by the hard slap she gave him right across his face. She had to reach high to make the necessary contact. Though intimately familiar with her person, Pip still would have reacted to such a hard blow—except that Pip was nowhere to be seen. As soon as they had reached the entrance to the medical complex she had elevated skyward to leave on some unknown errand of her own. Flinx was not concerned. He could sense that she was somewhere nearby. Whatever had drawn her away, she would not pass out of perception range of her friend and master.

Reaching up, he touched his stinging cheek where Clarity had struck him. "I missed you, too."

"All this time." She was staring hard at him, so tense that the muscles in her neck were twitching. "One minute we're fighting for our very lives at the shuttleport; the next I wake up immobilized in a hospital chamber. No sign of you, no kind word, no knowing if you're alive or dead. Eventually your big friend and your bug friend show up to tell me you've taken off yet again on your fanatical quest halfway across the galaxy."

Though appropriately abashed, he did not try to evade the issue. "A galaxy in need of saving, Clarity."

She nodded briskly. "Uh-huh. We talked about it, remember? We also talked about you and me. We talked about that, too." She indicated their surroundings, taking in the beurre lawn, the structural complex, the lake, and by inference the entire welcoming world of Nur.

"You were gone over a year. More than enough time for me to heal—physically. How long are you here for this time? A week? A month?" Her unhappiness was manifest in her tone as well as her expression. "I'm not letting you leave again. Ever. Not without me. I can't take it. I wouldn't have made a good wife to an ancient Terran sea captain, Flinx, waving understandingly as her husband disappeared over the horizon for two or three years to hunt cetaceans, or discover uncharted islands, or . . ."

She was crying now. Tenderly, he took her in his arms. One moment she was sobbing against his chest and the next she was pounding on it with both fists. "I won't let you leave me again, Philip Lynx! I won't! I'll have your heart if I have to cut it out and keep it next to me in a cryosac!"

He smiled affectionately down at her. "I've never met another woman capable of such an extreme degree of homicidal affection. You really think I would risk losing someone so unique? Okay."

Sniffling, furious at her own emotional vulnerability, she rubbed crossly at first one weeping eye and then the other as she frowned up at him uncertainly. "'Okay'? What the hell do you mean, 'okay'?"

"I mean okay, that I concur." He stared evenly into her damp eyes. "I'll never leave you again."

Anger and ardor merged in confusion. "You're giving up your search? For the Tar-Aiym weapons platform? But what about the Great Evil, the danger that's coming toward us from out of the Great Emptiness? You showed it to me, I know it's real. Have you given up all hope of somehow confronting it?"

What is it you want me to do? he thought in bewilderment. *Marry you or save civilization? Make up your mind.* He felt a headache starting, only this time the basis was utterly different from the one that usually plagued him.

"No, I haven't," he finally replied. "Here lately it seems I was always getting sidetracked by other matters, but that's all over and done with now. I've recommitted myself. I intend to do my utmost to relocate that example of ancient advanced technology—even though I don't think it will do any good. Not when pitted against what's coming this way. But I promised Tse-Mallory and Truzenzuzex that I'd try to find it, and that's what I'm going to do. With one adjustment."

She blinked, waiting. "Adjustment? What adjustment?"

"You're coming with me. Just as you were supposed to do before the fanatics from the Order of Null attacked us at the shuttleport outside Sphene." He lowered his eyes. "That is," he mumbled awkwardly, "if you still want to."

Staring back at him, she sounded incredulous. "You didn't stick around long enough for me to heal sufficiently or I'd have gone with you this last time. Do you really think I'd say no now?"

"I—I wasn't sure. After leaving you that way. . . . Clarity, everything was happening so *fast*. I felt I had no choice. Bran and Tru felt I had no choice." He met her gaze once again. Strolling staff and patients were staring at them, murmuring and pointing. He ignored them.

"I've learned more about myself since I've been away. A lot more. Some of those things I needed to know, like whether civilization is really worth saving. Some were things I didn't want to know. Some I had to know the answers to whether I wanted to learn them or not. I'm still struggling to deal with the consequences." He would tell her what he had discovered about his patrimony later, he decided.

She saw the pain in his face, heard it in his voice. "And," she whispered as she put a hand on his arm, "what *have* you decided? Are you continuing with this crazy search to fulfill a promise you made to your friends—or because you believe that civilization really is worth saving?"

He managed a smile. "Both, I think. But one of the things I realized is that I can't do this without support. For a certainty, not without you." He put a hand on each of her shoulders. "No matter where I was, no matter what outlandish world I was on—Arrawd, Jast, Visaria, Gestalt, Blasusarr—I wondered if what I was doing was the right thing, because everything I was doing and all that I was experiencing was without you." His fingers tightened. "I need you *with* me, Clarity. Not waiting for me if and when I finish with it. Whether I can find this artifact again or not, whether the finding of it portends anything effective or not, whether the whole galaxy, or for that matter the entire universe, goes to hell or not—none of it matters to me anymore if I'm not with you." Reluctantly he let go of her shoulders, dropped his arms, and looked past her, his gaze coming to rest on the quiet waters of the vast lake. His voice threatened to crack.

"I've been so alone for so long, Clarity. I just can't do it anymore. Not even to save the galaxy. Not even to save myself."

For a long while she said nothing. Then she stepped forward, put her arms around his waist, and drew him to her. A wide, warm smile spread across her face. "Philip—Flinx—you've never really been alone since the day I met you."

From where he was sitting on the air lounge down on the beach, Barryn had watched the reunion with slowly rising anger. Or at least he had since Clarity had slapped the stranger across the face. That initial delight had given way steadily to dismay, then to despair, and finally to antipathy. Who was this lanky red-haired outsider, to show up after an absence of so many months and try to steal away the woman on whom he, Tambrogh Barryn, had lavished so much time and attention? If it was indeed the shadowy individual known as Philip Lynx, he was in line to receive some choice words at the very least. Rising from the air lounge, his mounting resentment bolstered by righteous indignation, the medtech strode up the slope toward the embracing couple. That they took no notice of him until he was almost on top of them only served to further stoke his resentment.

A heavy, insistent hand tapped Flinx on the shoulder. "Look here, *thinp,* is your name Philip Lynx?"

The youthful redhead looked around and responded with an unexpectedly gracious smile. "My friends call me Flinx."

"All right then—'Flinx.' My name is Tambrogh Barryn and this lady is *my* friend." He took a step back, ready for anything. "I know who you are because I've heard her talk about you."

Flinx turned his smile on Clarity. "Is that true? You talk about me?"

She returned the smile. "You know how it is. Talk long enough and sooner or later every little thing gets mentioned."

He nodded, then lost the smile. "How good a friend is this gentleman?"

Clarity glanced over at the quietly fuming medtech. "Tam's been very kind to me during the late stages of my convalescence. I'll always be grateful for his company, his kind words, and his support."

Complimentary as her words were, they were not the ones Barryn wanted to hear. Instead of complaining, he turned his ire on the tall redhead. "I don't know where *you've* been all the time Clarity has been fighting to recover from her serious injuries, but *I've* been right here with her." Resting his hands on his hips, he struck a deliberately challenging pose. "Doesn't seem to me that anyone who really cared about her would disappear and leave her to recover all by herself. I know she has some odd friends who look in on her from time to time, but that's not the kind of attention and compassion she deserves."

The last vestiges of Flinx's smile fell away. "You're absolutely right. But it couldn't be avoided. There was"—and his gaze flicked back to Clarity—"some unavoidable business I had to attend to. I didn't want to leave her behind. But she couldn't travel. Promises had been made, and before I realized it circumstances led me to deviate even from those." Extending an arm, he indicated that the medtech should join him in stepping off to one side.

Barryn tensed but complied. He wasn't afraid of this stranger. His rival was taller but slimmer and younger. If the confrontation came to blows, the medtech was confident who would come out on top. Behind them, Clarity stood frowning and watching.

Flinx did not raise his hands, however. Nor did he raise his voice.

"I can't tell you the specifics of why I had to leave Clarity in the care of friends. I've had a difficult time since I've been gone." The smile returned, confident and, oddly enough, almost sympathetic. "There have been others before you. Now that I'm back, this time there will never be any more."

Barryn refused to be lulled by his challenger's easygoing manner or to be provoked by his quiet insistence. "And if I tell you that I plan on sticking around and that *I'm* not going anywhere . . . ?"

"You don't understand," Flinx told him quietly. "I've—had—a—difficult—time." His eyes peered directly into those of the other man.

He could have sought to project onto the medtech. He didn't have to. He certainly did not try to, at least not consciously. Whatever flowed outward from him to pass between them was for once unforced and involuntary.

Meeting that stare, Barryn found himself gazing upon a thousand years worth of sorrow and worry. There was pain there, and heartbreak. A sense of loss beyond anything he had ever encountered before. Knowledge, terrible knowledge, of matters beyond his imagining. Answers there for the taking to questions he shrank from asking. So much suffering, so much anguish, a wealth of bereavement. Failure, inadequacy, hopelessness, desperation.

An inescapable and palpable emptiness.

Swallowing hard, feeling a sudden dry tightness in his throat, Tambrogh Barryn retreated from that stare. "I—I didn't *know,*" was all he could mumble.

Flinx responded with the slightest of shrugs. "I didn't want you to have to know. The fewer who know, the better." He glanced briefly to his left. "Clarity knows. More than that, she understands. Hardly anyone else understands even a little. I need that understanding. Without it, I'm afraid that inside myself I'll shrivel down to nothingness. If that happens, a great many more mortals than me will learn things they don't want to learn and would be better off not knowing."

Barryn found himself nodding without thinking. "I'm sorry," he heard himself whispering. "I'm so very, very sorry."

Flinx's smile returned. "It's all right. I understand. You understand."

"Yes." With that, Tambrogh Barryn, who had never turned away from a confrontation or a challenge in his life, pivoted sharply and walked away, striding upslope at a rapid pace toward the nearest building.

Approaching from behind, Clarity slipped her arm through Flinx's as they both watched the medtech take his leave. "What did you say to him?" Her expression narrowed slightly. "You didn't threaten him, did you? He's like so many men, at heart desperately in love with himself, but he means well."

Turning back to her, Flinx let out a tired sigh. "I didn't say anything. I let him look into my soul a little bit. I know he's not a bad guy. If he was, he wouldn't have seen what he saw, or react to it the way he did. He understands."

She blinked. "Understands what, Flinx?"

"This."

Taking her in his arms, he used his mouth to forestall any more questions. Watching the two lovers, other patients and medical personnel smiled, or commented, or sniggered under their breath. None of it mattered to the young couple. It had been a long, long time, and they had a lot of catching up to do.

Out in the lake, a tree that had taken leave of its rooting was drifting unhurriedly southward. Something bright-winged and swift had coiled itself around one of its bare upper branches. The creature's iridescent emerald-green head tilted back to gaze upward as a slightly smaller version of itself dropped toward it from the increasingly cloud-filled sky. Rain began to fall as Pip loosened her grip on the branch, spread her wings, and took to the sky. At the last moment, the plummeting predator, which was one of her offspring, extended both wings to their maximum and braked dramatically in midair.

It was a festive reunion. Though the only sound that emanated from mother and son was the occasional joyous hiss, it was still noisier than the one that was taking place on shore.

There, conversation of any sort had ceased completely.

CHAPTER
13

With its eight limbs, a thranx can put up a formidable defense against any attacker. Large compound eyes provide excellent peripheral vision and allow it to see potential threats approaching from angles that would be invisible to a human. Feathery antennae detect new smells and sudden changes in air pressure.

Though he was advanced in years and not as sensitive to his surroundings as he had once been, Truzenzuzex was in remarkable shape for a thranx his age. So he was startled when he was taken completely by surprise from behind. He had not sensed the approach of his assailant. Probably he had been too relaxed. The secure surroundings of the underground park had caused him to lower his customary guard. Age breeds a sense of security that metastasizes with indifference.

The weight on his back sent him tumbling forward on the hiking path. Whatever had struck him was bigger and heavier than any thranx. As it followed him to the ground he was already working to identify the shape. It could not be AAnn, not here on New Riviera. Judging from the mass and texture it was most likely a human. But why the assault? Truzenzuzex's lower legs were pinned beneath the human bulk and his foothands had little room in which to maneuver. His truhands were all that remained free. Fragile though they were, he did not hesitate to strike out with both.

"Ow!" The offending human promptly rolled off the combative philosoph and clutched at its face. A thin red streak appeared on one cheek.

As he reflexively reached with one hand toward the long but shallow scratch, Flinx had enough presence of mind to grab an aroused Pip by the tail just as she started toward the scuttling thranx.

Scrambling up onto all four trulegs, Truzenzuzex used one foot-hand to pick up the compact reader he had been perusing while walking, picked up his dropped drinking vessel with the other foothand, and extended both truhands out in front of him as he assumed a fighting posture. Only then did he get his first good look at the intruder. Projector and spiral-mouthed goblet were immediately set aside.

"Grub, you are bigger each time I see you, and just as lamentably impulsive." With all four hands now free he was able to punctuate his observation with an elaborate and eloquent gesture of second-degree stupidity.

Hurrying up behind him, Clarity had arrived at Flinx's side and was examining the cut on his face. Having heard the commotion behind him, a grinning Bran Tse-Mallory had hurried back down the path to rejoin his friend. Standing behind Truzenzuzex, he carefully straightened a vestigial wing case that had been knocked askew in the course of the brief tussle.

"Whereas your reflexes aren't quite as slow as you, my friend," Tse-Mallory reflected aloud.

"Young fool!" Reaching up with a truhand to meticulously groom one downy antenna, the philosoph stared over to where Flinx was regaining his footing. "I might have killed him, *crr!ltt!*"

Flinx winced as Clarity touched the cut. Extending his upper body outward from his perch on her shoulder, Scrap let his tongue flick tentatively at the wound. Perceiving her master's composure, Pip ignored both. The graze was superficial and would heal quickly.

"Nice to see you again, too, Tru." The bleeding from the warning strike, Flinx noted, had already stopped.

Tse-Mallory stepped back from his insectoid companion. "I believe that with his leap from the bushes our young friend wanted to surprise you."

With great dignity the Eint Truzenzuzex straightened his legs beneath him, lowering his thorax so his foothands rested on the fastidiously manicured, fungus-covered landscaping that paralleled the path down which he had been walking. Once again he stood sturdily on all six feet.

"I accept the explanation. Consider me surprised." Ambling over to where Flinx stood, the philosoph leaned back on his four trulegs. Even in this altered, partially elevated posture, his head only came up to Flinx's chest. Antennae fluttered impatiently.

Bending at the waist, Flinx let the tips of both feathery appendages make contact with his forehead before he reached out to gently touch them with his fingertips. Informalities concluded, the thranx stepped back to scrutinize his friendly assailant.

"You have succeeded in startling me with your presence." The chitinous valentine-shaped head inclined in Clarity's direction. "It's evident that you've also already made contact with and no doubt also surprised your charming and now fully-recovered lady. I presume it would be too much to expect that you also intend to surprise us with the knowledge that your journey was successful and you have reestablished contact with the ancient weapons platform of the Tar-Aiym?"

"It would." *Strange,* Flinx thought. Despite all he had been through, everything he had experienced, and as much as he had matured, he still felt like a little kid in the daunting presence of Tse-Mallory and Truzenzuzex.

"You searched extensively, I imagine?" the thranx pressed him.

As always with compound eyes, it was difficult to tell precisely where they were focused. "Not as extensively as I could have, I'm afraid. I—I got distracted," he added evasively.

A scowling Tse-Mallory was clearly not pleased. "The fate of all civilization, of the entire galaxy, is potentially at stake and you allowed yourself to be distracted?"

Clarity turned quickly protective. "Let him explain. He's under a lot of pressure."

"No one here would deny that." Truzenzuzex's tone was as dry as the deserts of Blasusarr. "However, the gravity of the situation is such that there is little time remaining in which to indulge personal eccentricities." Aware that he might be sounding too harsh, he added, "What about your headaches? Have they been as debilitating as ever? As frequent?"

"They come and go," Flinx acknowledged. "Sometimes they're incapacitating, sometimes no more than irritating. I can never tell at the beginning when one's going to be really bad and when it's just going to fade away."

Tse-Mallory sat down gingerly on a nearby Otoidian fungus. The spongy brown and gray growth compressed beneath his weight but did not collapse. "You said you were distracted, Flinx. What distracted you?"

Sitting down on the stone path, Flinx crossed his legs and let his arms droop toward one another. Taking a seat, Clarity rested one hand possessively on his right thigh.

"At first it was just depression, a general malaise. The *Teacher* did its best to help me rise above it, but I found that the only solution was for me to immerse myself in civilization. In sentience. To learn some things about it, and about myself."

"And what did you learn?" Tse-Mallory inquired thoughtfully.

A pair of silvery *etelel* whizzed past between young man and mentor, their brushlike wings rotating madly to keep them aloft. Though they were indigenous to the cultivated underground gardens of Nur/New Riviera, they reminded Truzenzuzex of the similarly evolved subterranean fliers of his native Hivehom.

"I learned that humankind, and humanxkind, is worth saving. That whatever its faults and immaturities, the spark of intelligence is worth fighting to preserve." His gaze met that of the older man and locked. "Even if that intelligence is nonhumanx and hostile. I learned that sentience is essential to any kind of progressive evolution, irrespective of its origins. I learned"—he turned away from Tse-Mallory and back to Clarity—"I learned about myself."

"And what did you learn about yourself?" Tse-Mallory asked again.

Flinx hesitated a moment. Then he smiled at Clarity and at his old friends. On his shoulder, Pip snuggled closer. "That I can be happy. Maybe. But that I have a responsibility that, much as I might like to disregard it, I can't just set aside in order to selfishly further that happiness. And that if I'm to have any hope of fulfilling the responsibility I've taken on, I'm going to need the help and support of others."

Picking idly at a gaudy spray of spore-filled spheres growing near his feet, Tse-Mallory nodded understandingly. "It's a terrible burden you bear, Flinx. Tru and I worried and worried about how you would cope when you had to flee New Riviera alone and leave the rest of us behind." He looked up. "It's apparent from what you've just told us that you coped by avoiding. Well, from now on you won't have to do that. Tru and I will be with you at all times."

"As will I." Clarity's fingers tightened on Flinx's leg.

Hearing this, the terrible anxiety that was his constant companion did not vanish; Flinx knew it probably never would. But he felt better, more confident, than he had in months of wandering aimlessly around the Blight and then the sundry worlds of the Arm. The likelihood was that despite his best efforts he would never again make contact with the wandering Tar-Aiym weapons platform, and even if he did, any attempt to make use of it against the oncoming Evil would prove as futile as it seemed on paper. But at least now he would no longer have to carry on by himself, alone in the vastness of space-plus save for the faithful company of a considerate but soulless shipmind.

"You're not going to cry, are you?" Eyeing his young friend, Tse-Mallory looked suddenly alarmed. "Cry after the threat has been dealt with, weep once the danger has passed—but not now."

Flinx rubbed at his right eye. Or maybe he hit himself. In any event, no tears were shed. "It's just that I'm so glad to see you all again." Reaching over, he put an arm around Clarity and drew her to him. Forced together, the two flying snakes slithered petulantly in opposite directions in search of more individual space.

"This time there'll be no delay, no mistakes." Tse-Mallory rose from his seat. Though comfortable in the underground park, which was designed to accommodate thranx, he much preferred the warm sunshine of Nur's surface. "Tru and I can leave immediately." He turned his attention to Clarity. "What about you? Have you made any arrangements?"

"Some, yes, but I can't just vanish into the ether like you two. I need a little time to do it right." Disdaining Flinx's proffered hand, she rose easily to her feet. "There are people who would miss me and file reports if I simply disappeared."

His characteristic self-control notwithstanding, Flinx's expression darkened ever so slightly. "Tambrogh Barryn, for example?"

She made a face at him. "Don't be a fool. I have to alert and prepare medical personnel who've worked on my case, coworkers at Ulricam, casual friends, and others." She eyed Tse-Mallory. "We're not all of us famous, independently wealthy scientists, philosophs, or interstellar vagabonds who can just take off on a moment's notice to go gallivanting around the galaxy."

"I do not 'gallivant,'" Truzenzuzex commented primly. "I plan in haste."

Tse-Mallory smiled considerately. "Will a couple of days be sufficient for you to get your affairs in order?" When she nodded, he turned to Flinx. "And you?"

Flinx did not have to think. He had worked through departure procedures many times, on many worlds. "There are supplies and provisions the *Teacher* can't synthesize. There's no telling where we're going or how long we'll be gone. It would be good to be able to start the search again knowing the ship is fully prepared."

Instead of replying, Tse-Mallory glanced over at his companion. "Tru?"

The thranx gestured impatiently. "Humans invariably find a way to rationalize delay. But I suppose our young friend's logic is sound. Very well then. A couple of days. I will use the time until our departure to compose and plant certain situation-sensitive messages with professional acquaintances."

"What kind of messages?" Flinx asked curiously.

The thranx philosoph's great golden eyes rose to regard him impassively. "The kind that might prove useful to friends and colleagues in the event we don't come back."

Effrom was out of breath by the time he reached the rendezvous. It was out in the open, of course, the better to ensure both anonymity and privacy. As soon as he showed himself beside the public healthirl, the others began to steadily gravitate in his direction. As they did so, like the several dozen other citizens caught up in the healthirl's whirl, Effrom and his party breathed deeply of the supervised whirlwind's heady atmospheric cocktail. Today's broad-spectrum anti-retroviral was infused with the aroma of Terran peach. Effrom took care to inhale the respiratory prophylactic, though improving his health was not the reason for his visit.

Tuoela, Ambreleon, and the others were waiting for him inside the slow-speed domesticated cyclone. Drifting away from the other citizens, they collected in a small group near the center of the health-enhancing storm. There they could hear one another clearly while reasonably confident no one else could eavesdrop on their conversation, either in person or electronically.

"We received your alert." Tuoela ran a small business that supplied decorations imported from different worlds for everything from birthdays to ceremonial government dinners. On any of the capital's streets she would not have drawn a second look from the most suspicious policeman or chary government operative. Nor would any of her companions in the present circle. Their zealous ordinariness ensured their continued anonymity.

"Everyone is excited." Canodoce was only slightly younger than the woman floating next to him. "We've waited and hoped for this. You can really confirm?"

Though he was no less excited than his comrades, Effrom controlled his emotions. "The one who endangers the Purity has indeed returned. I have seen him myself on multiple occasions. There is no mistaking his identity." He breathed deeply of the invigorating, health-giving hurricane. "As if further authentication were required, the same small flying creature accompanies him."

Ambreleon's expression darkened. "That's the kind of verification I could do without." Reaching up, he touched the right side of his neck. Surgery had completely erased the damage he had suffered during the fight at the shuttleport, but no physician or medtech could eradicate the phantom pain that continued to haunt him. "The flying snake kills."

"We'll deal with it this time." Tuoela was full of confidence. Their patience had, at last, been rewarded. "Deciding to monitor the woman's recovery was genius. Our colleagues lost track of the man almost immediately. Based on what was known and could subsequently be learned, it was thought he might one day return to see her." She smiled thinly. "Love is such a proficient betrayer."

"It certainly makes it possible once again to carry out our sacred duty." Longing for the all-inclusive great death that might follow his own, Canodoce verged on the ecstatic. "We can now act to preserve the Purity that is to come."

"In order to do so we must separate the tall meddler from his small protector," Tuoela pointed out.

"'Protectors,'" an apologetic Effrom corrected her. "The others who were at the shuttleport and helped provide the cover that allowed him to get away have also returned."

Tuoela was not pleased. "More complications. Still, we will prevail." Squinting into the roaring wind of the rejuvenating airstream, she regarded her friends and colleagues. "We have waited too long for it to be otherwise. Let it begin here and now. First, to logistics." She turned to face middle-aged M'dbane. "While I have no more fear of dying than any of us, if possible I would prefer to live to greet the coming end. As I am sure you all would." Murmurs of agreement greeted her assumption. "Therefore I rule out suicide attacks unless we are left with no other choice. Such an attempt would likely fail in any event."

"Why is that?" Though bigger and stronger than any of them, Canodoce was comparatively new to the Order.

She caught his gaze. "It has been determined that the meddler can read feelings. The stronger the emotion, the easier it is for him to perceive it. Whether in isolation or a crowd, an incipient suicide would stand out sharply. To a certain extent one's emotions can be masked by medication. But while drugs can disguise feelings, they also tend to diminish skills. A proper balance must be struck." She shifted her attention to the rest. "That much we have learned from several failed attempts to eliminate the meddler. We cannot fail again. We may never have another chance."

"Bearing in mind our previous failed attempts to kill him, wouldn't he be exceedingly watchful now that he has returned to Nur?" Beulleu had a face that reminded others of a stranded fish, and a personality to match.

"He gives no indication of it." Effrom felt confident in sharing his assessment. "On the several occasions I observed him, I could not see that he was taking any special precautions save for keeping the flying creature always close by. Perhaps he feels that his elderly human and thranx friends are shield enough."

"Or more likely," Ambreleon declared, "he remains unaware of our strength and persistence and believes we were dealt a mortal blow during the fight at the shuttleport."

Tuoela nodded. "So much the better for us if he thinks we are all dead, disabled, or disbanded. It is entirely conceivable he cannot imagine the depth of commitment those of us who survived have to the Order." Muted but steadfast rumbles of affirmation rose from the congregation as she turned to a roly-poly employee of one of New Riviera's most respected research companies.

"What news of the Purity?"

"It still comes." The man's voice was high and squeaky, as if he dwelled in a state of perpetual fear. His ruthlessness and ability were not compromised by his vocal shortcomings, nor by the fact that despite his intellectual skills he qualified as a borderline psychopath. "Continued corroboration comes from our covert contacts on Earth." His eyes rolled heavenward. "Would that I might live to see its arrival and be drawn into the great nothingness! The meddler cannot stop it. Nothing can stop it." In a quiet paroxysm of semireligious ecstasy he lowered his gaze and shut his deep-sunk eyes tightly. "All will be wiped clean and remade."

"Nevertheless," Tuoela reiterated sternly, "we of the Order are committed to ensuring that the Purity encounters nothing that could prevent or slow it from fulfilling its destiny in this small corner of the cosmos. That means removing the meddler and the enigma he represents from the scheme of possibilities." As she addressed the gathering the fragrance of the wind whirling around them changed from peach to cupuraçu.

"This should not be so difficult, now that we have a better idea of what we are dealing with. We do not have to confront an army. Two men, two flying creatures, one woman, and one thranx. Several times we have underestimated the ability of this small group to forcibly reject absolution. It is a mistake we will not make again."

"How do you propose to proceed?" Though Canodoce dwarfed the rotund researcher, he did not consider himself the other man's superior. Within the Order, all were equal. In death, in the Purity, they would be exactly the same. It was a soothing thought. Those who believed their mission was to prepare the way for death did not fear it.

"We must deal with them separately." Tuoela was remembering. "When we tried to take them that day at the shuttleport they were able to concentrate their defenses and render help and support to one another. The big man and the thranx are clever, but they are old. I fear the small flying creatures more." She nodded in M'dbane's direction. "Though it seems that very little specific information is available on them, Olu has done some valuable research on the creatures that should aid us considerably when we confront them this time. The woman we nearly killed the first time. She presents no problem. It is the meddler himself who continues to present the real difficulty."

"How do you plan for us to take him?" Truth be told, while helping to maintain the watch on the healing woman, Ambreleon had not given the winding up of the business much thought.

"There are a number of options, all of which will be exercised if necessary." Tuoela's unbending confidence was an inspiration to them all. "This time nothing is being left to chance." She smiled grimly, more she-wolf than saleswoman.

"I have even made arrangements to bring in professional help."

CHAPTER

14

It was an odd group.

Tse-Mallory noticed them as soon as they entered the shop. In the back, the two sets of simple clothing he had ordered were in the process of being soft-cast from the holo the proprietor had taken of his customer. Tse-Mallory could have come back when they were ready, but since the entire process took less than twenty minutes from customization to conclusion, he had decided to wait. To kill time, he amused himself examining, trying on, and pricing the vast assortment of accessories available for the outfits he had ordered.

The peculiar troupe that had wandered in did not look like they wanted to kill time.

Their very blandness nearly caused him to let down his guard. That was their intent, of course. A couple of matronly women; a decidedly senior citizen who flaunted his long, double-pointed beard; a chatty younger couple, and a single street singer radiating music from his headband did not at first glance appear to pose a threat to anyone or anything. What gave them away was the incongruity of their congress: one would never expect to encounter the street musician, for example, in the company of the old man, or the younger couple with the pair of matrons. Had they entered the shop separately, Tse-Mallory might never have taken notice. But they all came in together, almost pushing to get through the single portal. As soon as they were inside, they went from the comparative silence of their collective entrance to all talking at once.

Culturally and socially it was a bit off. Just sufficiently skewed to set off internal alarms in someone like Tse-Mallory. Evincing no outward unease, he ambled toward the back of the store. Perfectly normal for someone in his situation to want to check on the progress of his order. Perfectly natural for him to step behind the counter. The member of the staff he intercepted started to say something. As she did so Tse-Mallory smiled, leaned toward her, put a finger to his lips, and whispered, "Get on the floor. Now."

Her eyes got very wide. "Is this a robbery? We have nothing to steal except equipment and fabric."

"I wish it were a robbery. I think it's something more. Something that doesn't involve you or your establishment." Out of the corner of an eye he detected movement behind him. "Not that it will matter to these people. Get down or get shot."

Then he was whirling, spinning, and ducking all in the same incredibly rapid motion as he drew a pistol from his pocket.

The first shot, fired by one of the two matrons, was overeager. Though she took careful aim, in her hurry to extract her weapon she had fumbled the draw. It was that motion that had alerted Tse-Mallory to the fact that the curious cluster of presumed patrons was intent on something other than casual shopping. The discharge from his pistol sizzled air as it cleaved her skull just above an elaborately shadowed right eye.

Chaos erupted inside the small shop. Harkening to Tse-Mallory's warning, the clerk had dropped to the floor. She had her hands over her ears and was undertaking, with some success, to scream. Sheltered behind the counter, constantly in motion, Tse-Mallory took out his assailants one by one. While it was apparent in the course of the firefight that all of them were experienced in the handling of arms, formal weapons training was not the same as actual battlefield experience.

Bits and pieces of counter and wall, but not of Tse-Mallory, went flying. One struck the poor prone employee hard enough to make her gasp. Her nonstop screaming was only one component of the auditory madness that filled the shop. In back, the proprietor and his assistant did the usual stupid thing by sticking their heads out to see what was happening. For their trouble the assistant acquired a hole in his chest and his employer a severe concussion.

Both of the older women were down. So was the senior citizen, who had proven surprisingly agile but far from invulnerable. The street singer's severed head lay in one place and his body in another. The headband continued to pump out music. As for the young couple, they rose from the little available cover they had found to charge straight toward the counter. It was a suicide rush. Tse-Mallory's interest in their motivation did not prevent him from rolling to his right out of their line of fire and shooting them both down.

Rising slowly amid the carnage, he took stock of himself. A couple of close calls had resulted in wounds that looked bad but were in reality little more than bloody nicks. Good thing he had new clothing on order, he mused. That was assuming he could persuade the stunned proprietor to finish the job.

Stepping out from behind the counter, pistol gripped tightly at the ready, Tse-Mallory checked those bodies that still had their heads. If these people wanted him dead so badly, why had they not simply bombed the entire building? But a bombing on peaceful New Riviera would doubtless have attracted investigative attention from all across the planet. Therefore it was reasonable to assume they did not want to draw that kind of attention to themselves. Which left hanging the critical question—who were 'themselves'?

A quick check of the pockets of the dead told him nothing. What information and identification he was able to access was consistent in its uniformity. Based on what he found, it seemed as if he had been marked for assassination by as mundane a bunch of citizens as could be found in the city.

That was when old memories gave birth to a terrible suspicion. Still holding the pistol, he lifted his left arm to his mouth and addressed the communit on his wrist. Sartorial replacement could wait. With luck, his fear would not be confirmed. As he spoke to the pickup he was heading for the door. Behind him, the stunned shop owner was trying to render aid to his badly wounded assistant and shell-shocked salesgirl. Tse-Mallory would have to let him get on with it by himself.

His own concerns ran much deeper.

They closed in around Truzenzuzex while he was in the park. Lacking the need for any additional personal supplies for the forthcoming journey, he had chosen to wait in more amenable and relaxing surroundings for Tse-Mallory to finish his business in the nearby shopping arcade. The philosoph was taking his ease on one of the many longitudinal benches set out in the park to accommodate his kind when he noticed the trio coming toward him.

Their approach was restrained—and they had probably rehearsed it thoroughly—but that could not keep them from occasionally glancing furtively in his direction. One or two glances he could appreciate. Nur/New Riviera was a human colony world. Thranx, while they could be found in numbers in the equatorial regions, were not to be encountered everywhere. But his presence in Sphene was not so extraordinary as to draw nervous, fleeting looks one after another.

Then there was the couple approaching from the opposite direction. Though ostensibly wholly absorbed in each other, they too cast sporadic glances in the direction of the elderly thranx sprawled on the bench. Raising his head, he idly surveyed the remainder of his surroundings. His peripheral vision, far superior to that available to any human, quickly detected several individuals coming toward him from still another direction. Taken together, it was clear to him that the trio, the couple, and the advancing individuals had one thing and only one thing in common.

They happened to be converging on the spot where he was lying.

Easing off the bench, he gathered all six legs beneath him and started off in the one direction that was not occupied by humans coming toward him. While this corner of the park was not deserted, neither was it crowded. The three and two and more who were closing in on him might be doing so with the intent of meeting up with one another. Or it might be nothing more than a mathematical coincidence. Truzenzuzex did not like convergences that placed him at the center of strange coincidences. In any event, it would be easy enough to find out if he *was* the focus of their attention. He would walk away from them, they would pass behind and ignore him, or . . .

The sonic burst that shattered the trunk of the small tree he stepped behind was more than enough to confirm that last suspicion.

He was virtually surrounded and there was nowhere to run. Seeing weapons being drawn, the few other visitors in the vicinity began running in all directions or ducked down behind decorative boulders and trees. Ignoring these panicky citizens, the humans who had been closing in on the elderly thranx charged toward their quarry. Several of the bystanders who had taken cover were already using their communits to report the violent encounter to the police and to the media. While their rapid responses were to be commended, they would do the target of the belligerent humans no good. The philosoph would be diced and sliced before the first police arrived.

Off to his right, the fleeing philosoph noticed a hole in the ground. He had no idea what it was or where it might lead, but to a thranx salvation instinctively lies below. Cutting in that direction, he dove into the opening as sonic and neuronic bursts ripped up the landscaping in his wake.

The tunnel was lined with smooth ceramic alloy. His feet would have clicked noisily against it if not for the several centimeters of dirty water that filled the curved surface underfoot. Patently unable to go back, he would go forward. As he ran he cursed his own self-confidence. Whereas his old friend Tse-Mallory never went anywhere without a weapon, the philosoph considered even a small gun an unnecessary encumbrance on a civilized world. Would that he were presently so encumbered!

Restive men and women gathered at the opening to the cavity. Heedless of his own safety, one man straightaway ducked inside. He was back in a couple of minutes, his clothes and hands stained with brown water and dripping muck.

"He's gone. I can't even hear him."

The scholarly-looking older gentleman who was the nominal leader of the attack squad wore a grim expression as he surveyed the landscaped terrain to the north of the opening.

"We'll never catch him in the conduit. Its diameter restricts us to advancing hunched over, but it's plenty high enough for a thranx to run full out."

"The philosoph is old," another man pointed out. "He'll get tired and slow down."

The leader turned to him. "You weren't at the fight at the shuttleport. I was. This is not your ordinary thranx elder." Turning back to the park environment, he studied their immediate surroundings. "The police are liable to be here any minute. We can't be found together. Spread out. North and east, I think, are the most likely places for this conduit to emerge. Search the near shores of Town Lake and Claris Pond, find where drainage empties out, and wait there. Sooner or later, he'll show himself."

The group promptly split up, some to search the shore of the nearby ornamental lake, others the park's decorative pond, two to wait by the opening where their quarry had taken refuge in case he decided to backtrack. The group leader was not worried about dividing his forces. A successful resolution to the ambush required only one weapon, one shot. As soon as the thranx stuck his antennaed head out of one of the conduit's openings, it would be blown off.

No one was more aware of that than their quarry himself. As soon as it became clear that he was not being followed, Truzenzuzex slowed his pace. The small beam that was part of the communit secured around his left truarm provided more than enough light for him to find his way. Waving back and forth above his head, his antennae kept him continuously apprised of the distance between his head and the conduit's ceiling. Unlike a human, he did not have to constantly look up to keep from bumping his skull.

While all of this was reassuring, it did not ensure his safety. If he was not being pursued down the drainage channel, he could simply halt and call for assistance from Tse-Mallory, Flinx, or the local authorities. On the other hand, if his attackers did come in after him, he would be trapped beyond help. And in the closed confines of the conduit their aim would not have to be very precise to take him out.

In such circumstances, waiting was rarely the best thing to do. Never concede the initiative to your enemy. He needed to get out. How to do that safely was a matter of some concern. He would be most vulnerable at the moment of emergence. The way forward might be devoid of assailants—or as soon as he stuck his head out he might find it locked in the crosshairs of their weapons. The trouble was that the only way to determine if there was any danger was to expose himself to it. From a very young age he had learned that inviting hostile fire was not the best way to ascertain the enemy's strength and position.

Squatting in the cold, dirty water he contemplated his options. He had come a considerable distance. There was no telling how far it was to the drain's exit. He certainly could not see the end. Confronted with such a situation a human would see itself as having two choices: to go forward or to go back. Since his attackers were all human, it was likely they would ponder the same two scenarios. However, he was not human. Other options were open to him. The sooner he settled on one, the more time he would have to explore its possibilities before it also occurred to his assailants.

While he was weaponless, his thorax pouch did hold a handful of useful instruments and tools. The cutter would be useful as a weapon only at very close quarters. Meanwhile, it did serve to burn a nice oval hole in the tough but thin ceramic ceiling of the conduit. Removing a meter-wide section and setting it to one side, Truzenzuzex began to dig. It was a skill at which his ancient ancestors had been especially proficient. Though there was not much call for it in the modern world, it was an ability that was innate and could not be forgotten. Helpfully, the soil overhead was soft and largely devoid of rocks—just what one might expect to encounter in a park that had been heavily and repeatedly landscaped.

More than an hour later, having avoided the attentions of the police who had been summoned in response to the earlier shooting, his intent pursuers were still guarding the entrance to the conduit where their quarry had vanished as well as the location where it drained into Claris Pond. They were fidgety but patient. The philosoph had to show himself sooner or later, via one exit or the other. When he did emerge they would be waiting for him.

None of them was watching the distant pedestrian intersection where Truzenzuzex rejoined Tse-Mallory. Having calmly covered the distance from the bloodbath in the clothing shop, Tse-Mallory had contacted his companion via communit. A few passersby glanced in the direction of the philosoph, their curiosity drawn not by his species but by his current personal appearance.

Upon first catching sight of his companion, Tse-Mallory reacted similarly. "What happened to *you*? You're a mess."

"And you, *tr!llk,* are bleeding." The philosoph gestured with a tru-hand at the shallow but unsettling crimson gashes that decorated his friend's arms and shoulders. "Were the choice up to me, I think I would opt for a tidier tailor."

Reaching up to his face, Tse-Mallory rubbed at one bloody patch of skin. "These scratches aren't a consequence of a bad fitting. A handful of Sphene's everyday upstanding citizens just tried to kill me."

The thranx nodded, a gesture his kind had long ago adopted soon after Amalgamation. "How interesting. Exactly the same thing just happened to me. What a coincidence—except that is most unlikely to be the case." Resplendent compound eyes peered up at Tse-Mallory's brilliant blue single lenses. "Average-looking citizens wielding an uncharacteristic array of weaponry attempt to murder both of us in broad daylight. Do such circumstances remind you of anything?"

Tse-Mallory nodded slowly. "A certain day and time more than a year ago. The fanatics of the Order of Null who wanted to kill Flinx to keep him from trying to stop or divert the Great Evil. The same kind of nondescript but obsessed people we had to contend with at the shuttleport."

He looked around. None of the pedestrians meandering through the intersection appeared threatening or on the verge of suddenly resorting to an orgy of unexpected violence.

Truzenzuzex gestured accord. "My feeling at the time was that once Flinx was safely offworld and on his way, then these deluded and confrontational folk would retire to whatever fatalistic conclaves they favor and we would hear no more from them."

Tse-Mallory nodded. "Plainly an incorrect supposition. The only reason they'd have for trying to kill us would be to prevent us from being of assistance to Flinx."

Antennae weaving, the thranx stood up on his four trulegs, the better to bring his face closer to that of his human companion. "Flinx can take care of himself, I think. He has matured considerably in the ways of society, and repeated conflict has heightened his special senses while sharpening his singular abilities."

Tse-Mallory looked troubled. "I wasn't worried—about Flinx."

As the human turned his attention to his communit the full meaning of his observation struck home to Truzenzuzex.

"Clarity . . . ," the philosoph clicked through clenched mandibles.

They waited until Scrap had descended to land on his mistress's shoulder. Previous experience and subsequent research had shown that the safest way to neutralize the dangerous Alaspinian minidrag was to incapacitate it at the same time as its owner. Taking no chances, the self-sealing net they released from the boat was big enough to envelop the woman, the flying snake, and the male friend riding the sunfoil parallel to hers.

They were too far from shore for anyone on the beach or the slope below the medical convalescent facility to hear her screams or his curses. When the two captives tried to contact local emergency authorities via their separate communits, they discovered that all outgoing signals in their immediate vicinity had been blocked. The net that had been employed had been chosen with great care. It was flexible yet sturdy, self-sealing but not dangerously constricting. Insofar as their research had allowed them to determine, the members of the Order charged with carrying out the abduction believed that the material was impervious to the corrosive effects of the minidrag's venom.

A net had been utilized instead of direct deadly force because it was vital to keep the woman alive. Long enough, at least, to serve the purpose.

Seeing that there was nothing to be gained by screaming, Clarity went quiet as she, Scrap, and Barryn were hauled in like so many netted fish. The delicate sunfoils made faint crunching sounds as the net collapsed around them. At the same time as she was concentrating on her fear, hoping Flinx would perceive it, she spoke hurriedly to Barryn.

"I'm sorry, Tam, to get you mixed up in all this."

In spite of Flinx's unexpected arrival he had insisted in seeing her through the last stages of her recovery. "I helped nurse you through the past couple of months," he declared, "and even if you dump me for this creepy offworlder, I'm not giving up on you until you marry him or run off with him."

She kept Flinx abreast of the medtech's persistence, of course.

"Give him credit for perseverance," Flinx responded. "Let him down easy. I don't like to see people hurt, and I know you don't either." For a brief moment his thoughts went somewhere else. "I've come to understand how complicated relationships can get, especially when you don't expect them to develop the way they sometimes do. Especially when you're apart from someone for a long time and thrust into difficult circumstances. Things—happen. We're all human. At least, I used to think so," he added ruefully.

"It's going to take a few days to reprovision and refit elements of the *Teacher.* Meanwhile you might as well be nice to him. But not *too* nice," he had concluded, admonishing her.

Struggling ineffectually with entangling strands of net as Scrap's wings beat alternately against her shoulder and his back, Barryn tried to twist around within their constricting prison to meet her gaze.

"Mixed up in *what*? What are you involved in, Clarity? Something illegal?"

"In a manner of speaking." She spoke as they were pulled through the water toward a waiting boat. "But not on my part. Or on Flinx's, even though it's him they want."

"'They'?" The medtech looked further confused. Then his expression darkened. "I knew there was something wrong with that skinny offworlder the minute I set eyes on him. I could feel it."

He could feel you, she thought, but said nothing.

Having unexpectedly dialed into a scenario that fit his hopes, Barryn was loath to let it go. "What is it? Illegal pharmaceuticals? Unregistered genensplices? Straightforward smuggling? What's his line, this *skewnk* Flinx of yours? And how are you mixed up in it?"

"They're going to try to use me to get to him," she explained with a serenity that was utterly alien to their present circumstances. "Or else maybe they're just going to kill me."

That quieted him for a moment. "What do you mean, 'get to him'? They want him? For what?"

They were very close to the boat now, she saw. Soon they would be hauled aboard. Or dispatched, though she was fairly confident her first assumption was the correct one: that their intention was to use her as bait.

"They want to eliminate him. Because he's trying to save the galaxy. Trying to preserve civilization. They call themselves the Order of Null." She swallowed water, coughed. How could she explain her personal involvement with the approaching apocalypse in the time remaining to them?

"There's something coming this way out of intergalactic space. It eats planets, suns, whole star systems. Whole galaxies. It will consume this one unless it can somehow be stopped or diverted. Somehow, in some way, Flinx believes he is the key to the one small, slim chance of doing so. Incredibly knowledgeable individuals of multiple species have confirmed this to me. They can't explain it, but they can confirm it." She cringed as an unseen winch started to haul them up out of the water, crumpled sunfoils and all. Several times she and Barryn were banged against the side of the capture boat. Fortunately it had a low freeboard and their bumpy ascent was a brief one.

Initially too stunned by her words to comment, Barryn finally found his voice again. It was commendably calm. Or his composure might have been attributable to simple shock.

"That's the most insane thing I've ever heard, Clarity, and I've spent a lot of time working with mental patients. How can you believe such nonsense? In all the time we've known each other I've never seen or suspected that you harbored anything like that kind of intellectual frailty. I mean, step back if you can and look at what you just *said.* You don't really expect me to believe any of it, do you?"

Swinging around toward the stern of the capture craft, the power winch deposited its catch brusquely on the smooth, seamless surface of the rear deck. Peering out between the net's resilient fibers, she noticed a quartet of onlookers staring down at them from the boat's upper level. If they were aware of Scrap's capabilities, they were doubtless keeping their distance intentionally.

"You can believe as you wish or not, Tam." She was tired from fighting the water and the net. The minidrag's wings beat furiously against her neck and shoulders as Scrap made futile efforts to free himself.

"Clarity Held!" Holding a small amplifier card in front of his mouth, a portly gentleman with a deceptively mild mien addressed her from the upper level. "We apologize for some roughness in the process of bringing you aboard, but this was deemed the safest and most inconspicuous way of remanding you to our charge. We are—"

"I know who you are." She cut him off. "You're fanatics of the worst kind. You have no respect for logic or reason and you worship death and destruction."

The man and his companions looked indignant. "We 'worship' nothing," he took pains to correct her. "Seeing filth and ignorance and waste all around us, we welcome the Purity that is coming. That is all. Our philosophy is entirely practical and scientific. In contrast, yours, that of the great mass of deluded sentients, and most importantly that of your friend Philip Lynx, is to deny the impending cleansing. It does not really matter because nothing can stop it.

"We believe in leaving nothing to chance, however, and as there is a very slight theoretical possibility that this individual might somehow be able to interfere with the efficiency of the cleansing, we feel it is our obligation to brush away even so minuscule a probability."

Struggling with the tangle of net, she managed to climb to her feet. The shroudlike nature of the overlapping folds did not escape her. "You've tried that before, more than once. Each time, some of you ended up dead."

The man stiffened, but his demeanor remained unruffled. "Mistakes were made. The abilities of this Flinx person were underestimated. We will not make such mistakes again. Nothing has been left to chance. He will die. He has to die. The only difference between him and the rest of us is that he will die a fragment of time sooner.

"We could have killed you soon after he fled from Nur, Clarity Held. It was decided not to do so because it was thought that under certain circumstances you might prove more useful alive than dead. Events are soon to confirm this supposition."

Where were Bran Tse-Mallory and the Eint Truzenzuzex? she found herself wondering. She was pleased when they had stopped hovering over her months ago. Now she felt their absence keenly. Had they already been slain by other members of the Order? Knowing man and thranx as she did, she found that hard to believe. But the Order was lethal, cunning, and most dangerous of all, subtle. After the battle at the shuttleport more than a year ago they had seemingly disappeared. With Flinx safely away offworld she had been lulled into what was now clearly a false sense of security. Despite their wisdom and experience, were her two venerable guardians equally susceptible to such deception?

A man and a woman emerged from the boat's forward cabin. Both were dressed in flexible, dull-gray security suits that looked robust enough to be military issue. As soon as they drew near enough, an enraged Scrap spat in their direction. The tiny stream of venom struck the suited woman square on her suit's faceplate. Startled, she stumbled backward a couple of steps. But the powerful toxin did not penetrate the special transparent alloy, although it did eat away a small part of the outermost layer.

As the man raised the pistol he was holding, a frantic Clarity moved to position herself inside the folds of the net between the muzzle of the projectile weapon and her pet.

"Don't shoot him! There's no need. I'll make sure he doesn't attack again."

"It doesn't matter." The man spoke casually to his companion. "The amount of venom it stores in its mouth is limited. Let him expel until the poison sac is empty and then we'll pull them out of the net."

Barryn finally managed to get his legs under him and step forward. Or at least as far forward as the enfolding net would permit. "Look, I don't know who you people are or what kind of lunatic farce Clarity says you've chosen to venerate, but neither she nor I have anything to do with whatever trouble that redheaded offworlder has stirred up." Using both hands, he held up two handfuls of the fine-mesh net in which he was imprisoned. "Just get us out of here and we can discuss whatever concerns you have like civilized human beings. If this Flinx person is mixed up in something illicit, maybe we can help you sort it, and him, out."

Clarity looked at him sharply. She turned toward him just in time to see the woman point the pistol she was holding at the medtech and blow his head off. Not off, precisely. More into glutinous blobs of flesh and bone. In any event the effect was the same. The headless body remained standing for a moment, blood spurting from the severed neck like some perverted fountain. Then it collapsed in a broken heap, not unlike the sunfoils.

Clarity did not scream. Some time ago, Flinx had introduced her to something that was genuinely worth screaming about: the very incarnation and manifestation of evil and annihilation whose approach these people sought to facilitate. So the explosive, messy demise of the man who had been standing next to her did not stagger her. Only filled her with emptiness.

"You didn't have to kill him," she observed in dismay. "He was just a medtech who liked me. You could have let him go. He didn't believe in you even when I explained who you are and what you're about."

"He saw us," replied the rotund speaker through his amplifier card. "He saw faces. You are going to disappear, and it was apparent that he was enamored enough of you to follow up on your disappearance. Above nearly all else, we of the Order value our anonymity. Sometimes distasteful steps must be taken to preserve it."

As the two suited figures reached the net and began working with the folds, Scrap kept spitting at them, trying to bring them down. His aim was impeccable, but the caustic venom could not penetrate the multiple layers of the military visors. As the man working the net had foretold, after a while the minidrag's store of venom grew exhausted. At that point they were able to handle the fighting, squirming serpentine shape without concern. Manipulated by four strong hands, Scrap was maneuvered into a transparent double-walled box whose airholes were offset to prevent him from spitting his toxin outside. Clarity had her wrists fastened behind her and her ankles secured with flexible straps to a small horizontal crossbar. Thus bound, she could walk but not run.

The forward cabin was large enough to accommodate all six of the boat's occupants. None struck her as experienced sailors, but on central Nur's placid and cultivated waters oceangoing skills were hardly a requirement for operating a watercraft. The boat's integrated automated systems handled any required seamanship, leaving its passengers free to enjoy the experience.

A large triangular *sprowel* had been thrown over Clarity's shoulders. As the thousands of filaments of the specially treated quasi-animate hydrophonic material reacted to the water on her skin and began to warm and dry her, firm hands guided her toward one of the boat's consoles. Beyond, through the craft's curving foreport, she could see the shoreline and in the distance the familiar profile of the rehabilitation facility where she had spent so many months and subsequent visits convalescing, healing, and recovering. For all that she could presently access, its facilities might as well have been situated in a different star system.

Poor Barryn, she found herself thinking. If she'd had any inkling the Order was still interested in Flinx, she would have shunned the medtech from the first day he had paid any serious attention to her. It had been his misfortune to become infatuated. With a start she remembered what Flinx had once told her: people who found themselves swept up in his orbit often came to an unpleasant end. Exactly that had happened to the well-meaning Tambrogh Barryn. Now it appeared that the same was to be true of her.

Having put away the no-longer-needed amplifier, the deceptively innocent-looking man spoke to her as his hands brushed over the quaint manual controls on the console.

"I'm sure by now you're wondering what has happened to the singular pair of guardians who have been looking out for you these past many months. We're about to find out." His smile was almost regretful. "As I said previously, sometimes steps must be taken."

Even if she could have broken free of her captors there was nowhere to run, and she could not swim with her wrists and ankles bound. She could only stand and watch and listen as the speaker contacted the first of the Order's two specialized assassination squads. Outwardly she was as calm and composed as anyone in her situation could be. Inside she was as frightened and scared as anyone in her situation should be.

If not exactly reassuring, the first words to echo through the cabin at least did not send her into a panic.

"What of the old thranx?" the portly man inquired of the image of a slender female shape that materialized above the console.

The attractive woman sounded peeved. "We had him surrounded in Claris Park, but he ran into a drainage conduit. We have both ends blocked. Eventually he'll have to emerge, and we'll be here. Of course, we're not waiting on that eventuality. We are presently assembling the appropriate materials to allow us to go in after him. One way or the other, the matter will be settled before tomorrow morning."

"Compliments and blessings." The speaker adjusted the controls. This time the image that appeared in the cabin was that of a young man who looked to be barely out of his teens—except for his eyes, which looked older than the rest of him.

"Salutations, passerby." Like his tone, the youth's expression was gloomy.

The speaker noted both immediately. "The esteemed researcher gave you trouble?"

The younger man's reply was remarkable for its impassiveness. He might as well have been reciting a grocery list. "You might say that. Six of the Order tried and true—dead. As to the target I can report nothing conclusive. He may be dead within the shop. Or possibly wounded and on the way to hospital. I don't know because we as yet have been unable to get one of our own inside to inspect the wreckage. The shop owner and his staff are reportedly traumatized and under constant police and medical watch. The police have also, not unexpectedly, sealed off the location and are proving uninformative. There is a lockdown on the scene that applies to the general media as well. As soon as we have more precise information it will be communicated."

Following a further brief exchange the speaker signed off. It was only when he turned to the eldest of the boat's passengers that Clarity realized for the first time that the man with whom she had been conversing was not the leader of the group.

The short, white-bearded senior to whom the speaker now deferred looked physically feeble. Despite the best efforts of modern medicine, he suffered from curvature of the upper spine. He had a long, lined, unyielding face that reminded her of a petulant camel. One hand rested on the rounded hilt of a cane fashioned from a dark copper alloy. Familiar as she was with the fanatical organization that had abducted her, she would not have been surprised to learn that the walking stick contained within its cylindrical body several self-propelled and highly volatile projectiles.

"Orel?" Along with the speaker, the attention of every acolyte on the boat was focused on the cane bearer.

The old man grunted softly. "The thranx is contained. The man is dead, injured, or on the run. There is nothing to be gained by delay. Events are put in motion. We should proceed."

A general sigh rose from the assembled members of the Order; an exhalation of contented decay. Resting both hands on the top of the cane, one on top of the other, the Elder blinked across at Clarity.

"Since you know who we are, you know that we must deal with the anomaly who calls himself Flinx. We are bound to do this. We have no

choice. Personally, I wish it could be otherwise. While the Order antic-
ipates and welcomes the Purity that is coming, sometimes there is
groundwork we dislike having to lay. The interference aura that has
been blocking your communit will be deactivated. You will contact him
and supply him with a location we will provide where he can find you."

"So you can kill him," she responded tightly.

The old man nodded resignedly. "Yes. So we can kill him."

"And then you'll kill me."

His response was a shrug. "Perhaps. Perhaps not. Your fate remains
a matter of some controversy. Once the anomaly has been eliminated,
the matter of your continued existence essentially becomes moot."

"Don't play with me," she growled defiantly. "You killed poor Tam
just because he could maybe identify some of you later. Why should I
think you'll do any different with me?"

Casting an eye in the direction of the speaker, the Leader shook his
head slowly. The latter looked abashed. "Poor tactics," the old man murmured as he turned back to Clarity. "Once this Philip Lynx is dealt with,
there may be some leeway in options. I can of course promise nothing
until then." And then, quite unexpectedly, his creased and furrowed visage broke out into an unmistakable leer.

Ever since she and Barryn had been seized, Clarity had felt a certain
degree of fear. This was the first time she had felt as if she was going to
lose her breakfast.

"I'm not going to call Flinx," she declared rebelliously. "If you contact him, I'm not going to say anything." She strove her hardest to make
the glare she bestowed on the vile Elder actually sear his flesh. "I'm most
especially not going to tell him to travel to any coordinates you provide!"

The hoped-for force of her glare had absolutely no effect on the old
man. "Yes you are," he demurred gently. Turning, he nodded at the
semicircle of acolytes.

A young woman came toward Clarity. In her severe and unadorned
fashion, the true believer was almost pretty. She was holding something
in her right hand. A device.

"Hold her," she instructed her associates. Ready hands moved to re-
strict Clarity's freedom of movement. Her muscles contracted as she
tensed. The device was pushed forward.

Out in the middle of the lake her shrieks went unheard except by a few startled, long-necked *pinsoir* gliders and a helplessly writhing, securely caged Scrap. While their volume was muted by the cabin's soundproofing, the pitch of the recurrent screams was shrill enough to make the broad-winged fliers veer off to the west and give the source of the frightful noise a wide berth.

CHAPTER
15

According to the readback the call-in was coming from Clarity's communit. But the visage that took shape above his wrist was not that of Flinx's beloved. Instead, he found himself gazing back at the countenance of a pleasant-faced, slightly rotund middle-aged man. Confused, he switched the image from full dimensional to flat.

"Who are you? And where's Clarity Held, the owner of the unit you're calling from?"

"All will be explained," the man replied soothingly. "My name is not important. All you need to know about me is that more than a year ago you tried to kill me at a regional shuttleport. You did succeed in killing or injuring several of my close friends and associates. Of course, we were at the same time trying to kill you, so it would be futile to waste time debating the situational ethics. At least, we feel so. We were not at all certain we would have the chance to kill you again. We thank you for returning to New Riviera so that we might have the opportunity to realize our earlier intentions."

Delivered in a calm, all but tranquil tone, this was such a dumbfoundingly frank declaration that Flinx found himself momentarily speechless. When he did finally manage to reply, it was to repeat the name he had already spoken.

"*Clarity.*" This time his tone was ominous instead of uncertain.

"Certainly," the man responded briskly. "It is implicit that you will do nothing in the absence of confirmation."

The image rotated as the other communit's visual pickup was re-aligned. It was plain from the way the viewpoint shifted that the unit it-self was being held loosely and was not presently on someone's wrist, least of all that of the portly individual who had greeted Flinx.

Very soon the scene steadied. It was clear and, as verified by his own unit, natural and unaltered. Clarity sat in a chair in the center of the image. Her arms were secured behind her. She looked—bad. Her hair was a mess, the very modest amount of makeup she utilized daily was blurred and streaked in spite of the fact that contemporary cos-metics were designed to prevent such distortions, and her eyes were red and swollen from crying. Her clothes were distressed. It was obvi-ous she had been seriously mistreated. There was no blood, no visual evidence of anything as primitive as breaking or cutting. Whoever had abused her was too subtle for that. Her captors' methods were efficient, not prehistoric.

Raising her head from his shoulder, Pip straightaway began search-ing for the source of her master's sudden distress. That it was nowhere to be sensed only served to unsettle the minidrag further.

"You're from the Order of Null." The accusation emerged from be-tween clenched teeth. The allusion to multiple killings and the shuttle-port location also fit the time frame the caller had cited. There was no doubt in Flinx's mind who he represented. The other man proceeded to confirm it.

"We are *of* the Order of Null." More than a touch of self-importance tinged the terse correction as Flinx's view of Clarity was once more re-placed by the face of the implacable speaker. "We have neither the need nor the desire to kill your partner. Her location will be provided to you. You will come there now, immediately, without detour or hesitation. If you bring another soul with you, if you attempt to contact anyone for misguided assistance, if you try to notify the authorities down to and in-cluding the city sanitation department, we will cut her throat. Even as we speak, you are being watched and your personal communications are being monitored. You will not attempt to utilize them in any way, shape, or fashion. That extends to and includes the need for you to shut down any emergency beacons or locators." Flinx did not bother to look around. "Your subsequent movements and actions will be recorded to the best of our abilities. These I assure you are extensive."

Another voice reached Flinx via the remote aural pickup. Though dimmed by distance, its source was unmistakable.

"Don't do it, Flinx!" Clarity was yelling. "They'll kill me anyway after they kill you. Call the police and . . . !"

Her words were interrupted by a sharp sound. She fell silent. Flinx fought hard to keep his breathing steady. There was nothing he could do from the opposite end of a communications link. He could not reach through the tiny pickup and clutch the self-righteous speaker by the throat.

"Don't hurt her," he swallowed, "any more. I'll do whatever you ask."

"Of course you will." The speaker's voice brimmed with confidence. "You're a young man in love. Your heart and your hormones command your brain. You are convinced that you will somehow rescue her and avenge her treatment—none of which, I assure you, exceeded that which was necessary to advance the cause of this conversation. Who knows? Perhaps you will succeed. Perhaps subsequent to your arrival here we will somehow find a way to reach an accommodation satisfactory to all." His voice dropped slightly.

"Regardless of future developments, one thing is certain. If you do not start this way the instant this communication is terminated, the woman Clarity Held will be dead within minutes. We know that you have certain perceptive abilities. That you attempt to use them in the service of preventing the inevitable arrival of the cleansing is regrettable. Possibly you can somehow employ them to convince us that you are right and we are wrong. You are certainly welcome to try."

You have no idea, an incensed Flinx thought, *what I am capable of and how I am going to try.*

But he could not do it standing there in the lobby, ignoring the occasional curious glances of other patrons of the hotel where he had been staying since his return to Sphene.

"Give me the coordinates," he snarled at the communit.

While they were being downloaded he surreptitiously scanned the lobby's other occupants. That woman supposedly gazing into her private entertainment wraparound. The young couple chatting by the entrance. The preoccupied entrepreneur striding quickly toward the lifts. None stood out as agents of the Order. None were marked by suspicious emotions. Was he really being closely watched or was the threat nothing more than a clever ploy? It was a chance he could not take. No doubt his enemies knew that as well.

There was little he could do, in fact, beyond double-checking the coordinates that had been entered into his communit.

He did not have to announce his departure to the human clerk working the front desk, but it was a reasonable move. As long as he kept the encounter brief, even someone assigned to watch him was unlikely to think he might be using the opportunity to contact the authorities. As he approached the desk Flinx did his best to shield what he was doing with his communit from possible prying eyes.

"I'm in twenty-twenty." As he mumbled to the attentive clerk, he slipped a fragment of dull black memory no bigger than a fingernail paring out of his communit and onto the countertop. "Please hold this for a friend who will come to pick it up."

Before the clerk could respond with a question or reply Flinx had spun on his heel and was heading for the exit. If his actions *were* being monitored he dared not risk lingering at the counter to explain further. Any extended conversation might raise the suspicions of the Order's malign agents—assuming any were actually present. With Clarity's life at stake it was a chance he could not take. Just the hasty passing of the memory splinter he had furtively slipped out of his own communit constituted taking a big risk. But he felt he had to do *something*. If the Order was indeed monitoring his communications, he could not chance trying to contact Tse-Mallory or Truzenzuzex directly.

Notwithstanding the blunt orders he had been given, he could have delayed. He could have tried to stall, could have waited to see if they would contact him again to voice their impatience. If only it were not the life of his love that hung on such decisions. Despite the speaker's threat, Flinx didn't think they would kill her out of hand even if he was a little late. If they wanted him badly enough they would be hesitant to throw away their bait. But again, he could not take that chance.

Anyway, patience had never been one of his virtues.

He had not heard from his mentors all morning. With luck they would check in with him soon. When he failed to respond, he knew they would follow up in person. The hotel would be one of the first places they would look for him. By the time they arrived, any agents assigned to monitor his movements would have long since left to follow in his wake. Failing to find him at the hotel, Tse-Mallory and Truzenzuzex would routinely query the staff. The memory splinter Flinx had left behind would be handed over to them. Bran and Tru would react accordingly.

At least, that was the scenario he hoped would unfold. Anxiously as he anticipated it, he could not waste time or energy hoping it would come to pass.

Upon arriving in Sphene he had rented a skimmer in order to be able to easily visit Clarity at the outlying medical facility where she was finishing her term of convalescence. Even as he was climbing into it in the garage adjoining the hotel, he was sending the vehicle's AI the coordinates that had been supplied to him. Moments later he was outside the structure and airborne, climbing to the maximum allowable commuter height. Its destination programmed in, the craft turned and headed north out of the city.

Following the instructions he had been given, Flinx deactivated his communit's communications functions. He would speak with no one and allow no one to contact him lest Clarity's kidnappers somehow intercepted such a transmission, panicked, and decided to carry out their threat. His continuing silence would further confirm the significance of the recording he had left behind for Bran Tse-Mallory and the Eint Truzenzuzex.

Given luck and perseverance, he would be able to put off any irreversible action on the part of his expectant assassins until his friends arrived. In the absence of any direct communication between him and his mentors, their unexpected appearance would be a nasty surprise for the members of the Order. Everything depended, of course, on a concerned Bran and Tru seeking him out at the hotel, questioning the front desk, and recovering the memory splinter.

His head was pounding. The last thing he needed now was one of his severe headaches. He had only a general idea of how, in the event Tse-Mallory and Truzenzuzex did not arrive in time, he might save Clarity and himself. As their speaker had remarked, the members of the Order now realized he was capable of Certain Things.

With nothing more to do until the skimmer reached its destination, he forced himself to settle back in the pilot's seat. The grand and peaceful surrounds of the city of Sphene disclosed themselves around him, the sun-washed urban serenity in stark contrast to the emotions that were boiling inside him. He was only partly successful in his efforts to calm Pip. Those who wanted him dead would have to cope with her, too, he thought dourly.

As for his ability to do things, the Order of Null was about to find out the full extent of that Talent.

"I'm looking for a friend."

The hotel clerk regarded the visitor equably. "I'll need a little more information than that."

"Of course you will. His name is Philip Lynx. It's possible he is registered under a different name. But I can describe him easily. Quite tall, red hair, green eyes; and he is rarely without his pet: a small, brilliantly colored winged creature that often rides on his shoulder."

The clerk's expression brightened. "Oh, yes. I know the gentleman." He glanced to his left. "His rooms are vacant of life-forms at the moment." The clerk hesitated. "Wait. You are his—friend?"

"Absolutely," declared the stranger with fresh interest.

"Just a moment." Reaching into a drawer behind the counter, the clerk removed a small clear plastic vial. "He said that a friend of his would come to pick this up." One hand slid the container holding the black memory splinter across the polished blackwood. The visitor eyed it thoughtfully. "You are that friend, of course."

The visitor hesitated momentarily, then brightened. "I suppose so." The memory splinter disappeared into a carry pouch. "Thank you for your help. When I see my friend I'll thank him personally for your assistance." With that, the visitor turned and headed for the front exit.

Always glad to be of help to a guest, the clerk turned back to his work, convinced he had done the right thing.

Not long thereafter a distinctive pair of beings entered the lobby and approached the same counter. One was a burly human, the other an elderly thranx. Looking up from his monitor projections, the clerk smiled at the newcomers.

"May I help you? Do you require habitation?"

"Just information." The human was curt without being impolite. "A friend of ours has been staying here. We've been unable to contact him, which is not unusual. What is unusual is that his communit appears to have been shut down completely."

"Completely?" The clerk was professionally sympathetic. "That is disconcerting."

Tse-Mallory uttered a bad word. "It's worse than disconcerting, I'm afraid. Where our friend is concerned, and based on the kind of day my multilimbed friend and I have had so far, it could be a matter of life and death."

"Our friend does not answer his personal communit and we have not been able to contact him via your interchange." Standing back on his four trulegs, the thranx was just able to peer over the human-height counter. "Can you send someone to check his room, or allow us to go there with a member of your staff to look at it for ourselves?"

Anxious to please, the helpful clerk's right hand hovered over the relevant instrumentation. "What is your friend's name again?"

Tse-Mallory provided the alias Flinx had used when he had registered with Nurian Immigration upon arrival. At the mention of the name the clerk needed to wave only briefly at his instruments.

"The gentleman left here earlier. He did not check out and he hasn't returned."

The two visitors exchanged a glance, the thranx punctuating his look with a sharp gesticulation the clerk did not recognize.

"Did he happen to mention his intentions, or where he was going?" Truzenzuzex inquired tersely. The clerk shook his head. "Did he happen to leave anything behind?"

At this the clerk smiled. "Yes. A memory splinter. A friend would come to pick it up, he told me."

Man and thranx relaxed visibly. Tse-Mallory extended a gnarled hand palm upward across the counter. "That's good. I'll take it now, thanks."

A bewildered expression came over the clerk's countenance. "You can't. That is, I mean—his friend has already picked it up. Quite a while ago, in fact."

The tension among the pair of unusual visitors that the clerk had sensed a moment ago abruptly returned in full. "If you wouldn't mind," the thranx enunciated in perfect, almost colloquial terranglo, "it's very important that you describe this 'friend' to us."

"Everything you can remember about him." The human's stare was so forceful that the clerk found himself awed—and a little frightened.

"Certainly—sure," he stammered. "First of all, it was not a 'he' . . . ."

CHAPTER

16

Flinx pushed the skimmer to its legal limits. Every additional minute it took him to cover the distance between the city and the coordinates he had been given was another moment that Clarity remained in the unpredictable, unpleasant hands of the fanatics of the Order of Null. While from the time of their first encounter long ago they had struck him as a group that tortured only for a purpose, he had no intention of relying on that initial impression. At the same time he had to take care not to draw the attention of the city authorities who regulated travel in Sphene's vicinity. The consequent enforced delay was agony.

Pip was all over him as well as the interior of the skimmer. Restless and edgy, she would dash from him to one part or another of the craft's transparent canopy and back again, searching for the source of her master's continuing distress. He tried to settle her down, with only limited success. Permanently joined to him empathetically, he could not calm her if he could not calm himself. And no matter how hard he tried, he could not do that.

The other airborne travelers he shot past might be ignoring his high-speed, somewhat erratic flight. Or they might be raging at him. With the rented skimmer's internal communications deliberately disconnected to comply with the instructions he had been given, he had no way of knowing. Nor could anyone contact him via the personal communit he wore on his left wrist. Also in accordance with the Order's commands, he had disabled all of its functions, including the integrated emergency locator beacon. He did not even reach out with his Talent to the passengers of the increasingly infrequent transports he passed.

Having programmed the coordinates into the skimmer and instructed it to take the fastest point-to-point possible, he raced across lake and river, greenbelt preserve and densely wooded low hills. The craft did not begin to slow until he unexpectedly found himself cruising within the boundaries of one of the capital city's most upscale precincts. Expensive custom villas dotted thickly vegetated hillsides above a gently meandering river whose banks had been channeled, landscaped, and decorated to resemble Earth's fabled Arno.

Descending, the skimmer settled gently to ground on autopilot, touching down on the oval landing pad that fronted one such residence. The structure's two-story portico was an incongruous, slightly absurd, but perfectly rendered reconstruction of the Nymphaeum at Sagalassos, complete to trickling fountains. There was nothing of the ancient Roman about the skimmer's acknowledgment of arrival and touchdown, however. And the generously proportioned middle-aged human who waited to greet him was not clad in a toga. Flinx recognized the man immediately: it was the representative of the Order with whom he had spoken earlier.

As soon as the engine shut down Flinx exited the skimmer and strode over to confront him. He paid no attention to the pistol the man was pointing at him. Exiting from the building's main entrance, several other armed men and women came forward to join them. Much as he wanted to lash out, to flay them with his Talent, to try to sow fear and terror among them, he held back. He dared not act precipitously, especially if they really did have some notion of what he was capable of doing. For one thing, he could not yet sense if Clarity was even in the vicinity.

While he held firmly on to Pip and kept her as calm as he could, one of the men searched him for weapons. His roving hands were quick and professional. After removing Flinx's tool-laden belt, the frisker stepped back.

"He's not carrying nothing dangerous. Nothing obvious, anyway."

The portly speaker nodded. Looking up at the much taller, younger man who had emerged from the skimmer, he opened conversation. His tone was brisk and unafraid.

"Since we want you dead, you're probably wondering why we don't shoot you right here and now. Or why we are even taking the risk to meet with you in person."

Flinx kept his expression as neutral as he could. On his shoulder, Pip squirmed, sensing quiet hostility all around her. "The thought had occurred to me."

"First of all, we of the Order keep our promises," his host explained. "When I communicated with you I said that there might be a way for us to reach an accommodation. While our beliefs limit the range of options that are open to us, some do exist. We are more open to discussion now that you are here and we can kill you anytime. Second, there is certain knowledge we would like to have that is apparently available only to you."

Flinx became aware that the individual members of the armed faction surrounding him were eyeing him with a most peculiar mixture of anger and awe. Knowing who they were and the rough outlines of their beliefs, he could make a reasonable guess as to what kind of information the speaker was after.

"You want to know about the Great Evil that's coming this way. The 'Purity,' as you call it. The 'cleansing' that you worship."

A couple of the men and one of the women surrounding him actually lapsed into silent prayer. It was left to the speaker to articulate their craving.

"Our contacts in Commonwealth Science have only been able to provide details of an astronomical nature. So many parsecs purified, so many suns and so much interstellar hydrogen swept away." Never overtly belligerent even when the talk was of killing him, the speaker's voice abruptly took on a hint of unexpected longing.

"We yearn to know more about that which we strive to facilitate. We feel certain it cannot be wholly and absolutely inanimate. Surely something so vast and all-powerful must be controlled by a consciousness of equal magnitude! A thought process that underlies and directs. Unquestionably there must be more at stake than mere annihilation. There must be purpose, direction, rationale." Eyes alight with the fire of fanaticism searched the face of the barely restrained young man standing before him.

Flinx finally nodded. "Yes. Yes, there is. You're right. I've seen it. I've perceived it."

Excited looks and whispers were exchanged by his guards, though they were careful at all times to keep their weapons trained on him and the flying snake that remained wrapped around his right arm and shoulder.

"Alas, our sources have no access to such extra-physical possibilities." With eyes as hungry as his intellect, the speaker stared at the prisoner. "You must, you *have* to share what you know with us."

"So I will," Flinx agreed. "I'll tell you everything. But first, take me to Clarity."

"Yes, yes, of course! Even those who serve the Purity must not neglect good manners." Turning, the speaker led the way into the villa. The other members of the Order formed up as an escort on either side of Flinx as well as behind him. Under this heavy guard he was marched into the building.

Slender jets of gel-infused water played in the artificial streams that flanked both sides of the central hallway. At the far end, high double doors opened into an antechamber whose walls and ceiling were decorated in the style of ancient Imperial Rome, albeit a Rome that had been lavished with the latest in contemporary furnishings. Faux Aurelian-era mosaics danced and played on both sides of Flinx as he was led inward.

The next room, the villa's central chamber, had been emptied of furniture, its animated wall mosaics and paintings deactivated. Still more members of the Order were waiting for him. Among them was a singular old man with a bent back. Flinx focused on him immediately. Physically, he was a relic. From the standpoint of emotional strength, however, he easily dominated everyone else in the room. It was also significant that he was one of the very few present who was not visibly armed.

Sitting off to one side on a bench of ersatz marble, a rectangular transparent box held a supine serpentine shape. In a flash Pip spread her wings and, despite Flinx's efforts to restrain her, bolted from his shoulder. The winged form imprisoned inside the perforated, impervious container was alert and active even before she landed atop it. Though they could not make physical contact, mother and offspring proceeded to engage empathetically.

The contemptible folk filling the room would take no more chances with her than they had with Scrap, Flinx realized. It didn't matter. Their number was not important and at least for the moment their armaments were of no interest to him. The only thing that mattered was the solitary figure sitting isolated in the center of the chamber.

Sunlight filtering through a circular pane in the ceiling lit Clarity from above. She looked much as she had sounded over his communit— exhausted and abused. The damage that had been inflicted was visible only in her face—and her eyes. It took them, and her, a long moment to recognize him as he rushed toward her.

"F-Flinx?" She shook her head, blinked, and tried without much success to sound angry. "You shouldn't have come. Now that you're here they'll kill us both."

"Maybe," he muttered as he knelt in front of her. "Maybe not." He wanted to take her in his arms. He could have tried, though in her present state it would have been difficult to get even those rangy limbs around her.

From the neck down she was completely encased in a dirty gray foam that had hardened to a plastic-like consistency. Other than her head and neck, only her hands and feet had been left exposed. He started to reach for the foam casing. Her eyes widened.

"No, don't touch me!" She was trying hard not to cry. "If you try to tear or break or drill through the foam in any way, it will blow up!" She looked toward the watching Order members. "At least, that's what they told me when they were spraying it on."

A deepening chill washed through Flinx as he straightened and took a step back. Her captors were taking no chances. She was encased in enough material to bring down the entire building: a possibility that apparently did not bother those who had gone to the trouble of fitting her with the untouchable, volatile sheath.

A voice sounded nearby. The Elder had come up behind him.

"Having become all too familiar with your peculiar combative abilities, young man, we of course have taken appropriate steps." He pointed the cane he was holding at the terrified, immobilized woman seated before them. "She is encased in a latex-based high explosive, which has been intermingled with sensitized nanowiring. Attuned to the microscopic cabling are four button-sized wireless detonators taped to her thighs, any one of which can by itself set off the entirety of the so-lidified amalgam. If you attempt to penetrate the material to retrieve the triggers, the material will detonate. The detonators themselves have been individually randomly coded and locked, so they cannot be deac-tivated remotely."

Flinx digested this. "Then how can she be freed from the foam without setting it off?"

"An optical wormgrip can be slipped through the slight gap be-tween her body and the encasement to safely remove the detonators. They can then easily be switched off." The Elder smiled thinly. "Some-times simple mechanical procedures are more expedient than complex electronics." He indicated their surroundings. "We intentionally do not have a wormgrip anywhere on this property so you cannot take one of us hostage and demand that we bring it forth. We cannot be forced to turn over that which we do not have." Eyes that had seen much and were the harder for it met Flinx's.

"Once you have unburdened yourself of the knowledge we seek, someone will be sent to obtain and bring back the tool necessary to free her."

Flinx scrutinized the hardened explosive spume that had been sculpted around Clarity, looking for a weakness, looking for something the Order might have overlooked. The casing was not skintight—the Elder had explained that there was a gap between foam and body. They had to leave her room to breathe, to sweat, and to twitch a little. But there was no way he could get a hand, much less an arm, into and down the narrow gap between the solidified sheath and her neck, ankle, or leg. He could not get up inside the congealed foam to remove the detonators without the kind of flexible, specialized probe the old man had de-scribed. Even if he could have slipped a hand up inside he knew he would not be given the time to try.

If the Elder was telling the truth, deactivating four simple mechan-ical switches would be enough to completely eliminate the danger to the immobilized, imprisoned Clarity. Except Flinx could not reach them. Nor could she.

How to neutralize their captors and free her? Engaging them in combat would not secure her release. Even if he did strike, all one of them had to do was shoot or strike hard at the foam casing to set off the sensitive material and kill them all.

There was nothing he could do. Nothing, it seemed, except stall for time by complying with their request. Their eagerness grew palpable as other members began to edge nearer to the human who had perceived the Purity.

"Tell us of the holy place." The rotund speaker was pleading even as he brandished a lethal handgun in Flinx's direction.

"Speak to us of the coming cleansing!" Hands outstretched, palms upward, a woman beseeched the tall young man in their midst whom she was sworn to kill.

"What is it like? . . . Does it have shape and form? . . . Can you do more than sense its presence? . . ."

The cluster of killers was pathetic in their zeal. Their expressions, their importunate stares, their forthright emotions hung eagerly on whatever he might say even as he could perceive their desire to witness his demise. Even the Elder exhibited unfeigned emotion. Looking forward to and dedicating themselves to the pending death of every living thing in the galaxy, they were desperate to know the particulars of the onrushing instrument of destruction whose arrival they had devoted themselves to facilitating.

"Why should I?" Folding his arms across his chest, Flinx regarded the closing circle coolly. "Clarity's right. When you've heard everything you want to hear from me, you'll kill us both."

The Elder's expression darkened and his lips trembled slightly as he spoke. "You said that you would tell us everything if we brought you to this woman."

Flinx shrugged indifferently. "What can I say? Maybe the prospect of imminent death has affected my memory."

Keeping his pistol trained on Flinx at all times, the portly speaker came up beside the Elder and whispered into his ear. The older man listened, nodding occasionally, until his associate had finished. Then he turned back to Flinx.

"We will make you a proposal. If you will tell us what we wish to know—everything that is of interest to us concerning the cleansing—we will allow both of you to live. But not to go free. I am sure you understand that we cannot let you go free so long as we feel that you may pose a threat, however slight it may be, to the triumphant approach of the Purity. So we will allow you to live out your natural lives together, in each other's happy company. But only if you agree to do so under our constant supervision." Leaning both hands on the top of his cane, he eyed Flinx intently. "Under the circumstances, I am sure you can see that this is an offer that is more than fair. Certainly it presents you with a better prospect than death at our hands."

It would, Flinx thought, if you weren't lying through your biochemically regenerated teeth. Able to read the emotions of those around him, Flinx knew immediately and without question that the Elder, the speaker, and their fervently impatient colleagues had absolutely no intention of carrying out or implementing any such seemingly benign proposal. As soon as he was finished talking, they would kill him, and Clarity thereafter. This realization handed him his first weapon for the clash to come.

They did not know that he knew.

He snuck a furtive glance in Pip's direction. She was wholly preoccupied with trying to find a way into the toxin-resistant box in which Scrap was imprisoned. If he called to her or shouted an order she would likely respond, but he held back. There were too many guns in the room. Too many of the Order for her to take out at once.

Some of the small tools on his belt, like the cutter, could double as weapons. But they had taken that before allowing him inside. It seemed they had left nothing to chance. Except Flinx himself.

To provide cover for his furious planning he started to talk, giving a simplified depiction of his essence traveling through space, his mind-self covering immense cosmic distances in a direction that had only been made known to him years ago. They listened raptly but did not lower their weapons or their guard. While a part of him rambled on with no particular attention to detail or accuracy, the rest of him concentrated on projecting a single dominating, overpowering emotion. Trapped in dangerous surroundings he would typically have tried to project an overriding fear, or perhaps unbridled confusion. He was afraid that the fanatical members of the Order would not respond adequately to the first or wholeheartedly to the second.

So, since they worshipped death and annihilation, he projected life.

Feelings that underscored the beauty of existence, the fulfillment to be had from simply existing, the joy and wonder of continuing consciousness poured out of the tall redhead to inundate the chamber in an emotive flood of intense, all-consuming, ardent delight at the sheer ecstasy of being—each emotion carefully and consciously counterpointed with what the loss of life really meant.

They resisted—he could feel them resisting the projection—but his choice of emotions had taken them completely by surprise. Perhaps anticipating the same kind of emanations of hatred or fear, panic or alarm, that he had projected on their colleagues in the course of the fight at the shuttleport more than a year ago, they were not prepared for an emotional plea for life. As the emotive antithesis of everything the Order stood for, it hit them hard, each and every one. "One by one, they began to fall to the ground in ecstatic reverie."

Only just conscious of what was happening as his colleagues began to slump to the ground, the speaker tried to aim his pistol at Flinx. Caught up in a surge of support for continued existence and happiness the likes of which he had never encountered or imagined, he failed to get off a shot. Instead, he fell to the floor like the rest of the acolytes and lay there, trembling with the thrill of knowing how good, how important, and how sheerly *true* the simple pleasure of being alive could be.

Of them all, the strongest resistance came from the Elder. More deeply indoctrinated in the philosophy of the Order than any of his presently helpless brethren, he stumbled forward and tried to swing his cane at the volatile foam encasing Clarity. Flinx had no trouble concentrating on and sustaining his life-affirming projection while knocking the old man's attempt aside. Thwarted in his effort, the Elder too finally succumbed to the tall young man's remorseless emanation of contentment.

Flinx surveyed the chamber with satisfaction. Wallowing in the joy he empathetically projected, every member of the Order now lay sprawled on the polished stone floor, each caught up and ensnared in a personal paroxysm of bliss that stemmed from the sheer joy of being. So powerful and focused was Flinx's projection that he felt confident the effects would persist for a good twenty or thirty minutes after he drew back into himself.

Though she had seen what he could do and knew what he was capable of, Clarity still found herself staring in amazement at the man who had come back for her.

"Flinx? What did you *do* to them?"

Bending to pick up the first of many hand weapons that had been set aside and forgotten by their owners, he smiled softly. "I challenged their thinking. And in so challenging it, I changed it. For the better, I think. It probably won't last. By the time the effect wears off, the most zealous among them, at least, will begin to recover their beliefs." He looked over to where she sat encased in her volatile, dirty gray prison.

"By then I expect you and I and Pip and Scrap will be long gone from this place. By tonight we should be well away from this entire world."

Without warning, something struck his right hand hard and hot. Flinching in pain and surprise, he drew his fingers back quickly from the pistol they had been reaching for and looked around to his left.

"Flinx . . . !"

Clarity's shout of his name was warning enough, but it was unnecessary. He had already located the new threat. As soon as he recognized and identified it he realized that the members of the Order, being aware of his unique abilities but ignorant of their extent, had anticipated their own potential inadequacies in dealing with him. So in the event their quarry somehow managed to overcome them despite their careful preparations, they had organized a backup.

The Qwarm was a brute, even for a member of the Assassin's Guild. Taller than Flinx, he outweighed the younger man by fifty kilos or more. Muscles bulged beneath the tight black suit he wore. The death's-head belt, the form-fitting skullcap covering the shaven pate, the crimson insignia: all served to identify the professional killer on sight. The black composite pistol he gripped almost disappeared in his huge fist. Flinx recognized the type. It fired a very focused, very narrow heat beam. Set to blister and not to kill, the perfectly aimed single shot had caused Flinx to pull back sharply from the pile of weapons he had commandeered from the members of the Order.

A loud humming filled the air. Alarmed, Flinx whirled and tried to warn Pip off—too late. Drawn away from Scrap's prison by the new threat to her master, she had soared ceilingward before launching herself at the Qwarm.

An ordinary assailant she would have taken out easily. There was nothing ordinary about the Qwarm. Reacting to her attack with lightning-like reflexes, the assassin raised his weapon. A desperate Flinx projected fear in the man's direction. It had no effect.

Like all the elite of his specialized, dedicated criminal Guild, the veteran Qwarm had trained himself until he was literally emotionless. Unable to feel anything, he did not respond to the emotions Flinx flung at him.

In all the years they had been companions, in all the brawls and scrapes and battles they had fought, Flinx had never seen anyone fast enough to intercept Pip with a weapon. That record was broken as a needle-thin beam from the assassin's gun ripped through her right wing. Though the shot missed her body, the partial loss of lift caused her to spiral to the ground. She landed hard, but alive and still full of fight. But she had landed too far away from her foe to reach him with her venom. Within his transparent prison a hysterical Scrap beat in a frenzy at the impervious walls.

As the Qwarm turned implacably back toward Flinx, Clarity cried out a fresh warning. Her alarm was hardly necessary. Flinx and his assailant were the only figures in motion within the circular chamber.

He studied his adversary. The man was big, powerful, and agile. Completely hairless, he looked to be about fifty. The suggestion of age was in itself unsettling. Unlike in popular fiction where professional killers tended to be youthful and attractive, the successful ones, the truly dangerous ones, were ordinary in appearance and lived to a respectable age. The handsome and reckless tended to die young. That this Qwarm was still alive and healthy told Flinx all he needed to know about his opponent's skill level.

He continued to try to force the issue emotionally, projecting a full and varying range of sentiments at the looming executioner. Fright, panic, alarm, loss, despair, friendship—empathetically, he ran the full gamut of feelings in his attempt to somehow, in some way, reach his assailant. Nothing had any effect. A walking emotional void, the Qwarm felt nil.

Flinx steeled himself. He was quick, long of limb, and in good condition. If he could get in underneath the killer's first shot, he could strike upward to deflect the arm holding the pistol. There was a distinctive thranx fighting move Truzenzuzex had taught him long ago that just might catch a human assassin, even a professional, off guard. But before Flinx could launch himself forward, the Qwarm did something entirely unexpected.

Moving slowly and deliberately, the assassin put his weapon aside, setting it down on a nearby padded bench. Then he straightened and eyed his target. And waited expectantly.

In one respect Flinx was fortunate. Any other opponent, any ordinary aggressor, would simply have tried to shoot him down where he stood. A professional, however, functioned according to a different code. The most professional of all their kind, the Qwarm followed strict rules of combat. If Flinx had been armed he would likely already have been shot. In contrast, by standing defenseless before a highly trained senior Guild member he acquired a certain degree of innocence. That would not grant him mercy, but according to the rules of the Guild it would allow for opportunity, slim as that might be. He was still going to die. The only difference was that it would be by the Qwarm's actual instead of metaphorical hands.

As he had throughout his life, he would take whatever chance was offered. He had received instruction in hand-to-hand combat from Tse-Mallory and Truzenzuzex. If he could not overwhelm his overmuscled executioner, maybe he could surprise him.

If you are out-sized, you counter with speed, he had been taught. Without waiting for a formal invitation, he threw himself at his assailant. Arms extended in front of him, the waiting Qwarm dropped into a fighting crouch. Beneath the gleaming black and crimson skullcap there was no eagerness in his countenance, no disdainful grin on his face. He was just doing a job. Guild convention required that it be consummated in a way that would take slightly more time than originally anticipated. No matter. The end would be the same.

At the last instant Flinx spun in midair parallel to the floor and kicked out, first with his right leg, aiming for the assassin's groin, second with his left, in an attempt to make contact with the blunt bridge of the man's nose. Neither strike was compassionate. Both were intended to disable or kill. In a fight for his life and Clarity's there were no rules. One could not lose gracefully. You won, by any means possible. Or you died.

Demonstrating extraordinary agility for one so massive, the Qwarm dropped onto his back. One scything hand blocked Flinx's first strike. The second kick passed over its intended nasal target as the assassin thrust sharply upward with both feet to strike the younger man solidly in his solar plexus.

As the air whooshed out of him Flinx found himself flying through the air. He landed hard on his back, fighting for breath. He would roll fast, kip to his feet, and attack again before the Qwarm could regain his . . .

Hands in striking position, the assassin was already standing over him.

How had he recovered so quickly? Flinx had barely hit the floor before the killer was looming over him. He readied himself as best he could to block the expected leg thrust or punch. Lying prone, he was vulnerable to all that and more.

Empathetic projecting had failed. Hand-to-hand combat had failed. What other weapons did he have available to him? He unleashed a stream of words. Already aware that emotion would have no effect on his designated assassin, he kept his voice steady and rational. Pleading, crying, begging, would weigh no heavier on the Qwarm in verbal form than they had emotionally.

"If you kill me," Flinx declared as calmly as he could, "then any descendants of yours, the entire Guild, and every living creature is going to die when something unimaginably vast and malevolent sweeps through this corner of the cosmos."

Perceiving no need to hurry, the assassin considered this most peculiar plea for clemency. "The unlikeliness of what you put forward aside, it does not sound to me like something a stripling like yourself could influence." A hand drew back, gathering force to strike a killing blow.

Flinx did something he had never done before in his life. He boasted.

"I am civilization's last hope."

Coming from a beaten young man lying on the polished floor of an exurban residence on the fringes of the city of Sphene, this was such a blatantly outrageous declaration that the senior Qwarm was disposed to pause, if only to deliver a final assessment.

"You do not look to me like the last hope of anything except your-self." The killing hand tightened.

Lying on his back gazing up at the assassin, his chest heaving, out of time and ideas, Flinx tried one last tack. Knowing what he did of the Qwarm he had little hope it would work, but he had to try.

"Whatever the Order is paying the Guild, I'll triple it. I have access to resources far beyond what you can see or imagine."

"He's telling the truth!" From her body jacket of explosive foam, Clarity pleaded with the killer. "About having money *and* about saving the galaxy."

The Qwarm allowed himself a single sigh. "I am sorry. I do not be-lieve the latter. As for the first, you should know that the Guild's reputa-tion is built on a cherished tradition of fulfilling each and every contract to the letter of the respective agreement. Even if I were personally at-tracted to such an offer, as a member of the Guild I could never agree to it. Were I to do so, my own brothers and sisters would hunt me down and swiftly put paid to any such idiosyncratic escapade." The killing hand rose higher. "Consider yourselves fortunate I was hired to dispatch you quickly and efficiently, and not to make your passing linger."

The fist started to descend toward Flinx's face, almost faster than the eye could follow. He barely had time to close his eyes. Encapsulated in explosive, Clarity screamed. Slithering toward the combatants, a grounded Pip desperately spat venom that landed more than a meter short of its target. The Qwarm's precise, methodical killing strike struck home.

And just brushed Flinx's left ear.

A heavy weight depressed his chest. His breathing had stopped, but not as a consequence of the assassin's blow. The man had collapsed on top of him and it was his great weight that was inhibiting Flinx's respi-ration. To the left of his head, the murderous strike had cracked the stone floor. Clarity was still screaming. Gasping and choking on her own anguish she stopped only when, grunting with the effort, he rolled the heavy body off to one side and slowly sat up.

"Flinx?"

"I'm okay. I'm alive. I guess." Sucking air, he eyed the massive bulk that was now lying motionless on the floor next to him. The Qwarm was unchanged, provided one discounted the hole that pierced his cranium from forehead to back. The hole was notably smaller in front than in the rear, indicating that something superfast and lethal had penetrated the skull. No sound had accompanied the lethal shot. A sonic stiletto would make a hole like that, Flinx knew. Or an inertia plug. Professional that he was, the Qwarm could probably have identified the source immediately. Except that it had been focused on him, and now he was dead.

A pulsing, cylindrical shape slithered into his lap. A quick check of Pip's right wing showed that the injury, while sufficient to bring her down, was not extensive. With appropriate treatment it should heal quickly. Lifting her, he slipped her carefully onto his right shoulder and waited until she had a good grip before he rose.

A voice parsing elegant symbospeech clicked melodically behind him.

"Still riding the *grizel*, I see."

Still a little unsteady, he turned and looked behind him. What he saw and recognized made him smile.

Deus ex thranxicum, he mused. Memories came flooding back.

CHAPTER

17

Her chitin glistening a pure and brilliant aquamarine, feathery antennae inclined forward, twinned ovipositors forming a pair of perfect parallel arcs above the back of her abdomen, the young female thranx stood facing the center of the chamber. In addition to the customary carry-pouch slung over her thorax and a larger satchel strapped to her abdomen, she held four pistols: one in each truhand, the others in her raised foothands. The display of firepower was impressive. Even more so was the realization that she had needed only a single shot to bring down the Qwarm. The presence of all four vestigial wing cases indicated that she had yet to mate. Inlaid into her right shoulder was the gleaming enamel insignia of a full padre in the security service of the United Church.

Flinx doubted she would have been able to bring down the assassin, despite her bearing, maturity, and sharpshooting ability, had he not been fully engrossed in preparing to finish off his quarry. That total absorption had been just enough of a distraction to allow the new arrival to get off the fatal shot. Had she missed, Flinx feared the outcome might have been very different. But she had not missed. Still smiling, he started toward her. As he did so, she neatly holstered all four of her weapons.

"Your reflexes have gotten better," he told her.

Standing on her four trulegs, she had to tilt her head back to meet his gaze. The maroon bands that formed horizontal stripes across her shimmering gold compound eyes were darker than most.

"And you've grown taller. You humans and your disorderly growth variations: it's enough to make those of other species who follow sane patterns of biological development believe your genetic code is packed with jokers."

"You wouldn't get any argument on that from me." Lowering his gaze, he eyed a truleg. "You still limp a little."

She clicked her mandibles and kicked out slightly with the indicated limb. "The occasional limp is a psychological reflex I have not been able to shake. Structurally, the leg is fully restored. A little regenerated natural chitin, a little synthetic, and everything was made good as new. Memories, however, aren't as easily repaired. Those are what sometimes cause me to miss a step." Almost as an afterthought, she leaned toward him. Bending low, he let the tips of her antennae caress his forehead. When he straightened, he extended a hand to contact them with his fingertips.

"You're still human, I see," she commented when she stepped back. "Meaning that you're still short the necessary number of appendages required to live a proper civilized life."

"My life has been anything but civilized." His tone darkened. "Or proper. I'll fill you in and do my best to skip over some of the greater excesses."

A foothand reached up to indicate the insignia embedded in her shoulder. "No need. As you can see, I'm no longer a padre-elect. Working for Church Security, one encounters plenty of excess on a regular basis."

"Um—excuse me?"

At the sound of Clarity's voice Flinx turned back toward her. In the excitement of the unexpected reunion he had momentarily forgotten that his beloved was still encased in a hardened container of highly volatile explosive material.

"You two *know* each other?"

"Sorry, sorry." Flinx indicated the self-assured insectoid standing poised in front of him. "Clarity, this is Sylzenzuzex. An old friend and a distant relative of Truzenzuzex. She and I originally met under— difficult circumstances. That was something like ten years ago." He looked back at the waiting thranx. Her b-thorax pulsed slightly as she breathed, taking in air through spiracles far more advanced and oxygen-efficient than those of any Terran insect. Her personal bouquet was even more fragrant than that of the average thranx. Frangipani and rose, honeysuckle and huckleberry. It was all coming back to him.

He gestured in Clarity's direction. "Syl, meet Clarity Held. The one human being in the universe who knows who and what I am, in more depth and detail than I used to think possible. She loves me in spite of that."

"That could change," Clarity growled, "unless you get me out of this coagulated goo before one of these fanatics wakes up and thinks to hit me with a rock, or a chair, or a good swift kick, and blow all of us to kingdom come."

"I do not know exactly what your intended mate is talking about, *srra!!aut*," Syl clicked, "but I can relate to the part about being blown up." Left truhand and foothand gestured in unison to take in their immediate surroundings. "What is all this about? Who are these people and how and why have they come to be so incapacitated?" She used a foothand to gesture back the way she had come. "There are others by the entrance and in the hallway. Seeing them in such a state and knowing you were somewhere here is what caused me to proceed with caution and weapons drawn."

"They're members of something called the Order of Null. I—incapacitated them. They want me dead."

Her right truhand and foothand pointed to the body of the Qwarm. "And are apparently willing to pay well to accomplish that."

Flinx joined her in staring at the assassin's mountainous corpse. "I'm glad you didn't switch professions. He wouldn't have given you a chance to explain yourself."

She gestured second-degree accord. "A senior Qwarm." Her gaze returned to search his face. "After all these years there are still those who wish you gone."

He shrugged. "Their identity shifts and changes, but not their intent. It's just my life, Syl. Later, when we have more time, I'll tell you more about it than you want to know." He mustered up his earlier smile as he turned and started toward the immobilized, increasingly impatient Clarity. "Just as you have to tell me how you came to be here, and how you found me."

She nodded and moved off to check on the condition of the traumatized, fetally curled, and still overwhelmed members of the Order, as he hurried over to Clarity.

The Elder had told him that there were four of the small, disk-shaped detonators taped to her thighs and electronically attuned to the hardened foam. They would set off the explosive amalgam if anyone attempted to cut or break through it or if it was struck hard enough. He did not need the beseeching look in her eyes to tell him that whatever he did he would have to proceed with the utmost caution. As with the Qwarm, if he made a mistake there would be no second chance. For either of them.

But if the detonators were simply taped to her body . . .

Smiling encouragingly, he stepped behind her and tried to slip his right hand down her front, starting at the neck where the foam stopped. No matter how hard or how carefully he wiggled his hand and no matter how deeply she inhaled, he could not get more than a finger or two into the restrictive space between her throat and the inside layer. Fearful of cracking or setting off the gray amalgam, he was reluctant to push too hard. He could not take a chance on triggering one or more of the detonators.

He had no better results when he lay down on the floor and tried to slip a hand up a leg. The Order had done their work well. He couldn't free Clarity without splintering or splitting the encasing foam. Doing that would undoubtedly set it off. And if the Elder was to be believed, the "simple" mechanical triggers taped to her upper legs could not be deactivated electronically without the risk of initiating the deadly reaction.

He needed something thin, narrow, and flexible that had a strong grasp, like the wormgrip the Elder had referred to. He could send Sylzenzuzex off to obtain one and bring it back, but that would leave him having to guard Clarity against any surprises the recovering acolytes might produce. Even disarmed they might prove dangerous. With the right tools he could shift both Clarity and her volatile sheath, but what if in the process of being moved it accidentally struck a wall or fell to the ground? The result would be as explosive as if he tried to cut into it.

As Syl continued to gather up the last of the Order's weapons and communits, he wracked his brain for a solution that would not only be viable but quick. It finally struck him that he had at his disposal a tool that was even more flexible than a wormgrip. Turning and walking away from Clarity, he started searching through the pile of instrumentation Sylzenzuzex had collected. Clarity watched him intently.

"What are you doing, Flinx? You heard what the crazy old militant said: the detonators on my legs can't be switched off electronically. They're simple on-off switches. In order to disable them you have to get them off me." An edge crept into her voice. *"Why aren't you getting them off me, Flinx?"*

"Because I can't reach them without splitting or cracking the foam and setting it off. But there's someone who can."

Digging through the growing pile of sequestered weaponry and personal instrumentation, he evaluated and discarded one item after another before finally settling on a miniholo disk. It was round, it was small, and it was the closest thing to a button-sized detonator he had been able to scrounge from the pile. As a puzzled Clarity looked on, he grabbed Pip gently by the neck and drew her head downward. He showed her the disk, emphasizing its importance by emanating concomitant heightened emotions of longing and desire. Then he dropped it down the front of his shirt.

Clarity had heard him talk to the minidrag on numerous occasions. This, however, was the first time she had ever heard him use the word "fetch."

For an alien non-Terran pseudo-reptiloid whose body shape was an excellent example of interstellar parallel evolution, Pip was moderately intelligent. Even so, she was no dog, far less a dolphin. Flinx had to repeat the demonstration several times before she got the idea. His feeling of accomplishment when she finally wriggled down his shirtfront to recover the dropped disk and then slithered back out his open collar holding it in her mouth was the equal of any triumph he had experienced recently.

Leaving the mound of confiscated gear, he returned to Clarity. Gently unwinding Pip's coils, he placed her on Clarity's left shoulder with her triangular-shaped head facing the slight opening at her neck. Holding the miniholo disk in his other hand, he mimed dropping it into the narrow space between her throat and the hardened explosive foam. Wings folded tightly against her sides, the flying snake immediately ducked down into the opening and disappeared into the gap.

A moment passed. Clarity's expression contorted. She gave every sign of trying to move, to get away, but imprisoned within the solidified froth she was unable to do little more than twitch. Flinx was suddenly concerned. She had not raised any objections to his serpentine stratagem, and living as she did with Scrap the last thing he expected was for her to show any kind of irrational fear of intimate proximity to Pip.

"What's wrong? Try not to move so much—you might accidentally impact the foam and set off a reaction."

"I *am* trying!" she shot back, just before she lapsed into uncontrollable giggling. "I can't help it—she tickles!"

The laughter subsided along with the stimulation when Pip's head reappeared beneath her chin. Flinx broke out in a wide grin. Gripped firmly in the minidrag's sharp teeth, the thumbnail-sized detonator trailed shreds of the tape that had secured it to her right thigh. The empathetic warmth that now passed between man and minidrag was as deep and true as any spoken expression of satisfaction.

He examined the recovered detonator closely. It was small, but not so small that it couldn't conceal within its slim plastic body some kind of backup triggering system. He laid it carefully aside. At his urging Pip made three more trips down Clarity's front, bringing forth the remaining three detonators along with concurrent bursts of uncontrollable laughter that gradually faded in intensity. When all four detonators had been recovered, he induced the flying snake to make one more exploratory slither. This additional excursion took three times as long as any of its four predecessors. Finally emerging, the minidrag radiated concern and uncertainty. Picking her up and settling her on his shoulder, he proceeded to soothe her both mentally and physically.

There was always the risk, he explained to Clarity, that the Elder had been lying. "Couldn't take the chance that there might have been five detonators," he told her, "or more. Don't worry. If there were, Pip would have found them."

Gathering up the four detonators, he turned and headed for the hallway. Behind him, Sylzenzuzex was busily trussing the hands and feet of the recovering Order members with a spool of wire-thin makesafe that was standard issue equipment for a Church Security operative.

His rented skimmer was parked where he had left it. Ten minutes later he was forty kilometers away and hovering a centimeter above the center of a small, shallow lake. Slipping out of his clothes, he picked up the detonators one last time, took a deep breath, and plunged into the cool water. Reaching the bottom, he proceeded to shove them as deep into the mud as he could. Lastly, he moved a large flat rock over the top of them before returning to the surface to gulp air.

Moments later he was back at the Order's villa. No smoke rose from the middle of the building and insofar as he could tell, the central atrium had not collapsed. His relief was not complete, however, until he was once more in the central chamber.

Emerging from the individual paroxysms of pleasure induced by Flinx's emotive projecting, the now bound and secured members of the Order were suffering from varying degrees of emotional hangover. The Elder in particular looked especially distraught. None of them were in any condition to confront him verbally, far less physically. Her training had taught Sylzenzuzex how to secure detainees. None of the Order members could stand, much less mount an assault.

"What do you want to do with them, Flinx?" One antenna waved in his direction while the other indicated the prisoners. "What did you do to put them in this condition, anyway—drug them?"

"Something like that." Years ago, when they had met on Ulru-Ujurr, his Talent had still been in its infancy. He had only been able to infrequently read the emotions of others—not to project his own onto them.

He realized with a start that dealing with the Order posed a tricky problem of its own. Their organization might be secretive, but that did not make it illegal. Attempted murder, of course, was another matter. But declaring the attempt on his life would require registering a formal complaint with the Nurian authorities, giving a relevant deposition, appearing before an adjudication automaton, and answering the kinds of questions he preferred not to answer. On the other hand, if he and his friends simply departed and left them bound as they were, eventually they would free themselves and come after him again. Perhaps less precisely next time: say, by locating him in a public place in downtown Sphene and then bombing it. That risk he could deal with, but not the prospect of endangering innocents.

It was Sylzenzuzex who proposed a solution. One that was temporary, to be sure, but temporary was all that was required. The members of the Order needed to be neutralized only until he and his friends were safely away from New Riviera.

"In my capacity as a Church Security officer I am allowed a certain amount of operational leeway." A truhand indicated the bound and now increasingly active throng of believers. "If I file a report stating that these confrontational humans are members of a potentially dangerous organization, they can be taken into official custody until the truth of the claim is adjudicated one way or the other. It is not necessary for me to mention that they have attempted murder and hired a Qwarm to do so. It should be enough to keep them in custody for a couple of days. Will that be sufficient for your purposes?"

He would have hugged her except that he was afraid of breaking a delicate truarm. He settled instead for swiping his hand across the tips of both antennae.

"Go ahead and file the necessary report. I'll see to Clarity."

Recovering his service belt, he returned to where she still sat encased in the congealed sheath of explosive foam. Her tone, like her expression, had lost none of its impatience. "What was that all about?"

"I had to find a way to make sure that both these fanatics and the authorities wouldn't interfere with us for a little while. At least long enough to allow us to leave Nur without having to chance another battle at the shuttleport." He turned his head to his left. "Syl assures me she has enough rank to take care of it. Hold still. And you might want to take a deep breath."

While Pip looked on with interest, he drew a small cutting tool from his belt. Under his experienced fingers it flared to life.

"Why take a deep breath?" she wondered aloud. "If this doesn't work and you set off the amalgam it's not going to matter how much oxygen I have in my lungs. Or you have in yours, either."

"Good point." He moved the dynamic end of the tool toward her left shoulder. The beam made contact and began to slice into the hardened grayish material. In spite of himself, he winced. But the beam continued to cut and nothing, least of all his life, flashed before his eyes. He was careful to work at an angle that would keep it well away from her skin.

Proceeding with care it took nearly an hour to free her from the last of the casing. When the final cut was made and he was able to remove the last piece of foam from her right leg, she collapsed forward into his arms. Unable to do more than twitch inside the sheath, her muscles were badly cramped. She was content to sit as he tenderly massaged her arms and legs, and he was more than happy to do so.

As soon as she was able to sit upright by herself he extracted a medikit and went to work on Pip's damaged wing. Strands of all-purpose synthetic organocarbon bound the edges of the wound together as cleanly and expertly as if the repair had been woven by a spider with an M.D. A spray of mistskin was applied to sheath the fibers. Sitting back, he eyed his handiwork. The membrane should heal quickly as the flying snake's own tissue replaced the artificial fibers and mistskin.

Returning to where Clarity was continuing to rub sensation back into her thighs and upper arms, he addressed the recovered communit that once more encircled his left wrist. The response to his call was immediate.

The image the unit projected in front of him showed a man and a thranx. Both evinced extreme agitation that began to diminish only when they saw that the caller was in good health and under no visible duress.

"First positive." Truzenzuzex was visibly relieved. "You are not dead."

"Yes, I can confirm that," Flinx replied blithely.

"And your consort?" Tse-Mallory added quickly.

"Clarity's fine," Flinx assured him. "We're all fine. Sylzenzuzex is here, too. Did you know anything about that?" Raising his arm and turning his wrist, he allowed the communit's sensor enough room to image Clarity and then the young thranx.

At the unexpected sight of his youthful relation, Truzenzuzex promptly unleashed a stream of clicks, whistles, and wordings too fast and too furious even for Flinx, who was fluent in both High and Low Thranx, to decipher. Using her own communit, Sylzenzuzex latched on to the relevant channel and replied in kind. This alien dialogue continued until Flinx felt compelled to interrupt with his own version of what had just transpired. Tse-Mallory and Truzenzuzex listened in silence until he was finished.

"While your chronology is compelling and the details satisfying," the elderly thranx replied, "I can't escape a feeling in my sphincter that certain important minutiae are missing. For example, while I am of course relieved to hear that my Eighth-Once-Removed has succeeded in rescuing you, I am much more interested to learn how she came to *find* you."

"As am I," Flinx told him. "In fact, I think I'm going to ask her to explain that right now. We'll rejoin you very soon. And Tru—you and Bran need to make preparations to leave Nur immediately."

"Interesting," Tse-Mallory's image replied. "Tru and I were about to make the same suggestion to you. You see, we just had our own separate run-ins with the happy folk of the Order."

That explained why they had not come to his aid, Flinx surmised. It did nothing, however, to explain how and why Sylzenzuzex had done so.

"You'll have to tell me all about it," he responded, "when we get back to Sphene."

"Wait!" As Tse-Mallory tried to maintain the link, Flinx cut his old mentor off—something he would never have thought of doing as recently as just a few years ago. But he was tired and sore, and concerned for both himself and for Clarity. There would be plenty of time for conversation and reflection later, once they were safely away from both New Riviera and the murderous Order of Null.

A hand touched his shoulder. Looking around, he saw Clarity gazing up at him. "Thanks for closing the conversation. Your fatherly friends are wonderful, and caring, and they watched over me all through my long convalescence." She smiled ruefully. "But they *do* like to talk."

"I know. Just, whatever you do, don't ever call Bran Tse-Mallory 'fatherly.' Or Truzenzuzex either, for that matter." On his shoulder Pip was squirming for attention. When he turned to eye his serpentine companion, she lifted her upper body away from him and used her head to point.

"O'Morion's Mother!" he exclaimed contritely. "I forgot about Scrap."

The transparent container that restrained the young minidrag might be fashioned of impervious material, but it was secured by a pair of straightforward mechanical latches. Flinx unsnapped them and opened the box. Wind from the flying snake's humming wings brushed the human's hair as the Alaspinian rocketed past his liberator's face. Darting about like an oversized hummingbird, the joyful minidrag swarmed Clarity.

"All right, all right!" she laughed. "I'm glad you're out of that box, too!"

Reassured that his human was unhurt, Scrap zipped over to confront the more mature minidrag resting on Flinx's shoulder. Pip snapped playfully at her offspring as the other flying snake nipped in and out, his pointed tongue flicking at her as he danced blissfully in the static air of the circular chamber. Eventually exhausting himself, he finally settled back down on Clarity's right shoulder. Reaching up and stroking him, she cooed softly to her pet as he folded his multihued wings against his ribs and rubbed his head against her bare neck.

Flinx walked over to Sylzenzuzex as she finished securing the last of the recovering Order members. Turning toward him, she gestured with a poise and confidence that had not been present in the young padre-elect whose insecurities he well recalled from a decade ago.

"Don't worry," she assured him in perfect, crackling symbospeech. "I've been careful to disarm them all, and in any case they are well bound, *kss!lpp*. A task that is much simpler when one is securing beings with only four limbs instead of the normal eight." She indicated her communit. "I have summoned a security team to take them into custody." Gleaming in the light from overhead, golden compound eyes looked back into his own single-lensed oculars.

"I wasn't worrying about your work," he told her. "You still haven't explained your sudden, unexpected, and extraordinarily timely reappearance in my life."

She whistled archly: thranx laughter. "I can see where you would find it something of a surprise." She gestured with a truhand. "But I'm afraid the explanation is entirely prosaic.

"A couple of years ago, as a matter of family and clan etiquette, I finally made contact with my Elder Eighth-Once-Removed, the esteemed Eint Truzenzuzex. A polite correspondence ensued. Limited, as you would expect, by the twin exigencies of distance and expense. In the course of this ongoing communication he mentioned that he was in regular and close contact with someone who turned out to be a mutual acquaintance—you."

Flinx nodded. "I remember my surprise years ago when you told me you were related to Tru."

She gesticulated understanding. "Time passed. Among the many postings available to those who work in Church Security, one eventually opened up here on Nur/New Riviera. I applied for it and was delighted to have my request honored. I am sure that hailing from the Hive Zu and having a renowned relative with the rank of Eint did not hurt my application. I was elated. The transfer offered an opportunity to finally meet and interact with my eminent Eighth-relation." Feathery antennae alternated switching slowly back and forth.

"It was also, I hoped, an opportunity to encounter once again the singular young human with whom I had shared so much trauma and travail so long ago." The valentine-shaped head looked him up and down. "You are less young. In many ways, I think."

"We're all a lot less young, in many ways," he commented somberly.

She indicated third-degree concurrence. "While I had no difficulty making contact with my Eighth, I was disappointed to learn from him and his companion that you had left Nur to engage in vital research. I was told you had departed under difficult and rushed circumstances." She indicated the struggling bodies littering the floor of the chamber. "Conflict was alluded to, but this Order was not mentioned.

"More time passed. Then I was informed by Truzenzuzex that you had finally returned in advance of resuming your important research." As she declaimed the latter she gestured with a truhand and a foothand to where Clarity was continuing to play with Scrap. "And other matters."

"If Tru told you I was back," Flinx murmured, "then he must have also told you where I was staying. Why haven't you come to see me?"

"Believe me, *cr!!akk,* I was eager to do so, but my Eighth suggested that I remain in the background for at least a little while. In order to give you time to recover from your long journeying and"—she gestured in Clarity's direction—"to mate."

Flinx had the grace to blush. "Remind me to have a word about semantics with a certain elderly thranx."

Sylzenzuzex continued. "Once these and other issues had been sat-isfactorily dealt with, the intention was to surprise you with an unantic-ipated appearance on my part, *chlakkt.* I waited for my Eighth to announce a time. Alas, he is old and older, and I think my eagerness to see you again kept slipping his mind. Tiring of his continued unrespon-siveness, I chose to set aside his plan and decided on my own initiative to reunite with you today.

"I went to your hotel intending to do this, only to discover that you were away. Oddly, the attendant gave the impression I was expected. My initial reaction to this was that my Eighth had finally told you of my presence on Nur without so informing me. Though somewhat confused, I took the information splinter you had left behind for a 'friend.' When I perused the contents, it provided me with your intended destination. Nothing more." She gestured second-degree regret. "Had I known of the circumstances, I would have brought half a dozen police skimmers with me."

So that was what had happened. Nodding to himself as much as to Syl, Flinx remembered leaving the memory splinter "for a friend." When she had identified herself as such, the clerk had passed to her the coordinates that had been intended for Bran and Tru. With their full at-tention occupied by the Order, they had been unable to get to the hotel earlier to check up on him and retrieve the splinter. Not that the mix-up on the hotel clerk's part had worked out badly in the end.

But—after waiting so long at Truzenzuzex's behest, why had Syl fi-nally decided to go to the hotel to make contact with him *today*?

When he asked, she gestured second-degree bafflement. "I could not say, Flinx. As I told you, I was tired of waiting for my Eighth to set-tle on a date for a reunion. All I can tell you is that today the time felt right."

Standing nearby, Clarity reflected on their close escape as she con-tinued to caress Scrap. The youthful minidrag was finally winding down from the excitement of being freed and reunited with his master and his mother. She shook her head knowingly.

"You don't see it, do you, Flinx? You project your emotions even when you don't know you're projecting. Maybe you were broadcasting your anxiety all over the place and Syl picked it up, and that's what led her to try and make contact with you today."

He considered the theory. "If that's the case, then why didn't Tru or Bran react?"

Clarity smiled tightly. "Maybe they were too far away. Maybe having to deal with the Order's attempts on their own lives overrode their sensitivity to anything you might have been sending out. Maybe you have a deeper emotional relationship with this thranx." She eyed the impassive Sylzenzuzex. "Maybe it was just a fortuitous coincidence. Such things do happen, you know. Are you asking *me* to try and explain you to you?" When he failed to reply she added, "If you weren't such a wonderful human being and I wasn't so acutely in love with you, I think I'd be scared to death of Philip Lynx."

He met her gaze somberly. "You know what, Clarity? Sometimes I'm scared to death of me, too."

While her command of terranglo was very good, Sylzenzuzex found this exchange inordinately puzzling. "Though I understand your words and there is nothing the matter with my hearing, I have the feeling that I'm missing something. Just as there were times when I thought I was missing something, Flinx, when you conversed with the natives on Ulru-Ujurr so many years ago." She sounded wistful. "I wonder how their tunnel digging is progressing."

Flinx had to smile at the remembrance. "A few millennia yet to go, I should imagine."

"'Ulru-Ujurr'?" Clarity moved over to join them. "'Tunnel digging'?" She looked up at Flinx. "Maybe you could fill me in on what you two are reminiscing about?"

"Maybe so," Sylzenzuzex agreed, underscoring the comment with whistling thranx laughter.

More old memories came flooding back to Flinx. As was usual with his remembrances, not all of them were pleasant. "Syl and I have some history together," he told the curious Clarity. "I suppose I better explain."

"That would be helpful." She did not add that, given the obvious depth of feeling that existed between him and a female with whom he had evidently shared a great deal prior to meeting her, it was also helpful that Sylzenzuzex belonged to an entirely different species.

It was a long story replete with details that Flinx decided not to elaborate on until he had a lot more time in which to do so. It was enough that Clarity learned how, in the ongoing search to unravel the secrets of his parentage, he and Sylzenzuzex had found themselves thrown together on the edicted world of Ulru-Ujurr, that they had struck up an enduring friendship with its extraordinary natives in the course of doing battle with unscrupulous exploiters and a distant relative of his, and that upon surviving numerous potentially fatal encounters they had subsequently gone their separate ways.

"It's all part and parcel of my long, strange, jagged journey," he concluded. As he put a hand on the shoulder that was not occupied by the minidrag Scrap, the sounds of arriving skimmers drifted in to them from outside. "A journey that's led me to some answers, to more questions, to a lot of knowledge and maybe a tiny bit of wisdom, to a partial understanding of the monstrous thing that's approaching our galaxy, and most importantly of all—to you." Leaning forward, he lightly kissed her upturned lips.

She was smiling when he pulled back. "If that 'tiny bit of wisdom' involves knowing how to properly conclude an explanation, I find I'd have to agree." Pulling his head down toward her, she kissed him again; harder this time.

Sylzenzuzex looked on with the combination of tolerance and quiet amusement her kind reserved for much of what passed for intimate social interaction among their bipedal mammalian allies. As far as the average thranx was concerned this involved the exchange, in varying amounts according to the particular activity involved, of far too much in the way of bodily fluids. A delicate brush of antennae, a truhand caress, struck her as a far more sensible and civilized way to achieve a similarly intimate result.

It was all a matter of contradictory cultures, she knew. No doubt it had much to do with physiology as well. When pressed together, soft and flexible human flesh tended to meld, whereas performing the same action with part of a chitinous exoskeleton only resulted in potentially disfiguring blemishes and scrapes. Then there was the whole business of ovipositors versus . . . and . . . well . . .

The time available for such captivating speculation vanished as a team of alert and armed Church Security personnel arrived on the run. Identifying herself, she detailed the reasons behind her emergency call-in and explained what needed to be done. As a full padre, her authority to do so and to direct that the members of the Order be placed in custody was not questioned. That could very well come later, but it was not a concern of the newly arrived security personnel. Instructed to ignore the sometimes passionate protestations of those being detained, they rounded up the recovering members of the Order with a proficiency and single-mindedness that was a credit to the Church.

As he watched his nemeses being led away, Flinx knew that in a couple of days, at least a few members of the Order were likely to be released. Formal grievances might then be lodged. But by the time the Nurian judicial system fully engaged with that of the local Church hierarchy and consequent summonses could be issued, he and his friends would be aboard the *Teacher,* far out in space-plus on a vector for deep into the Blight, safe from both the homicidal machinations of the minions of the Order of Null and the tentacles of meddlesome Commonwealth bureaucracy.

At least, he hoped so.

Flanked by two burly Church operatives, the portly speaker was being hustled toward the hallway that led to the villa's entrance. Now fully recovered from the bewildering effects of Flinx's emotive projection, he was visibly less happy than he had been when lying on the floor immersed in its influence.

"This isn't over!" Twisting in the grasp of his escort, he turned to shout back at Flinx. "There are more of us than you know, more than you can imagine! Others of the Order will find you. The Purity will arrive unhindered and the cleansings will be done! But first, you and those around you will be . . . !"

"Quiet!" It was the Elder, roaring with surprising strength as he was ushered out ahead of the speaker. "You idiot!" the old man added for good measure. Thus chastened, the speaker lapsed into a petulant silence.

Clarity clung to Flinx, the two minidrags flicking pointed tongue-tips at each other from the shoulders of their respective masters, and watched as the rest of the trussed acolytes were led out.

"I know we'll be gone before they're released from detention, Flinx, but they still scare me."

He shrugged, doing his best to make light of her concern. "Extremists are always frightening, Clarity." He offered a reassuring smile. "With luck, though, we'll never see any of them ever again. It's a big

Commonwealth." He turned to Sylzenzuzex. "Do you have to go with the security team, Syl? To make your report?"

Gesturing a negative, she skittered up alongside him. "I'll file it via my communit. What do you want to do now?" Thoughtfully, she leaned slightly to her right to make eye contact with the woman who was holding on to his left arm. "Both of you."

Flinx considered. Though few preparations were required before he could leave New Riviera, some could not be avoided. The *Teacher*'s AI could handle most of the necessary procedures. A couple of days were all it would take. Meanwhile . . .

"Why don't we have that reunion?" Reaching out with his right hand, he swept his palm across the middle of her antennae, bending them forward.

As they snapped back, Sylzenzuzex reflected that a male thranx who had done such a thing uninvited would have risked a swift strike to the b-thorax. Coming from a human, however, the gesture carried no such social baggage.

With a female on each arm, Flinx followed the last of the security team out of the villa.

CHAPTER
18

Sylzenzuzex's Church-registered skimmer was far faster than Flinx's rented vehicle, so he instructed his skimmer to return to its base station on autopilot while he and Clarity joined the padre in returning to Sphene. For Flinx it was one of those rare journeys when he did not have to constantly monitor his course or destination, much less keep a lookout for private, government, or alien forces seeking his capture or death. He used the atypical opportunity to enjoy the views of the tranquil Nurian countryside with his companions.

Later, while Flinx lingered near the rear of the craft, entertaining Pip and Scrap, Clarity wandered forward to take the seat alongside their driver. While Sylzenzuzex straddled the familiar thranx bench, Clarity availed herself of a standard human-conforming chair. It felt strange to be snakeless. Though she missed the familiar weight on her shoulder, she understood her pet's desire to spend as much time as possible with his often absent parent.

"You could not have timed your arrival much better," she murmured in symbospeech by way of opening conversation.

Since the skimmer, once programmed, more or less flew itself, Sylzenzuzex was able to turn her attention away from the height-adjustable console and to her passenger.

"So it seems to have been." A foothand gestured toward the back of the craft. "From the time we first met, it struck me that there existed a more than casual bond between us."

"I can empathize with that. Because Flinx and I are also deeply bonded."

What am I saying? Clarity found herself thinking. Was she jealous? Because Flinx had known and bonded with Sylzenzuzex before he had known her? That was absurd! Their timely rescuer was a *thranx*. Clarity knew she should be feeling nothing but gratitude. Or was female jealousy something capable of crossing species?

You, she told herself quietly, *are being a world-class fool. Rectify it.*

"I haven't had a chance to actually thank you. For saving us."

A thranx could not blush, but the padre made the equivalent gesture. "Flinx saved my life. I suspect he would have survived this time even in my absence."

"How can you know that?"

Antennae fluttered gracefully. "Because according to my esteemed Eighth, he always does. For example, despite the many difficulties and concerns that are unique to him, the many curious challenges and dangers and personal troubles he has endured, he still somehow managed to find the time to find you."

Now Clarity not only felt like a prize fool, she was ashamed.

"He's been out of my life more than he's been in it." She looked toward the rear of the skimmer. A brilliantly hued minidrag on each shoulder, Flinx was staring out the transparent canopy, enjoying the view as the skimmer entered Sphene proper. Despite his height, his appearance and manner were still boyish. One got that impression whenever one was around him, she knew. Provided you didn't look too deeply into his eyes.

"I'm sure he hopes that will change." Click-whistling to the console, Sylzenzuzex made a minor course adjustment. The skimmer obediently turned slightly to starboard.

"We both do." Clarity came to a decision without even realizing she had been debating the issue. "I know you two go back a long way, and I know you must have a lot to talk about. If you'd rather converse in private . . ."

The thranx looked over at her. "Wouldn't a private conversation automatically include Flinx's prospective mate as well as him? Or are your prenuptial standards so very different?"

"No," Clarity murmured in reply. "No, I guess not." With that classically cogent observation by Flinx's old friend, the last vestiges of incongruous resentment on Clarity's part vanished completely.

The sprawling extended-stay residence had been designed and built to accommodate, insofar as it was physically and socially viable, visitors to New Riviera from as many worlds as possible. Mindful of traditional thranx tastes, some of the facility was located belowground. It was in a spacious habitat on the third subterranean level that they reunited with Tse-Mallory and Truzenzuzex.

After formally greeting his young and suitably deferential female relative, the esteemed Eint walked over to Flinx. Having to bend low to clear the ceiling when he walked, Flinx had taken a seat on a floor cushion of a type designed to provide visiting humans with some degree of anterior comfort.

"My boy, you invite trouble," the thranx muttered, "the way a distillation of pheromones attracts the sexually vigorous."

"With consequences that are significantly less gratifying." Tse-Mallory was seated cross-legged on the other side of the room.

"It's not by choice or by design, as you both well know," Flinx responded glumly.

"No, no, of course not. You are just unlucky," the Eint observed with characteristic sarcasm. Turning to face the watching Clarity, he executed a bow whose grace belied the absence of a flexible backbone.

"I am very relieved to see that you suffered no harm, my dear. Bran and I blame ourselves for not keeping closer watch over you. Especially since Flinx's return."

She smiled and shrugged it off. "Even the most attentive of nurses can't keep watch every minute of every day. Forget about it. I'm fine, Scrap's fine, and Flinx is fine."

"And we will be more fine," Flinx added, "once we're safely off New Riviera and in space-plus."

Sylzenzuzex gestured agreement coupled with understanding. "I've insured that those who abducted Clarity and desired to kill Flinx have been removed from contact with them and with society for at least a couple of days." The sardonicism in her voice reminded Flinx immediately of her older Eighth-relative Truzenzuzex. "My report insists that their detention is vital to the continued public health."

"Clarity and I being the public," Flinx concluded with satisfaction.

Tse-Mallory eyed him from where he sat. The old man was nearly as tall as Flinx and much heavier of build. Even with his legs crossed in front of him, his closely cropped white hair nearly scraped the slightly concave ceiling.

"Flinx, while you were gone on the *Teacher*, Tru and I were kept busy not only looking after your enchanting lady but monitoring the progress of that evil that threatens to devour all. As it draws nearer the galaxy our contacts in both Commonwealth and Church Science Central have been able to track its direction and progress to a degree that is as increasingly despairing as it is increasingly precise."

"It continues to speed up," a somber Flinx guessed.

Tse-Mallory nodded grimly. "According to the latest report we've received, last month the leading edge of the darkness made contact with the very minor star cluster known as MC-3048b. Hardly worthy of the designation 'cluster,' the grouping in question contained eight stars in four single and two double systems." He paused for emphasis. "All but one of the binary systems has since disappeared."

A new voice interrupted, the bemused clicking of Sylzenzuzex. "Would it be too much, venerable Eighth, to ask what you are all talking about?"

"Yes, *csillkk*, it would," Truzenzuzex told her brusquely. "All will be explained in due course." She went silent as he turned back to his lifelong companion. "Continue please, Bran."

Tse-Mallory nodded briskly. "The light of half a dozen suns—gone, just like that. No plasma flare-up, no ensuing nova, no punctuating outburst of X-rays or gamma radiation. Nothing. One by one these stars have simply vanished. Swallowed up, as an immeasurable quantity of additional matter has been, by what Flinx has so eloquently yet simply described to us as the Great Evil."

Truzenzuzex leaned impatiently toward the tall young human in their midst. Having known him for a long time, the Eint knew he could ask him anything he wished, directly and without precondition or preamble.

"What more can you say of the threat, Flinx? Have you perceived it recently? What news can you impart, what hope can you deliver?"

"Very little of either of those, I'm afraid," he mumbled unhappily.

Seated next to him Clarity reached over, took his right hand in hers, and squeezed gently. It was such a simple, uncomplicated gesture. What it communicated silently was exactly what he had missed more than anything else during his nearly two years of journeying. Human warmth. Openness. Unquestioning love.

Truzenzuzex did not take Flinx's hand, but he could gesture first-degree sympathy and understanding. "Expecting little, I am neither surprised nor disappointed by your response. At our end, nothing has changed for us or for those few others who know the secret. Despite much pondering and theorizing by minds better than Bran's and mine, the massive disguised weapons platform of the extinct Tar-Aiym that you encountered and interacted with still presents the only means and method any of us consider worth pursuing as a possible defense against the overwhelming extragalactic threat that approaches."

Tse-Mallory nodded agreement. "Not only is nothing humanx-derived perceived as even remotely capable of affecting something so vast as the Great Evil, we cannot even envision or imagine anything capable of doing so."

In the ensuing silence Truzenzuzex proceeded to voice what he and Tse-Mallory had so far been reluctant to ask. "Are Bran and I correct in assuming from the time and manner of your return to Nur that you have been unable to reestablish contact with the greatly sought-after artifact in question?"

The philosoph's assumption relieved Flinx of having to confirm what was plainly an anticipated disappointment. "I'm afraid so. But," he added quickly to forestall their deepening disillusionment, "it's not like I spent all these past months looking for it, either."

Tse-Mallory's gaze narrowed. "Then what have you been doing—boy."

Flinx flinched, but otherwise accepted the scold without comment. From a commonsensical standpoint Tse-Mallory was entirely correct in voicing the censure. Flinx would have been the last one in the room to claim that during the past year or so he had behaved in a wholly rational manner.

"I needed—I had to find out some things." He looked for support to Clarity, to whom he had already confessed the reasons behind his wandering. "About myself, about intelligence in general, about worthiness."

"Dear me," Truzenzuzex murmured, "and is it now safe to believe that with the fate of the galaxy and all sentience at stake you have finally managed to satisfy your personal requirements?"

"I think so." Flinx was too abashed to respond directly to the philosoph's sarcasm. Though in the past months he had dealt efficiently with murderous humans and belligerent AAnn, with hostile environments and would-be assassins, in the presence of the two senior scientists who had been his mentors since his early youth he felt like little more than a wayward child.

"You 'think' so, *kijaa!kt*?" Truzenzuzex harrumphed. "To think that the fate of everything should rest on the shoulders of one so young, self-centered, and unstable!"

Clarity had heard all she could stand. Locking her arm in Flinx's and leaning protectively against him she glared at the philosoph, unintimidated by either his considerable accomplishments or fearsome reputation.

"That's enough! What about everything Flinx has gone through on behalf of this lunatic quest you sent him on? What about the recurring headaches that sometimes nearly kill him? He doesn't know what a normal life is and he hasn't had any peace since he was a child—and even then he sometimes had to steal just to eat." Her gaze swung back and forth between the two scientists. "You're both famous, successful, honored representatives of your respective species. You have the freedom to go wherever you want, when you want." As Scrap adjusted his position on her shoulder she pressed close against the man beside her.

"Everyone wants something from Flinx: private individuals, companies, the great families, government agencies. Or else they want to kill him. Or dissect him." She looked up at the young man who had already lived several lifetimes. "All he wants is to be left alone—and maybe to be happy, just simply *happy,* for a little while before he dies. You can't, any of you, imagine the pressures he is under every moment of every day."

Peering down at Clarity, Flinx swallowed hard. He had been right to come back here. He was not so sure he had been right ever to leave.

For a while it was quiet in the underground room. When Truzen-zuzex finally spoke again his symbospeech was shorn of the usual abrasive clicks. But his words were underscored with as much resolve as ever.

"It's not that Bran and I don't feel for our young friend, Clarity-bearer, or that we fail to understand and sympathize with his challenging physical and mental condition. But the threat we face is far, far greater than any individual or any individual concerns. Everything—everything including personal happiness—must perforce be sacrificed in the attempt, however futile it may seem, to deal with this oncoming danger. Otherwise we abrogate our responsibility as sentient beings, to civilization and to the generations yet to come." Downy antennae dipped in her direction.

"Do you think that I am 'happy' having to devote to this peril what little time remains to me? Considerably less time, may I point out, than remains to you or to Flinx. Do you think I do not ponder what may become of my own scattered progeny if it is not overcome?" Glistening compound eyes regarded each of them in turn. "We are all of us here among the few who are even aware of the monstrousness that is sweeping toward our home, our Commonwealth. And among that few, we know that we have only one realistic possibility of confronting it. Without Flinx's intimate involvement, we have not even that." His golden gaze eyed her unblinkingly.

"In light of all that, my dear, I am afraid that individual concerns, no matter how poignant or involving or intense, must necessarily be set aside."

This time the ensuing silence lasted even longer than the one that had preceded it. For a change it was Flinx who spoke up first.

"Uh, actually, I have an idea."

Tse-Mallory took a deep breath, exhaled slowly and deliberately.

"I'll take that as encouraging. An idea about what, Flinx?"

"How to find the artifact—the Tar-Aiym weapons platform."

The older man frowned at him. "You've said from the time you left Nur months ago that you thought it would be impossible for you to track it in the vastness of the Blight. That you would have to embark on a random search pattern fueled by hope. It was the best any of us could expect from you."

Flinx reached up to stroke the back of Pip's neck. "And that's still the case. But while I don't think *I* can locate the artifact, it has occurred to me that there's another who might be able to do so."

The two scientists exchanged a glance. "You are the only individual who has been able to establish any kind of contact with the device," Truzenzuzex reminded him.

"No," Flinx insisted, "there's another."

"Who?" a startled Tse-Mallory demanded to know.

Flinx's lips creased in a thin smile. "It's not a who—it's a 'what.'"

"The boy plays mind games," Truzenzuzex muttered. "Explain yourself."

Flinx let his gaze shift from philosoph to soldier. "The original Tar-Aiym Krang. The one we found so long ago on the world called Booster, in the Blight. Remember, I activated it once."

"Indeed you did," admitted Tse-Mallory.

Flinx warmed to his proposal. "I'd be astounded if you two neglected to record the coordinates. If we can find Booster once more, and if I can make contact with the machine again, perhaps I can get across the need to contact the much bigger weapons platform. Maybe what it takes to locate one alien machine is another alien machine. All we need to get from the Krang is the platform's position and course."

Truzenzuzex looked thoughtful. "Use one weapon to locate the other. Why shouldn't weapons converse? A better prospect, certainly, than simply striking out blindly through empty space." He eyed his companion. "Bran?"

"I wholeheartedly concur." Deep blue eyes regarded Flinx. "Your ship has been adequate for all your personal searching. I presume it can make the journey to Booster."

Flinx's smile widened. "To this day I still don't know all of the *Teacher*'s capabilities. The Ul . . . its builders endowed it with all kinds of abilities I'm still learning about. I don't doubt for a minute that it can make the trip to Booster."

"Excuse me," Sylzenzuzex put in, "but what is this 'Krang' you keep talking about?"

"An ancient artifact of the long-extinct race known as the Tar-Aiym," her Eighth informed her. "A legendary device that was rumored to be a great weapon—or a musical instrument." His antennae quivered as he remembered. "To our astonishment and edification, it turned out to be both." He gestured in Flinx's direction. "Our inimitable young friend here, who was considerably less mature at the time, possesses the only mind we know of that is capable of activating the alien mechanism. If all goes well we'll be seeing it again soon enough."

"Whatever happens, however this turns out, I don't care as long as we're together." Clarity abruptly let go of Flinx's arm. "You're not thinking of going off without me *again,* are you?"

He pursed his lips thoughtfully. "The idea had occurred to me."

Her expression tightened. "Then you won't have to worry about the Order of Null, because I'll kill you first!"

He held the mock-serious expression as long as he could before releasing it as laughter and sweeping her up in his arms. "Do you really think I'd leave you behind, after nearly losing you to those crazies twice? Of course you're coming with me."

Tse-Mallory nodded approvingly. "Tru and I will of course also accompany you, as was the intention prior to the assault at the shuttleport that resulted in the serious injuries suffered by Clarity. Earlier, you told Tru and me to be ready to leave Nur 'immediately.' We are ready now. How soon can your ship be prepared for departure, Flinx?"

Still holding Clarity, he regarded his mentor. "I think we can leave tomorrow morning. Any additional provisioning or repair that needs to be carried out can be done at another world lying along the same approximate vector—safely away from local assassins."

"Then it is settled," Truzenzuzex declared with satisfaction.

"Not quite settled, *syrrlnn.*"

Everyone's attention immediately shifted to Sylzenzuzex. She regarded them evenly. "I'm coming along also, you know."

Her Eighth turned to her. "No, we do not know that, shining sweet. It is no pleasure jaunt, no tourist outing, this dive into the dead worlds of the Blight. I already anticipate enough things to worry about in the course of such a passage."

"Rest assured I will not be among them." Arching high above her abdomen, her ovipositors vibrated tautly. "I am not the youthful padre-elect of years past, esteemed Eighth. I am a fully hardened operative working in Church Security. While my skills and abilities may not begin to approach yours, and differ greatly, they can only supplement and assist in this effort." Gleaming in the overhead light, her great compound eyes turned to Flinx. "Besides, the decision is not yours."

Unexpectedly finding himself caught between relations, Flinx hesitated. In the resulting stillness it was Clarity who spoke up.

"Myself, I don't see any reason why Syl shouldn't come with us. She's already shown herself to be a practiced truhand with a weapon. On a less functional note, I personally would like to have another female along for company."

Relieved to have been given an out, Flinx shrugged. "There's certainly enough room on the *Teacher*." He eyed the philosoph. "If anything were to happen to you, Tru, having another thranx along would be . . ."

"I can take care of myself, thank you," his insectoid mentor responded stiffly. "Still, the vessel and the responsibility are yours. If you feel comfortable having yet another aboard, I will not object further. My personal feelings aside, Sylzenzuzex is no longer a sub-adult."

Reacting to this concession, Sylzenzuzex executed a gesture Flinx knew well. Her senior Eighth did not respond either verbally or with a gesticulation of his own. But Flinx knew that, at hearts, Truzenzuzex was not displeased. Quite the contrary. Though the crusty old philosoph would not admit to it, he was glad that his "niece" was coming with them.

Flinx knew this because his Talent allowed him to perceive it.

As with everything else on the paradise world of Nur, the exterior of the detention center located on the outskirts of a far commercial exurb was designed to soothe the eye and reassure the mind of any passersby. Likewise, the interior was calculated to pacify and ease. Rather than to extract revenge, the intent was to heal and repair those with antisocial tendencies who had been committed to the facility's care. Penal care on New Riviera differed considerably from that practiced on, say, Visaria.

Notwithstanding its dedication to the rehabilitation of its inmates, the detention center was a modern and secure facility designed to keep those assigned to it from interacting with the public outside the bounds of its smartly landscaped exterior. The unassuming guards carried weapons that would immobilize without killing. Though it presented many of the aspects and qualities of a convalescent retreat, the center's principal purpose remained as one with its earliest predecessor, the gaol that still stood on the south bank of an ancient Terran river called the Thames.

In accordance with and proportionate to their crimes and sentences, detainees had certain rights and privileges. Absolute freedom of movement was not among these. Those who claimed membership in the Order of Null and who had been committed to confinement until the Church order that bound them into custody could be reviewed were not allowed to stray outside carefully marked and fenced boundaries. The majority of the facility's inmates would have happily traded places with those belonging to the Order, knowing that the representatives of the newly arrived group were likely to be released uncharged within a day or two.

It was that same modest time frame, however, that was driving the Order members to distraction. Unless they could quickly regain their freedom to act, the main reason to do so would surely be on his way offworld.

No one imagined that the legal representative who came to converse with the speaker and the Elder would attempt to smuggle weapons into the facility itself. In addition to subjecting him to much more serious criminal prosecution, doing so would automatically and permanently void that individual's professional certification. What the designers of Nur's law enforcement system could not foresee was the utter dedication of the members of the Order of Null to their beliefs, and the fact that their legal agent might subscribe to them with as much fervor as those he sought to defend. The members of any organization dedicated to advancing death have little fear of prosecution, and are quite content to utilize the existing legal system to advance their own extremist ends.

So it was that the visiting counselor managed to slip a handful of shift weapons to half a dozen of his colleagues and lead them out of the facility as their unarmed brethren sacrificed themselves to delay pursuit and facilitate the flight of the seven. Considering how hastily the escape had been organized, it was carried off with considerable expertise. It was greatly aided by the fact that no police officer claiming even marginal insight into criminal behavior would have anticipated a violent jailbreak by inmates incarcerated for only two or three days. Who in their right mind would chance being sentenced to a year's imprisonment or more in order to avoid a couple of harmless nights in stir?

Where authority failed was in assuming that the members of the Order of Null were in their right mind.

While word went out from a dazed constabulary that six hitherto harmless-appearing short-term detainees and their legal defender had shot their way out of the detention facility, the escapees had utilized the counselor's skimmer to plunge deep into the heart of Sphene. Though the city was not a center of heavy industry, there were still commercial districts where those in flight could lose themselves. The escapees proceeded to do so, but only briefly. Having likely sacrificed a considerable amount of future freedom for the opportunity to act fleetingly now, they had no intention of wasting the little time that was available to them.

Their counselor had not acted alone. In addition to those who had helped him with the actual jailbreak, others were waiting attentively at the old warehouse that swallowed the skimmer.

Once safely inside and out of sight, the speaker, the Elder, and the other four high-ranking members of the Order who had fled the detention facility moved fast.

"You have something for us, I believe, Companion Delahare?"

The somewhat frumpy middle-aged woman the speaker queried had the look and demeanor of a contented homemaker whose days were filled with raising teenage progeny, swapping otherworld recipes with neighborhood friends, and ensuring the cleanliness and welcoming appearance of her household. In fact, she did all of this and more. Notable among the "more" was a penchant and a talent for working with explosives. The package she passed to the speaker was barely big enough to hold a pair of shoes.

"I worked through the night and all through this morning, ever since the request came down through channels, and managed to put this together." Her voice indicated unmistakable pride in her accomplishment. She might as well have been discussing the preparing of a favorite recipe. In a manner of speaking, she was. "I hope it will fulfill the needs of the Order."

The speaker took the package gingerly. "Will it destroy a shuttle-craft?"

The woman was apologetic. "There was no time for moderation. It will destroy a good part of the entire shuttleport."

Neither the speaker nor the Elder standing nearby voiced any objection to the potential overkill. Why worry about collateral damage that might run into the hundreds or even the thousands when everyone and everything, blessed be the coming cleansing, was going to die anyway? Studying the package, the speaker knew that whoever delivered the device to its intended target would perish along with it. It would be an honor. Nothing mattered so long as it put paid to the one potential threat to the coming Purity. Like his cohorts, he had no fear of death.

"I will come, too," the Elder informed him solemnly, "as long as I can keep up."

"My overweight will cancel the effects of your age, honored sir." The speaker smiled. The Order's objective was noble, and he had always been ready to perish on behalf of the noble cause.

No one objected when the counselor who had arranged their escape chose to remain behind. It was necessary that he survive so that his skills could be utilized in the future. Though with the one called Flinx eradicated, the Order would be able to relax, melt back into the smug, self-satisfied culture of New Riviera, and placidly await the coming destruction. The speaker was mildly disappointed that he would not have the opportunity to participate in that forthcoming repose. But what did it matter, when martyrdom awaited?

As for the many innocents who would perish at the shuttleport when the package performed its own humble, localized cleansing, they would simply die a little sooner than otherwise. In the eyes of the Order, time was nothing more than a variant that served at its whim.

No police vehicle shadowed the counselor's skimmer as it rose from the warehouse exit and headed for the city's main shuttleport. No official craft fell in behind as it wended its way cautiously between as many shielding structures as possible. The skimmer arrived at the shuttleport undetected.

The most dangerous time was behind them now, a thankful Elder pointed out to the attending acolytes. If their colleague's work was as scrupulous as she had claimed, their lingering irritant would be removed very soon indeed.

One of their number politely queried a port worker, who proceeded to check the register she carried with her. Yes, a shuttlecraft of the type described was parked on the tarmac and had been for a number of days. Monitors in its vicinity had recorded little or no activity since its arrival. It was registered as private transport. Might there be an image or physical description of the owner/operator? the Order member inquired courteously. It was a matter of some urgency. Much was at stake.

The worker apologetically avowed that she could not give out such information to those who were not cleared to receive it. Closing in discreetly around her, two of the other escapees resolved the standoff by wrenching the register from her hand. When she objected and tried to take it back, one of them quietly shot her in the back.

A minute's work with the register was sufficient to tell them everything they needed to know. By the time Port Security was made aware that a murder had been committed within its jurisdiction, the group of six was already hurrying down the appropriate corridor.

Since the pedestrian passageway accessed that portion of the port tarmac that served private craft, security was minimal. Having participated in a ferocious firefight in a similar corridor many months ago, the Elder and the speaker each experienced a profound sense of déjà vu as they huffed and puffed to keep up with their associates. Unlike on that previous occasion, this time there was no skillful senior soldier to surprise him and his colleagues, no many-limbed thranx to unleash multiple hand weapons in their direction.

This time there would be no mistake, even if their talented bomb maker had overstated the explosive potential of the contents of the package being carried by the Order's speaker. If their quarry was already aboard his shuttle, they would set it off beneath the craft, or close enough nearby. If he had not yet arrived at the port, they would conceal themselves close to his craft and wait. If Port Security interfered, several of their number would stage a noisy diversion. He, for one, would readily participate in any attack necessary to divert attention from whoever took final possession of the cleansing package.

"We're here!" the man who had shot the unsuspecting port worker announced.

Designed to handle small cargo as well as passengers, the lift carried the six of them from the depths of the subterranean corridor up to the surface. Stepping out onto the tarmac and into the warm, pleasant sunshine of New Riviera, the Elder looked to his right toward the nearest shuttle. Somewhere below, armed security teams were now racing down the corridor in pursuit of those who had violated and murdered. From different directions a pair of Port Security skimmers could be seen speeding toward the line of parked shuttles. Several other shuttlecraft, whose origin and ownership were of no consequence, gleamed nearby.

The pad where, according to the stolen port register, the shuttle belonging to the young man known as Philip Lynx had been parked was now empty.

As the others drew their weapons and crowded in behind him, an increasingly agitated speaker turned to the Elder for advice. "It's not here!" He looked around wildly. "Could we have taken the wrong access corridor?"

The man holding the stolen register performed a hurried recheck. "No, not a chance. PA-Fourteen—this is the right place!" He turned a hasty circle. "It should be *here*."

The two approaching security craft were slowing, dropping surfaceward as they neared the place where the Order members had emerged from the belowground service corridor. Confused, angry, and resigned, the speaker fondled the lethal package. Three contact switches protruded from the bottom and a fourth from the top. His fingers hovered in the vicinity of the underside.

"Honored Elder, should I proceed with . . . ?"

"No." The Elder's decision was firm. "Our lives may be needed yet. Put the device down." Turning, he regarded his loyal colleagues. "All of you, set your weapons aside. Dying is inevitable, but it should not be wasteful."

"But what of the anomaly, the one who would try to interfere?" one of the others wondered dejectedly. "What went wrong? How did we come to the wrong place?"

"We did not come to the wrong place." After the marathon run through the access corridor the Elder was feeling the full weight of his years. His weariness was compounded by failure. "Despite our haste, despite our best efforts, it appears that we just got here a little late."

Turning away from them he tilted his head back. Using one hand to shield his eyes from the bright afternoon sun he gazed skyward. The telltale trail of a shuttle heading hell-bent for the Rim of space drew his full attention. It might be the shuttlecraft belonging to the anomaly, or the young man's craft might have departed even earlier. It did not really matter. Not now. The fading track was a marker that mocked their best efforts.

Weapons drawn and leveled, Port Security was closing in around him and his associates. If he gave the word, the speaker would trigger the package and obliterate them all, members of the Order and security personnel alike. While undeniably dramatic, such a gesture would be useless, futile, and worst of all would focus attention on the surviving members of the Order. That would be counterproductive, the Elder recognized. If nothing else, a peaceful surrender might at least preserve some anonymity and deflect attention from those who would remain free to continue the necessary work.

Moments later, as he was being placed in restraints, he reflected that his life would soon be over anyway, albeit long before the coming cleansing arrived from the far reaches of the intergalactic void. His only regret was that he was not going to live long enough to experience that great day. That gratification would be bequeathed to others. The Order would go on, until its watchfulness was no longer needed. As he and his colleagues were taken away he consoled himself with the knowledge that the efforts to eliminate the singular impeder were probably unnecessary anyway. Nothing could stop, or slow, or hinder the inexorable arrival of the Purity. Nothing!

It bothered him, though, that he could not stop himself from occasionally glancing skyward in the direction taken by the recently departed shuttlecraft.

CHAPTER

19

"It's a beautiful world."

Clarity expressed her feelings as the shuttlecraft began the long drop surfaceward. Her reaction upon glimpsing the view on the shuttle's monitor was identical to Flinx's upon his first sight of Booster so many years ago.

"It is." Reaching over from the pilot's drop seat, he took her hand and squeezed it gently. "Mostly ocean, and the one big continent where we're headed. A nice place to live—if you're a Tar-Aiym. They're built a lot heavier and more solid than we are."

She glanced over at him. "It looks inviting on the readouts. A lot of free helium in the atmosphere, but otherwise perfectly breathable. What's wrong with it?"

From the seat behind her Tse-Mallory offered an explanation. "It's just a bit breezy," he told her.

"When Bran and Tru and I were here before," Flinx explained further, "we had to locate the Krang from orbit. Now that we know its location I'm going to try and set down close enough so that we can reach it by skimmer, instead of having to use a heavy land vehicle. Which is important, because the *Teacher* doesn't carry a crawler."

"I'm sure there'll be no—oh!" She let out a short gasp as the shuttle rocked violently and her lounge protectively locked her down.

"Breezy," Tse-Mallory quipped from behind her.

Though he was not nearly as good a pilot as Atha Moon, who had managed the first humanx landing on Booster, Flinx's shuttle had the advantage of more advanced electronics. As they passed through the upper jet streams the ride smoothed out, the ship's systems compensating for the incessant winds. The rest of the descent held steady enough so that, when the concentric crescents of the ancient city below finally came into view, Clarity and Sylzenzuzex felt safe in leaving their seats to enjoy the nonelectronic view out the main port.

Immediately, they found themselves drawn to the towering, dull yellow-white, rectangular pyramid that soared skyward from a bluff near the center of the city. It dominated everything, natural and artificial, as far as could be seen in any direction.

"Is that it?" Clarity's tone was subdued. "The Krang?"

Though the shuttle was more or less flying itself, Flinx kept his attention on the instrumentation in case his input was needed. "Three kilometers high and each side at the base is more than a kilometer. Five hundred million years old, give or take a few million. And when we were here before, we never did really figure out what it was made of. We do know it contains a lot of incredibly dense, unidentifiable ceramic alloy."

Standing alongside Clarity, Sylzenzuzex clicked in symbospeech. "That's the tallest artificial structure I have ever seen. I don't think there is anything like it even on human worlds—and your people adore tall buildings."

"I assure you, dear Syl," Truzenzuzex clicked, "that its height, *sili!!ppk,* is the least of its extraordinary characteristics."

Passing swiftly over the remnants of what must have been a spaceport of immense size, the little shuttlecraft set down cleanly at the base of the bluff dominated by the tower of the Krang. The airstream outside read thirty-four kph. On either side of the shielding bluff it rose to a steady hundred and twenty, with gusts as high as two hundred. Even that constituted nothing more than a stiff breeze compared to the shocking gales that ripped around the planet's equator.

Prior to disembarking, Flinx made sure that Clarity donned a pair of protective goggles. Tse-Mallory had his own, and Tru looked after his young relative Sylzenzuzex. Collecting daypacks filled with basic supplies, they filed through the *Teacher* and into the skimmer waiting in the holding bay.

Following the irregular layers and ledges the ceaseless wind had cut into the bluff, they rode the skimmer up to the base of the Krang. Sheltered in the lee of the massive structure, they set down directly in front of a vitreous, dull gray, thirty-meter-high metal door.

An all-too-familiar dull pounding had started up at the back of Flinx's skull. *Not now,* he cursed himself. Not here. But there was nothing he could do about it except try to rest—and he had no intention of resting here and now.

Clarity was staring out the front of the skimmer's transparent dome at the gargantuan doorway. "How do you get inside? How did you open it the last time?"

The throbbing at the back of his head kept Flinx from smiling. "We didn't. It sensed us and opened for . . . there it goes now!"

He was more relieved than he cared to admit when the two halves of the colossal portal began to part in front of them. If the doorway had not opened of its own accord, he and his companions would have been obliged to try to find an alternate means of entry. Forcing their way into the Krang was not a prospect he would have looked forward to with delight.

He was worrying needlessly. They were in.

Rising, they moved cautiously through the portal. Once they were inside, the twenty-meter-thick metal barrier commenced to slide silently shut behind them. Clarity looked uneasily at Flinx. When he did not react to the blocking of their exit, she quite rightly assumed the action had been anticipated. Returning her attention forward, she got her first view of the interior of the Krang—and sucked in her breath sharply. Resting nearby on all six legs, Sylzenzuzex let out a long, low whistle.

Remembering his own first sight of the Krang's core, Flinx smiled to himself. The headache was not worsening and the pain was manageable—for the moment. Behind him, in the center of the skimmer, Tse-Mallory and Truzenzuzex were reminiscing aloud as they identified salient points of the alien edifice's extraordinary interior.

Though viewed this time through the eyes of a world-weary adult instead of those of an awestruck child, the sight that spread out before the skimmer was every bit as remarkable to Flinx as it had been the first time he had seen it. Visible through the intensifying but still diffuse blue-green artificial light that was concentrated in wavelengths intended for nonhuman eyes, wisps of cloud hovered near the impossibly distant ceiling of the colossal structure's hollow heart. Soaring a hundred meters high and more from the floor and extending downward toward the core of the planet itself, arcane machinery and alien instrumentation lined all four inner walls. Above that rose an infinitude of tubes and protrusions of every imaginable size, shape, and length. Some no bigger than a finger, others great enough in diameter to swallow a small ship.

Within the impenetrable walls of the Krang there was no wind. It was dead quiet. Half a million years dead quiet, Flinx reminded himself. Unlike the previous visit, when he and his companions had been forced to hike across the vast space, this time they traveled across the immense amphitheater, passing its alien chair-lounges, to the far side of the structure in the seats of the comfortable skimmer. Their destination was a platform that rose slightly above the rest of the yellow-white floor.

He threatened to drown in the flood of memories that washed over him at the sight of it.

After the skimmer set down gently, he waited until everyone else had disembarked. Overcome by the sights surrounding her and by the moment, even Clarity did not linger to wonder what was holding him back. She and Scrap exited along with the others.

He followed in due course. The two scientists discoursed on their surroundings and how accurately they corresponded to their respective recollections. Clarity and Sylzenzuzex stood and marveled. But Flinx's attention was focused on the glassy, transparent dome that formed a canopy above the Tar-Aiym resting place. Like the rest of the Krang's interior, the platform was exactly as he remembered it: tilted slightly toward the amphitheater, a second smaller dome suspended above the lower, fibers and filaments and strands of alien conduit running from its pedestal to vanish into the walls and ground.

This had all happened yesterday, he told himself as he stared fixedly at the unassuming nexus of power and contemplation. In reality it had all happened more than a decade ago.

His, Bran Tse-Mallory's, and the Eint Truzenzuzex's memories were not the only ones that were stirring.

Deep within the heart of the unimaginable complexity that was the

Krang, an awakening had begun. In response to the arrival of sentient beings, long-dormant connections were reestablished. Quiescent links flared to life. Illumination manifested itself in photonic blinks and flashes whose significance would have been lost on human or thranx. Bit by bit, section by section, element by element, core components of instrumentation that to an outsider would have appeared to owe their functionality more to magic than to known physics began to return to life.

At its core was a synthetic consciousness that was as different from the artificial intelligence that ran the *Teacher* as that simulated mind was from the brain of a fish. For the Krang, hardly any time at all had passed. Recently ("recent" being, to the Krang, in itself a highly relativistic term) there had been certain developments of significance on its watch. It divined that more of these were now in the offing.

The great machine that was the Krang had been conceived and fabricated to protect its builders and itself from external danger. The threat that now loomed, distant but all too real, was beyond its considerable capability to defeat. In consequence of that it had periodically reached through realities other than space-plus and space-minus in hopes of finding allies that might serve to counter the oncoming menace. In its devout and consistent searching it had located two. Both, it developed, were also aware of the threat. Both by themselves were equally as helpless as the ancient Tar-Aiym weapon to offer up or propose a defense against the danger.

Operating in unison offered more promising possibilities. Particularly if a force able to bind all three of them together could be found. Unfortunately, such a unique and specialized link capable of functioning over such great distances could not be engineered—certainly not in the time remaining before total annihilation arrived.

Astoundingly, unexpectedly, unpredictably, it turned out that such a force already existed. Incredibly, the necessary trigger, the requisite input, had already been contrived. Made aware of its astonishing existence, all three inconceivably disparate entities had for years toiled with subtlety and sensitivity to raise the trigger's awareness of itself and of what was at stake. To some extent the effort had clearly been successful. In exceedingly minute increments, progress had been made. The key had, if nothing else, been made cognizant of itself and its importance.

Whether it would function effectively remained to be seen.

Clarity had moved to stand next to Flinx. As she talked softly, Pip and Scrap engaged in a feint fight from their perches on their respective masters' shoulders. Iridescent triangular heads darted sharply forward only to withdraw from each counterthrust as pointed tongues flicked harmlessly.

"The Tar-Aiym Krang." As befitted the surroundings, Clarity's tone was suitably subdued. "As many times as you've mentioned it to me, as often as you've tried to describe it, I don't think anything even you could have said, Flinx, could prepare someone for the reality."

Staring at the familiar tilted platform that beckoned from beneath the twin transparent domes, he nodded thoughtfully. "Images wouldn't have helped much, either. There's just too much of everything."

"And the weapons platform constructed by the same race, the one Tse-Mallory and Truzenzuzex want you to try and find again," she went on, "is the size of a small planet and has dozens of such devices?"

"Maybe hundreds," he muttered. "I didn't have time to take the full measure of it, Clarity. When I was on it I was—preoccupied."

She considered before replying. "How can something like this—building—do battle against the menace you've shown me?"

"It can't, by itself. But I'm hoping"—he nodded toward where Tse-Mallory and Truzenzuzex were conversing with Syl—"that the artificial intelligence in control of it can make contact with the corresponding AI that controls the weapons platform and obtain its coordinates and course." He indicated the resting place beneath the dome. "That's where the operator, or performer, lies. I've occupied that place myself, and another one very much like it on board the weapons platform." He looked down at her. "We're here so I can try to make contact again."

Her eyes met his. "What happens if you fail, Flinx? What if the intelligence that directs the Krang is no longer functional?"

"I believe it will still be functional, Clar. It survived lying dormant for half a million years. I don't think it will have stopped working in the past ten. It can't have changed that much in so short a period of time." He looked back toward the empty, beckoning platform. "On the other hand, I have."

"For the better," she insisted, putting a hand on his arm.

"Maybe." A sharper stab of pain shot through the back of his head.

The throbbing that had commenced outside the entrance to the Krang had returned, with fervor. "We're likely to find out."

As she leaned close against him her voice dropped to just above a whisper. "Don't lie to me, Flinx. Don't try to make things easy, or mollify me with evasions, or patronize me out of love. How dangerous is this?"

Preempted by her directness, he could do nothing but resort to irony. "I'm going to try and make mental contact with a half-million-year-old alien war machine built by a battle-loving species that, when activated, is capable of projecting a Schwarzchild discontinuity strong enough to swallow starships and, for all I know, maybe entire planets." Putting his left arm around her shoulders, he squeezed firmly. "No danger there."

She smiled encouragingly. "Maybe you haven't changed as much as you think."

While he and Clarity were immersed in each other, his old friends and frequent mentors had arrived to rejoin them. Sylzenzuzex stood beside her Eighth, ready to lend support to both Flinx and the expedition's other female.

"Well?" was all Bran Tse-Mallory said dryly.

That was what the bold, ebullient merchant Maxim Malaika had exclaimed on numerous occasions during Flinx's first visit to this place, so many years ago. Well, it was time to move on. He was going to the well to see what kind of water he could draw. Well he would be if he survived. Well, well, and well.

What the hell, he thought cynically. All he could do was die.

He climbed the dais to its skewed summit and paused there, peering underneath the transparent canopy at the vacant, waiting platform. Everything looked exactly as he remembered it. That much could have been anticipated. What mattered was, would everything *feel* as he remembered it. Having previously been exposed to unimaginable, unknown forces beyond human ken, he had reacted and responded instinctively. Could he do so one more time and perhaps this time retain some control? Taking a last impassive breath he stepped forward and eased himself beneath the edge of the canopy.

On his right shoulder Pip immediately went taut, alerted to something commanding and unseen. The pebbly surface beneath Flinx's feet began to vibrate. From somewhere far below emerged the first inklings of a deep, pulsating mechanical moan that grew progressively more audible. The throbbing in his head grew abruptly more intense.

He considered stepping back, then steeled himself. There *was* no going back, really. Not now, not here. Ignoring the pain and a growing dizziness, he stumbled forward until his legs bumped up against the platform. Leaning forward, his hands resting on the edge of a superficially simplistic structure that was designed to accommodate a much larger body, he shook his head as he fought to retain balance and control.

Seeing him falter, Clarity started forward, only to find herself restrained by both Tse-Mallory and Truzenzuzex. Her worried gaze remained focused on Flinx. He was starting to sway, and not because of the increasingly frequent tremors under their feet.

"Let me go! He's in trouble, he's . . . !"

". . . Doing what needs to be done, child." The philosoph's gleaming compound eyes regarded her sympathetically. "Collect yourself, have courage, and watch."

Unable to break free of the combined human-thranx grasp, there was little else she could do.

"It hurts. . . ."

Trembling slightly, Flinx reached one hand up to his forehead. This wasn't how it was supposed to be. This was not how he remembered it. This . . .

A voice, or words, or a sudden thought. Somewhere between migraine and migrant. Inside his head. Inside his own thinking, but not his. Yet for all that, familiar.

WELCOME—BACK.

Just like that, his headache was—gone. Evaporated like spit on the sun. His skull still throbbed, but there was no pain. Refusing to dwell on the apparent contradiction, he climbed up onto the platform and lay down, positioning himself in the center. Slithering upward from his shoulder, Pip bundled herself into a tight coil near the top of his head. In a normal prone resting position she would have done so on his chest or his stomach. Reaching up, he stroked her muscular shape affectionately. She was and always had been his friend. His companion. His protector.

Also an empathetic lens, involuntarily and reflexively focusing his peculiar Talent.

Taking a deep breath and using his heels, he pushed both of them upward. Up, until his head emerged beneath the second smaller, inner dome. He shut his eyes. Or perhaps they were shut for him.

Looking on from outside, Sylzenzuzex vocalized a sequence of clicks, whistles, and exclamations the likes of which she had never intoned before. Nearby, Clarity's eyes got very, very wide. As for Tse-Mallory and Truzenzuzex, they simply stood flanking her while providing the comfort of their physical presence. They had seen it all before.

The inner dome above Flinx's head began to pulsate with metallic bursts of the most intense deep purple. The outer dome exploded in a blistering burst of color in every conceivable hue: scorching crimson, crushing azure, fluorescent pinks, and electric greens. At unpredictable intervals balls of colored lightning swelled to form bulges on the upper curves and crest of the dome. When they reached a certain blazing, crackling volume, they detached themselves and rose like electrified balloons toward the distant apex of the Krang's interior.

All that only signaled the beginning.

The great pipes and cylinders that lined the kilometers-high walls had sprung to life with sound as well as color. While bands of intense color ran up their towering flanks like flights of electricity from God's own van DeGraff generator, something deeper and harsher, wilder and more profound than the rumble underfoot began to fill the vast interior space. It caused Clarity to cover her ears, and then it made her drop her hands and listen. The vibrations penetrated her flesh and being and soaked directly into her bones.

"That's music!" she shouted, trying to make herself heard above the martial alien thunder.

Next to her Tse-Mallory nodded, leaning close to yell into her ear. "Tar-Aiym music. Alien harmony and dissonance. Instrumentation of a scale and scope unequaled anywhere in the Commonwealth." He put a hand on her shoulder. "Contemplate it: mass as Mass."

She raised an arm toward the dome that was now fully enveloped in opaque, coruscating color. "What about Flinx? Does he hear it?"

On her other side the venerable philosoph turned from shout-whistling at Sylzenzuzex. "Only Flinx knows what he hears! And what he hears, *Kssa!!lk,* is barred to the rest of us. What we learned on our previous visit, so many years ago, is that this relic of an ancient people is both a musical instrument *and* a weapon."

Indicating that she understood, she returned her attention to the color-masked platform. Beneath the two domes occasional glimpses of her beloved flickered within the maelstrom of color and light. She assumed he was still alive and all right. She assumed so because she had to.

Flinx kept waiting for the pain in his head to return. It did not. Instead, he experienced a lucidity of perception he had come into contact with only rarely before. Experimentally, tentatively, he tried reaching out, as he had done when lying on a similar platform beneath a similar structure inside the great space-traversing Tar-Aiym weapons platform itself. There had been no pain then, either. He had communicated successfully, albeit briefly and with notable directness and simplicity. This exchange would be more difficult, more fraught with uncertainty. His intention was not merely to make and maintain contact, but to ignite nothing less than a conversation.

WELCOME BACK.

He was positive that was what he had heard. Or felt, or sensed. The Krang was still alive. *He* was still alive.

Now he had to make his attempt while keeping it that way.

Above his head a coiled Pip twitched and spasmed, the unthinking Alaspinian minidrag serving as a lens to focus and intensify her master's feelings. As he had on the weapons platform, Flinx tried reaching out. He was but dimly aware of the vast play of light and sound that was going on around him. Would the ancient artifact respond to his mental push with more than just color and harmony and the tintinnabulation of alien percussion?

"You remember me," he struggled to project. To *feel*. It was the mental equivalent of expectantly spreading his hands to his sides.

It was sufficient.

Naisma was established.

CLASS-A MIND . . . I REMEMBER YOU. YOU COME SEEK-

ING HELP TO DEAL WITH THE THREAT THAT APPROACHES FROM BEYOND THE RIM.

Having no time to waste on it, Flinx withheld his astonishment. *"You know of it?"*

IT DOMINATES. IT LOOMS. IT THREATENS ALL OF EVERYTHING. HOW COULD IT EXIST UNOBSERVED?

Enthralled, he thought back to one singular experience of the past several years—and then to another, and another.

"You've been with me, of me. You pushed me to perceive the Evil."

ISELF, AND OTHERS.

"What others?" Flinx contorted slightly on the platform.

OTHERS WHO KNOW YOU. OTHERS YOU CAN KNOW BUT I CANNOT. OTHERS WHO ARE AS DIFFERENT FROM ONE ANOTHER AS YOU ARE FROM I. BUT OTHERS WHO ALSO KNOW AND FEAR THAT WHICH THREATENS ALL. SOMEHOW YOU ARE THE KEY TO THE ONLY CHANCE OF STOPPING IT. YOU ARE THE ONLY LINK THAT EXISTS BETWEEN US.

The key. Flinx had heard that before. In dreams both asleep and awake. What was he now? Asleep? Awake? Or drifting in a state of which no physiologist had dreamed and for which there was therefore no definition.

"Why me?" he asked, not for the first time.

YOU ARE AN ANOMALY. YOU ARE A SINGULARITY. NOTHING THAT CAN BE PREDICTED CAN HALT THE ADVANCE OF THE THREAT. WHAT YOU ARE IS—NOT PREDICTABLE.

"I understand. I and my friends have given much time and thought to possible ways of stopping or diverting the menace that comes for all. There is another like you, another built-mind of the Tar-Aiym. I have seen it, been on it, communicated with it. Its structure contains multiples of yourself and the great force you can project. I and my friends believe it may be strong enough to stop the Evil."

I CANNOT MOVE. I AM FIXED TO THIS PLACE, AND TO THE CORE OF THIS WORLD THAT POWERS ME. I CANNOT FIGHT THE INVADER. NOR CAN THE OTHERS. NOT ALONE. PERHAPS TOGETHER WE MIGHT DO SOMETHING—YET WE

DO NOT KNOW HOW. AS THE KEY, WE HAVE THOUGHT YOU MIGHT KNOW THE WAY.

The way? What was the Krang talking about? The only "way" Flinx knew was the possible one he had debated with Truzenzuzex and Tse-Mallory.

"I do have one idea," he explained solemnly. *"Reach out, if you can. Seek the individuality that is akin to but greater than yours. Define and locate and enlighten it. Give me the coordinates. I and my friends will go to it. I will lie therein as I lie here, and give that of myself that no one and nothing else seems able to give—be it some kind of 'key' or whatever. If you and the triad of my dreamings can be there with me, at that moment, then we will see if the combining of our thoughts and minds somehow works to stop what is coming to destroy all."*

As sound and color raged throughout its structure, the Krang within was silent. Then: IT SEEMS TO ME NOT THE WAY. IT SEEMS TO ME NOT ENOUGH STRENGTH. IT SEEMS TO ME NOT ENOUGH OF ENOUGH. BUT . . . YOU ARE THE CLASS-A MIND. I WILL COMPLY. MEANWHILE . . . BE STILL, AND AT PEACE, AND . . . WAIT.

Outside the dome Clarity was doing her best to restrain herself. So intense was the all-enveloping color and so luminous the lightning that she could no longer see Flinx where he lay on the interior platform. Primordial alien harmony continued to hammer at her ears and assault her sanity. In the shadow of Tse-Mallory's and Truzenzuzex's continuing composure, she forced herself to stay calm.

But as the light storm shattered her senses she could not keep her fear from continuing to deepen.

"Are you sure he's all right?" she yelled at Tse-Mallory.

Eyes of deepest, clearest blue peered into her own. "We can't be sure of anything here, Clarity!" A long arm waved to take in their heaven-storming surroundings. "We can't know anything for certain until this stops!"

It was no comfort, no comfort at all. But she was too focused, too engaged, and frankly too enraptured by what was swirling around her to cry.

Flinx could feel himself being drawn outward. He did not marvel or wonder at the sensation, having experienced it numerous times before.

Born on the strength of the Krang's projection, he soared through space. Stars passed by in the wink of a mental eye, sprawling nebulae appeared and vanished in an instant of thought. Seeking, searching, uniting— until at last a connection was made. Feeble at first, it strengthened quickly when a response was received. There came a kind of joy he could not share as artifact made contact with artifact. He was present at the exchange, he perceived, but even though his facilitator tried, little of what transpired could be imparted to him.

Two machine minds were exchanging communication. Two artificial intelligences that had previously been unaware of one another's existence. After five hundred thousand years, like was communicating with like. It was curt, it was efficient, it was enabled. Much simplified, it was two weapons talking to one another. Two weapons, at least one of which had the capacity to destroy worlds. The entire passage of information, during which the equivalent of many complete libraries was exchanged, took less than one minute.

Key, he thought. *Trigger.* Such power as the wandering Tar-Aiym platform represented. Would it be enough? The Krang didn't seem to think so. But it had to be tried. There was nothing else.

It was over as soon as it had begun. He felt himself receding, falling back, his perception shrinking. Down past suns and worlds unknown, through vortices of energy and disks of dark matter; back, back toward a single dead world circling a long forgotten sun.

He opened his eyes. Actual purple momentarily replaced visual purple, and then both were gone in a double blink. An echo of symphonies unimagined echoed briefly in his ears, already fading to pianissimo. The voice that was replacing it and growing rapidly stronger was familiar.

"Flinx, Flinx!" Clarity was atop the dais and at his side as soon as he straightened and slipped out from beneath the inner dome. He would have reached for her except that he felt a weight falling from his head. Extending his arms, he caught Pip just as she tumbled. The minidrag was completely spent, completely limp, and if possible even more exhausted than her master.

With him holding the flying snake it was difficult for Clarity to kiss him, but she did her best. Tse-Mallory was next at his side, helping support him. Behind them Flinx saw the two thranx looking on and gesturing concern. Above and in the distance, colors were fading as they re-treated like pale syrup down the multitude of cylinders that lined the towering interior walls of the Krang.

Tse-Mallory didn't waste time. "Anything? How did it go? Famil-iar, new, shocking, reassuring—say something. Talk to me, Flinx."

Heedless of both the sociologist's physical size and intellectual stature, Clarity interposed herself between him and his subject. "Leave him alone—for a while, anyway. Can't you see that he's completely drained?" Without waiting for Tse-Mallory's response, she turned back to Flinx. "Are you all right? Can I get you something from the skimmer?"

He took a step and nearly fell. Between Clarity and Tse-Mallory, he did not. "Water. Water would be—good."

Whirling, she raced down the dais to where they had stacked the supplies they had brought from the skimmer. Following more slowly, Flinx and Tse-Mallory were joined by Sylzenzuzex and her Eighth.

"What was it like, Flinx?" With both left hands Syl gestured back at the now dormant platform. "What happened there, under all that noise and light and color?"

"Contact occurred," he told her weakly, "and it was tiring."

"I can see that. You were a brave boy, once," Truzenzuzex told him. "Now that bravery is backed by maturity."

A weary Flinx smiled down at his old mentor. "Don't count on it. How many minutes was I under?"

"Minutes?" The philosoph looked to his human companion. "Do I misinterpret the chrono?"

"You do not," Tse-Mallory assured him. He met Flinx's quizzical gaze. "You were lying in state for just under four hours, my young friend."

Pondering the disparity between perception and reality, Flinx summed up with an observation that was wholly typical. "That would explain why I'm starving as well as thirsty."

As soon as they were clear of the dais, his companions helped him take a seat on one of the impervious benches that had once served as resting places for Tar-Aiym. Despite his exhaustion he refused to lie down, preferring to remain upright as he drank, ate, and slowly regained his strength. A little water and some appropriate nutrients were enough to revive Pip.

"You said that contact occurred." Sylzenzuzex was so close that in his weakened state her distinctive perfume threatened to overpower him. "What kind of contact? With the Krang?"

"No. First, there was interchange between myself and the Krang." He looked up over the water bottle he was holding at the two attentive scientists. "I explained our need. Though doubtful as to its potential, the machine complied with my request. It extended itself. Contact was made with the wandering relic."

Truzenzuzex and Tse-Mallory exchanged elated murmurs. "You learned its location?" Flinx nodded. The philosoph turned to his human colleague. "We must make preparations to leave here and set out on the relevant vector as quickly as possible."

Clarity immediately moved protectively closer to Flinx. "What's the matter with you people? Look at him! Don't you realize how frail he is? He needs time to rest and regain his full strength." Her tone darkened. "He's not an instrument, damn it!"

Tse-Mallory did not blink, did not look away as he replied to her. "I'm afraid, my dear, that he is."

"Well, I don't care what you think. I've been exposed to this impending horror in more depth than any of you, and I know it won't be here tomorrow, or the next day. There's nothing that can't wait a day or two."

"The weapons platform whose assistance we seek may not wait," Truzenzuzex told her. "In a day or two it may travel millions of units of distance. In a week, tens of millions." He eyed Flinx as the latter sipped from a flexible, self-chilling liquids container. "One does not dawdle with the fate of civilization at stake."

"It doesn't matter." Draining the last of the bottle's contents, Flinx leaned against Clarity. Sliding downward, he ended up with his head in her lap. Pip took the opportunity to slither onto her master's body, forming a series of solid serpentine coils on his stomach.

In the absence of eyelids Truzenzuzex's gaze could not narrow, but his tone conveyed the same effect. "What do you mean, 'it doesn't matter'? Are you once again sliding into depression even as you slide backward on your fundament?"

"No, not at all." Flinx gazed contently up at Clarity, who bestowed on him the smile that never failed to improve all manner of injuries, physical and otherwise. "I mean that it doesn't matter because we don't need to hurry to make contact with the weapons platform."

Tse-Mallory eyed the ever-unpredictable youth uncertainly. "Why not? What Tru just stated holds true."

"I realize that." With a pained sigh Flinx closed his eyes, this time, he hoped, to see, feel, and experience as little as possible. "I mean that we don't have to hurry to make contact with the weapons platform because it's coming here. . . ."

CHAPTER

20

Flinx knew what was coming because the Krang had communicated that much to him and because he had sensed it for himself, but a time frame had not been part of the exchange. The weapons platform was coming to Booster. If the Krang was to be believed, that much was a certainty. *When* it would arrive the great machine could not say. When Tse-Mallory gently suggested to Flinx that he go back under the dome and try to find out, Clarity Held went up one side of the brawny sociologist and down the other. Flinx himself had no way of knowing what another attempt so soon at communication with the ancient alien device might do to him. It might result in him receiving a dose of cerebral enhancement, as had the original connection years earlier. Or his simple organically wired human brain might finally snap under the strain.

So they waited. While they did so, Clarity and Flinx and Sylzenzuzex took to exploring the sprawling dead city while the two scientists amused themselves trying to extract harmonic fractals from the recording the skimmer had made of the Tar-Aiym music.

A week passed before the *Teacher* relayed an alarm from shuttlecraft to the skimmer and onward to their individual communits.

"Something has emerged from space-plus to assume a position beyond this system's outermost planet."

"I know." Flinx hastened to reassure his vessel's wary AI. "The visitor is expected."

"Recognizing it and recalling its capabilities, I am most relieved to hear that, Flinx. Its parameters appear to be unchanged. It is as we encountered it previously, some six years ago. The exact time of concurrence . . ."

"Not necessary," Flinx told his ship. "I remember."

"You remember everything." The ship was not trying to flatter, merely stating fact.

"The luxury of forgetfulness is one that always seems to escape me." Twisting his head, he glanced down at Pip. The minidrag was sleeping soundly on his shoulder. Seeing his pet so often at peace, he regretted being unable to change places with her.

Rising from where he was sitting deep at the edge of the amphitheater, he tilted back his head to take what might well be his last look at the interior of the Krang. The strangely persistent fog that hung near the distant apex, the ranks of cylinders and pipes that lined the inwardly inclined walls, the operator's dais: sights and memories that had been with him since early adolescence had now been refreshed in adulthood. He would carry them with him always. As the *Teacher*'s AI had just reminded him, he never forgot.

Because they were leaving this place behind physically did not mean it would be out of his mind any more than it had been absent from his recurring, often cryptic dreams.

Having had the newly arrived Tar-Aiym artifact described to them by Flinx, Tse-Mallory and Truzenzuzex were eager to see it for themselves. In her capacity as a security officer for the United Church, Sylzenzuzex had a professional interest in any kind of unauthorized and unrecorded weapons system. And while Clarity was primarily interested in Flinx's health and well-being, she had to admit that she was not entirely devoid of curiosity regarding the visitor herself.

"It's really that big?" she asked as they stepped out of the shuttlecraft and back into the holding bay in the underside of the *Teacher.*

"No." He didn't smile and was not joking. "It's bigger. You'll see."

Booster's tired and now distant sol-type star boasted the classic array of rocky inner worlds and outer gas giants. Heading outsystem in normal space, they passed several of these uninhabited, unnamed orbs.

It was not necessary to skim so close in order to make rendezvous with the artifact, but the two scientists would not hear of leaving without using the opportunity to make at least a few nominal measurements in passing.

When the *Teacher* began its approach, everyone gathered in the ship's control room to have a look out the main foreport. Despite what Flinx had told them of the relic, Sylzenzuzex still confessed to bemusement as she gazed upon the spherical object that occupied the space forward and slightly to port.

"Where is it, *tlacchk?*"

"You're looking at it." Standing behind her, Flinx gazed out at the alien sphere from which he had barely escaped with his life some half-dozen years before.

"You mean," she clicked, "it's in orbit above the surface somewhere?"

"No," he told her. "I mean that's it. The vessel. The Tar-Aiym weapons platform."

It did not matter that he had described the artifact to them. Saying that a vessel was planet-sized was one thing. Trying to comprehend the actuality of something so immense was, as he knew well, entirely different.

It looked just as he remembered it from the encounter years ago, when he had been forced to explore its outermost level while being pursued by human assassins, rapacious AAnn, and—one other. He forced himself to push the disturbing memories into the past, to file them in the overflowing folder of similar unsettling incidents from his history. It was all over and done with, and for the sake of everyone he needed to concentrate on the present.

As a planet the cloud-swathed globe was not especially impressive. As a ship, an artificial construct, it exceeded anything humanxkind had ever contemplated except in moments of drugged engineering fantasy and conceptual delirium. Stippled with flecks of yellow and dark red, the thick gaseous cloud cover shone a dreary bronze in the faint light of the distant sun. Leaning over the forward console, Clarity pointed as an irritated Scrap struggled to keep from slipping off her left shoulder.

"Look there, in the northern hemisphere. Is that a storm?"

Flinx looked to where she was pointing. He knew what the vortex she had singled out portended. The storm was as artificial as the colossal mechanism that had created it.

"I'm pretty sure it's a sign that our presence has been acknowledged," he told her. What he did not add was that the Tar-Aiym artifact, which was twice the size of the Earth, might be putting forth a welcome because it remembered him from last time.

The *Teacher* might subscribe to the same theory, but all it said was, "I am receiving a directional signal."

"Follow it," Flinx replied crisply. Clarity looked over at him.

"I know you've had contact with this—vessel—before, Flinx, but shouldn't we be taking some kind of precautions before going down? Shield activation, maybe, or initiation of—"

"Of what?" He interrupted her gently, nodding out the port at the immense mass of cloud, metal, and who knew what else. "Weapons? I've told you what the Krang can do. This world-sized ship is probably capable of generating a big enough discontinuity to swallow a whole system. At least, that's what we're hoping. Otherwise there's no point to this encounter. What would you suggest as a defense if it decided we were deserving of a hostile response?"

She considered his words, then nodded slowly. "Faint praise, maybe. I see your point."

As a tiny portion of the swirling, dense, synthetic atmosphere was sucked away by gigantic intakes, a portion of the surface of the weapons platform became visible to those huddled in the control room of the *Teacher*. There were no gasps of incredulity, no mutterings of astonishment at the sight thus revealed. The relic was simply too big, too overwhelming, to inspire any more than an abiding, awed silence. External edifices of metal and ceramic, crystal and metallic glass, and other exotic materials came into view. Some of the structures were the size of cities, others as big as bits of continents. Illuminatories in all colors and hues flashed to life where the veiling methane haze was drawn away.

"It's not just big," Sylzenzuzex murmured. "It's *beautiful*. To think that somebody built it, that it's a construct and not a natural object, would try belief if I wasn't looking at it myself."

On Flinx's shoulder, Pip was stirring. "Don't forget that it's a weapon," he reminded her. "Quite possibly the biggest weapon ever built."

Standing at his right side, Clarity eyed the artifact as the *Teacher* began to descend. "I once saw a picture of an ancient Terran weapon, a metal projectile gun that dated from an era well before Amalgamation. It used combustible powder to propel a piece of lead toward a target. What struck me was not the primitive technology; it was the ornamentation. Gold filigree, gemstones, and ivory inlay." She studied the view outside. "Why do so many sentient species find weapons worthy of decoration?"

A curious Flinx pondered her question as he turned to lead the way to the shuttle bay. "What's ivory?"

Bolts of lightning kilometers high slashed through the thick atmosphere in the vicinity of the downward-spiraling vortex that was clearing a path through the clouds down to the surface. As the *Teacher*'s shuttlecraft descended, jostled and rocked by the surrounding synthetic cyclone, an opening appeared below it as a portion of the surface irised open to welcome the diminutive arrival. The aperture was more than wide enough to admit the visitor. It was more than ample enough to admit any city on Earth, had one possessed the means and the inclination to embark on such a visit.

"If the solitary Krang on Booster is powered by the energy of the planetary core itself," Tse-Mallory was speculating aloud, "then what could possibly drive an artificial world of these dimensions? Not to mention the multiplicity of comparable destructive devices it supports."

"Plainly an energy source beyond our limited ability to engineer, *kissaltt*." Truzenzuzex was gazing raptly out the foreport. "Some sort of matter-antimatter drive, which has long been theorized and sought after. Or perhaps the vessel is able to channel the energy of a small white hole for which its builders were somehow able to devise containment." The valentine-shaped head inclined toward his old friend. "We hardly have the theoretical mathematical underpinning from which to begin to envisage such technology."

A miracle of alien engineering itself, the vast acreage of alloy that comprised the portal began to close behind and above them as the shuttlecraft dropped down onto a vast, open, and otherwise unoccupied deck. The *Teacher* promptly informed those on board that outside gravity was tolerable and the external air pressure was rising rapidly.

"There are some unusual trace gases here," Flinx informed his companions, "but it's essentially the same atmosphere we breathed on Booster. The Tar-Aiym may have looked nothing like us, but they sucked the same air."

Truzenzuzex fixed his inflexible gaze on his young associate. "How do you know what the Tar-Aiym looked like, Flinx?"

"I found out last year. On Repler. It was an awkward time for me. Part of my journey to learn about my fellow man and to find myself. Turned out I found out about some other things as well." He shrugged. "That always seems to be the way of it." As he spoke he was careful not to look in Clarity's direction.

"Ah," murmured Tse-Mallory, "you came across some sort of hypothetical reconstruction of the Tar-Aiym themselves."

"Something like that." Uncomfortable with the line of questioning, Flinx indicated their immediate surroundings. "I don't know if this is the same portal I entered through the last time I was here, so I don't know how soon it narrows down, but we should be able to set down close to one end of the landing area. After that there should be corridors and then . . ." His words trailed off as he remembered.

"And then?" Clarity prompted him.

He finally looked over at her. "Then we have to find another operator's platform like the one I utilized on Booster. So I can try and make contact."

They touched down without incident. Outside the shuttle, the vast empty expanse of the landing deck seemed to reverberate ever so slightly with the echoing roar of hundreds of long-vanished craft. When the shuttle's AI announced that the atmospheric pressure outside had reached normal levels, they shouldered daypacks stuffed with supplies and disembarked via the ship's unloading ramp.

Standing together at its base, Clarity and Sylzenzuzex marveled at the distant metal sky. The airlock was spacious enough to accommodate every ship in the Commonwealth with plenty of room to spare. It was big enough to hold its own weather. There was none because, as with every other aspect of the artifact, conditions within were carefully programmed.

As Sylzenzuzex confronted her Eighth and Tse-Mallory, Clarity joined Flinx. "You told Tse-Mallory that you know what one of the beings who made this looked like." She hesitated. "I'm going to hazard a guess that they didn't resemble mammalian bipeds."

He nodded in agreement. As he studied the nearest of the multiple, branching, high-ceilinged corridors that led away from the landing deck and into the bowels of the alien craft, he was already reaching out with his Talent. He sensed nothing, but that did not mean they had landed in an area devoid of accessibility. They would just have to don packs and commence a physical search. At least this time when he found himself in unfamiliar passageways and tunnels he would be able to proceed safe in the knowledge that he was in the company of friends and not fleeing from those who wished him dead.

"They were bigger than us," he told her. "Impressively but not monstrously big. Much tougher of body and build, too." Remembering the survivor Peot with whom he had worked to defeat the Vom on Repler, he tried to build an image for her. "Cross a giant super-intelligent crab with a bear, give it four eyes and silvery fur, projecting tusks, and a permanent air of melancholy, and you have a Tar-Aiym."

"Sounds intimidating," she commented when he had finished.

"When evaluating another sentient you always have to get past appearance." Settling on a corridor, he shouldered his pack and started forward. "That's what humankind had to deal with when we first made contact with the thranx."

"Not to mention," Sylzenzuzex observed dourly as she followed behind him on all six legs, "the shock and disgust we had to overcome subsequent to our first encounters with human beings."

The passage Flinx had chosen was high and wide enough to accommodate several large cargo skimmers traveling in tandem. Despite Flinx's assertion that the Tar-Aiym themselves had not been all that much bigger than humans, Clarity found herself intimidated by their surroundings. Some of her concern was mitigated by the harsh alien splendor they encountered. Tar-Aiym technology was not so alien that the inherent elegance of its design went unappreciated.

From time to time the walls flanking them were made up of sweeping curves, while in others the corridor contracted into a quilt of sharp angles. Though much of the material of which their surroundings were fashioned reminded her of metal, Tse-Mallory and Truzenzuzex assured her that it was something else entirely. Carbonate or silicate alloys, perhaps, or ceramics of a kind unknown. A good portion of it appeared more organic than inert. There were tubes and conduits, protrusions and concavities whose function the visitors could only guess at. Flinx was as ignorant of their purpose as his erudite mentors.

They did not have to advance in darkness or by artificial illumination. Light was everywhere, much more than Flinx remembered. Of course, on his earlier visit the gigantic vessel had undergone a return to life after half a million years of relative dormancy. Now that it was once more entirely awake, full functionality had been restored.

Not only was the interior illuminated, it was agitated with constant noise. Squeaks and squirps, buzzing and humming, whistles and crackles and pops accompanied the visitors as they trekked deeper into the ship. Clarity entertained herself trying to match unfamiliar sound to imaginary function. Her inventions owed more to fantasy than physics.

Flinx had no time for such amusements. *The story of my life,* he reflected as he led the way onward. Despite his concerns he was careful to moderate his pace, aware that his stride was significantly longer than that of any of his companions with the exception of the burly Tse-Mallory. Even as he led the hunt for a point of contact he knew the possibility existed that they could walk for the rest of their lives and explore only the tiniest fragment of the ship's interior without ever coming across one of the sought-after operator's platforms.

Now and then they would find themselves confronted by free-floating congruencies of light. "Ambient lambent," a buoyant Tse-Mallory called them. These wandering luminosities randomly manifested all colors of the spectrum. Some were so pale as to be little more than blinking wraiths. Others sustained an intensity that verged on the solid. Discussing the nature of the perambulating phenomena, Flinx and the two scientists felt confident that the corridor also enjoyed visits from similar entities that dwelled in the infrared and ultraviolet and were therefore invisible to human or thranx sight. The role of the dynamic drifting lights remained unknown, though for reasons Flinx could not fathom he found himself shying away from the occasional floating sphere of a particular blue hue.

Corridors led to rooms, and rooms to chambers without any sight or sign of the kind of contact dais Flinx had utilized before. One such passageway led to a gigantic cavern that Tse-Mallory characterized as a "circus for domesticated lightning." Even with face guards or goggles on it was difficult to gaze for more than a minute or two directly at the dazzling display of prodigious electrical discharges that were continuously erupting across a vast open expanse the size of a large city. Even more astounding than the sight itself, all the clashing, flaring energy went about fulfilling its unknown purpose in near-complete silence. Unable to glimpse a safe way through or around the awesome yet mystifying display, they were forced to retreat slightly and turn down another corridor that led in a different direction.

The longer they walked, the deeper they penetrated into the artifact and the farther they found themselves from the immense airlock. Attuned to the location of the shuttlecraft, their equipment kept them from losing their way. The problem, as Truzenzuzex pointed out, was that they had no "way." They were simply probing and poking, hoping to find a domed platform of the kind Flinx had managed to activate previously. Undoubtedly there existed other methods and means of communicating with the gargantuan Tar-Aiym vessel, but neither Flinx nor the scientists had any idea what such instrumentation might consist of or how they might identify it. For all they knew they might already have passed a hundred beckoning perceptive communicators without recognizing a single one of them.

In place of a setting sun or the timer on board the *Teacher*, exhaustion told them when it was time to stop for the day. They made camp (strange, Flinx mused, to think of "making camp" inside a starship) in the middle of a long corridor that in contrast to many they had explored was almost dark. The gently bowed ceiling and floor were as black as space while the opposing walls were shot through with shimmering coppery veins that surged and flowed like animate glycerin. Humming softly to themselves, these supple embedded streaks supplied the only illumination from one end of the otherwise dark corridor to the other. Reaching out to touch one such glistening stripe, Clarity avowed that it felt warm to the touch, like gilded blood.

Duplicating the action, Sylzenzuzex declared she could feel no such thing. To Tse-Mallory's touch each of the pulsating sinuous lines felt as cold as ice. Alternately hot and frigid, ductile and wending their way through the ebony material of the walls, the mesmerizing contours might have been carriers of energy, communications, or scrolling Tar-Aiym script. To the visitors, one supposition was as good as another. Regardless of their true function, the mystery of the radiant stripes served at least one useful purpose: they kept the two scientists occupied as everyone else prepared for sleep.

All they needed was some dry wood with which to build an open fire, Flinx mused, and the incongruity of their situation would be complete.

The hard ceramic floor was not accommodating, but everyone was so tired it didn't matter. While Flinx would rather have gone to bed in his cabin on board the *Teacher,* at least he had Clarity, Pip, and Scrap for company. Settling on a spot beside one wall, he slid his daypack beneath his head and did his best to convince himself it was a pillow. Laying her head on his chest, Clarity benefited from padding that was considerably softer but less immobile. The two minidrags made out best of all, each curling up atop a soft, warm, familiar human.

"I was just thinking," Clarity whispered thoughtfully as she closed her eyes against the reddish glow from the enigmatic lines that veined the nearby black wall.

"Dangerous in a place like this," he riposted in the half dark.

Her closed fist playfully thumped his sternum. Mildly irritated, a disturbed Pip glanced over at her for a brief moment before settling back down within her pink and blue coils.

"I'm serious! What if we can't find one of those operator's platforms, or something else that can be used to make contact with this relic? Calling it here to the outskirts of this system will have been a waste of time. Do we go back to Booster and try to get the Krang to do something?"

"I don't know." He shrugged underneath her. "I haven't thought that far ahead."

She knew he was telling the truth. His whole life had been predicated on not thinking too far ahead because every moment of it had been fraught with danger or conflict, uncertainty or confusion. Still, she told herself, there was always a first time.

After all, he had never stopped thinking of her.

"If we can't make contact," she went on, "and we have to give up and return to New Riviera, what happens then?"

She could feel him shifting beneath her, trying to get comfortable. "You and I get married, move somewhere the Order of Null can't find us, raise a family, have a life, grow old together, and die. Depending on how and if the Great Evil continues to accelerate toward the Milky Way, some time after our death it impacts on the outermost fringes of the galaxy and begins to devour one star system after another. Eventually this galaxy disappears and the entity, in all probability, moves on to the next."

Lying against him in the dim red light, she was quiet for a while. "I never thought that if my happiness was guaranteed, I wouldn't be happy. Is that too much of a contradiction?"

"Not if you care about the fate of humanxkind, the Commonwealth, and every other sentient creature regardless of shape, size, or culture. Sometimes I wish I didn't care. Wish that I could forget all this and for a change be entirely selfish." In the diffuse glow he raised his head slightly to look down at her. "I've tried, you know. For a little while I was so disgusted with everything I saw around me that I actually worked at it. At being selfish."

"You failed," she told him perceptively.

The rise and fall of his chest gently lifted and lowered her head. Resting against him, she found the steady movement oddly comforting.

"I'm afraid so," he admitted. "It's what comes of realizing that in the scheme of things, a single individual is utterly unimportant. Your own life is meaningless. What matters is the survival of sentience, of the continuation of conscious thought somewhere in the cosmos."

Something small, pointed, and slightly damp struck her cheek several times.

"We'd better shut up. Scrap is getting tetchy with me." In the feeble luminosity cast by the flowing, radiant lines running through the black walls she could just make out Flinx's faint smile.

"Then it's likely Pip will be telling me to be quiet any minute now, too. Good night, or good whatever it is, Clarity."

"Good night, Flinx." Reaching up with her right hand, she drew it affectionately down his cheek and then closed her eyes, sighing against him. Lulled by the purring walls and her own exhaustion, she was asleep almost instantly, as were the two minidrags.

As he lay contemplating their impossible surroundings, Flinx felt his own eyes growing heavy. His head did not hurt. It was enough. Very soon he was as sound asleep as his love.

Not long thereafter, a drowsy hard-shelled shape moving on multiple legs bumped up against him. In searching for her avuncular Eighth, Sylzenzuzex had come across a human instead. She was not displeased. Humans radiated more heat than thranx. When Flinx did not stir or push her away, she was more than satisfied to tuck all six legs underneath her abdomen and thorax, entwine her antennae for safe sleeping, and lie down beside him. The press of her body against his caused Flinx to stir restlessly for a few moments before quieting. A thranx was as hard as the floor.

Other than the mellifluously humming walls, it was silent in the lengthy corridor.

Time passed. Tired from hours and hours of hiking and searching, human and thranx did not stir. So they did not notice the tiny lights, each no bigger than a pinprick, that began to emerge from the lambent lines in the surrounding walls. Flashing as many colors as their elongated corridor-traversing brethren, they drifted toward the two groups of sleeping figures like so many sentient dust motes. They were few at first.

Soon there were hundreds.

Slitted eyes flicking open, Pip raised her head. Half a dozen dots of refulgence danced in front of her face. They hovered there, making no noise, occasionally changing color. The minidrag eyed them for a moment. Then she yawned hugely, lowered her head back down against her master, and went back to sleep. Beneath her relaxing coils Flinx stirred but did not wake.

There were now several thousand of the minuscule, intense lights dancing above the sleepers like so many cybernetic fireflies. Every so often several of the phosphorescent pinpoints would meet and merge. On other occasions one would split to become two. They did not linger long. After some ten minutes spent in what might have been silent inspection of the intruders the lights began to drift away. One by one, they fused back with the flowing streams of luminance that striped the opposing walls. Beneath a ceiling blacker than the night sky on any world, the visitors slept on.

The next morning, immediately after breakfast, they found a contact dais.

CHAPTER
21

Located at the far end of a large, but not overpowering, cone-shaped, red-gold chamber with a sloping, ribbed floor and a pockmarked ceiling, the tilted platform was familiar in shape and size but not design. The gently slanted slab was roofed by four instead of the usual two transparent domes. Nestled one inside the other, these rose to crests that were acute instead of gently curved.

"I don't know about this, Flinx." Tse-Mallory was clearly unhappy as he studied the configuration. "The design and layout is noticeably different from the operator's pulpit inside the Krang on Booster."

Gazing speculatively at the beckoning rostrum, Flinx found himself nodding in agreement. "It's different from the one I utilized when I was on this artifact previously, too. But it *has* to be a communicator-contact." He gestured in its direction. "The composition of the platform, the general size and shape—everything beneath the multiple domes is exactly the same."

"Perhaps this arrangement is designed to allow even better communications and more control." Truzenzuzex sounded hopeful as his antennae waved in the dais's direction.

Clarity stood close to Flinx. "Or maybe it requires more experience and skill to operate." She looked up at him. "We can keep looking for a platform like the ones you've used before."

He considered the options. Yes, they could keep looking. Yes, he would feel more comfortable placing himself beneath the twin transparent domes with which he was familiar. But in more than a day of probing they had encountered nothing else even remotely like a contact platform. Here right in front of them, almost as if it had been dropped there in response to their wishes, was something sufficiently similar to be worth a try. Maybe Truzenzuzex was right, and its apparent greater complexity would allow for cleaner communications and improved control. Certainly the atypical layout of the chamber hinted at something out of the ordinary.

That's me, he taunted himself in an effort to stiffen his resolve. *Something out of the ordinary.* If one proceeded from that premise, he was in exactly the right place.

"I'm going to give it a go," he told Clarity and the others. "If it doesn't work, we'll keep looking. If it does, that doesn't necessarily mean I can contact anything from here. This room might be nothing more than an elaborate Tar-Aiym classroom, or kitchen."

"It could also be a suicide chamber, or a specialized niche for performing some kind of religious self-immolation," Clarity counseled him.

"That's my girl," he shot back, "always encouraging."

"Clarity's my name and Clarity's my game," she countered in all seriousness. "I just don't want to see you end up dead because you chose to try activating a different piece of Tar-Aiym instrumentation without thinking it through as thoroughly as possible."

"Then we're in complete agreement." He found Tse-Mallory staring back at him. "Sir?"

The sociologist-soldier did not hesitate. "If you think there are sufficient similarities to the apparatus you have already operated, then I have to agree with Tru." Raising an arm, he gestured toward the platform. "Greater schematic complexity implies a higher, not a lesser, level of importance. If you can't activate it and it looks like it's giving you trouble, Tru and I will be standing by to pull you out."

Left unsaid were the potential adverse side effects, mental as well as physical, that he might suffer from such an abrupt and violent disconnect from the alien instrumentation. He did not raise the possibilities for discussion, nor did the two scientists, or Clarity, or Sylzenzuzex.

There was no need to hold forth on an uncomfortable possibility of which everyone was already aware.

He conferred a kiss on Clarity, said nothing, found himself pulled back for a second, longer embrace. Thoroughly familiar with the peculiar courtship rituals of humankind due to the length of time he had spent among the species, Truzenzuzex paid no attention to the seemingly interminable physical give and take. In contrast to her jaded Eighth, Sylzenzuzex looked on in unabashed fascination. She was captivated by the intricacies of an affectionate exchange whose physical malleability no chitinous thranx could emulate.

Flinx finally forced himself to disengage. Lightly touching a forefinger to the tip of Clarity's pert nose, he murmured tenderly, "If we keep this up I won't be in any condition to attempt the contact."

Her lips bonded briefly with his finger. "If we keep this up I won't let you."

A last hug and he turned away, heading purposefully for the dais. She knew he had to do it, and the inexorableness found her hating the universe entire. She forced herself not to cry, not to call out. Why Flinx? Why not Bran Tse-Mallory, or Truzenzuzex? They were older, their lives were already on the downside of the inescapable slide to eternity. Why not them, or some other, instead of the only man she had ever loved? She knew the answer, of course, just as she knew it could not be any other way.

As for the universe, it did not care.

Unwittingly, she found herself edging closer to Sylzenzuzex. Did the female thranx feel this same kind of affection for a mate? What emotions emerged from larvahood that allowed one of them to bond with another of the same species? For all their common sense and sympathy, their goodwill and intrinsic kindliness, their gentle touch and exquisite body fragrance, one could not escape the fact that thranx still resembled giant bugs. Inside, deep inside, did they really feel anything like a woman did for the man she loved?

She felt something touch her. Looking around, she saw that the security officer had inclined both of her antennae to the right so that they could make contact with Clarity's bare left arm. It was like being caressed by a pair of fine-quality feather dusters. It also answered her question.

Flinx had approached to within a couple of meters of the raised platform when a subtle vibration in the floor reached him through his boots. At the same time the largest and outermost of the four domes came to life, turning translucent as light the color of thick cream washed over and through it. Flinx halted immediately. Never before on the three previous occasions when he had utilized such platforms had any luminescence manifested itself until he was within the outermost dome. Simultaneously alert, Pip raised her head off his shoulder and stared. The tension in the minidrag's coils pained him as they tightened around his shoulder.

This was new. What it portended neither he nor anyone else could tell. Was the preflux radiance a warning to keep away? Reaching out with his Talent, he felt, sensed, perceived nothing. The dais awaited. Behind him, Clarity and his friends looked on anxiously but said nothing. They were leaving him to his deliberation. Leaving him, as usual, to make the decision alone on how or whether to proceed.

Nothing to be gained by standing and dithering, he knew. There never was.

A voice finally sounded behind him—the august soldier-sociologist Bran Tse-Mallory. "Get a move on, boy. Apocalypse waits for no man."

Flinx nodded and resumed his advance. As he drew close to the dais, tiny sparks of ashen lightning began to jump from the whitened outermost dome. One landed on his bare left wrist. It burned and left a small scar as he hastily brushed it away. Not an auspicious beginning.

Get under the domes and lie down, he thought sensibly, *and you'll be shielded from such discharges.*

Climbing up onto the platform as the flickering intensified, he wasted no time in turning his back to the slab and lying down. As soon as his head made contact with the smooth surface Pip contorted and lunged upward. Contracting into a series of tight concentric coils, her body came to rest against the top of his skull.

An instant later a numbing electric shock tore through Flinx. His body spasmed and went still. Sight, sound, touch—all sensation vanished. It happened so quickly he did not even have time to think he might be dying, or to be scared. Yet he found he was not frightened. He felt completely at peace.

What transpired beyond ken of his now deadened senses was rather less pacific.

Tse-Mallory and Clarity threw up their hands to shield their eyes and the two thranx turned away as all four of the domes abruptly erupted with light and color. Letting out a cry, Clarity tried to run to the dais. Truzenzuzex caught her and held her back.

"This is as it is supposed to be, *crl!!kk!* And if it is not, there is nothing you or any of us can do now! Stand and hope, Clarity Held. Stand and hope!"

The philosoph was right, she realized as she peered through clenched fingers at the now fiercely illuminated podium. There was nothing she could do for Flinx. He lay out of reach of her reassuring touch, out of hearing of words of encouragement or support. She could only hope that wherever he was now, wherever he had gone to, the essence of him was still whole and intact. And that he would come back to her.

"Will he be okay?" She had to yell to make herself heard to Tse-Mallory above the crackling chaos that now filled the chamber and echoed off the curving walls.

"I don't know!" Bending, he placed his lips closer to her ear. "I hope so. Don't ask of me absolutes. I'm neither a pacifier nor a solipsist. Tru and I have survived as long as we have by responding only to reality and not to wishes." Squinting against the cyclic detonations of light that continued to assault their eyes, he nodded in the direction of the dais, which was fully enveloped in erupting radiance. "That's all we can do. That's all any of us can do now!"

The deep-throated mechanical drone that filled the chamber was periodically interrupted by explosive discharges of energy. As the innermost dome above Flinx turned a shimmering, impenetrable violet, the outer three blazed with a continually shifting combination of hues that were shocking in their brightness. Flaring from formerly transparent surfaces, goblin globes of coherent energy and streaks of crazed lightning exploded in all directions. Even contained and restrained, the least of them fronted enough energy to reduce every one of the stunned onlookers to dust. But every time it seemed that one of the powerful discharges was flaring in their direction, it veered off or faded away.

So much free-flowing energy would have blown apart the walls of an ordinary room, or engulfed anything combustible in flame, or simply torn apart their simple organic molecular structure. But there was nothing ordinary about the chamber in which they found themselves. As soon as a blast of liberated force made contact with walls, ceiling, or floor, it was absorbed, soundlessly and without any visible damage to their surroundings. Gradually coming to the realization that they were not about to be instantaneously blasted out of existence, Clarity and her companions did not exactly settle down, but they did relax enough to marvel at the display. Though it continued unabated, they could detect no effect on their surroundings. There was one, however. Of some significance. Due to their present location it understandably escaped their notice.

The planet-sized Tar-Aiym weapons platform had begun to move.

Outside the room, past the enormous airlock, beyond the artificial atmosphere that shrouded the gigantic ancient artifact, the *Teacher* immediately detected the change that escaped those within. The ship's sensitive instruments reported readings that were unprecedented in its existence. Under different circumstances it might have tried to alter the existing equation, might have commenced some kind of rescue attempt. Two conclusions mitigated against doing so.

First, there was no indication from its master that he was in any kind of danger or difficulty. And second, there was very little a ship even as powerful as the *Teacher* could do against an artificial construct twice the size of the Earth. One might as well ask a paramecium to forcibly deflect the intrusion of the bacteriologist observing it.

So instead of trying to attack or follow, the *Teacher* maintained its position relative to Booster's sun while the great weapons platform began to slowly but unmistakably accelerate outsystem. If Flinx chose to go somewhere without notifying his ship, the ship assumed he would eventually return to resume command. No other reasonable course of action was open to it. Even had it wished to follow, the *Teacher*'s controlling AI noted that the gigantic structure was propelled by an unknown drive system. Nothing like a colossal Caplis generator was in evidence. Whatever powered the ancient war machine, it was not a derivative or variation of the familiar KK-posigravity drive.

Just before the sphere vanished completely, the *Teacher* thought it detected a disruption in the continuum that was more nearly an effect of space-minus rather than space-plus. Communications and nothing else traveled through space-minus. No engineer of any intelligent species had ever been able to shunt anything more complex than a series of waveforms through space-minus. It was considered impossible, space-minus being a realm or dimension that was implacably hostile to anything solid.

It also appeared to be a transportation problem that the martial and endlessly creative Tar-Aiym had solved.

Once the weapons platform had gone, the *Teacher* was left to itself on the outskirts of Booster's system. It stayed there, isolated and alone, and settled down to wait for whatever eventuality should present itself. It was in no hurry and it did not lament its range of possible fates.

Unless specifically programmed to do so, artificial intelligences do not suffer from loneliness.

Flinx neither saw nor felt nor experienced any of the luminous pandemonium in which he, Pip, and the control platform on which they were lying were currently engulfed. It was as if he were peacefully asleep but in control of his dreams. The one containing him at the moment included a distinct point of light, which he immediately recognized as Pip. There was also another presence. It was stark, forthright, immense, and yet shallow. It was also familiar because he had encountered it once before, though without the present degree of transparency and precision.

CLASS-A MIND. He was informed in direct tones that bore no relationship to the reverberations of modulated air currents. WE REACH TOWARD THE DANGER THAT THREATENS ALL. A LESSER OF MYSELF HAS PROVIDED THE NECESSARY INFORMATION.

Flinx knew that the Krang on Booster had communicated with the colossal craft. That meant he would not have to explain anything. He began to wonder if it was necessary for him even to be aboard. Could he and his friends have remained behind on Booster while the weapons platform sallied forth to do battle with the oncoming Evil? Positing the question produced an immediate answer.

THERE ARE CERTAIN THINGS I CAN DO WITHOUT DIRECTIONAL ORGANIC INPUT, the vessel explained. I CAN SEARCH. I CAN TRAVEL. I CAN HIDE AND DEFEND. I CANNOT ATTACK.

Trigger, Flinx remembered. That's me. I'm the key, the trigger. It was what he had been told in his dreams by the Krang and by at least two other concerned and involved entities. Evidently that was what he was going to do and why his presence was necessary on board this immense ship. And yet—and yet—something about that explanation did not feel quite right. Not quite—complete. He set his unease aside. The Tar-Aiym planetary platform, perhaps the ultimate weapon that ancient martial species had ever built, needed the involvement of a Class-A mind in order to engage in battle. As a kid growing up in Drallar, on Moth, he had played more than his share of the ancient Terran childhood game of tag.

Unambiguously, he was *it.*

Lying on the contact platform, asleep and yet aware, he had no notion of or feel for the passage of time. It might have been moments; it might have been years. It was conveyed to him that the ship was capable of covering far greater distances at a much higher velocity than anything powered by a mere KK-drive. Despite that, it would take far too long to physically impinge on the oncoming Great Evil. That force still lay far outside the Milky Way, separated from the Commonwealth by distances measurable in tens of thousands of parsecs.

But the planetary weapons platform *could* reach the Rim and utilize its weaponry to try to make an impact from there. The incredible destructive force it was capable of projecting would not travel through normal space. The disruption of reality created by the weapons platform's combined discharge would warp the continuum itself. The discontinuity it would emit would fold space and allow it to strike its target in chronoparts equivalent to real time.

Flinx grasped only the minimal amount of what he was being told, but it was enough to give him an idea of what was going to happen. He did not need to know the exact how and why of what the ship was going to do, only if it worked. Lying on the platform, feeling neither thirst nor hunger, pleasure or pain, he had time to wonder what it might be like to exist thus. Casually putting the query to his ancient physical and mental host, he was somewhat surprised to receive a reaction.

YOU CONJECTURE BOREDOM ON MY PART. THAT IS AN ABSTRACT CONCEPT. I DO NOT FEEL BOREDOM. I DO NOT

FEEL. I EXIST AND I REACT TO MY SURROUNDINGS. NOTH-
ING MORE.

"It's like that for you for millennia?" Flinx wondered silently in his
sleep.

FOR FOREVER, the ultimate weapon of the Tar-Aiym told him.

"I have one other question," Flinx thought.

ASK.

Flinx considered carefully as he shifted his body slightly against
the smooth surface of the platform. Above his head, Pip reacted
accordingly.

"What, exactly, is a 'Class-A' mind?"

The planet-sized ship showed him.

"He moved! I saw him move. I'm sure of it!" Rising so abruptly from
where she had been sitting that a startled Scrap had to spread his wings
to keep from falling off her shoulder, Clarity lunged toward the crackling, flaring, energy-engulfed dais. Heedless of any danger, she ignored
the lambent, writhing bolts of distilled lightning exploding all around
her.

Using both foothands and truhands, a pursuing Sylzenzuzex caught
the distraught Clarity and gently but forcefully drew her back.

"It doesn't matter that he may have moved," the security officer
click-whistled. "I agree that any sign of life is a good sign. But we must
wait to celebrate until he sits up and waves."

Recognizing the truth of the thranx's observation as well as the danger inherent in approaching the furiously flaring platform too closely, a
despondent Clarity reluctantly restrained herself.

Having lost contact with the *Teacher* and unable to influence the
airlock exit, they had been moving back and forth between the shuttlecraft and the chamber containing the galvanized contact platform for
over a week now. The shuttlecraft's limited stock of supplies had compelled them to ration their food and drink. Carefully allocated, they had
enough to last several additional weeks. After that . . .

Meanwhile, the vivid electrical fury enveloping the dais and the
young man lying at its center gave no indication of abating.

"I just wish I knew what was happening." Pulling her knees up to her chest, Clarity wrapped her arms around them and lowered her face forward until her chin was resting on her forearms.

Though no less vexed, Sylzenzuzex tried to raise the spirits of her human friend. "You said that you saw him move."

Clarity's head came up to meet the young thranx's multilensed gaze. "I did. I'm sure of it."

"Then at least we know he's still alive." Sylzenzuzex gestured second-degree encouragement.

"I regret to say that we know nothing of the sort."

Truzenzuzex had walked over to join them. "The fact that Flinx's body may have moved is inconclusive. The nervous system of humans and thranx alike can continue to function for some time after the brain, for example, has been permanently shut down."

"Thanks for that encouragement." Clarity dropped her head back onto her arms.

"I did not say that was what I think to be the case." Truzenzuzex gestured disapproval of her acrimony. "I only point out what is possible." Looking past her, he gazed at the continuing barrage of light and sound. In his compound eyes was reflected a wealth of ejected color. "I believe that shrouded inside that wellspring of erupting energy Flinx not only lives but carries on."

Wanting desperately to be encouraged, Clarity raised her head. "Carries on doing what?"

Reaching out, the four chitinous digits of a delicate truhand came to rest perceptively on her shoulder. "I'm sure Flinx will tell us when he emerges."

The observation being optimistic without being in any way conclusive, she chose to take it with a grain of salt.

Several more days passed. To the watchful Clarity's increasing dismay Flinx did not move again. As to what was happening outside the minuscule fraction of the great ship they had explored, they had no way of knowing. The capabilities of the shuttlecraft's limited internal instrumentation had long since been exceeded. They had been able to deduce only that the immense weapons platform was moving and that it had passed beyond range of shuttle-to-*Teacher* contact. Unless the city-sized portal that closed the airlock off from outside showed signs of iris-ing open, they could not even use the shuttlecraft to explore the exterior of the alien vessel in their vicinity.

There was very little they could do, in fact, except husband their supplies, speculate on what was happening outside and around them, try to get some sleep amid all the sound and fury being discharged by the contact platform where Flinx lay, console one another—and wait.

CHAPTER

22

The intergalactic void. The space between galaxies. Stars becoming few and far between even when measured by interstellar distances, until at last only a few scattered and isolated rogues and wanderers remain. A place seen but not experienced, vastness on such a scale that attempting to measure or quantify it becomes meaningless, just as the numbers one attempts to assign to it become meaningless. A region observed and studied for centuries by humans and thranx alike but never actually visited or touched upon.

Until now.

With his eyes closed Flinx saw by other means. The ship showed him, entering the perceptive information directly into his brain.

Behind: an immense disk of stars and nebulae, pulsars and novae, neutron stars and X-ray stars, and the entire panoply of other highly evolved stellar phenomena. Energy and life and consciousness all thrown together in a spectacular swirling spiral of existence and experience.

Ahead and far distant: much more of the same.

Except in one region. Except in one still far-off section of the cosmos closed to view by the Great Emptiness. Behind that and on the verge of emerging, a void so utter and complete that not even the glow of a match could be discerned within a square parsec of its lightless, menacing self.

WE GO NO FARTHER. EVEN IF I COULD CROSS THE GULF,

WHAT CONFRONTS US IS NOT A MATTER OF DISTANCE BUT OF TIME.

Flinx did not venture a thoughtful response. He was too awed by the vision offered up by the weapons platform. He and his friends were the first of their kind to step outside the realm of the Milky Way. The first to be able to view the home galaxy from outside and not via artificial constructs or artfully imagined images. It was big, it was beautiful, it pulsed with the fever of stars dying and being born. It was life itself. It could not be allowed to be extinguished, like a candle casually snuffed.

He was only one man, and biotechnically not even that. What could *he* do? Lying on the slant, he twitched slightly. He could do what human beings had always done.

He could try.

"Are my companions seeing any of this?" As always, he framed the thought carefully before allowing it to drift outward.

NO. I CANNOT PUT IT INTO THEM. THEY HAVE NOT THE RIGHT TYPE OF MINDS.

What a shame, Flinx reflected sadly. So much beauty and it could not be shared. He would have to describe it to Clarity and the others as best he could when he emerged from his present state. If he emerged. Another might find it unsettling, being forced to lie motionless and helpless while contemplating the possibility of imminent death. Not Flinx. He'd been there before.

"Why are we stopping here?" he inquired. He thought he had an inkling of the answer, but he wanted to hear it. The ship did not disappoint.

TO SAFELY DISCHARGE THE ENERGY FROM ONE OF MY WEAPONS I MUST BE A CERTAIN MINIMAL DISTANCE FROM ANY SOLID OBJECT. TO FIRE ALL OF THEM SIMULTANE-OUSLY, TO GENERATE A COHERENT EFFECT, I MUST BE AT A CONSIDERABLY GREATER DISTANCE. HERE, FAR BEYOND THE NEAREST STAR, IS THE SAFEST PLACE.

"The Great Evil lies much farther away still," Flinx pointed out. *"I've touched upon it, but only through means I don't pretend to understand, and certainly not physically. I presume that to affect it, it must be impacted physically. Given the extraordinary distances involved, how can this be done?"*

I HAVE TRAVELED HERE THROUGH THE SUB-DIMENSION YOU CALL SPACE-MINUS. IF A SUFFICIENT FORCE IS UN-LEASHED THROUGH THAT IDIOSYNCRATIC INTERPLAY OF THE COSMIC CONTINUUM, IT WILL ACCELERATE EXPONEN-TIALLY. DISTANCE ITSELF, AS YOUR KIND UNDERSTANDS IT, CEASES TO HAVE MEANING. TWO POINTS IN SPACE-TIME CAN, FOR A BRIEF INSTANT OF TIME, BE MADE CONGRUENT. THE CONSEQUENCES CAN BE OBSERVED IN REAL TIME. BUT NOT BY ME. ONLY BY YOU.

Flinx swallowed. Sitting, talking, passing time away from the refulgent contact platform, none of his companions noticed the brief movement in his throat—not even Clarity.

"You're going to boost me out there mentally to perceive the result, aren't you?"

I—AND OTHERS.

"About these others . . . ," Flinx began. He did not have time to finish the inquiry. The immense sphere was already focusing its energies elsewhere.

Deep within the core of the planet-sized machine, engines of destruction capable of generating energies that belonged more to the realm of poets than of physicists ignited for the first time in half a million years. Out on the methane-shrouded surface of the globe first one Krang came to life. Then two more, then a dozen. With no one in a position to note the spectacular, in less than a day more than a hundred of the towering devices were vibrating with readiness. Eons ago, when the Tar-Aiym did battle with their ancient enemies the Hur'rikku, the intent was for only one Krang at a time to be discharged. Such was the power of each radiant spire. Nothing in its design or programming prevented the gargantuan weapons platform of which they were a part from unleashing the energy of all of them simultaneously, however.

It did so now.

Each minuscule Schwarzchild discontinuity projected by a Krang was capable of swallowing an entire fleet. Several combined could implode an entire world into nothingness. More than a hundred discharging at once—there was no predicting what their combined effect might be because such an assault had never been unleashed before. There had never been the need for such a concentration of collapse. Defensively or offensively, a discontinuity of such scale would have amounted to serious overkill.

Flung outward through space-minus instead of existing normality, the energy of the hundred-plus Krangs pooled at a safe distance from the hovering weapons platform. A slight quiver ran through the body of the entire ship. It was the only hint of the immense discharge. Blessed with more sensitive feet and a lack of intervening footwear, Sylzenzuzex and her Eighth experienced it as a negligible tremor, one so insignificant that neither thought it worthy of mention.

As soon as the collated strike had been hurled on its way, the ship relayed the information through a different fold of space-minus back to the single Krang situated on Booster. That device in turn contacted not one but two other entities with a deep interest in both the attack and its outcome. Responding, they merged their efforts to reach outward to the vessel that was drifting beyond the edge of the galactic disk. Taking hold of a certain singular mind they found there, the amalgamated tripartite entity boosted it outward at the speed of thought.

Flinx felt that he had prepared himself and that he was ready for anything. But he never was. How could anyone, regardless of whatever twists and tricks had been implanted or had evolved in their unique mind, be ready for such a literally mind-bending alteration of consciousness?

As he had on multiple previous occasions he felt his inner self being thrust outward. Already beyond the edge of his own galaxy, he had the sense of racing past others. Great glowing orbs and disks, whirlpools of gas and energy, sped past his awareness like so many snowflakes drizzled on black velvet.

The dark shadowed section of space that was the Great Emptiness drew near. That, at least, he was ready for because he had penetrated it before. Within lay an immensity of nothingness. Beyond, on the far side, lay that mindless smothering of reality it was better for sane minds not to acknowledge. Instinctively, he shunned it, turned away from it, tried his best to ignore its baleful existence.

As he struggled to keep his pitiful inner self clear of the crushing malevolence, he perceived via his massively attenuated but in no wise diminished core essence something impacting that galactic pool of horror. For the first time since he had been compelled to awareness of it, a light appeared at its forefront. Glowing argent, the collected projected discharge of the Tar-Aiym weapons platform struck the Great Evil and sliced a curving trail along its leading edge. The gash that was extending itself before Flinx's real-time acuity was hundreds of parsecs in length—and no greater in diameter than his thumb. As the space-time rip lengthened in both directions like a flash of lightning against a moonless sky, the first glimmer of radiance ever to appear on that dark shadow began to eat into it.

The Evil screamed.

Had Flinx been present physically that reaction would have shredded the atomic bonds holding together his being. It would have sent stars into overload, with novae breaking out everywhere like radiant popcorn. But in that darkness there was nothing extant, nothing solid to be destroyed. His sanity was protected by the very inimitability that allowed him to be present and to observe in the first place.

A small portion of the unidentifiable thing that was the Evil was destroyed. The parsecs-long silvery split flickered, and then faded to blackness. Having no center, no nexus, the oncoming horror could not be shattered by a single well-directed assault no matter how powerful. As a questing filament of darkness reached for him Flinx felt himself falling, falling, being drawn swiftly backward and away. Back through the Great Emptiness. Back past intervening galaxies. Back to reality. Though still in the comatose state induced by the fiery contact platform, all of him was soon back within himself.

Lying there, breathing long and deep, he remembered what he had perceived. As always, the strenuous mental journey left him sweating, exhausted, and instilled with fresh insight. The galaxy had always seemed immense. But whenever he passed witness to thousands more, it was reduced to homeliness.

WHAT CONSEQUENCE?

It took Flinx a moment to realize that the great planetary weapons platform was asking for *his* assessment of what had just transpired. It was seeking the opinion of a lone and lowly dust mote composed of water and a few twisted proteins that dared to aspire to cognizance.

"You hit it," he thought without hesitation. *"You hurt it. But not enough, I'm afraid. It's still coming."*

The gigantic machine voiced no disappointment. Guns do not sulk when they fail to kill.

SUCH WAS THE PREDICTION. BUT IT HAD TO BE TRIED. IT IS DIFFICULT TO FIGHT SOMETHING THAT EXISTS OUTSIDE OF THE KNOWN LAWS OF PHYSICS.

Flinx twisted slightly on the platform. *"Can't you attack again?"*

SEVERAL TIMES, YES. BUT OPTIONS ARE LIMITED. IF NO SUBSTANTIAL DAMAGE WAS DONE THIS TIME IT IS UNLIKELY ADDITIONAL EFFORTS WILL BE SIGNIFICANTLY MORE EFFECTIVE.

"You have to try," Flinx entreated.

NO I DO NOT.

It was a perfectly cold and perfectly valid response. A device, the ship saw no reason to sustain an effort that was unlikely to produce a desired result. To do so would be to waste energy and effort. But not to do so, Flinx knew, meant subscribing to the inevitability of the demise of everything, the ship itself included. Then he realized that was not necessarily the case. Able to travel through space-minus at speeds no humanx vessel could begin to approach, the weapons platform could take itself elsewhere. Out into the intergalactic gulf, perhaps even far and fast enough to avoid the oncoming Evil. The designers and builders to whom it owed allegiance were half a million years dead. If not for him, Flinx realized, the Krang on Booster and the weapons platform would not even have made the failed attempt.

He had tried. The weapons platform had tried. It was over, it was done. There was nothing left to do.

No, he told himself, that wasn't quite true. There were two things left to do.

"Take my friends and me back," he projected. *"Back to the system of Booster, back to my own ship. And one other thing."*

DECLARE.

"Let me wake up—please."

CHAPTER

23

So inured by now to the constant flaring lights and continuous underlying roar in the chamber were Clarity and the others that it was more of a shock when both abruptly ceased than it had been when they had initially exploded to life. The sudden, unexpected silence echoed almost painfully. Eyes that had become accustomed to the ubiquitous bursts of multihued lightning strove to readjust to far more muted illumination. Despite the transformation in their surroundings, her first thought was for the young man who had been lying so long on the alien platform.

Her concern was rewarded when he slowly sat up, wincing. Rocketing off her shoulder, Scrap shot across to the dais and was soon snuggling and sharing his body warmth with Pip. For the moment, the two minidrags totally ignored their respective humans.

Clarity shared more than body warmth as she all but threw herself against Flinx, hugging him and covering his face with kisses.

"I was starting to worry that you might not be coming back." Her eyes glistened with moisture as she looked up at him. "I knew you weren't dead because you kept twitching and moving. But you didn't respond to words, and Tse-Mallory and Truzenzuzex warned me not to go under the domes while they were active."

Rubbing at the back of his head, Flinx found it an effort just to sit up. She eyed him fretfully.

"One of your headaches?"

"No, not this time. I'm just tired." Turning to his right he extended an arm. Disengaging from her reunion with her offspring, Pip used the limb like a pole as she slithered slowly back up to her familiar resting place on his shoulder. "And famished," he added. "I feel like I haven't eaten for a week."

Whirling, Clarity yelled back toward the anxiously watching other members of the little group. "He's okay! He's hungry!"

Leaning over, Tse-Mallory murmured to the two thranx standing beside him. "That's a human for you. No matter how farsighted and intellectually accomplished, we never forget the physical aspects of our being."

"Our supplies grow dangerously low." Truzenzuzex eyed the dais where Clarity was helping Flinx to stand. "Let us hope that despite the travails of his trial our young friend leaves something for the rest of us."

In the restored silence the philosoph's words carried to the platform. "No need to worry about that, sir." Though he was giving a reassuring response, Flinx did not smile. "We're already on our way back to the Booster system. We'll be back aboard the *Teacher* in a few days."

It was not surprising that those on board had failed to notice the latest change in the weapons platform's position. Within the planet-sized sphere there was no sense of acceleration or movement.

Even with the fate of civilization at stake, the two scientists had patience enough to wait until their former charge had wolfed down two complete emergency meals before they began pressing him for particulars. Wanting a full and accurate report from the recently deployed instrument, they knew from experience that it was better to wait until the device in question was ready to operate on a full charge.

He was downing the last drops of a half liter of liquid supplement when Sylzenzuzex could stand the delay no longer.

"*Srall!tt,* Flinx—what happened? Talk to us! Where did we go? What is the result?"

Lowering the partially imploded, pressurized drink container, he blinked at her. "You don't know?" He looked around at his companions. "You didn't see anything?"

Putting a hand on his arm, Clarity offered gentle clarification. "We only saw you lying under the dome and its spectacular reaction to your being there." She nodded in the direction of the corridor that led back to the landing deck. "When it became clear that you might be under for an extended period of time, Bran and Tru hiked back to the shuttle. None of its ranging instruments were able to take any readings beyond the airlock." She smiled hopefully. "We couldn't tell what, if anything, was happening outside."

Stepping forward, Truzenzuzex brandished impatient antennae at the tall young man. "Your comatose presence on the operator's platform spawned a great deal of impressive ancillary activity. Bran and I presume it was not merely for show. What, if anything, of consequence was accomplished during your period of unconsciousness?" A truhand gestured in the direction of the corridor. "We know only that we moved out of range of contact with your ship. *Did* you succeed in making contact with this artifact?"

It struck Flinx forcefully that his friends had absolutely no idea of the momentous events that had transpired while he had been, to their eyes, insensible. He considered how best to enlighten them.

"You could say that. Yes, I made contact. The situation we all face was discussed. The weapons platform agreed to a plan of attack." He tried to meet each of their gazes in turn. "You're correct in assuming that our position changed. While I was—elsewhere—the artifact was not static. We took a little trip. In order to mount a maximum effort, the ship traveled through space-minus, or something akin to it, to a location outside the galaxy."

"'Outside'?" Tse-Mallory was staring evenly at him.

Flinx nodded. "It was very beautiful. Even under the circumstances I was able to look back and see—everything."

"Outside the galaxy." Truzenzuzex gestured a mix of awe and disbelief so radical that Flinx was unable to identify it. "The first humanx to travel beyond the Rim, and we have not even a crude image to commemorate the visit."

"There may be nothing to memorialize." Tse-Mallory was less given than his old friend to the need for memorialization. "You spoke of the ship mounting a 'maximum effort.' This was done?"

Flinx nodded again. "The artifact brought together the combined energy of all its weapons systems and unleashed them through a nonconforming variant of space-minus at the oncoming threat. I was able to observe the consequences in real time."

Tse-Mallory did not hesitate. "And the consequences were—are?"

Flinx did not try to hold back or to minimize what he knew. There would be no point, and he doubted he could deceive either of the highly perceptive scientists in any case, even if he believed doing so might be to their benefit.

"I'm afraid there weren't any. No," he corrected himself, "that's not entirely true. There were some corporeal consequences. The Evil was affected—a little. It was slightly damaged. An insignificant amount, I think. Insofar as I could tell, both its structure and its course remain intact." He glanced down. "It's still coming this way."

The two scientists conferred briefly. "You say it was damaged." Truzenzuzex used all four hands to indicate their surroundings. "What went wrong? Could the great weapons platform not sustain the attack?"

"It could," Flinx told the philosoph, "but it won't. It believes that any further assaults would be useless. It says that it can't effectively do battle with something that exists outside known physics."

"Known Tar-Aiym physics," Tse-Mallory pointed out. "Not that the distinction matters if it stated that it won't continue to fight. I presume that you did your best to try and convince it otherwise." Flinx said nothing—and in so doing, said a lot.

"It's taking us back to the Booster system," he finally announced. "That much it's willing to do."

Tse-Mallory exhaled resignedly. "Well then, I guess that's that." Raising his gaze, he surveyed their extraordinary surroundings. "This artifact was our last, best hope of overcoming the annihilation that's heading toward us. Tru and I have felt that way ever since you first told us about it." Reaching out, he lightly tapped a nearby wall. "Compared to the forces this relic can bring to bear, every weapon in the Commonwealth is little more than a conventional firecracker. If the best it could do was irritate the menace, then I expect we all may as well make plans to live out the rest of our lives and enjoy them as best we can in the time we have left to us. As for our descendants . . ." He left the inevitable unsaid.

"No."

Everyone's attention shifted to Truzenzuzex. The philosoph was standing on his four trulegs, rising as tall as he could.

"I refuse. So long as consciousness remains, so long as cognizance holds sway, so long as I can function as a thinking being, I repudiate the notion of capitulation." Gleaming compound eyes fixed on his longtime companion and fellow researcher. "However fruitless the effort may appear, we will continue to search for possibilities, my old friend. We will do this not because we must, or because we see avenues that may lead to success, but because it is what we do. Evolution has given us the ability to reason. If we choose to abjure it, we surrender the one thing that makes us worthy of continuance."

A somber Tse-Mallory stared down at his wholly inhuman, chitinous counterpart. Then he nodded, once.

"Up the universe," he murmured, and broke out in a wide grin.

"Up the universe," the philosoph echoed, not at all solemnly.

While the moment was inspiring for the two scientists, it had less effect on their younger companions. By the time they had all returned to the landing deck and their waiting shuttlecraft, a sense of dour inevitability had settled over Flinx, Clarity, and Sylzenzuzex.

"At least we won't see the stars go out in our lifetime," the padre whistled softly. "With luck, it won't happen during the life terms of my own offspring."

"There's no way of telling." Flinx was helping to sort their remaining supplies that had been laid out next to one of the shuttlecraft's landing skids. "Every time Tru and Bran's contacts in Commonwealth Science think they have its velocity verified, it keeps accelerating."

Clarity wore a contemplative expression. "Life must have been so much easier and more relaxing before Amalgamation, back in primitive times when people were confined to one world and believed it constituted the whole universe." She shook her head mournfully. "They never had reason to be afraid of the stars. Their only concern was first to look out for their own survival, then that of their tribe, then their village or nation. They never had to worry about the survival of a civilization composed of dozens of star systems and species."

"True," Flinx agreed, "but they also believed that shape, or smell, or language differences or belief systems were important. They didn't know that all that matters is sentience and sensibility."

"None of it will matter for long." Tilting back her head, Sylzenzuzex looked up toward the sweeping roof of the immense airlock. "When that *thing* gets here, it will all disappear. Everything. No more consciousness.

No more exploration and explanation." She eyed Flinx. "According to what you've told us, there'll be nothing but—nothingness."

It was too depressing a précis on which to terminate the conversation. He nodded over to where Truzenzuzex and Tse-Mallory were conversing.

"Tru's not ready to give up. If he's not, then I'm not either."

"You saw what's coming," Clarity commented from nearby. "You, more than anyone, know what it's like. Dark and emotionless and horrible." She held back the hysteria that threatened to rise and engulf her. "I know you, Flinx. I know that you're a realist. Your life has made you that way, more so than most people. Given all that you've been through and all that you know, after all these years how can you find even a shred of optimism to cling to now?"

He considered briefly. "Old habit," he finally confessed. "Maybe that bit of DNA was manufactured into me, too. Special optimism gene. One more twisted strand of warped customization." He bent to pick up a water container. "How about giving me a hand here?"

"'Manufactured'?" Sylzenzuzex inquired quizzically from nearby. But Flinx did not hear her. Or maybe he did.

The weapons platform emerged from space-minus back into normal space far enough beyond the orbit of the Booster system's outermost world and high enough above the plane of the ecliptic that its gravitational influence did not perturb any of that system's attendant planets. That was fortunate because it also did not disturb the *Teacher*.

Flinx did not have to make formal contact with the Tar-Aiym shipmind to ask that they be allowed to leave. As soon as they had boarded their shuttlecraft and lifted from the vast deck, the barrier overhead irised open. Their departure was not contested as they accelerated outward. Once clear of the surface they were able to look back as the synthesized methane atmosphere coalesced above their point of departure, once more concealing the actual artificial shell from any simplified external view.

"It's moving again," Flinx quietly informed his friends.

"Yes." Along with everyone else, Truzenzuzex was staring out the forward port of the *Teacher*'s control room. "Have you any idea where it might be going this time, Flinx?"

"It didn't say, and I didn't think to ask it. I imagine that its programming includes contingencies for self-preservation. It can travel through space-minus, or some kind of similar physical anomaly, so I guess it's heading—somewhere else. Maybe starting on a long journey outward, away from our doomed galaxy."

"If we had planet-sized ships like that," Clarity speculated, "we might be able to save enough of a remnant population to reestablish humanxkind somewhere else. Someplace out of the path of the monster."

"Next address, Andromeda." Flinx looked glum. "But we don't have any ships like that. Nobody does. Even the Tar-Aiym could only build one, and it's not exactly programmed for shuttle duties."

"A course, Flinx?" It was the *Teacher*'s AI. Though his ship was perfectly content to sit in one place, it knew from experience that its human was not. Flinx forever favored moving forward.

"I have no idea," the master of the ship muttered. What should they do now? What should he do now? He might have lost a galaxy, but he still had Clarity. Should they look for a quiet place to settle down on another world, perhaps even on Moth? His homeworld might be obscure enough to allow them to avoid the attentions of the misbegotten members of the Order of Null. Should he try to embark on the halfway normal life he had often dreamed of?

It would be the sensible thing to do. It would be the easy thing to do. The *Teacher* was his ship and would follow only his commands. He could do as he pleased.

Instead of making a decision on his own he put the question to his mentors. Beginning with Mother Mastiff, he had always found it prudent to listen to the advice of his elders. He might not do as they suggested, but he always listened.

Though visibly disheartened by the failure of the Tar-Aiym weapons platform to destroy or even deflect the oncoming menace from its seemingly immutable course, the two scientist-soldiers listened sympathetically to Flinx's quandary. They were in agreement in their response.

"There is always time for mating and egg-laying," Truzenzuzex pointed out. "Or for its messy human equivalent." Antennae fluttering, he glanced at Tse-Mallory, who nodded, and then turned back to the attentive Flinx. "We would beg of you a little more time in this unique system, Philip Lynx."

Flinx looked over at Clarity, who shrugged. "It's your decision. Staying here a little longer won't bother me, as long as we're together." Turning, she smiled at the philosoph. "You want to carry out what studies you can in a place you're not likely to ever see again. I've known you long enough to expect that."

Truzenzuzex gestured second-degree gratitude mixed with gentle appreciation. "Bran and I thank you for your understanding, Clarity Held. Our objective in remaining here awhile longer is not merely to indulge scholarly pursuits, however. We wonder if further study of the Krang and the ancient city that surrounds it might lead to a hint of another possibility for fighting the oncoming threat." Both truhands described opposing circles in the air. "We have nothing else to try, and are bereft of other ideas for defense."

"Expending one's efforts and energies on a long shot," Tse-Mallory added tellingly, "is better than doing nothing at all, even if the only eventual real benefit is psychological."

It was settled, then. Raising his voice slightly, Flinx addressed the *Teacher.*

"Did you hear that?"

"My aural sensitivity is acute. I hear everything," the shipmind replied tartly. "I continue to await a course—from you."

Flinx sighed. AIs were so literal. "Take us back to Booster. Prep the shuttle for another landing. Same surface coordinates as before."

"Complying."

They set up a sleep and study area just inside the entrance to the Krang. Returning to Booster after having communicated at length with the massive and now-departed weapons platform, Flinx half expected the Krang to fill his mind with all manner of queries and thoughts as soon as he stepped through the alien edifice's lofty entrance. Nothing of the sort eventuated. Inside the great vaulting tower, the relentless winds of Booster were blocked, the soaring pipes and conduits silent and cold. Reaching out with his Talent, he molded a mental query. There was no response. He eyed the distant dais and its overarching domes. It was a lesser platform than the one he had made use of on the simulated methane dwarf, but more familiar.

The Krang was a device. For all its planetary dimensions, the departed weapons platform was nothing more than a bigger device. The Meliorare-engineered extreme multipolar neuronic connections within Flinx's telencephalon that gave rise to his singular Talent were not duplicated by alien hardware. To in any way match his abilities, complex instrumentation was required.

He considered placing himself once more beneath the domes—and demurred. In the absence of a specific reason, without a driving need, he saw no reason to subject himself to what was unfailingly an enlightening but always exhausting and potentially dangerous exercise. If consulted, Clarity would certainly agree with that conclusion. Subjecting himself to the domes and to intimate mental congress with ancient Tar-Aiym instrumentalities in hopes of saving the galaxy, or even just himself, was one thing. Doing so for purposes of asking general questions or just having a conversation seemed needlessly dangerous. So he avoided the beckoning platform and spent the ensuing days with Clarity, with whom he shared an entirely different and far less stressful mental connection.

They enjoyed their time together as best they could, given the stark solemnity of their surroundings. Meanwhile, Sylzenzuzex assisted her revered Eighth and the ever-stolid Tse-Mallory in their research. This often took the three of them outside the Krang and into the deteriorating city proper. Flinx and Clarity were left behind to admire their alien surroundings, the silent mist hovering high overhead, and ponder a future fraught with an ominous mix of problem and promise.

They spent a week thus. As a locale for what they half jokingly decided to call a pre-honeymoon it was decidedly out of the ordinary. Under such exotic conditions most men would have given little thought to anything but assuring their own continued survival. With the weight of all of civilization pressing down on his shoulders, that was not a luxury that had ever been afforded to Flinx.

Clarity knew him well enough to realize that as much as they were enjoying having some time together without anyone trying to shoot, paralyze, or blow them up, issues other than their relationship were preying on her beloved's mind. One morning after the usual rudimentary early meal she determined to press him on it.

She found him sitting just inside the cavernous entrance, staring out at the decomposing metropolis of the long-vanished Tar-Aiym, looking lost in contemplation. In a way that was encouraging, since he so often looked simply lost.

Settling herself down beside him on the crest of the outermost arc of amphitheater resting slabs, she snuggled as close as she could. Outside the soaring portal, the ceaseless winds of Booster wept for a civilization long-gone and all but lost to memory.

"I'd ask if there was something on your mind," she murmured, "except that the answer to that question is always the same."

"What?" His surprised exclamation confirming her assertion, he glanced down at her and smiled. "You're what's on my mind, Clarity."

She grinned. "I'd better be. But I know there's something else. Something more than the usual restlessness has been bothering you these past couple of days."

He looked away. "It's just a thought."

"Uh-huh," she observed knowingly. "When you have 'just a thought,' there's no telling what's at stake. Empires could crumble. Worlds could stop spinning on their axes."

He grunted softly. "Might just be gas."

She shook her head. "Not this time, unless you're running a secret internal chemical analysis. I know you. You're too deep into whatever it is you're currently into."

He waved a hand at the silent city that was slowly succumbing to the ferocity of the relentless wind. "I've been thinking. Tru and Bran hope to find something here that might point them to another means of combating the approaching menace. They've had no luck. They don't expect to have any luck, but it's in their nature to keep fighting, to not give up. I'm kind of the same way."

She slipped her arm around his back. Mildly irritated, Scrap slithered across the back of her neck to take up residence on the opposite shoulder. "I know. I understand."

"They're not likely to find anything," he continued. "I'm thinking that the only thing that might have a chance of working against what's coming this way is a completely different approach. Another way of thinking. An entirely different take on physical reality."

Drawing back, she frowned at him. "You think differently from most people, Flinx, but not entirely differently. Not enough to do what you say."

"Not me." Shifting around so that he was facing her, he said with a perfectly straight face, "Take out your gun."

Her expression was something to behold. *"What?"*

He repeated himself. "Take out your pistol and point it at me. Try to summon up some hate. Think of what you dislike about me. I know that you love me. The corollary to love is the ability to recognize the faults in whomever you love."

She pursed her lips. "When I said that you think differently, I didn't mean to imply that you'd gone completely over the edge."

He nodded. "I know what I'm doing—I hope. The only way this works is if there's a conviction that I'm on the verge of being killed." He stared hard at her, his eyes imploring. "You have to make it seem real, Clarity. You have to make it *feel* real."

She was shaking her head slowly. "Maybe if you'd explain to me what this is about, I might . . ."

"No!" The vehemence of his response startled her. It unnerved Pip as well and the flying snake took to the air. Concurrently, Scrap unfurled his wings and lifted clear of Clarity's shoulders. "The more you know, the less genuine the effort will feel. Get mad at me, Clarity! You've had several opportunities to live a satisfying, normal life. I've taken all that away from you. I've exposed you to constant danger. Truly wicked people have tormented you, have tried to kill you. That's what you have to look forward to if you stay with me!" He leaned toward her and she drew back without thinking.

"Draw your gun!" Reaching up with a forefinger he tapped himself forcefully between his eyes. "Aim it here, right here! Here's where the source of all your troubles lie. Here's where the source of all *my* troubles lie! Do it, Clarity! Put an end to it! Save us both!"

The pistol was in her hand, though how it got there she was not sure. What was wrong with him? Had he gone completely mad? Had the failure with the weapons platform driven him over the edge, unleashed something deep within him that was previously unseen and unrevealed? Though her fingers trembled slightly she had full control of the weapon. In a gesture of pure reflex, one finger was on the trigger. Looking on from above, Scrap and Pip whirled about in utter confusion. Confronted by the conflicting emotions being projected by their respective masters, each was unable to decide how to react or what to do next.

"Shoot, Clarity! Finish this! Put an end to all your troubles! SHOOT, YOU STUPID BITCH!" His fist came forward, aiming for her face.

Wild-eyed, she pulled back on the trigger.

Several things happened at once. An unbelievably deep rumbling echoed in her ears. To her left, a hole appeared in the air; a perfectly smooth, circular black disk. Something warm, heavy, and rife with musk slammed into her. Stunned, she felt herself tumbling. At the same time she heard a frantic Flinx yelling, "Don't hurt her, don't hurt her! It's okay, it's a sham! Pip, Scrap—stay back!" On his feet, he was shouting and crying and waving his arms all at the same time.

Her vision blurred and her thoughts rattled from the force of the impact she had just absorbed, she retained consciousness just long enough to make out a shape standing over her. Enormous yellow eyes glared into her own. A muscular seven-fingered hand adorned with glowing rings was reaching down.

As she blacked out, it struck her that she had seen that same daunting alien visage somewhere before. . . .

CHAPTER
24

"Clarity. Clarity!"

She mumbled something incoherent. As consciousness slowly returned and she once more became aware of her surroundings, she realized that Flinx was holding her up with one arm beneath her back. Above him, Pip and Scrap continued to circle in confusion, utterly bewildered by what had just transpired below them. Tears were running down Flinx's cheeks. He looked thoroughly, completely, absolutely miserable.

Good, she thought.

The first thing she did when she regained full control of her senses was to smack him across the face as hard as she could.

"What was *that*?" she growled wrathfully as she sat up, pushing his arm aside. "Yelling at me like that, trying to get me to shoot you. . . ." Furious, she looked around. "Where's that gun? Give me another chance. . . ."

Her words trailed away. Searching for the pistol, her gaze encountered a third visage. Memory came racing back. Though the face she was staring into was not human, she thought she could put a name to it.

"Fluff?" she mumbled hesitantly.

The giant Ulru-Ujurrian smiled hugely, showing gleaming white teeth. His kind being the only true telepaths ever discovered, he replied to her straightforwardly and without hesitation.

"Clarity-friend! Good to see Flinx-friend's best friend again!" Paws that could pulverize rock embraced her, pulling her close to a furry chest and threatening to smother her. When Fluff finally let her go she was gasping for air. "Sorry hug you so hard." The Ulru-Ujurrian's mental apology reeked of genuine contrition. "Sensed life-danger to Flinx-teacher and had to come quicklike." Marvelously and quite unexpectedly, the huge ursinoid winked. "Always still keeping an eye on Flinx."

He stepped back and she saw that he was not alone. Flinx's hulking savior was flanked by three other familiar figures. She recognized them as well: the thoughtful Moam, the appropriately named Bluebright, and Softsmooth, festooned with more rings than any of her companions. A fourth stood off by himself, glaring at her.

"Interruptions. Always interruptions." An Ujurrian of few words, Maybeso promptly folded himself and disappeared into the hovering disk that constituted a dark hole in midair. Having done his job of locating Flinx, the most enigmatic of all the ursinoids had returned to wherever it was he went when he was not participating in the communal tunnel digging.

Rising shakily to her feet, she extended an arm to provide a perch for a returning Scrap. As soon as the poor minidrag landed and coiled around her extended arm, she began to stroke and reassure it. Her bewildered serpentine companion was trembling with insecurity.

"It's all right, Scrap. Everything is all right," she whispered soothingly. Her gaze shifted to the watching ursinoids. "I'm fine, Fluff. I understand now what happened and why you did what you did." Turning, she glared at Flinx. "You I'm still mad at."

"I'm sorry, I'm so sorry, Clarity!"

She put her free hand to her head. "Okay, okay! Stop projecting on me or I'm going to start crying myself."

"It was the only way," he told her helplessly. "Remember how Fluff and his friends responded when I was in danger from Coldstripe's people, back when you and I first met? Fluff and the others reacted again when I was on Visaria recently and was threatened there. I figured—I hoped—they would come to my aid once more if I could initiate similarly threatening conditions. But," he mumbled contritely, "the threat *had* to be real."

"Fooled us," Bluebright declared, her loud-thinking buoyantly cheerful.

"Fooled me, too." Clarity gazed across at Flinx. "What would have happened if your friends hadn't responded to the apparent danger and come to your aid? What would have happened if they'd been—late?"

"I would have projected onto you." His tone was as serious as she had ever heard. "Tried to deflect your intention, or at least affected your emotions enough so that your shot would have missed."

She was staring at him. "Are you sure that would have worked?"

"No," he told her quietly, "I was not. But when I commit to something, I commit wholeheartedly. I don't know how to do anything halfway." He paraphrased Truzenzuzex. "With all of civilization at stake, extreme measures are justified."

"You committed to *me*," she reminded him forcefully.

He swallowed hard and looked away. "I said I was sorry."

She was quiet for a long moment. Realizing they had intruded on something profound, the normally inquisitive Ujurrians responded with uncharacteristic silence.

"I'm sorry, too, Flinx," she told him firmly. "Not necessarily about failing to shoot you. That remains to be determined." He stared blankly at her taciturn expression. She managed to hold it for a moment longer before throwing herself into his arms. "The galaxy may die, the galaxy may survive," she declared soberly, "but one constant remains unchanged throughout: the profound obtuseness of the human male."

The quartet of Ujurrians looked on as the two human-friends embraced.

Moam thought frankly at Softsmooth, who was standing next to him. "This is all part of the human game. Not civilization game. It is less important."

"No—*more* important." Softsmooth was insistent, and the four of them immediately fell to soundless arguing.

With the traumatized minidrags once more put at ease and Clarity (more or less) reconciled to Flinx's desperate effort, he did his best to explain to the curious Ujurrians the rationale behind his ruse.

"I had to make you think my life was in danger." He tried not to lose himself in the plate-sized yellow eyes that were staring candidly back at him. "The last time that happened, on Visaria, you came through one of your tunnels in time to save me. You also did it years ago, at Coldstripe. Now I need your help again." He paused. "*Everybody* needs your help."

"The big danger is coming." Moam was making an observation, not asking a question. "We know. We showed you."

Flinx nodded. "There was a weapon devised by the people who once inhabited this world. I was able to convince it to attack the oncoming Evil. It did not have enough of an effect to deflect the danger. So I thought I would ask if there's anything more you can do." He tried to sound encouraging. "Maybe you could 'dig' one of your tunnels in front of it and it would fall in?"

A sequence of amused grunts emerged from deep within Bluebright's chest. Nearby, Fluff was apologetic.

"Cannot dig a hole that big, or at that distance, Flinx-teacher. Maybe in few billion of your years. But do not have that kind of time. Do not have enough minds or hands." The rings on his fingers pulsated softly, emanating subdued internal hues. "We have done all we can do by passing along the warning, which we got from the dead people's alarm machine on world you call Horseye and local people call Tslamaina."

Stepping forward, Softsmooth loomed over the two humans. A massive but soft seven-fingered paw came down to rest on Flinx's unoccupied shoulder. Huge eyes full of wisdom that were at once childlike and incomprehensible peered down into his own.

"We can do no more and there is no more we can do, Flinx-friend. Outcome of all games, end of biggest game, is in your hands now. You were the key, you are still the key."

Flinx suddenly felt both small and vulnerable, and not because the hulking Ujurrian was so much larger than he was. He spread his arms helplessly. "The key, the key! You keep telling me that, but I don't know what I'm supposed to be the key *to*! Or the trigger: it's all chaotic and confused."

"Is usual condition of life and universe," Moam pointed out without hesitation. "You have seen and experienced enough of it to know that, Flinx-friend. Only help we can provide is keep you alive."

"That's not good enough." His frustration threatened to broker a return of one of his devastating headaches.

Clarity leaned toward him. "Be thankful for small favors, Flinx."

Fluff came forward. Standing side by side, the two ursinoids were a dominant presence. "We simple folk, Flinx. We play at our game. We keep you live. We dig our tunnels. That what we do."

A new thought caused Flinx to pause a moment before responding. "Maybe that's what happened to the Xunca. The race that built the alarm system that's centered on Horseye. You told me years ago that they 'went away.'" He eyed each of the Ujurrians in turn. "Maybe they made a tunnel similar to the kind you're digging, and they went 'away' through it."

The Ujurrians exchanged looks along with thoughts. "Our tunnels can go far places through interesting ways. Or interesting places through far ways. But not far or interesting enough to get away from evilness that is coming."

"If we could do that," Moam added, "we would already have made the going. And asked you to come with us," he added as an afterthought. "Would miss Flinx-friend, Flinx-teacher." Turning, he lumbered with great dignity toward the hole that was hovering in the atmosphere. "Cannot save ourselves, Flinx-friend. All falls to you."

"But I don't know what else to *do,*" he wailed earnestly. Clarity put an arm around him while Pip snuggled closer against his neck. Each, in their own different and distinctive way, sensed and was reacting to the suffering he was undergoing.

Contrary to his hopes, the only thing the Ulru-Ujurrians had left to offer was compassion.

"Flinx-friend hurts." Reaching out, Softsmooth patted down his red hair with a paw that was large enough to cover his entire head. "We hurt for Flinx-friend. But this is a tunnel he must dig for himself." She shook abruptly, fluffing out the fur that covered her head and upper body. "You are the key. Find what you must unlock, or this game will be the last game. Ever."

Pivoting, she moved to rejoin Moam. Bluebright followed. Only Fluff lingered a moment longer. The thoughts he projected were tinged with heaviness and regret.

"So much burden for one small thinking fella-being. I sorry it you, Flinx-friend. I glad it not I. Try avoid situations like just now." Enormous eyes shifted to Clarity. "Next time maybe we not dig fast enough to save."

One by one the Ujurrians stepped or jumped back into the opening in the aether. A deep rumble followed Fluff's disappearance, following which the hole snapped in upon itself like a circlet of interdimensional elastic and was gone. Nothing remained to indicate that anyone other than Flinx, Clarity, and the two minidrags had ever been there.

Well, almost nothing. Bending down, Flinx picked up half a handful of gray-brown fur and lifted it to his nose. It smelled strongly of myrtle and musk: Softsmooth. Turning, he found himself once again surveying their implausible environs. Any xenologist in the Commonwealth would gladly have given up several years' stipends for the privilege of spending a single day in such surrounds, and here he could not enjoy it for a moment because—because he was some kind of stupid, enigmatic, inscrutable key.

He shook his head. Following procrastinating visits to worlds as diverse as Visaria and Jast he had resolved to do whatever he could to try to save the Commonwealth. Someone else might have said "to fulfill his destiny"—except that he did not for an instant believe in such nonsense. It was all so much superstition and silliness.

There was nothing nonsensical about the Great Evil, however. His reluctant, innermost self had been thrust outward to perceive it. It was as real and remorseless and dangerous as his dreams of a normal life were wish fulfillment.

"Flinx? Are you all right?" Clarity was looking at him with concern. Such a simple gesture. Such an essential one.

"I'm unchanged," he responded carefully. "Whether that makes me all right or not I don't know and I no longer much care. But since you ask—yeah, I feel 'all right.'" His words relieved her evident alarm.

Alarm.

He thought back. Back to when he had gone to New Riviera to reunite with Clarity. What was it that Tse-Mallory and Truzenzuzex had told him a small coterie of their fellow researchers had learned about that mysterious apparatus that had been left behind on Horseye by the long-vanished Xunca?

He remembered. *Two* sources had been recorded. Down through the millennia the incredibly ancient mechanism had been monitoring not one but two locations. One was, of course, the threat represented by the Evil that was coming out of the Great Emptiness. The other was something unknown that was located in a unique region of space known as the Great Attractor. A point in the continuum that all local galaxies were shifting toward. An inexplicable physical anomaly with the energy of ten thousand trillion suns. It was utterly unique in the universe. No known physics or mathematics could account for such an incredible concentration of energy.

Could the Xunca?

Contemplating the anomaly, Flinx and the two scientists had previously speculated on whether the Xunca had actually considered constructing something capable of moving entire galaxies, including their own, out of the path of the oncoming menace. It had remained just that, nothing more than speculation. But what if, he found himself wondering, the Great Attractor, or something at the heart of that fantastic force, was actually designed to do something else? The instrumentality on Horseye not only monitored both sites, it also sporadically sent some kind of signal through a deviation of normal subspace toward an unknown third location. According to Tse-Mallory and Truzenzuzex the scientists studying the Xunca mechanism had not even been able to determine how the information was being sent, much less what was being transmitted or what might be on the receiving end.

Constant monitoring of the approaching threat he could understand. Constructing and monitoring something capable of moving an entire galaxy, much less several, out of the way of that threat was a physical undertaking that could barely be comprehended by mere organic entities. But why the third signal? What did it consist of, where was it being beamed, and what was it intended to accomplish?

Perhaps nothing, he told himself. Maybe it was an unintentional byproduct of the monitoring/alarm system. Maybe it was only an inadvertent leak of deformed radiation into subspace. Having latched on to the thought and fallen into speculation, he could not let it go. Always, ever, eternally curious, and usually to his detriment, he needed an answer. Where and how to find an answer to a question that some of the Commonwealth's finest scientists had only recently learned to ask? He was stuck on an uninhabited, long-dead alien world in the middle of the sterile Blight, cut off from any planetary information shell, with access only to the library that was part of his ship's mind.

Not quite a dead world, he reminded himself. Something was tugging at his arm.

"Where'd you go?" Clarity asked him intently.

"Hmm?" He blinked. "I've been right here."

"No." She smiled perceptively. "I know that self-inflicted stasis. You went somewhere. I'm sorry to break in, but I couldn't take it anymore. The silence, and the distance."

"Sorry," he apologized. "Something one of the Ulru-Ujurrians said got me to thinking."

Her expression twisted. "I don't think I like the sound of that."

"It just sparked a question," he explained, a little too quickly, a little too disingenuously. "Not a solution. Just a question." Looking past her, he nodded in the direction of the Krang's silent contact platform. "The only drawback is that I have to ask it of the machine."

She looked around sharply, then back at him. "Again? If I didn't know you better and appreciate what putting yourself under those transparencies costs you in terms of physical and mental wear, I'd say you were getting addicted to the experience."

He had to smile. "Hardly. It's every bit as tiring and draining as you say. But I don't have any choice. Even if we had access to the Terran Shell itself, the answer I need isn't available there. Or from any humanx knowledge resource." His expression reflected the helplessness he was feeling. "I *have* to try, Clarity. It might be the last thing I can think of to try."

She chewed her lower lip. "I wish you'd wait until the others are back."

He shrugged. "Why? Would Bran somehow make the experience easier? Is Tru's presence going to lessen the strain? Can Syl find a way to keep me from burning axons?" He shook his head. "I'd rather do it and get it over with than have to listen to their advice and deal with their worries."

Her tone was subdued almost to the point of inaudibility. "What about *my* worries?"

Reaching out, he did his best to reassure her. "This will be the least amount of time I've ever spent on one of those contact slabs, I promise. I'll just make contact, pose my question, receive an answer or a rebuff, and slip back out."

She looked up at him. "You make it sound as harmless as requesting a zoning change on a piece of undeveloped property on Nur."

"Okay," he acknowledged, "so there's some risk involved." He indicated their alien surroundings. "Look where we are. Consider where we recently were and what I experienced beyond the Rim. Compared to that and everything else you and I have been through, soliciting the answer to a single question from an alien machine I've already been in contact with counts as a minor diversion."

She sniffed. "I don't know why I bother to raise concerns: you're going to do what you want to do anyway."

He straightened. "I'm going to do what I *have* to do, Clarity. You, of all people, should know that." Reaching up to stroke Pip, he started deliberately past her. As he headed down the wider-than-human aisle toward the distant dais, she watched him go.

It seemed like she was always watching him go.

As soon as the skimmer settled gently to ground and its loading ramp deployed just inside the entrance to the alien monolith, Truzenzuzex, Tse-Mallory, and Sylzenzuzex disembarked. Seeing the human female sitting by herself, Syl wandered over and proffered politeness.

"*Sirrintt,* Clarity. You are feeling well?"

"As well as can be expected, Syl." She nodded past the thranx in the direction of the two senior scientists. "How did it go? Did you find the solution to everything—or anything?"

"I'm afraid not." Settling back on all six legs, Syl used both truhands to pull down her right antenna and commenced preening. "There's certainly much to see and learn—there is an entire city to explore, after all—but we found nothing more remarkable than what was expected. As a xenoarchaeological expedition it has been a great success." She gestured regret. "Insofar as finding something to use against the advancing threat, it has been a total failure." Continuing to groom, she looked back over her thorax. "My Eighth and his companion try to exude optimism, but at hearts they are realists."

Clarity nodded understandingly. "Well, as long as they search without expecting to find anything they won't be disappointed."

"*Chilarr-ah-Ksa!!tt,* so true it is," the security officer agreed. Looking past Clarity, she found herself searching the area immediately behind her friend. She could not frown—inflexible chitin rendered thranx facial expression virtually nonexistent—but she gestured her sudden distress.

"Where is Flinx?"

"Speaking of optimism . . ." As her voice trailed away Clarity raised a hand and pointed.

Sylzenzuzex had no difficulty identifying the distant solitary figure mounting the dais. Responding to her loud, sharp whistle of exclamation, Truzenzuzex and Tse-Mallory hurried over to see what was happening.

Clarity sighed knowingly as they approached. "I guess we'd better get ready for another concert."

"But what is he doing?" As he tracked the progress of the familiar tall biped, Truzenzuzex could not hide his puzzlement. "Why is he going to submit himself to the stress and strain of reconnecting with the alien device? It has already indicated it cannot do anything to inhibit the advance of the approaching peril."

"I believe," she explained, "that he intends to ask it a question."

Tse-Mallory was also tracking the progress of the tall redhead. "What kind of question? A question about what?"

"I don't know. Flinx doesn't tell me everything that goes on in his head. I think he's doing his best to spare me." She gestured in the direction of the platform. "You can ask him yourself when he's finished. Maybe he'll even get an answer to his question."

"He didn't say what the question was?" Truzenzuzex persisted.

"No." Despite telling herself that this time she was not going to watch, she felt herself turning to join the others in gazing at the distant dais. Flinx had assured her he was not going to be under its influence for very long. That was small comfort, but she would take what she could get.

"But doesn't . . . ?" Sylzenzuzex began. Then her antennae flattened back against her head as she winced.

Thunder filled the Krang's interior as tame lightning emerged from the structures protruding from its walls and began to crawl ceilingward. The deafening, clashing howls of alien music assailed their ears even as flaring bursts of luminosity skipped off their retinas like stones on the flat surface of a lake. The Krang was alive again; with sight, with sound, and with presentiment. Beneath the inner of the double domes, Flinx could be seen sprawled out on the operator's platform, Pip coiled tightly above his head. Young man and ancient machine were talking again.

Reduced to the status of mere onlookers, his companions could only shield their eyes and ears and wait for the esoteric conversation to end.

AGAIN, CLASS-A MIND. I HAVE COMMUNICATED WITH THE SHIP OF THE BUILDERS. THE ATTEMPT FAILED.

"Yes." Flinx spasmed slightly beneath the inner dome. Above his head Pip twitched and contorted, acting as a lens for his projections.

YET YOU SEEK AGAIN. I AM A WEAPON. I HAVE NOTHING MORE TO OFFER.

"I disagree. You have knowledge. I would posit a question."
ASK.

"There is a world inhabited by three indigenous intelligent species. My people call it Horseye, the locals call it Tslamaina. Buried near one of its poles is the visible portion of an extensive instrumental complex that was put in place by a race called the Xunca, who dominated this entire portion of the galaxy before the time of the Tar-Aiym and the Hur'rikku."

I HAVE KNOWLEDGE OF THE XUNCA. SOME. THEY WERE A GREAT PEOPLE.

Already the Krang had confessed to knowledge beyond the fragments that had been laboriously accumulated over the centuries by Commonwealth xenoarchaeologists. So excited was Flinx by the machine's revelation that he put aside the question he had come to ask in favor of another. *"What—what happened to them?"*

THEY WENT AWAY.

Went away. The Ulru-Ujurrians had said almost exactly the same thing.

"How did they 'go away'?"

THAT IS NOT KNOWN.

Dead end. He returned to his original question. *"It's thought that the instrumental complex on Horseye is part of an incredibly old and advanced warning system. Even though those it was intended to warn have 'gone away,' the device they left behind continues to function. My people have been able to determine that it is monitoring the approach of the Great Evil and also the most energetic, dynamic region of known space, a phenomenon that we call the Great Attractor. But in addition to monitoring and recording these two events, the system also sends out a sporadic signal whose meaning and content we have not been able to decipher.*

"I want to know, I need to know, where this signal is directed and if possible, the purpose behind it."

The half-million-year-old machine that was at once an instrument of war and an instrument of art did not hesitate. Hesitation was a defect reserved for organic sentients.

SEARCHING NOW.

Flinx waited. Something remarkable happened.

Nothing happened.

It happened for a moment, then several moments. The several moments stretched into a period of time lasting longer than any comparable period of time he had spent on a Tar-Aiym operator's dais without anything happening.

Was it possible that just then and now, at that particular instant of time, the half-million-year-old mechanism had finally failed? It was a possibility he was allowed to ponder for barely an instant before a response was forthcoming. When it did, there was no indication on the part of the instrumentality in which he lay that anything unusual had transpired.

MUCH TO SEARCH. THEN HAD TO SIFT WHAT WAS SEARCHED.

"Did you learn—anything?" Muscles convulsed as Flinx arched his back against the unyielding composite material beneath him.

LEGEND. OF THOSE WHO WENT AWAY.

Flinx was patient. *"Can you be more specific?"*

ONE SIGNAL TO MONITOR THREAT. ONE SIGNAL TO MONITOR DEFENSE. ONE SIGNAL TO LINK THE TWO.

Was it possible? Was it even conceivable? Had the Xunca, before they "went away," built something they believed might be capable of defending against the oncoming Great Evil? If that was the case, why hadn't this hypothetical weapon already unleashed its unknown potential on a threat that had now shifted nearer than ever? Flinx thought hard.

A menace looms. The threatened man raises a defensive weapon to protect himself. But he has a choice: he has time to flee. So instead of firing, he simply runs away. A safer option than standing and fighting when the outcome of the clash is unpredictable.

And in his haste to run away, he leaves his unused weapon behind. But the unfired weapon remains bound to the danger. Sporadically, if the Krang was to be believed.

Where was the weapon? *What* was the weapon? The Great Attractor? How did you fire, how did you pull the trigger, on a cosmic phenomenon that blazed with the energy of ten thousand trillion suns?

Very carefully, he decided. That was assuming the fantastic inferences he was making were in any way, shape, or fashion accurate, and he was not just wish-dreaming.

"The signal that intermittently reaches out from Horseye—it's not designed to activate the defense?"

NO.

"Why not?"

ASK THOSE WHO MADE IT.

Back to square one. *"Do you know where this defense is?"*

I CAN PROVIDE COORDINATES.

Flinx's spirits rose. Something solid, something tangible, at last!

"Please provide."

Though the *Teacher* essentially flew and maintained itself, years of crisscrossing the Commonwealth and the AAnn Empire had given Flinx a certain amount of insight into the basics of interstellar navigation. When the Krang offered up a simplified set of stellar coordinates, Flinx quickly set them against what he knew. They made no sense. He projected his confusion.

I WILL SUPPLY VISUAL REFERENCE.

An image formed in Flinx's mind. It moved and shifted, changing size and perspective. Slowed, enhanced, enhanced again. Eyes shut tight, locked in communicative stasis, he inhaled sharply when it finally resolved.

"Useless," he finally thought. *"Impossibly far away. Of what conceivable use is something situated at such a distance?"*

ASK THOSE WHO MADE IT.

Infuriating. If he did not know better he would have thought the machine was mocking him. It was doing nothing of the kind, of course. Simply responding with minimal waste and delay to his inquiries.

"I am patently unable to do that," he replied as calmly as he could manage, *"since those who made it have 'gone away.'"* Almost as an afterthought he added, *"Perhaps you can suggest another means or method of ascertaining the potential usefulness of this hypothetical defense?"*

The last thing he expected was a response. No, that wasn't quite correct. The last thing he expected was a *positive* response.

GO THERE.

Being locked in cerebral stasis did not prevent Flinx from coughing slightly. *"I'm afraid I don't have adequate means of transportation. Even if I did, I wouldn't live long enough to complete the journey."*

BOTH LIMITS ARE WITHIN REACH.

If he had been in full control of his body, he would have sat up. *"What did you say?"*

THERE EXISTS A POSSIBILITY.

"I don't understand. Can you explain?"

TO ACTIVATE THE DEFENSE, THOSE WHO MADE IT HAD TO BE ABLE TO REACH IT. THEY LEFT BEHIND THE DEFENSE. THEY LEFT BEHIND THE WARNING SYSTEM. THEY LEFT BEHIND A MEANS BY WHICH SUCH THINGS WERE LINKED.

THE DESTINATION OF THE THIRD SIGNAL.

Flinx could hardly contain his excitement. His elation communicated itself to Pip. Her coils began to contract against the top of his head, playing havoc with his red hair.

"How can we tell if this link still works?"

The Krang's response was typically terse. GO THERE.

"How is that possible?"

I CAN PROVIDE COORDINATES.

For the second time in the past several minutes Flinx found himself mentally articulating an anxious appeal. *"Please provide."*

The Krang proceeded to do so. This time Flinx was able to reference the location. Not only was it nowhere near as extreme as the set that had been given for the Xunca defense, the locality lay virtually next door, within the boundaries of the Commonwealth itself.

Somewhere to go. Something to seek out. Not a solution, not an answer, but at least a bona fide destination. He fought to make his muscles work, to slide free of the platform and out from beneath the blinding, binding influence of the glowing, luminescent domes overhead. Locked to his thoughts, sensitive to his emotions, the Krang sensed his struggle.

DO YOU WISH TO TERMINATE EXCHANGE?

"Yes!" Flinx all but shouted silently. *"Terminate contact now, please."*

COMPLYING.

There was a brief instant of delay, a second of disorientation, and then he felt himself starting to emerge from stasis as contact was broken. At the last possible instant of contact, something remarkable occurred. It was not that the ancient weapon/instrument offered concluding words to the exchange so much as it was the nature of that parting, which was unprecedented in Flinx's experience with both the Krang and the much larger but related weapons platform. It was, however, characteristic in its conciseness.

GOOD LUCK.

He blinked. Gazing upward, he found himself looking through twin domes that were once more untinted and perfectly transparent. He could see the distant, permanent haze that hovered near the top of the Krang. His recovering ears still rang with the dying echo of ancient alien music. Sitting up, he swung his legs off the dais and stood. When he started to stumble, he heard a voice calling out to him from a figure that was now running in his direction.

"Flinx, Flinx! Are you . . . ?"

"I'm fine!" he shouted back to Clarity. "Just a little shaky, but okay!" Extending an arm back to the platform he waited while Pip used it to climb up onto his shoulder. All around him the Krang was silent and still. And conscious, though he alone of his entire species had shared thoughts with that cold, primal intelligence.

Mounting the dais with long, graceful strides, she was in his arms in a moment. "Please," she pleaded as she hugged him tight, "please don't do that anymore! I can't take watching you lie there writhing and twisting like you're in constant pain all the time. If you have to talk to someone, talk to me. Leave sentient alien weapons to themselves." Drawing back, she met his eyes and he could see the quiet anguish in her face.

"It's aging you, Flinx. Every time you subject yourself to its influence, every time you make contact, you come out a little older."

Bending down, he kissed her gently on the forehead and ran a hand down the back of her hair. "Clarity. Clarity, charity, emotional parity, if there's one thing you should know about me by now, it's that I was *born* older."

CHAPTER
25

As soon as Tse-Mallory set the skimmer down close to the dais, Truzenzuzex disembarked and hurried over to help Clarity. Sylzenzuzex was right behind her Eighth, and Tse-Mallory joined them moments later. The philosoph looked up at his visibly fatigued young friend.

"You've been chatting with the eons again, I see. I'm curious to know why and what for."

As a weary Flinx proceeded to explain, the two scientists and Sylzenzuzex soon found themselves enthralled. When he finally finished it was left to Tse-Mallory to restate the obvious; something humans were more inclined to do than thranx.

"A functioning Xunca defense!" The sociologist-soldier's eyes glittered as he considered the potential ramifications. "Is it the Great Attractor?"

"No," Flinx had to tell him. "It might lie in that area, but it's not the Attractor itself."

Tse-Mallory was staring at the ground while thinking out loud. "No reason for some kind of defensive weapon to be located so far away unless there's *some* kind of connection." He looked up. "The Krang did not describe one, I take it?"

Flinx shook his head. "'Go there,' it said. It mentioned a possible means of doing so." He eyed his friends hopefully. "I know enough to be sure that the coordinates for this hypothetical link lie within the borders of the Commonwealth, but it's a locality I've never visited myself, not in all my travels."

"You are about to, I think." Turning, a gleeful Tse-Mallory slapped his longtime companion hard on the back of his thorax. The sound of flesh striking chitin was percussive. "It would appear, my old friend, that the annihilation of civilization is not yet a certainty!"

"My mobility will be, *kral!l!l,* if you keep hitting me like that," Truzenzuzex clicked sharply. Given the number of friendly smacks the philosoph had absorbed from his friend over the years, the complaint rang hollow.

As they were breaking down the temporary camp near the entrance and preparing to leave the Krang and its age-weathered world of Booster behind, Tse-Mallory paused in the packing to confront a busy Flinx. The younger man stopped what he was doing and looked up.

"Bran?"

"Those coordinates." Tse-Mallory looked almost expectant. "If you can remember them without having to check your communit, could you recite them to me again?" Flinx did so. When he was finished, the soldier-sociologist nodded slowly to himself. "I could swear—I'm almost certain that I *know* that place."

"I haven't done an overlay yet myself. Is it Horseye?" Flinx was hopeful. After all he had heard about that multitiered world and its three native intelligences he would have been glad to pay it a visit and see the excavated part of the Xunca warning system for himself.

Tse-Mallory disappointed him. "Not Horseye. There was a report filed with Science Central on Denpasar a little over a year ago by a couple of second-level xenologists. In addition to the expected material it came with a very strange supplementary attachment. Knowing of our interest in such matters, one of our contacts in the Church passed it along to Tru and me. Preoccupied as we were keeping watch over a recovering Clarity and awaiting your return, we weren't able to go over it in depth or request a follow-up. Those coordinates, though . . ." His words trailed away as he struggled to remember.

Ten minutes later everyone's work was interrupted by a violent exclamation from Tse-Mallory. By the time Flinx arrived at his side, Pip having to tighten her grip on his shoulder to keep from being jounced off, the two scientists were deep in excited conversation the details of which Flinx could follow only slightly.

Clarity jogged up alongside him. "What are they jabbering about this time?"

"I don't know." Risking impertinence, he raised his voice. "Bran, Tru! If you've figured something out it would be nice if you shared it with the rest of us."

The two old friends immediately ceased their rapid-fire dialogue.

"Of course, my boy, of course!" Turning to Flinx, Tse-Mallory whacked him enthusiastically on the back. Annoyed, Pip spread her wings in case she had to take flight. As for Flinx, it was not the first time he found himself sympathizing with Truzenzuzex. Both had suffered from Tse-Mallory's effusiveness.

"Those coordinates." There was a glow to the old scientist's expression Flinx had not seen there in some time. "They're in the Senisran system! They aren't for that water-world itself but for the outlying asteroid belt—the system has two, one between the third and fourth planets and the other proximate to but outside the orbit of the tenth and last." He wagged a thick finger in Flinx's direction. "It's most remarkable. Everything you learned from the Krang ties in with the recently received report I alluded to earlier."

"How?" Sylzenzuzex wanted to know.

A little of the older human's ebullience receded. "I'm not sure. As I told Flinx, the report was—odd." He brightened anew. "Of course," he added facetiously, "what we hope to find could not in any way, shape, or fashion be considered 'odd.' Oh, no." Turning away from the youngsters, he hurried to share the rest of his revelation with Truzenzuzex. Moments later the venerable thranx was all but turning cartwheels there in the soaring entrance to the Krang.

At least, Flinx mused thoughtfully, his mentors were encouraged. At the risk of diminishing their enthusiasm, he was compelled to point out that the Krang had prefaced everything it had passed along to Flinx by declaring it to be legend.

"It will be a good deal more than 'legend' if it conflates with certain aspects of that report, my boy," Tse-Mallory assured him.

"Me, I'd like to know a little more about this mysterious report." As always, Clarity's first concern was for Flinx's well-being. "What life-threatening, mind-tormenting exercise do you intend to get him mixed up in next?"

"This is not just about Flinx, I think," Truzenzuzex told her. "We are all of us in this together, for certain and final, for good or ill, until the next egg." As he reached out with a foothand, four hard-surfaced digits gently gripped her forearm. "Bran and I spent more than a year looking after you while you returned to health, Clarity. Rest assured we are not about to cast aside all that hard work casually."

"Even if the fate of the galaxy is at stake?" she asked him. But he had already turned and skittered off to resume working on the breakdown of the camp and packing the remainder of their supplies. He had not heard her parting comment—maybe.

In the course of the tedious journey out of the Blight and back into familiar Commonwealth space they had plenty of time to discuss a range of options. Everything, of course, depended on whether there really was anything at the locality that had been provided to Flinx by the Krang or if he had merely been given the coordinates of a myth.

The report that had found its way to Science Central on Earth, however, was no fable. It had been compiled and recorded by two respected xenologists in the course of their diplomatic and anthropological work among the natives of Senisran. Full of anomalous elusions and hypotheses, it was hardly enough to justify the immediate dispatch of a larger, better-equipped, and more costly research team to that watery world. For one thing, in the event that such an expedition were to be mounted, the natives who had provided much of the information that was contained in the report had promised to destroy the important relics the xenologists had described by dispersing them across a wide area of deep ocean. It was apparent that anyone wishing to carry out a formal follow-up to the initial report would have to proceed with extreme caution.

None of which concerns troubled those aboard the *Teacher,* since they were not going to touch down on Senisran and had no expectation of having to deal with its prickly natives.

The outer asteroid belt where the Krang-given coordinates lay was far enough from its sun so that it might as well have been in interstellar space. A visitor happening upon that circumstellar ring of rock and mineral, compacted dust and water ice, would have been forgiven for thinking that was exactly where he was, save for the dominating presence of a Jovian-sized gas giant nearby. Nearby in the interplanetary sense, that is. The enormous planet lay far enough away so that, while its roiling storms and double rings were clearly visible from the section of the asteroid belt where the *Teacher* came to a stop, its radiation, powerful magnetic field, and gravity well would not pose any danger.

"We have arrived." The *Teacher* was not much given to excessive celebration even in the best of times.

Orbiting in concert with the majority of rocks and boulders and planetoids that comprised the outer asteroid belt, the ship continuously monitored its surroundings lest something small, solid, and moving faster than its fellows threatened to pose a danger to it and its fragile organic inhabitants. During the following first week of searching it had to use its weaponry to reduce several such minor course-crossing hazards to powder. By the second week Flinx almost hoped something (small and essentially harmless but noisy) would slip past the *Teacher*'s sensors and strike the ship. It could hardly pose less of a danger than the ennui that was threatening to overcome them all.

"It would help if we knew more precisely what we were looking for," Clarity pointed out to him on the last day of the second week of searching the coordinates the Krang had provided.

"We're looking for a link." Flinx was standing by the forward console, staring out the main port. At the far end of the *Teacher,* its Caplis generator was dark. They could not use the KK-drive field this close to so many sizable solid objects, nor was there any need to do so.

"Like I said," Clarity reiterated with uncharacteristic exasperation, "it would help if we knew more precisely what we were looking for."

His retort was sharp. "I am *so* sorry. I had this perfect tridee image of a four-hundred-million-year-old Xunca alarm-weapons link in my pocket, but I seem to have dropped it somewhere." Her reaction left him immediately contrite.

"I'm sorry, Clarity. I apologize." As he started toward her, she put up a hand to forestall him.

"Forget it. Weeks of searching and finding nothing have left us all frustrated and on edge." She looked around to make sure they were still alone. "Have you seen Syl lately? She's so wound up she's chewed a couple of centimeters off the ends of each of her ovipositors."

The *Teacher* was doing its best, Flinx knew. But like any AI, even one equipped with symbolic logic, it remained at its core a literal device. It could and would search diligently for anything—if they could just tell it what to look for. On that note the Tar-Aiym Krang had been lamentably uninformative.

Surely they would find something, eventually. It was simply a matter of scanning and analyzing the objects that comprised the asteroid belt until they came upon—what?

"We will know it when we see it," an optimistic Truzenzuzex insisted. "The complex on Horseye would not continue sending, however intermittently, a composite signal to a corner of empty space."

At least they did not have to circle the distant sun and search the entire asteroid belt. They only had to examine the portion facing the outer gas giant, in the vicinity of the coordinates the Krang had provided. But visually, at least, there seemed nothing to differentiate one square kilometer of drifting dead rock from the next.

As the third week of searching crept toward its end, the *Teacher* continued its relentless examination. The less patient organic life-forms on board, however, were approaching terminal boredom.

"This isn't working." Truzenzuzex clicked impatiently as his four opposing mandibles finished masticating the last of the early meal.

"An unassailable observation." Tilting her head back slightly, Sylzenzuzex drained the last of the blue liquid from a spiral-tipped cylinder. The normally even-tempered security officer's mood was becoming as touchy as that of her venerable Eighth.

These days none of them, Flinx had to admit, was in a very good mood. The promise that had drawn them here from distant Booster had been lost to weeks of endless ennui interrupted only by the venturing of the occasional bad idea. Now it seemed that the philosoph was about to put forth another one. Among his companions, disinterest was universal.

Until they heard it.

"Nothing of value was learned on this journey, *dr!app,* until Flinx communicated with the Krang. It occurs to me that we are faced with a similar situation here."

As Tse-Mallory pushed his chair back from the table he was careful to avoid crushing the large spatulate leaves of the trio of decorative growths behind him. Some of the imported flora that bedecked Flinx's private lounge had done so well that he had transplanted shoots and buds elsewhere within the *Teacher*. The spread of greenery certainly brightened many purely prosaic corners of the ship.

"If that were the case and there was some sort of similar device adrift here," the soldier-sociologist conjectured, "wouldn't it have responded to Flinx's presence by now?" Turning from his friend, he looked over at the silent subject of the conversation. "You haven't sensed anything since we've arrived here, have you, Flinx? An alien presence, something akin to the Krang or the wandering weapons platform?"

Flinx shook his head as Clarity passed him a ship-conjured pastry filled with simulated cloudberries. "No, sir, nothing," he replied as he ate.

"I am thinking," the philosoph mused aloud, "that perhaps his proximity to the rest of us might somehow mute or dilute his sensitivity. Or conversely, confuse the perceptiveness of that which we are looking for."

Tse-Mallory was intrigued. "You're saying, in so many words, that the rest of us might be jamming the signals."

"A crude analogy for what we must presume, if it exists, is an exceptionally advanced interaction, but yes."

"How do you suggest we overcome this theoretical blockage?"

Both antennae inclined in Flinx's direction as Truzenzuzex regarded their young host. "We should experiment by isolating him from the possible source of disruption, which is us. Flinx, I am of the opinion that you should take an extended walk while the ship moves to another position."

Flinx paused with the remnants of the pastry halfway to his mouth. Responding to his abrupt emotional reaction, Pip and Scrap looked up sharply from where they had curled up together among the comforting vegetation.

"I've got an idea." Flinx stared back at the philosoph. "Why don't the rest of you go for a walk and I'll stay with the ship."

Seated beside him, Clarity jabbed him in the ribs. Perceiving that neither the blow nor its perpetrator were representative of the beginnings of actual conflict, both minidrags went back to sleep. "Me, too, Red?"

"No, of course not you, Clarity." Caught between a woman and a theory, Flinx sensed that neither was immediately resolvable. Perched on the resultant dilemma, he turned to Tse-Mallory. "Bran, what do you think? Is what Tru suggests a viable proposal?"

The powerfully built sociologist did not hesitate. "Nothing else is working. I don't see what harm could result." He studied the younger man. "Unless you have a fear of being outside by yourself."

Flinx shook his head. "I've spent too much time traveling through space to be afraid of it. Respectful, yes. Awed, surely. But it's not something I fear." He looked back to Truzenzuzex. "When do you want to try this experiment, Tru?"

The philosoph gestured with all four hands. "Yesterday's searching was devoid of discovery. Extrapolating from our previous probing, tomorrow's searching is likely to be devoid of discovery. Let us schedule an exception for today. Of course, if you feel you need time to acclimate yourself to the idea . . ."

Swallowing the last of the pastry, Flinx rose from his seat. "I'll instruct the *Teacher* to ready a survival suit." He looked down at Clarity. "Are you all right with this?"

She hesitated momentarily, eyeing the two expectant scientists. "If Bran and Tru think it's safe, then I guess we ought to try it. I don't like the idea of you making contact with *any* kind of device from *any* ancient alien civilization. Much less via an interface that might take you away from the ship." She looked reconciled. "But that's what we're here to try and do."

Smiling, he reached over and lightly tousled her hair. She responded by making a face. "Don't worry. I won't do anything stupid. And I'll be thinking of you the whole time."

Truzenzuzex shook his head sadly. "Unhelpful. While you're outside you should be trying to think like a Xunca."

Flinx would have been happy to comply—except that no one knew how the Xunca thought, and had not done so for hundreds of millions of years.

Stepping outside the ship was more interesting than he had anticipated. While over the years he had viewed the *Teacher*'s exterior from every conceivable angle, he had nearly always done so from the comfortable confines of one of its two shuttles. He could not remember the last time he had ventured outside in deep space in nothing but a survival suit.

The stars were very bright, and the looming striped mass of the system's outermost gas giant was brilliant and colorful.

"Everything all right, Flinx?" Tse-Mallory's voice emerged muted and modulated from the survival suit's cranial speaker.

"I'm fine. Let's get this over with. Ship?"

"Flinx?" the *Teacher* responded promptly.

"Withdraw to distance. Follow the honored Tse-Mallory and Truzenzuzex's instructions unless contradicted by me."

"I will continue monitoring your vitals for any evidence of abnormality," the shipmind replied. "For example, your blood pressure currently is . . ."

Flinx cut it off. He knew how the *Teacher* could go on. Especially when it was concerned about him. "You can recite all the statistics when I'm back on board. In order to conduct the philosoph's experiment appropriately, I should be left in silence."

Another voice reached him: Clarity. "I know you're supposed to be reaching out for a Tar-Aiym contact or something like that, Flinx, but— just watch what you wish for."

"I'm wishing I was back on the ship," he offered by way of reply. "I'm wishing I . . ."

"Flinx . . ." Truzenzuzex's perfectly modulated terranglo was both stern and suggestive.

"I know, I know. Try to think like a Xunca. Going to silence," he muttered.

The *Teacher* began, very carefully, to move away. The acceleration was extremely measured. Activating his suit's propulsion unit, Flinx headed off in the opposite direction. The sensation of weight dropped off quickly until, once clear of the ship's artificial gravity field, he felt himself floating, falling, adrift among the asteroid belt.

He chugged past his first planetoid some ten minutes later. It was about the size of the chair he had been sitting on during the early meal. The lump of dark flinty material looked comparatively solid. Not an aggregate, then, he decided. Utilizing the suit's propulsion system, he pivoted—and experienced a moment of mild panic. The *Teacher* was nowhere to be seen.

It took him a moment to find it—a point of light moving away at an angle to all the other drifting shapes. How much distance would Truzenzuzex think was necessary to put between it and him? He had not been boasting when he had told the philosoph that he was not afraid of being out in deep space by himself. The *Teacher* knew where he was every nanosecond. It would not, could not, lose track of his position.

Could it?

Could he, despite every precaution, end up lost and alone, doomed to drift forever among the shattered shards of an alien planetary system, floating free until his suit's air could no longer be satisfactorily recycled, dying forgotten among . . .

Stop it, he scolded himself. *The Teacher knows where you are at all times. It's right over there, just over that way. Distant now yet continuously aware of your presence, your location. You are not isolated. You are not abandoned.*

You are not fulfilling your mentor's straightforward request by wasting your focus on such nonsense, either, he reminded himself.

Settling down, calming himself, doing his best to transmit reassuring readings of his blood pressure and all other relevant biological indicators to a concerned *Teacher,* he forced himself to start concentrating on the reason for the solo excursion. He projected outward as best he was able, trying to recall and offer up the same state of mind he entered when he was lying beneath receptive Tar-Aiym contact domes. Unfortunately, the unidentified whatever that he was trying to make contact with was not of Tar-Aiym origin. Very little was known about the Xunca other than the fact that they had existed. Nothing whatsoever was known of their works except what little had been learned from study of the alarm complex on Horseye.

As his body drifted, so, inevitably, did his thoughts. He found himself looking away from the larger asteroids, away from the Jovian giant, and outward toward the stars. Stunning they were in their own right, joyous in what they represented. It was horrifying to think of them disappearing, snuffed out one by one like so many candles as they were sucked down and absorbed by the malevolent immensity that was even now rushing this way.

The contrast with the dreary rocks among which he was drifting was striking. Dull and lifeless, these precessed uneventfully in their primordial orbits. Making slight adjustments to his velocity, he fell in among them so that he was now drifting at the same speed as the majority. Several came quite close. Carefully extending an arm in the zero gravity, he reached out and wrapped his fingers around the nearest. His fingers caused the particulate matter that had collected on the hard surface to float away from the stone's minuscule gravitational field. A little of it clung to his gloved hand.

Using his other hand he flicked the dust away, then idly brushed at the fist-sized rock itself. More dust floated off, adding to the number of orbiting objects without altering their collective mass. Blinking, he brought the potato-shaped rock closer to his face. Was that a hint of color there? Murmuring a command, he activated the external light that encircled the suit's faceplate.

There was unquestionably some color there, he decided. Where he had brushed the dust away the stone showed a distinct shade of green. Well, the mineral olivine was a known component of many asteroids and meteors. Its presence here was not surprising. Releasing the stone and letting it drift free, he plucked another from its orbit. This one was the size of a melon. Finger-swept, it too revealed the same dark greenish tint. As he was examining it more closely, something out of the corner of his eye caught his attention.

The first stone was coming back to him.

Startled, he let go of the rock he had been examining and put up a hand to ward off the first stone, but his intervention wasn't necessary. It turned out that the rock was not moving in his direction, but toward the second, larger piece of rubble he had been holding. Coming together in total silence, the two stones seemed to fuse. In the process green sparks flared briefly, illuminating the borders. Fascinated, Flinx would have studied the two rocks in more detail if he had not been distracted by another unexpected phenomenon. Looking around, he saw that other stones untouched by him were now also beginning to move in his direction. As they approached, some changed course away from him to intersect the vector of another, resulting in a melding luminously similar to the first two.

Adjusting his position, he commenced a slow pirouette. What he saw caused his jaw to drop in amazement. It looked as if every pebble, every stone, every planetoid within range of his vision, was now in motion.

Some of those that had already merged had begun to glow with a pale green efflorescence.

Hurriedly, he addressed the suit's communit. "Ship, I think you'd better come and pick me up. There's something happening here. Some of these stones around me, they're moving. A number of them are starting to commingle, or fuse—I'm not sure of the methodology involved."

The *Teacher* responded immediately. "I am already on my way, Flinx. I have detected initiation of the same unidentified processes here. I will arrive at your location as rapidly as is feasible and safe."

"I don't think there's a need for any special hurry as long as you're on your way." Flinx looked on enchanted as more and more of the stony matter around him began to come together. The process seemed to be accelerating. "I don't see any danger. While a great deal of the material is in motion, it also seems to be avoiding me."

"Best not to take any unnecessary chances, Flinx," the ship told him. "While you have not yet been impacted, it is not possible to assure that all of the many orbiting objects will continue to steer clear of you."

"I'm not concerned." Inside the suit, Flinx smiled. "You're pretty good at predicting the movement of objects."

"That is so," the *Teacher* replied. "However, the number of orbiting fragmentational objects that are currently in motion exceeds my capacity to keep track of them."

Flinx's smile gave way to a frown. The *Teacher*'s computational and predictive abilities were exceptional. "I don't understand." He looked around again. "How many of the stony objects are moving toward me?"

"All of them."

He was silent for a moment, uncertain he had heard correctly. "I'm not sure I understand, ship. All of the objects in my vicinity are moving toward me?"

"That depends on how you choose to define 'vicinity,' Flinx." The *Teacher*'s voice was dry and dispassionate "They are *all* moving in your direction. The entire asteroid belt, billions and billions of individual objects, is now in motion and giving every indication of commencing a slow but accelerating collapse. You are in the approximate center of it."

Flinx looked around uneasily. It did not unsettle him that as far as he could see into the void, rocks and stones of every size and shape were rushing in his direction. It did not bother him that as more and more of them slammed into one another and melded together, a great green glowing shape was taking on contour and character not far from where he floated. Emerald sparks flew in all directions, lighting the darkness. It was as if he were drifting across the top of Vulcan's anvil.

It was only when a trio of asteroids each of which was at least fifty kilometers across appeared out of the dark and came tumbling toward him at high speed that he finally comprehended the enormity of what the *Teacher* had told him.

CHAPTER

26

Once back on the ship Flinx could hardly wait for the lock to cycle shut to begin struggling out of the survival suit. Clarity and Sylzenzuzex were waiting for him on the other side. They had to wait their turn until a brilliant pink and blue winged shape finished caressing him with her pointed tongue.

"Flinx, you're all right? You didn't get hit?" An anxious Clarity was looking him up and down as if unable to believe he had not been crushed or otherwise injured.

He shook his head as Pip settled down on his shoulder. "I'm fine, Clarity, fine. Not so much as a scratch. There was stuff all around me, yes, and some of it was starting to move really, *really* fast by the time you arrived. But not one of them touched me. Not one."

Sylzenzuzex was staring at him. "You activated something while you were out there, Flinx. Something that responded to your presence while also deliberately avoiding it. Truzenzuzex was right."

He nodded as he started for the control room. "I'm beginning to think so. But right about *what*?"

Truzenzuzex and Tse-Mallory barely acknowledged his arrival. They were far too absorbed in the view out the foreport. Around them, images projected by the *Teacher* provided various views with the ship as its locus. No matter which direction one studied, the spectacle was the same.

From planetoids the size of cities to gravel splinters no bigger than a fingernail, the entire asteroid belt that ringed the outer reaches of the Senisran system was collapsing toward a single point. Not one of the incoming objects had hit Flinx. Not one struck the *Teacher*. Those that looked as if they might do so swerved over, under, and around the ship as they sped toward rendezvous. Tse-Mallory was quick to comment on the seemingly conscientious evasion.

"Something is not as it appears. Chondrites don't have built-in avoidance systems," he muttered.

"These do." Truzenzuzex was studying a floating image close by his right shoulder that supplied a view astern. "They'd better."

Bearing down on them was a rectangular cliff face twice the size of the *Teacher*. Even if Flinx had given a command to do so, there was no time to move out of the oncoming monster's course. A moment later, when it was less than a dozen ship-lengths distant, it changed course. They could follow its progress easily as it shot past. Braking at the last possible instant, it rotated forty degrees and with incomparable delicacy slipped into a notch in another drifting planetoid even bigger than itself. The hurtling cliff face fit the empty notch as perfectly as a tooth fit its socket. The massive merge was accompanied by a blinding but brief burst of intense greenish lightning.

Only when exhaustion finally overcame fascination did they withdraw, one by one, to their cabins to rest.

When Clarity awoke, Flinx was no longer beside her. Rubbing sleep from her eyes, she gathered up Scrap and tracked him back to Control. Sylzenzuzex was standing nearby. For the most ephemeral of instants Clarity recognized and shamefacedly cast aside a flicker of irrational jealousy.

"Where are your mentors?" she asked as she came up beside him.

"In the lounge," he told her, "noisily disputing statistics while toying with irreconcilable data among the ornamental flora." He nodded forward. "Have a look."

At first she thought the object floating in front of the *Teacher* was nothing more than the consequence of a great many stones large and small coming together to make one big one. Peering harder, she saw that the fused rocky debris now formed a shape with a distinctly regular silhouette. Vaguely conical in shape, it flaunted an enormous dark maw at one end while the other tapered to a blunt, somewhat indistinct tip. Though more and more rocky detritus continued to arrive and add additional bulk to the drifting mass, the surge of material had markedly diminished. She found herself gazing at a massive, stark, simplistic configuration that radiated a subdued but steady green light from somewhere deep within. A tapering cone large enough to accommodate every starship in the Commonwealth. Simultaneously.

"Okay," she heard herself murmuring softly to the man standing beside her, "as Syl said yesterday, you've definitely gone and activated *something*. It was made aware of your presence, and it's aware of *our* presence. But what is it?"

"That's one of the things Bran and Tru are arguing about." He put his arm around her, forcing both minidrags to shift position. "It's beautiful, though, isn't it?"

Though glad of the comforting arm, its gentle grasp did not change her opinion of the enormous unidentifiable structure. "I don't know if I'd go that far. Dark green's not my favorite color, anyway."

Voices sounded behind them, coming closer and growing louder. Tse-Mallory made himself heard before he and the philosoph entered the bridge.

"Tru and I have spent hours pondering the possible nature and function of the object. We think we know what it is."

Flinx turned immediately. "What is it, then? What does it do?"

Truzenzuzex flicked the tip of one antenna in his direction. "Bran said that we know what it is. He said nothing about knowing what it does."

"We believe that it is," the sociologist-soldier declaimed importantly, "the receptor of the occasional transmission from Horseye. Your ship has checked and rechecked the relevant readings for us. There is no mistaking the confluence. The signals pass directly through the point in space now occupied by the assembled contrivance."

"That's most interesting, esteemed Eighth," Sylzenzuzex observed. "I confess, however, that I'm unable to see how this discovery has any practical ramification."

Looking over at her, he switched to Low Thranx. "That's because we remain ignorant of it. But both Bran and I are convinced there must be one." With his right truhands and foothands he gestured toward the port. "Otherwise, all the intriguing activity that we have been witness to here represents nothing more than a grandiose expenditure of energy in the service of no purpose."

Flinx had a sudden thought. "The Krang is both a weapon and a musical instrument. Could this be a work of art?"

Tse-Mallory frowned at him. "Why beam intermittent signals all the way from the Horseye system to here just to identify the location of a piece of art? Though I have to admit that I, personally, certainly find it pleasing from an aesthetic as well as an engineering point of view."

Truzenzuzex was not about to be sidetracked. "We have already had this argument, Bran. It *must* do something! And furthermore, *fss!is!kk,* it must do something of significance. It is too big, too impressive, and too joined to the Xunca alarm system to be nothing more than a diversion."

"That's your opinion." Tse-Mallory continued to play devil's advocate. "A Xunca might view the arrangement differently."

"How do we find out?" Flinx looked down at the philosoph.

"Bran and I have been debating that all day." The subdued light of the control room gleamed mirror-like from the dozens of individual lenses that comprised the venerable thranx's compound eyes. "Your physical and/or mental interaction with the orbiting matter galvanized, provoked, or otherwise set in motion the extraordinary orbital assembly process that has resulted in the new astronomical object we now see before us." He did not hesitate. "It follows that if anything is likely to stimulate further activity on the part of the object, it will be your presence."

Flinx swallowed. "You want me to put the suit on again and go out there—*into* there?" This time it was Clarity who put a protective arm around him.

Tse-Mallory nodded firmly. "Not alone, though. At least, not initially. We'll enter together. Then, if nothing happens and we can't come up with a better idea, that's when we will ask you to continue by yourself."

Clarity blinked at the old soldier-scientists. "'Enter'?"

Human and thranx nodded in tandem, though it was Truzenzuzex who spoke. "Bran and I have concluded that we should take the *Teacher* into the large opening." He gestured in the direction of the enigmatic alien construct. "There's certainly more than enough room. It may be that an apparatus that encloses such a considerable volume is in fact intended to act upon a single individual—but it seems, even for the Xunca, unnecessarily profligate in terms of expenditure. There is no reason not to take the whole ship inside. Unless"—and he executed a broad gesture of deference in Flinx's direction—"you choose not to. It is, after all, your vessel, and therefore your decision."

Flinx considered his mentors' words carefully. He hated the thought of risking the *Teacher*. On the other hand, he told himself, if he chose to enter in a suit, alone, and something untoward happened, of what use would be his wonderful ship? Bran and Tru were watching him closely, Sylzenzuzex was watching her Eighth, and Clarity— Clarity at that particular moment looked as if she would rather be anywhere else in the universe, as long as it was with him. In fact, of all those present, only one had not yet ventured an opinion regarding the philosoph's request.

Twisting his head down and to his right, he murmured, "Well, Pip? What do you think? Do we take a dive into the alien well or do we try something else?"

Raising her gaze, the minidrag looked up at him and blinked. Then she yawned, dropped her head back into her upper coil, and went back to sleep.

"That's what I thought you'd say." He turned back to the patient Truzenzuzex. "If you and Bran think it's something we should try, then I suppose we ought to go ahead and try it."

"Sure," an unhappy Clarity muttered, "just plunge ahead and hang the consequences."

"What?" He looked over at her. "If you object, Clarity, or think we should try something else first . . ."

She sighed and shook her head. "Don't listen to me. I'm just tired, that's all." She offered a wan smile. "My area of expertise is cosmetics, remember? Not of much use when it comes to trying to save civilization. As far as deciding how and when to experiment with alien artifacts, I'll be the first to admit I don't have any qualifications."

"Sure you do," he contradicted her. "I'm an alien artifact, and you've experimented with me."

She gaped at him. Figuratively, he gaped at himself in self-inflicted shock.

I—I made a joke, he thought numbly. *A joke about my genesis.* Try as he might, he could not remember having done anything of the sort ever before. His origins had always been a matter, to himself and to others, of utmost seriousness. Unsurprisingly, it had been left to Clarity to extract for the first time a scrap of absurdity from it.

Experiment, he thought dazedly to himself. That was the origin of Philip Lynx. Serious, somber, stern, severe—and if you looked at it a certain way, from a particular angle, just possibly also a little—silly?

They were all staring at him. As much to his surprise as that of everyone else, he smiled. "All right. Let's go see what's inside the big glowing green stone thing. Maybe it's a Xunca surprise."

"Let us hope it *is* a Xunca surprise." Truzenzuzex whispered under his breath, his spiracles barely pulsing. "Otherwise we will be reduced to drifting mentally as well as physically while formulating hopeful hypotheses from nothing."

Semisentient as it was, the *Teacher* might have been expected to raise an objection or two of its own to the scientists' proposal. It was sufficiently advanced, however, to recognize that the experiment was one that had to be tried. If its master and his fellow organic intelligences were willing to risk their continued existence in the service of such investigation, then as a properly programmed AI it could hardly do less.

The vast chasm at the enlarged end of the asteroidal aggregate loomed even bigger as the *Teacher* approached it. Not a hint of the soft, almost comforting green glow was apparent within. A sequence of barely visible silvery striations lining the interior were all that interrupted the otherwise interminable starless dark. As the ship moved deeper and deeper inward, Flinx could not shake off the sensation of being swallowed.

He forced it from his thoughts as the ship moved deeper. It was a foolish analogy anyway. There was not the slightest suggestion of the macrobiotic about the alien assembly whose immense curving walls now fully engulfed them. It was cold, dead, and manifestly unalive.

Which led him to wonder at the source of the faint violet glow that appeared directly ahead.

At first he thought his eyes were playing tricks and that the purple was visual, not external. Standing beside him, however, Clarity raised an arm and pointed toward the same glimmering.

"Flinx, do you see that?"

He nodded. "There's some color there." He looked sharply to his left. "Bran, Tru?"

"Something there for sure." Tse-Mallory moved forward until he was leaning against the smooth surface of the main console, as if the additional bit of space he had walked might bring him close enough to the flickering color to allow him to identify it.

Further reflection was interrupted by the *Teacher.* "Flinx, we are accelerating."

"I didn't give that order." He had not taken his eyes off the distant speck of profound purple. "Do you feel a need to or have evidence that suggests we need to increase our forward velocity?"

"It would not matter if I did," the ship replied uninformatively. "I note only that we have begun to accelerate. Rather dramatically, if I may say so."

Flinx and Clarity exchanged a glance, then looked across at the two scientists.

Tse-Mallory looked bemused. "I don't sense any increase in speed. Tru?"

The philosoph was likewise noncommittal. "I perceive nothing. Flinx, ask the ship to elaborate."

Flinx needed no prompting. Except in cases of obvious emergency it was unlike the *Teacher* to take such action on its own initiative. In response to his query the ship replied readily, though as far as a rationale was concerned its explanation was no more illuminating than its initial announcement.

"What's our speed?" Flinx asked. "How much faster are we moving?" He continued to stare out the foreport. Had the splotch of purple refulgence grown slightly larger?

"We are not moving faster," the *Teacher* replied. "In fact, we are not moving at all. Space, however, is. As to our speed, by my instruments, it is zero."

"You're not making any sense." An increasingly irritated Flinx glared at the nearest visual pickup. "If we're accelerating, how can we not be moving?"

He broke off. Additional detailed explication could wait until later. In fact, everything could wait until later. He felt pressure at his waist. Clarity was hugging him, hard. The two humans standing shoulder to shoulder allowed Pip and Scrap, mother and offspring, to push up against one another. Off to their left Bran Tse-Mallory, the Eint Truzenzuzex, and his relative Sylzenzuzex joined the two humans in staring straight ahead.

They did not know what they were seeing. They did not understand what they were seeing. They knew only that they could not turn away from it.

The *Teacher*'s confusing and seemingly contradictory attempt at explanation notwithstanding, it appeared that they had entered some kind of tunnel. A tunnel or corridor composed entirely of energy that was simultaneously volatile and unwavering. It was as if, Flinx reflected in awe, someone had taken an entire galaxy in all its glory, replete with suns and nebulae, pulsars and masers, black holes and X-ray bursters, and attenuated it until it was no greater in diameter than the coruscating tube they were presently speeding through. The curved walls that enclosed them flung successive waves of electric crimson, intense cobalt, and eye-bending yellow at their stunned retinas. Some emerged from astern to overtake and blast past the ship itself. He had the feeling that if the *Teacher* was to drift to the left or right, up or down, and make the slightest contact with that scintillating, flaring cylinder of encircling energy, the ship and everything within it would evaporate like a cough in a hurricane.

"Some kind of plasma tunnel." Tse-Mallory had found his voice. He spoke in that tone of barely controlled excitement scientists reserve for those special moments when they realize they have come across something that truly justifies the employment of the word "new."

"Irrespective of what the ship says, I can't tell if we're moving through it or if it's moving around us."

"I can tell you *this, cri!l!kk.*" Truzenzuzex's antennae were quivering like violin strings at the height of a Bartok arpeggio. "We are *traveling. Sitashk,* we are traveling! What I would not give to be able to pause and step for a moment outside these sculpted walls of dynamic conveyance."

Occasionally they had glimpses of other loops of force that might have been similar corridors. There were not many, and they were widely dispersed, but they materialized often enough to show that the one that was conveying them was not the only one of its kind. Glimpses of other such tunnels rapidly became fewer and fewer. Before long the occupants of the *Teacher* found themselves utterly alone, speeding down a channel formed of unfamiliar energies toward an equally unknown destination.

"I guess the Xunca," Sylzenzuzex observed hours later as they forced themselves to break away from the eye-numbing view out the foreport long enough to eat and drink something, "liked to get around."

Seated across from her, Clarity was hand-feeding Scrap slightly burnt bread crumbs. The minidrag would rear back and strike from her shoulder, dispatching one piece of toast after another as if he were stalking prey deep in the sweltering jungles of distant Alaspin.

"I wonder where we're going?" she ruminated.

"I think I can hazard a guess." Tse-Mallory sipped the hot drink the ship had prepared for him. "The end of the road. The last station on the line. The definitive terminus." He peered over at Flinx. Their host was neither eating nor drinking as his imagination worked overtime. "The place that the Tar-Aiym Krang told Flinx was coupled to the Xunca warning system on Horseye. The locality of . . ."

" . . . the defense," Truzenzuzex finished for his friend. "*If* we are lucky. And maybe also if we are not lucky."

Clarity blinked at the thranx. "I don't follow you, Tru."

The philosoph looked back at her. "We are traveling through a transportation system whose technology is at least as old as the last of the Xunca. Say, roughly half a billion terrestrial years." A truhand gestured toward a projection hovering conveniently nearby. It displayed the view forward of the ship: a seemingly infinite corridor of energy and light.

"That something so old still functions is in itself almost beyond belief. Yet if Flinx's exchange with the Krang was accurate, it is conveying us toward a construct, a device, beside which this astonishing example of ancient engineering must appear little more than a sandy path by comparison."

Clarity nodded pensively as she passed Scrap a piece of crust. "I wonder when we'll get there. Wherever 'there' is."

"I will happily settle for arriving before we're dead," Sylzenzuzex volunteered.

It took nearly a month. Given the speed at which they were traveling (or not traveling, if the seriously confused shipmind was to be believed), the expanse they must have crossed exceeded anything previously traversed by humans or thranx by many, many orders of magnitude.

"I think we're slowing down."

Flinx's general call caused everyone to drop what they were doing and race to the control room. Finding him seated in the command chair, his companions joined him in staring out the foreport. At first glance nothing seemed different: it looked as if they were still traveling inside the endless tunnel of glowing plasma. As everyone's perception adjusted, however, a number of other realizations became obvious.

Most immediately, it appeared that the diameter of the channel had been greatly enlarged. Though the *Teacher* was still fully enveloped, the enclosing walls were farther off. The corridor had ballooned into a bubble big enough to hold a hundred ships the size of the *Teacher.* Set alongside other megastructures Flinx had encountered in his journeying, the spherical structure of shimmering iridescent energy was not large. Compared to something like the Tar-Aiym weapons platform its dimensions were downright modest.

What *was* impressive was what could be discerned just beyond the borders of the bubble that enclosed them: an all-pervasive luminosity.

They were surrounded, insofar as he could see, by light. Beyond the barrier of the plasma sphere there was only radiance. He queried the ship.

"I have already been analyzing the omnipresent broad-spectrum phenomena—or attempting to do so, given that my instrumentation is exceedingly inadequate for such a purpose," the *Teacher* explained. "It is virtually impossible to impart an explanation in words. I myself can only just begin to appreciate the true nature of the phenomenon through the application of pure mathematics."

"Give it a try," Flinx urged his ship. "In words. Simple words."

"A contradiction that I fear may be impossible to resolve," the ship-mind replied. "Outside the enclosed plasma spheroid in which we presently find ourselves, in all directions and to a distance I am unable to measure, there is nothing but a solidity of gravitons."

Tse-Mallory blanched at the explanation. "That really is a contradiction in terms. Gravitons have zero mass and no charge. They're closed strings in special low-energy vibrational states. You can't catch them, you can't see them, and you certainly can't collect them in one place, much less in anything resembling a 'solidity.'"

The *Teacher* was not perturbed. "I told you that the reality I am perceiving crosses over into the inexplicable. Remember that as closed strings without endpoints, gravitons are not necessarily restricted to this brane. Or if you prefer, to what is referred to as the immediate physical universe in which we exist. They are perfectly capable of existing in and traveling through other branes as well as the greater Bulk."

"My head's starting to hurt," Clarity muttered.

"It does not matter," Truzenzuzex objected. "What Bran said about gravitons holds true."

"In this universe, yes," the *Teacher* agreed. "But much as we know about this brane, we know nothing of others. As has long been theorized, the laws of physics in other branes may be completely different from those in ours. A proton in another brane, for example, might have no mass. A wave or particle like a photon that could possibly exist in both might exhibit entirely different properties in another brane. In the L-brane, O-brane, or another, such a particle might possess mass, charge, or both.

"Some physicists and mathematicians have long believed that branes are not fixed within the infinity of the multiverse or Bulk, but that they are in constant motion—at least at the edges of the branes themselves. Where the ripples of two such branes impinge upon one another insistently enough, you get a bang. Sometimes a Big Bang. If that theory is to be believed, new universes contained within their own new branes are being born all the time—universes upon universes within universes.

"Envisage a technology so advanced that it could bring about such an interaction between a pair of branes, but under controlled conditions and on a manageable scale."

Truzenzuzex's mind was awhirl with the possibilities. "*Cr!!lk,* perhaps that's where the Xunca went. Through a congruency of two branes, from this one into another. The ultimate escape. Perhaps they traveled in craft propelled by focused gravitons—or composed of them."

An equally enthralled Tse-Mallory was not averse to taking the impossible another step further. "If they could influence such processes on such a scale, maybe they manipulated the degree and extent of the interaction in order to generate their own made-to-order Big Bang." Raising a hand, he brought thumb and forefinger toward one another to illustrate his point. "A little Bang, say. The result would be the creation of a new small universe contained within a customized brane. Nothing ostentatious. Insignificant, really. Say, a thousand available and unoccupied new galaxies they could explore and colonize at their leisure."

"An entire civilization?" Clarity was whispering without knowing why. "To escape what's coming toward the Commonwealth they moved their whole civilization to another *dimension?*"

Tse-Mallory smiled softly. "Tru and I are just speculating. If there was a Xunca around, I'd ask it. But they're not here anymore. As Flinx says, they went away. Only some of their works remain behind to hint at what little we know of them." With a wave of his arm he encompassed the view forward. "The plasma tunnel transport system. This place. The quantum impossibility it somehow holds at bay."

The shipmind was not finished. "But before they learned how to do whatever it was that they finally did, they rendered this brane and another barely proximate in an attempt to try and accumulate what they thought would be enough energy to counter the oncoming menace, which itself I have come to believe is quite likely an intrusion of another kind of matter-energy from still a third brane."

Truzenzuzex whistle-clicked softly. "I would need to do the math, but the juxtaposition of our brane with another could possibly provide an explanation for the Great Attractor's unbelievable energy."

"All that effort and science to create a defensive weapon became unnecessary," the *Teacher* continued, "when the Xunca found a way to step from this brane to another, or to create their own. Either means of escape would have rendered this weapon superfluous."

"But," Flinx pointed out, "they left it behind."

"Yes," the shipmind concurred. "They left it behind."

"Too big to move," Flinx found himself thinking aloud. "No need to move it, anyway." He eyed his companions. "Or maybe—maybe they left it behind, and intact, so that whatever civilizations and intelligences arose after them would have a chance to fight this thing that's coming toward us."

Clarity was not convinced. "If they wanted to help, why didn't they leave a signal that would lead us to the same brane where they've taken refuge?"

Tse-Mallory chuckled softly, shaking his head. "It wouldn't have mattered if they had, m'dear. In order to get to an island, you first have to have a proper boat. Maybe a quantum boat. It's not just that humanxkind is still learning how to swim: we don't even know what the water is like." He looked over at her. "What's the point of a signal you can't follow?"

"Oh, right," she murmured in sudden realization.

Turning away from the statistical illogicality visible through the foreport, Truzenzuzex spoke without looking at any of them. "The ship's speculations offer explanation not only for the Xunca defense, but perhaps also how the destructive Evil that we must confront can exist in our brane. It is background independent."

Flinx regarded the two scientists. "What does that mean? From a practical standpoint?"

Tse-Mallory explained. "It means that the oncoming menace flows through our brane without being a part of it, swallowing up matter and not acting like a normal part of our universe because it's *not* a part of it. It—leaked in. Or punched its way in. Or for all we know, deliberately gnawed its way in from some incredible, impossible, much larger 3-brane where such perversions of physics are an accepted and natural occurrence. As such, not being subject to the physical laws of this universe, it likely cannot be destroyed. Not in the sense that we understand destruction. Therefore the only way to stop it is by forcing it back out. Back into its own brane, or into another."

Flinx slumped in the command chair. Clarity came up behind him while Pip's tongue flicked out from her perch on her master's shoulder to lightly caress his cheek.

"I don't," he mumbled wearily, "feel much like a plumber."

Tse-Mallory offered a hopeful, encouraging smile. "Try not to let yourself become overwhelmed by the scale involved." Turning, he gazed out the foreport. "We've moved beyond that, anyway."

Flinx looked at his old friend and mentor. "No worries there, Bran. How can I be overwhelmed by something that's beyond comprehension?" He murmured under his breath, "So I was right all along: certain kinds of evil *are* quantifiable." Raising his gaze, he looked toward the nearest visual pickup.

"Ship, why haven't we been torn apart, crushed down to nothingness, or snapped out of this existence and into another one by the kind of forces that are at work here?"

"The unique bubble of energy that encloses this one small sphere of normal space shields us," the *Teacher* informed him. "Otherwise we would no longer be. All here—you, your companions, myself—would be compacted down to a single subatomic particle. Or something less than a waveform. Or perhaps we would be kicked out of this universe and into another one. My own feeling is that by compressing our protective bubble, the energy of the solidity that surrounds it actually makes it stronger by forcing its bonds tighter together."

Tse-Mallory was nodding to himself. "The Xunca not only knew how to fashion one hell of a transportation system, they knew how to build walls."

"To keep the 'water' out," Truzenzuzex added.

"Maybe they had to go elsewhere and didn't use this defense because—it doesn't work," Clarity could not keep from wondering.

Tse-Mallory nodded. "That's possible. I believe, however, that in addition to everything else they abandoned, they also left behind the means by which we may find out." Moving to the foreport, he leaned to his right and pointed.

No one had noticed the object before. Or maybe it had not been present until just then and it was their arrival that had caused it to appear. Or possibly, Flinx thought a little wildly, it had drifted out of this brane and into another and back again. If Bran, Tru, and the *Teacher* were to be believed, anything was possible here. They were in a space-place unprecedented, a minuscule bruise on the skin of the space-time continuum that teetered on the cusp of outrageous calculation. Anyone attempting to state for certain why something was happening, or even why something *was,* might as easily be right dead as dead right.

Careful, he told himself. Concentrate on the knowable. The *Teacher.* Pip. Clarity. Those were solid things, those were real things. They consisted of actualities he could hang on to. Or were they and himself and everything else he believed to be real nothing more than transitory expressions of the tortuous, convoluted physics and mathematics of some whimsical long-vanished species?

At least what Tse-Mallory had singled out looked real enough.

It was a hemisphere. Translucent red, it was so dark it was almost brown. Flinx was not surprised when the *Teacher* revealed that it occupied the exact center of the plasma bubble. At his direction, the ship cautiously adjusted its position to move closer—but not too close. That the *Teacher* could maneuver at all in such an outré environment was in itself surprising—and encouraging. It was with relief that he saw that not every law of nature had been abstracted in this place.

As they drew carefully nearer the hemisphere, which was the color of fine burgundy, they saw that it contained, hovering within it, a lump of some wrinkled maroon material shaped like a kidney bean. Three loops of what appeared to be gold wire but were undoubtedly something else encircled the object lengthwise like slender hovering halos. At no point did they come into contact with the material or each other. The center of the bean shape was occupied by a prominent concavity.

A mesmerized Flinx studied the object intently. If the depression in the center was intended to cradle a living entity, its dimensions suggested that the Xunca had been physically much smaller than the Tar-Aiym, smaller even than humans. Though the long-since-departed master engineers were closer in size to the thranx, he had no doubt who was going to be asked to take up a position within that beckoning indentation. His initial trepidation began to diminish even before the issue was brought up for discussion. After all, wasn't this what he had come all this way for?

Staring absently out the port, he found himself remembering a slightly built redheaded youth who with his pet minidrag had once innocently and without a care haunted the byways and back alleys of bustling, beguiling, aromatic Drallar. A boy who had worried only about staying one step ahead of the authorities, having enough to eat, looking after his elderly adoptive mother, and learning, learning, learning absolutely everything there was to know.

What a long, strange journey it had been.

CHAPTER
27

It was Clarity who voiced what everyone was thinking. "That depression looks like it might be about the right size and shape to accommodate a body, Flinx." Lips pressed together, she looked over at him. "I don't want you to find out if it is, but I know you have to."

He nodded slowly and peered past her. Tse-Mallory, Truzenzuzex, Sylzenzuzex—eyes single-lensed and compound stared back at him with equal intensity. No one said anything. No one had to. They were waiting on him.

He hugged Clarity, and that made him not want to go, too. As they gently disengaged he turned back to his mentors, one human, the other not. "I don't know what to do." He gestured at the object visible through the foreport. "I don't even know if it's designed to do anything and if it is, what it's *supposed* to do."

"Remember the first time you lay down on the operator's dais inside the Krang?" Tse-Mallory spoke encouragingly to his young friend. "The same lack of comprehension applied." He indicated the hovering, motionless hemisphere outside the ship. "I see no sign of anything like a switch, dial, button, headset, or even the overarching domes that allow activation of the Krang. Clearly this is not a Tar-Aiym device. It was made by a race as far in advance of the Tar-Aiym as they were beyond us." The soldier-sociologist shrugged helplessly. "All you can do, Flinx, is go out there, fit yourself to the beckoning concavity as best you can, and see what happens."

Flinx nodded. He had already reached the same conclusion. But it didn't hurt to hear Tse-Mallory confirm it.

"We're wasting time, and the more I think about it the less of a mind I have to want to do it."

They took turns helping him to suit up. There was no atmosphere, breathable or otherwise, inside the plasma bubble. In fact, as near as the *Teacher*'s instruments could tell, there was nothing at all within the sphere that kept untold forces at bay except for the claret-colored hemisphere. They were surrounded by the most perfect vacuum imaginable, devoid even of a hint of interstellar hydrogen. Beyond, the plasma container seethed and churned enough energy to shred the electrons from their orbits around the nuclei that composed their bodies, and then reduce the resultant basic particles to the subatomic equivalent of dust. Inside the ship inside the bubble, everything remained scandalously normal.

Pip went with him, of course. Pip almost always went with him, whatever the circumstances, whatever the danger. The flying snake was as much a part of him as an arm or a leg. The minidrag had been crucial to his contact with the Krang and with the Tar-Aiym weapons platform. It was impossible to know whether she would or could perform a similar function here, but to Flinx that was not what was important. What mattered was that he had his friend with him. There was plenty of room in the survival suit.

It was more than a little disconcerting to be traveling in a survival suit through a spatial vacuum that was pure white instead of jet-black. As he jetted away from the *Teacher* he spared only occasional glances at the curved, enfolding walls of force that held total annihilation at bay. The greater part of his attention was focused on the reddish-purple hemisphere looming steadily larger in his vision.

Halting his forward momentum within arm's length of the artifact, he commenced a circumnavigation, examining it closely from all sides, underneath, and from above. Tse-Mallory's distanced assessment proved accurate: there was nothing visible in the way of a control or any kind of instrumentation. Just the three encircling gold wires, if wires they were. The future of his civilization, of his galaxy, might depend on his ability to make this incredibly ancient relic respond in some way. But how?

Only one way to find out, he told himself unenthusiastically.

Skillfully manipulating his suit's thrusters to avoid the floating wires, he eased himself over the upper edge of the hemisphere and down toward its midpoint. Lowering himself carefully, he eased downward until he made contact with the half-moon-shaped indentation in the center. The object seemed to exert a very slight gravitational pull. Turning off his thrusters, he let it draw him in until he was lying on his back. Encased as he was in the survival suit he had no way of ascertaining the composition of the material beneath him, other than that it exhibited no give. Relaxing as best he could, he gazed out through the pure whiteness of his surroundings at the protective arc of the plasma bubble. At least, he thought to himself, there was one thing about his present condition he knew for a certainty. He knew exactly where he was.

He was alone. Again.

Except for Pip. Slithering up his left side, she stretched herself out between the inner lining of the survival suit and his chest, her iridescent emerald-green head facing his chin. Raising up, he looked down at her. Did the tenets of convergent evolution allow for the presence of an alien snake in an alien Garden of Eden? If that was where he had fetched up, where then the tree, where the apple? He was certainly no Adam, but he knew exactly where Eve was. Back on the *Teacher,* waiting for him to come back to her. Waiting for him to do—something.

He closed his eyes, tried to concentrate, struggled to reach out with his Talent as he had so many times before. He reposed like that for minutes, for half an hour, for an hour plus additional minutes.

Nothing.

No response of any kind was forthcoming. There was no splendid display of coruscating light, no thundering blare of alien music. Whatever kind of artifact was currently cuddling him, it bore no operational relationship to a Krang contact. The same silence that had greeted him when first he had lain down within the smooth-sided concavity still echoed in his ears. Extending himself through his Talent he could perceive Clarity and the others on board the *Teacher,* so he was confident his facility was functioning. But there was nothing else to be perceived. Nothing more.

Yet there *had* to be something more. Else why the entrée tunnel, why the enclosing protective sphere, why the hovering relic?

Try again, he told himself. *Go to sleep. You can do that, can't you? It's peaceful, it's comforting. You're exhausted anyway. Why not have a nice nap? The worst thing that will happen is that you'll wake up, the universe will be exactly as you left it, but you'll be rested and refreshed. Is that not an end greatly to be desired in and of itself?*

Why shouldn't he? he mused. Nothing else was happening. Tse-Mallory and Truzenzuzex would chide him for squandering an opportunity, but Clarity would understand completely. Once again he closed his eyes against the all-pervading white space.

So quiet. So still. He felt himself go limp as he let go for the first time in days. So much accomplished and learned, perhaps to no avail. His time to sleep, to take a mental break, was past due. He had earned the right.

A shock ran through his entire system as if a mischievous interloper had suddenly pressed one of his toes against a power transmission plate.

He and Pip were no longer alone.

On board the *Teacher,* Clarity gasped as she pointed out the fore-port. "Look. Oh, look."

The hemisphere in which Flinx had stretched out had become a solid sphere that glowed like a ruby lit from within. From the newly formed orb the crimson radiance extended outward perhaps ten meters in all directions. The artifact's original translucency had given way to opacity and he was no longer visible.

Pressure on her right arm caused her to look over and down. Sylzenzuzex was standing beside her, her left truhand and foothand gripping the soft flesh of the taller human. The thranx could not smile—but Clarity sensed that the security officer was doing so, even if only internally.

"You don't have to watch this." Sylzenzuzex's tone was somber. "Something is happening. Knowing Flinx, something more is likely to. Whatever the outcome, good or bad, you watching will not alter it."

Clarity considered a moment, then nodded appreciatively. "I'm going back to the cabin. Our cabin. You can tell me when everything is—over."

Antennae bobbed and a truhand gestured understanding. "If you would like some company, I'll come with you. At awkward times and in difficult circumstances my kind always prefer to have others nearby. It's what comes of subterranean living in close quarters."

Clarity nodded understandingly. "My kind didn't evolve underground, but I'd be glad of your company, Syl." Heading for the master's cabin, the pair abandoned the control chamber to Truzenzuzex and Tse-Mallory. So immersed in what they were seeing were the two scientists that they didn't even notice their companions' departure.

No longer alone, a startled Flinx realized. Furthermore, the entity identified inside his mind had a familiar feel to it.

IT IS GOOD TO BE WITH YOU AGAIN, FLINX-MAN, the voice in his dreaming declared. IT IS WELL THAT THIS TIME HAS FINALLY COME.

"I know you," Flinx found himself thinking. *"You've been with me before. Several times you helped push me out to perceive the danger that threatens us all."*

US ALL, the voice concurred. WE ARE COUSINS, YOUR KIND AND MINE. WE CANNOT REACH OUT AS YOU CAN—BUT WE CAN PUSH. WE CAN BOOST. THAT WE HAVE DONE.

"Who are *you?"* he inquired, not for the first time but more adamantly than ever before.

An image took shape in the theater of his mind. A picture of a world of few humans but of many—cousins. Long separated by corporeal evolution, but not by intelligence, they kept to themselves and to their new world. The sentiment he received, the emotions that flooded over and through his self, enveloped him like a warm, protective blanket.

I know that world, he realized with sudden excitement.

"Cachalot," he thought.

WE ARE ONE WITH YOU TO HELP. WE WILL BE AS A CUSHION FOR YOUR MIND.

AND I WILL HELP TO DIRECT AND GUIDE YOU.

The source of the second presence did not necessitate speculation. He had communicated with it only recently.

The Tar-Aiym Krang.

The triangle, he remembered. In order for him to have a chance of countering the oncoming peril, a cooperative triangle of different minds and means of thinking was required. Though not a part of the triangle itself, he was supposedly the trigger, the key, to something greater still.

What and where was the still missing third part? Of what did it consist and what minds lay behind it? If a Tar-Aiym itself, then there was no hope. Peot, the last living Tar-Aiym, had expired near the world of Repler not long ago. The Xunca? They had gone away. What then the third and last constituent of the triangle, and where to look for it?

Seek and ye shall find, he told himself. He reached out anew, as forcefully as he could, in concert with the two minds that had now joined themselves to his. Reached out—and made contact. With something as unexpected and utterly alien as it was near. It was waiting for him.

There was a relay. On his ship.

As his Talent had grown and matured, Flinx had encountered many minds. Human and thranx, AAnn and Quillp, Sakuntala and Tolian. The ancient machine-mind that was the Krang and now the group-mind of the cetacea of Cachalot. But he had never come across, had never even imagined, the bizarre cognitive processes that now invaded his awake-dreaming awareness. They sprang from a unified consciousness that encompassed an entire world yet could focus as tightly as the mind of a single individual. It was necessary for millions, perhaps billions of individual life-forms to come together to generate this sentience, which was as different from his or from those of any other he had encountered as was his from that of a stone. Except that a stone did not have consciousness.

Yet in spite of all that, in spite of an alienness that was clearly conscious but outside ordinary concepts of cognizance, he recognized it. Like the soothing group-mind of the cetacea, like the straightforward machine-mind of the Krang, it had been with and a part of him once before. In fact, he had walked among it.

The whales of Cachalot came to him with warmth.

The Krang came to him with an icy clarity.

And the untranslatable, inexplicable, globe-girdling greenness of the world-mind of Midworld came to him with—power.

The triangle was complete. How the Xunca would have replicated it he did not know and had no way of knowing, but that did not matter. He felt the energy flowing through him in a torrent. Though he could not see it or sense it, he could perceive through others and especially through the twisting, twitching serpentine shape lying on his chest that something was stirring Outside. Beyond the bubble. Like a shiver on a clear winter morning, something was working its way through the immense fabric of the Great Attractor. Lying there guarded by the combined minds of the cetacea, guided by the Krang, and energized by the verdant world-mind of Midworld, a semiconscious Flinx steeled himself for whatever might come to pass.

With every iota of his being thus preoccupied and mentally walled off and isolated from the rest of the cosmos, it was hardly surprising that he did not notice or sense the arrival of another ship.

Those on board the *Teacher,* however, did. Or rather, the *Teacher* detected the emergence of the visitor from the mouth of the plasma tunnel and hastened to notify Flinx's friends.

"Impossible!" Tse-Mallory blurted out as he and Truzenzuzex gaped at the instantly recognizable image that had arrived within range of the *Teacher*'s sensors. "No one else knew about the Xunca terminal at Senisran. It didn't even exist until Flinx brought it back into being."

"Which means that this vessel and whoever it holds must have been following very close." Truzenzuzex could not believe his own conclusion, far less what he was seeing. "But that makes even less sense. No one can track or follow a KK-drive ship through null space. This is not possible."

Tse-Mallory inhaled heavily. "My friend, we are in a place where the not possible is made real. Like you, I begin to doubt the evidence of my own senses." He turned to the nearest pickup. "Ship, is that truly another vessel we are seeing? Or could it be a corrupted duplicate of yourself, or an optical illusion generated by something in our surroundings?"

"It is another vessel." As ever, the *Teacher*'s reply was cool and assured. "A transport of Commonwealth origin. The externals and markings suggest a commercial craft of advanced design."

The two scientists exchanged a long look before a grim-faced Tse-Mallory addressed the ship again.

"Destroy it."

"I cannot do that." The shipmind sounded almost sympathetic even as it was unyielding. "Only Flinx, my master and guide, can give such a directive. It is one of many security measures installed at his command."

"Cannot the command be overridden if he is in imminent danger?" Truzenzuzex wondered tersely.

"There is no evidence that this new arrival presents any threat to him."

Tse-Mallory ground his teeth helplessly. Even the most advanced AI could be damnably literal. "Why else would this craft have followed us here?"

"I believe we are about to find out. They are hailing us now. I will saturate the transmission."

A communication holo appeared in the appropriate spot near the forward console. The image that formed was that of a middle-aged man. He did not look particularly threatening, Tse-Mallory thought. That meant nothing.

"Ship," the man declared, "stand at rest to receive visitors."

Tse-Mallory took it upon himself to reply. "Thanks just the same, but we're a little busy right now and we've no time for company. Who are you? How did you discover the plasma tunnel? What do you want here?"

By way of reply the man offered a thin smile. "All questions will be answered in due time. If you refuse to allow us to board, we will fire upon the radiant sphere that contains the individual Philip Lynx, perhaps better known to you as Flinx."

Tse-Mallory found himself stunned into silence. This was madness! How could they know that Flinx was inside the luminous red orb? Between its softly pulsing brilliance and increased opacity it was impossible to peer within, far less see that it presently held a single individual.

"Ship," Truzenzuzex declared, "the new arrival threatens your master! I say again, obliterate it!"

"I cannot." The *Teacher*'s tone was almost sad. "The threat is purely verbal. In any case, the visitor has halted itself on the other side of the luminescent orb precisely in line with our present position. At this point any unleashing of my weaponry in the direction of the new arrival would risk striking the sphere itself. I confront too many logical contradictions and practical difficulties to respond as you request."

"Then ask Flinx! Inform him of the changed state of affairs and ask him what you should do."

"I cannot," the ship responded. "When the visitor first manifested itself I attempted to do just that. He is right there before me yet completely out of reach."

The two scientists conferred anxiously. "We're going to have to allow these people to board, *s!!laksk*," Truzenzuzex insisted. "We will engage them in conversation. Whatever they want, we can and will keep them occupied for as long as possible." He indicated the incandescent crimson sphere. "It is evident that Flinx has succeeded in initiating a process of some significance. We must not allow it to be interrupted."

"Flinx has to know what's happening," Tse-Mallory muttered.

"You heard his ship, my friend." Antennae bobbed restively. "He is out of contact with us. These visitors, whoever they are, want to come here. We should let them. As long as they are here, we can talk. As long as we can talk, we can delay."

Tse-Mallory considered. "They may kill us."

"Certainly they may." Leaning back so that he stood only on his four trulegs, the Eint Truzenzuzex stood as tall as evolution allowed. "What happens to us does not matter. We are nothing. The process Flinx hopefully has inaugurated is everything. The longer we can keep these people busy, the more time it will give him to rouse—something."

Tse-Mallory nodded slowly. "Well, death is an old acquaintance." He smiled fondly. "Almost as old as you, bug."

Truzenzuzex trilled a thranx laugh. "I will issue the invitation. Up the universe, pulpskin."

Tse-Mallory offered an appropriately acerbic rejoinder as the philosoph turned to the nearest visual pickup.

There was nothing noteworthy about the appearance of the shuttle that detached from the new ship and made its way toward the *Teacher.* It was automatically guided into the appropriate bay. Then there was nothing for the two scientists to do but wait.

The visitors arrived on the bridge within moments. A dozen men and women, they were armed with neuronic weaponry that was not only viciously efficient but could safely be employed inside a ship without any risk to the integrity of its hull. They were also, Tse-Mallory reflected as he sized them up one by one, a somewhat motley-looking group. While a few individuals moved with the ease and grace of those who have had martial training, others appeared unsure of themselves and in questionable physical condition. The control chamber had become crowded, reducing the advantage of numbers in any conflict. Mentally, he started listing options. Doubtless Truzenzuzex was doing the same. He and his friend were old, but in a fight an elderly well-trained soldier is always a better bet than a young and inept civilian.

Then one more figure stepped into the room and everything he had been thinking was overturned.

The woman was tall and striking, with close-cropped blond hair and jet-black eyes. Tse-Mallory would have said that those corneas offered a window into her soul, except that he did not perceive the existence of one. Though she moved with the animal authority of a Qwarm and projected a barely contained ferocity, there was nothing else to indicate whether she might be a member of that murderous Guild. Certainly her attire was far removed from that favored by the professional assassins.

Those who had preceded her made way for her. As they did so they exhibited a deference that went beyond what was normally accorded a leader or chief. It took Tse-Mallory a moment to categorize the reaction he was observing.

They were afraid of her.

Halting, she stood silently as one of the armed but patently less threatening men stepped forward to confront the two scientists.

"We are of the Order of Null," he announced calmly.

Tse-Mallory kept his expression unreadable. "I know you people. You're the ultimate nihilists."

The man smiled slightly. "We have our beliefs, yes." Looking past man and thranx, he indicated the glowing red sphere that was visible through the foreport and beyond the great disk of the *Teacher*'s Caplis generator. "We require, nay demand, the death of the person presently within that scarlet orb."

Truzenzuzex could no longer stand the not-knowing. "How are you aware of his presence there, *sil!!ak*? How do you know his name? And how did you find the means for traveling to this place?" His wing cases fairly shook with frustration. "You could not have tracked this ship all the way from the depths of the Blight! You could not have tracked it the instant we initiated changeover and entered space-plus. Such a thing is not possible!"

At his words, the striking woman came forward. Tse-Mallory noted the deference the much larger and stronger speaker displayed as he stepped aside for her. The sociologist also noted, perhaps even more significantly, that among all the boarders she alone was not armed.

"You're right, insect." She employed the insult casually, as if unaware of its import and indifferent to its possible effect. Truzenzuzex ignored it. Contenders within his chosen fields of expertise regularly employed far more stylish invective. "It is impossible to follow a ship through space-plus. The obvious corollary therefore is that we did not follow your ship."

When neither scientist responded, she laughed loudly. With proper modulation the sound could have been as attractive as the rest of her, Tse-Mallory reflected. Except that it was cracked and broken, more a musical bray than an expression of delight.

"If you didn't follow the ship . . . ?" he prodded her.

Obsidian eyes looked right through him. "It seems that subsequent to our last encounter six years ago, I find it has become easier and easier to locate my brother."

Sociologist and philosoph gaped. In his conversations with them, Flinx had more than once made offhand mention of a half sister. He had told them that she was an Adept like himself, the only other survivor of the outlawed and disbanded Meliorare Society's genetic experiments, a girl of unknown abilities. Except that the person standing before them was no longer a girl.

"You are," Tse-Mallory whispered as he stared back at her, "Mahnahmi."

"Not the same Mahnahmi Flinx has told you about." Her gaze raked the room. "I'm older, stronger. More in tune with myself. I'm sure you're aware that as Flinx has aged he has gained more control of his abilities. Though we are different, in that respect we are the same. I can do things now that I could only inexactly envision the last time he and I—met. This, for example."

Something caught Tse-Mallory's brain in a vise. Reaching up, he grabbed at the side of his head and staggered. Next to him, Truzenzuzex had half collapsed to the floor. The philosoph's antennae stood out straight and stiff from his skull and a steady low whistle emerged from his collapsing spiracles. As fast as it had hit, the pain went away.

Blinking to clear his blurred vision, Tse-Mallory stared at her. She was not smiling, not laughing quietly. Just studying the two of them the way he and Tru would have devoted similar attention to any experiment.

"Six years ago I was just learning how to do that." She spoke as calmly as if she had just used a tissue to wipe at a speck of dirt. "I'm much, much better at it now." She started toward him. A defiant Tse-Mallory held his ground, but she was not interested in a physical confrontation. Walking past him, she stopped to gaze out the foreport at the hovering, luminant red sphere.

"My brother. The only one like me. The only one who could reasonably give me trouble or cause me grief. My mind is linked to his. He's like a disease I can't shake. His continued existence infects me when I'm in important meetings, announces itself to me when I'm trying to make critical decisions, wakes me when I sleep." She turned back to the two attentive scientists.

"Sometime after our last meeting I learned of these good people here and of their organization. Through various means and channels I informed them that there was one individual who might, just might, somehow be able to interfere with the impending apocalypse they revere. At first they didn't believe me. Nothing merely mortal, they insisted, could possibly affect in any way the coming cleansing. I was able to show them certain things, provide information that would otherwise have been unavailable to them. Though not all were convinced that he posed a danger to their agenda, I succeeded in convincing enough of them that there was no harm in taking precautions.

"Unfortunately, despite everything I told them and showed them, despite my warnings and admonitions, they did not prepare adequately when they attempted to eliminate Flinx on New Riviera. When I arrived, in hopes of cleaning up the mess they had made, I discovered that he had left for a world that, while not a part of the AAnn Empire, was dominated by it." She turned introspective.

"I completely lost track of him there, on a world called Jast. It was exceedingly strange, almost as if he had died. For the first time in a very long while I was unable to perceive his presence. Though unable to verify his apparent passing, I departed and returned to looking after my considerable interests.

"It was about a year later that I sensed his existence anew. It shocked me, I can tell you. How could I have been so stupid? I should have known that my brother could not be guaranteed dead until I saw his body and verified its demise with my own eyes. As soon as I was able to do so, I went after him. I missed him at Repler, then at Visaria, and lastly at Gestalt. I lost him again when he disappeared with you into the Blight." Now she did smile again. "But when you emerged I thought I was ready again. I and my friends of similar intent raced to the Senisran system only to have my intimation of Flinx's continued existence vanish. Nothing remained of him to be perceived.

"But in lieu of his presence there was a device. The sort of mechanism for which my brother demonstrates a remarkable and repeated affinity. We explored it, we entered it, and it brought us here." She gestured toward the foreport and the intensely luminous sphere beyond. "The instant we emerged in this place I recognized this ship of his—and simultaneously perceived his presence." Turning away from the two scientists, ignoring them as if they did not exist, she stared once more out the port in the direction of the resplendent red orb.

"Now it will end here. *He* will end here. And I will at last be free of the nuisance he represents. Of the last two Adepts propounded by the Meliorares, only one will survive."

Tse-Mallory didn't hesitate. "If you've associated yourself with these people, then you know full well what they believe and support. You've said as much. If the abomination that's headed this way from outside our galaxy is allowed to proceed unchecked, it will annihilate everything. Every world, every sun, every civilization. The entire galactic disk will disappear into it, after which it will move on to devour others."

Cocking her head slightly to her right, she studied the burly sociologist. Her tone was appallingly, unspeakably, indifferent. "I know. But by then I'll be dead. My life will have been a glorious one, replete with individual aggrandizement and the accumulation of personal power. Small payback for what the Meliorares made of me." Her gaze narrowed sharply. "For what certain individuals did to me. I won't allow Flinx or anyone else to jeopardize my recompense. It is my due. I am owed."

"What about civilization, the lives of hundreds of billions of other sentient individuals? What are they owed?"

She shrugged. "A one-way ticket to the hell of their choice, for all I care. Let them all perish. Let so-called civilization return to dust. Allow the Order's descendants to happily greet the apocalypse. It means nothing to me and I care nothing for any of it."

She spoke so nonchalantly, Tse-Mallory thought. Having been compelled to contemplate destruction on a galactic scale, he now found himself confronting egocentricity of similar magnitude. It was scarce to be believed. But in discussing the ultimate horrors she so casually dismissed she was being absolutely truthful. He could hear it in her voice, see it in her eyes.

So badly hurt had she been, so deep and immutable was her personal fury, that she *wanted* the universe to go to perdition.

That was when Truzenzuzex, with the still formidable power of all six of his legs, launched himself.

Several of the Order members brought up their weapons. They were too late. Notwithstanding his advanced age the philosoph was astonishingly quick. But not, alas, quicker than the mind. Something came out of the woman Mahnahmi—something as poisonous as it was powerful. It caught Truzenzuzex and threw him across the control chamber to smash into the far wall. As he lay there twitching, alive but hurt, Tse-Mallory rushed to his side. He did not try to take advantage of his friend's attack to make a similar run at Flinx's half sister. The soldier-sociologist was brave, but not foolhardy. It would do no one any good, least of all an unaware Flinx, if he too was injured.

Truzenzuzex was whistling his pain, but nothing appeared to be seriously damaged. A human thus flung aside would probably have broken bones. A thranx's chitinous exoskeleton could take tougher punishment. Tse-Mallory looked back over his shoulder at the beautiful deformation that was the product of another of the Meliorares' many biological missteps.

"If your aim is Flinx's death, why bother to board this ship? If you know that he's inside the red orb, why didn't you just destroy it the instant you arrived?"

The tip of her tongue stroked first her upper lip, then the lower. "All in good time, old man. A death delayed is a death magnified. A demise shared is a demise savored. I've worked a long time to reach this moment. Don't try to talk me out of my pleasure." She indicated their surroundings. "I know those who built this vessel for him. I wanted to see it for myself. I wanted to see what kind of friends he had made." She locked eyes with the irate sociologist. Did she ever blink? he wondered.

"You will watch him die," Mahnahmi murmured contentedly. "Then I will kill you both. After that I will try to make a prize of this ship. If not . . ." She shrugged again. "It will be enough to have made the attempt. As for this astonishing place, whatever it is, wherever it is, it will return to the obscurity from which my brother has only momentarily resuscitated it."

Rising from the injured Truzenzuzex's side, Tse-Mallory favored her with a stare of wizened incredulity. "You don't realize the significance of these surroundings, do you? You followed Flinx's ship without having the slightest notion of where it might lead. As we stand here talking you still have no idea how far you've come or what wonderment surrounds you."

"I don't know and I couldn't care less," she shot back. "If I can't exploit it for my own ends, then as far as I'm concerned it's just another grandiose alien folly. Like most follies, one probably better off forgotten."

She would have continued—except that the ongoing, rambling, half-mad declamation that preoccupied her and claimed her full attention was interrupted by a pair of unexpected arrivals. The newcomers to the conversation were not members of her entourage and did not subscribe to their beliefs or to their leader's objectives. Having carried out a necessarily hasty but nonetheless efficient reconnoiter of the state of affairs extant in the *Teacher*'s control chamber, the newcomers proceeded to take steps to rectify them.

CHAPTER
28

As a fully anointed padre in the Security Services of the United Church, Sylzenzuzex never traveled anywhere without the personal armaments that were part of her private kit. She would have felt naked without them. Opportunely, though each was designed to be manipulated by small, four-digited thranx hands, at least one of the weapons was sufficiently undemanding that Clarity could operate it.

With their ordnance tuned for in-ship combat, the two females used the entry portal for cover as they fired repeatedly into the control chamber. Their fully-charged shockers brought down several members of the Order of Null before the survivors managed to find some cover of their own and return fire. Adding to the confusion, Scrap had launched herself from Clarity's shoulder. Streaking around the bridge just below the ceiling, dodging the panicky shots of increasingly flustered Order members, the flying snake spat death at those attempting to conceal themselves.

Holding herself aloof from and ignoring the pandemonium swirling around her, Mahnahmi's eyes narrowed as she sought the source of the unexpected counterattack. But dominant as she was, she was no different from her brother in at least one respect: she could only concentrate on one threat at a time. As she prepared to squeeze Clarity's mind to a lump of enflamed meat incapable of conscious thought, a heavy male body slammed into her from behind. Though as an offensive strategy the primitive assault harkened back to tactics that had been employed since dawn of humankind, it was still uncompromisingly effective. As chaos and death filled the ship's control chamber and raged around them, Tse-Mallory and Flinx's half sister went down in a heap.

His awareness that something was amiss having been stimulated by the arrival and subsequent actions of his half sister, Flinx had little by little grown dimly aware of the confrontation that had now given way to out-and-out combat onboard his ship. While a small part of him continued to agonize over the conflict that was physically out of his reach, the bulk of his concentration remained focused on sustaining the bonds that were beginning to stir the incomprehensibly vast forces swirling around him.

With Flinx and Pip at its core, the triangle of concentration held firm and continued to function.

On board the *Teacher,* an enraged Mahnahmi let loose the full fury that was herself. The uncontrolled ferocity picked up Tse-Mallory and tossed him aside as if he had been flicked away by a giant invisible hand. Reaching out with her misshapen mind, she came down hard on Sylzenzuzex with the mental equivalent of a blow from a hammer. Dropping her weapons, the padre fell to the deck unconscious. A force akin to that which had pitched first Truzenzuzex and then Tse-Mallory into the far wall slammed Scrap straight up into the ceiling. When it drew back, the minidrag fell to the floor insensible.

Surrounded by the dead and injured, Mahnahmi stepped over moaning or motionless bodies as she advanced on the entrance to the control room. Seeing her coming, Clarity swung the muzzle of her weapon around to fire at the malevolent, commanding figure. Before she could depress the trigger, something set fire to her optic nerves. Crying out, she dropped the thranx pistol and fell backward, clutching at her burning eyes. As she lay on the floor, sobbing and moaning from the pain, Mahnahmi halted between her and the comatose Sylzenzuzex.

"Two females." Flinx's half sister sniffed contemptuously. "Two different species. Two fools. The only question remaining is, do I kill you slowly for the damage you've inflicted on my pitiful but still occasionally useful associates, or do I not waste the time and dispatch you with alacrity?" Kneeling, she picked up the weapon the now helpless Clarity had dropped. Handling it as if it were a jewel-encrusted necklace, she turned it slowly in her fingers as she admired the typically fine thranx workmanship.

"A toy from Evoria. I like toys. Let's see what this one does." Straightening, she aimed it at the back of Clarity's skull as her forefinger felt for the trigger.

Within the increasingly active sphere whose periphery was now blowing off scarlet sparks like a miniature red sun, Flinx found that he was gradually able to recognize more clearly what was happening on board the *Teacher*. He perceived Clarity's terror, fended off Mahnahmi's hatred, touched upon the pain of friend and foe alike whose bodies were scattered throughout the control chamber. They all needed his help, but Clarity's immediate situation took precedence over everything else.

Everything—except what he was doing. Everything except what he had come for. The future of civilization and the fate of the galaxy was at stake.

So—was—his—future.

STAY WITH YOURSELF, the cetacea of Cachalot counseled him uneasily.

BE WHAT YOU ARE, the Krang on Booster ordered him.

!!#*ζζωωω!, insisted the green pervasiveness of Midworld.

Clarity! He felt himself drowning in anguish. What good to save everything and everyone else if he lost the only thing in the cosmos that really mattered to him?

STAY—BE— *!!!^* the tripartite power resounded inside his head.

Something was on the verge of igniting. Not igniting, he told himself restlessly. It was on the cusp of exploding. No, it would not be an explosion either, he realized. Something magnificent, something unprecedented, something on a scale so vast it could only be even faintly comprehended within the realm of mathematics humanxkind had yet to discover.

HOLD ON, the cetacea exhorted him as they embraced him tighter in the depths of their warmth.

HOLD ON, the Krang commanded with the cold authority of eons.

!!☼!!, somehow elucidated the Midworld world-mind.

On board the *Teacher*, keeping the recovered thranx pistol pointed at Clarity's forehead, Mahnahmi pulled her communit and addressed it with serene iciness.

This child's play has gone on long enough, she decided brusquely.

"Caron, proceed as we discussed and obliterate that ball of blushing energy, or whatever it is. Use whatever means you think necessary. I'll be returning shortly." She glanced around the control chamber before returning her attention to the hurt, quietly moaning woman lying on the floor. "Just a little cleaning to finish up here." She started to slide the pistol's trigger.

Something yanked her off her feet.

Landing hard on her back, she found herself being dragged down the corridor between the unconscious female thranx and the weeping woman. Raising her head to look down at her feet she saw that several strong vines had wrapped themselves around her ankles. One was a striking cyan while the others were mostly dark green striped with yellow. The vines stretched all the way around the far end of the corridor.

How absurd, she thought as she was pulled along. *Another futile, time-wasting interruption.* Would the thranx weapon have an effect on the inexplicably aggressive vegetation? Raising the pistol and aiming it at the tugging green creepers just below her feet, she was impatient to find out.

On board the other ship, crew and members of the Order of Null prepared to fulfill their superior's directive. Potent armaments that did not belong on a commercial transport, that should not even have been in private hands, were activated. As these were brought to bear on the shimmering, fiery red orb that floated between them and the captured vessel, one of the innumerable crimson sparks that were being cast off from the side of the sphere came scintillating and spinning toward the visitor. Caron saw it coming. He frowned, then shrugged. While dazzlingly bright, the spark was no bigger than his little finger. Lifting his communit to his lips, he prepared to give the order to fire.

The spark touched the ship.

From Caplis generator to living quarters, from bridge to shuttlebay, the sturdy, ample craft was engulfed in primordial flame. In the space of several seconds—during which those aboard did not even have time to scream—it was reduced to a handful of blackened cinders floating in emptiness.

There's something else I have to do, Flinx thought forcefully.

This time no objection was flung back to him. Not from ocean-dwelling deliberators, not from calculating alien machine, not from convergently coherent alien flora.

Maybe it was too late for everything already, he told himself. Maybe his fractional loss of focus had weakened the trilateral nexus to such an extent that carrying on was impractical. He decided it did not matter. He had made his decision. He would try to do the impossible. He would try to concentrate on two things at once.

The triangle—held. He could not tell if its continuing coherence was for real or only an illusion he generated in his own mind to lend encouragement to what he was about to do.

He reached out one more time. Not to presences distant and alien but to something that was very close at hand. Close to him in more ways than he would have wished or could have explained.

Mahnahmi. Sister-half.

Having cut the vines holding her and once again standing over the increasingly feeble Clarity, the other surviving progeny of the Meliorares suddenly blinked and swayed slightly. The muzzle of the weapon she gripped wavered and her finger did not depress the trigger.

Get out of my head, brother!

I won't let you hurt anyone else.

Try and stop me. Go ahead—kill me if you can. I know that you can't. You couldn't aboard the alien artifact at Pyrassis. I don't think you can now.

The raw fury within her threatened to overwhelm him. It was primal, uncontrolled, and rife with feral intelligence. He fought back. It was if he was fighting himself.

Don't do this, Mahnahmi. Kill me if you must, but do it later. When I am finished with what I came to do here. Kill me, but let the galaxy live.

The emotional underpinnings of her reply were those of a soul ragged and torn. Lying against Flinx, a distraught Pip tried to filter that acid and agony.

Die now, die later; everything dies. Galaxies collide, suns go out. The universe is a cruel, dark, uncaring place. What do I care, what does it matter, if a little death arrives a little sooner for one insignificant pin-

wheel of stars? Let chaos and disorder sort out the consequences between them, I say, and damn the collusion of apathetic elements that brought me into being!

Her declamation was accompanied by the emotive equivalent of an all-encompassing sneer.

I'm going to kill this woman lying here before me, she continued remorselessly, *and next, the female bug lying next to her, and then your senile friends, and then I am going to kill you, brother. I'm going to do it because, unlike you, I can. What are you going to do about it?*

This, he told her. *I'm going to do it because, unlike you, I can.*

He reached out with everything that he was, everything that he had become in his too-long twenty-six years of hard existence. Everything that was in him, everything that was of him. He sensed her mind harden as she threw up her defenses.

And felt her recoil from his compassion.

It was the last thing she expected him to send her way.

His effort was not a solitary one. The cetacea were there with him. They draped around her an inescapable cocoon of such warmth, such sympathy, such understanding, that despite her mental howls of protest she could not ignore it. The Krang made itself known as well, saturating her mind with hundreds of thousands of years of lost history. It showed her the destruction of entire worlds, the unending war between the Tar-Aiym and their hereditary enemies the Hur'rikku, and the desolation and ultimate futility that was the eventual result of that ghastly colossal conflict. Lastly the group-mind of Midworld weighed in, an all-engulfing greenness that was at once the projection and representation of an entire planet whose globe-girdling organisms were bound together by the universal need simply to survive. Exploiting Flinx as a vector it reached out to enfold her.

The inexorable power of all that collective compassion beat back the interminable rage, smothered the blind fury, suffocated the bitterness that drove and nourished his half sister. She fought back ferociously, striking out blindly at the understanding that threatened to throttle her.

Nothing could withstand the force of that collective empathy. Not all the hate in the galaxy. Not even the embittered, shrunken soul of one as driven and obsessed as Mahnahmi. Her rage finally gave way.

Uttering a last defiant cry of hate she shook her fist at the heavens, and began to tremble. Sitting down slowly on the deck she put the gun carefully to one side, drew her legs up to her chest, wrapped her arms around her knees, and began to whimper. After a moment she started to rock back and forth, side to side. Deep inside her something had been exposed and, once exposed, could not be nonchalantly shoved aside or casually put back the way it had been.

Breathing hard, the pain behind her eyes finally beginning to subside, Clarity found herself staring at the devil-woman. Nearby, a bruised and battered Sylzenzuzex was starting to regain consciousness. After a few moments a hesitant Clarity started forward on hands and knees. Reaching out, she swept the thranx weapon aside. It skittered roughly across the deck. The striking blond woman made no attempt to grab for it.

Jet-black eyes rose to meet Clarity's own. Their gaze was blank, utterly blank. There was no maliciousness in them now, no visceral loathing, no homicidal yearning. There was just—nothing.

The woman leaned toward her. Clarity started to draw back, hesitated, and held her ground. The moans of the injured filled the control chamber. Advancing on hands and knees, the woman came closer, closer. Halting, she dropped her head and lay down on her side. With her head in Clarity's lap she drew her knees all the way up to her chest and lay silently, staring into oblivion. All the hatred within her had been asphyxiated, leaving nothing behind but a riddle.

Within the crimson sphere, where there was no time and no space, Flinx in his near-comatose state recognized that Clarity was safe. A great surge of relief rushed through him, a relief born of the exhaustion that arises out of desperate circumstances. Meanwhile, the cetacea held him together, the Krang held him up, and the greenness became one with him. On his chest, the emotional lens that was Pip convulsed as all that care and concern flooded through that inimitable part of her master's mind that marked him as a unique and unduplicatable accident.

Clarity's okay, he thought. He could refocus, redirect, rededicate himself. He proceeded to do so with everything he had and all that was in him. The result was that for the first time, the triangle opened fully to the key. The composite force of the multiple mind sources was unleashed. The fabrication the Xunca had contrived was activated.

The trigger was pulled on the Great Attractor.

For something that existed in the minds of the most advanced intelligences only as an abstract mathematical concept, the sudden surge of pooled charged gravitons had a decidedly quantifiable effect. So immense was the shaped thrust of forces that they punched a hole in the continuum itself.

In another part of the cosmos the brane that was the known universe split. Pressing forward at a velocity slightly more than incredible, the onrushing intrusion of another reality Flinx had called the Great Evil flowed into the unforeseen fissure. Before it could slow itself, before it could react, before it could even recognize what had happened, each and every iota of its annihilating malevolence spilled into the newly ajar congruent universe. The resulting shock wave was so powerful that it sent a ripple through all of space-time. The path of galaxies was slightly altered, including that of the local group of which the Milky Way was but a part.

Though this greatest single burst of energy since the universe formed was highly localized, its aftereffects would still have shredded groups of galaxies for millions of megaparsecs around—if not for the fact that within nanoseconds of its advent it commenced to collapse back upon itself. The fracture in the continuum closed and the impossible-to-measure flow of charged gravitons was sucked back into the very cleft they had created, leaving an improbably straight line of newly forming stars and nebulae in their wake. Upon discovering this singular astronomical phenomenon some time in the future, human physicists with a spiritual turn of mind would dub it God's Ruler, not realizing that its agent was actually a long-dead representative of their own kind.

Subsequent to The Event, several seemingly unrelated occurrences took place simultaneously throughout the length and breadth of the Commonwealth.

On its inner border, a powerful automated distress call suddenly flashed outward through space-minus from a world notorious for winking in and out of reality. Responding to the unexpected call from Quofum, a Commonwealth peaceforcer dispatched to that anomalous world found three scientists who had been marooned there. Two human and one thranx, they had been reported missing four years earlier and had been presumed lost.

In his official report, the commander of the rescuing vessel made a point of emphasizing two anomalies: for individuals who had been deprived of humanx company and resources for such an extended period, the trio were in good, even remarkable health. Additionally, and despite repeated scanning and the carrying-out of a thorough search, he and his crew had been unable to establish the actual source of the mystifying distress signal.

On the world called Comagrave, a xenoarchaeologist named Arleen Mapelle was hard at work at a well-known subterranean site, one of several where the famous technologically advanced preserving mausoleums of Comagrave's inhabitants had been excavated. At that moment she was busily entering information into a sybfile that would later be uploaded to her department's allocated segment of the planetary shell.

It was late and she was nervous. Not because of her striking environs: in the course of her monthlong stay on Comagrave she had grown used to the breathtaking solitude and grand surroundings of the vast underground chamber. No, as a recent graduate embarking on her first field assignment, she feared making a mistake or incorrectly entering data into the relevant sybfile.

The strange feeling that now crept over her caused her to turn from the communit over which she was laboring.

One of the hundreds of thousands of identical transparent cylinders that lined the interior of the immense underground chamber stood nearby. Tinted indigo, swathed in fragile vitreous golden filaments like fossilized baby's breath, it had been carefully removed from its place among its ranked fellows so that it could be studied more easily. The difficult move had entailed stretching and repositioning the dozens of delicate conduits and strands that connected it to the row from which it had been extricated. Held in suspension within the cylinder, or pod, was a slender, long-faced being of somber mien and spindly build.

Searching for the source of the odd sensation that had caused her to interrupt her work, she eventually found herself looking down at her feet. A dark wetness had pooled up beneath her left sandal. When she inclined her foot to one side, the dampness made contact with her bare skin. Frowning, she bent over to examine the liquid. It had not come from the protein drink that still sat upright on the console in front of her: the container was intact. Then what was its source? Raising her gaze, she followed the shadowy trickle. It led sideways to the base of the cylinder. Her eyes suddenly got very, very big.

The cylinder was open. Seeping out the bottom was the rest of the gel it had contained. The elongated horizontal eyes of the slender being inside were wide open and staring straight back at her. As she looked on, too frozen to scream, yell, or say anything, one of the being's two upper limbs started to twitch.

Rising from her chair she stumbled backward, tripped over a storage case, and fell. Dazed, she picked herself up. As she did so, her gaze happened to fall over the side of the walkway that was occupied by the archaeological station. Beyond stretched the immense preservation chamber, one of many buried deep in the bedrock of Comagrave. Like the others, this one held several million of the planet's indigenous inhabitants, each conserved for posterity in individual, highly oxygenated, gel-filled cylinders.

Row by row, tier by tier, room by gigantic room, each of them was opening.

Dimly, in the back of her simultaneously enthralled, terrified, awestruck mind, it occurred to her that this defining moment might make a worthwhile subject for formal observation. But despite her excellent training she was too paralyzed by the sight to pick up her communit or her recorder. No one would have blamed her.

Before her eyes, in their ritual gowns and ceremonial preservation attire, the Sauun of Comagrave, who for hundreds of thousands of years, out of collective racial fear of some unknown, irresistible peril had sealed themselves away far beneath the surface of their planet, were starting to wake up.

Donning survival suits, Tse-Mallory and Sylzenzuzex went out and brought Flinx and Pip back to the *Teacher* the instant the resplendent red sphere vanished. No explosion marked its passing and nothing remained in its luminescent wake to indicate that it had ever been. One moment it hovered in the exact center of the protective plasma bubble; the next it was gone, leaving behind only a lonely figure in an unscarred survival suit floating in white emptiness. Whatever had obliterated the vessel crewed by members of the Order of Null had not harmed Flinx.

Upon determining that his warped, crazed half sister Mahnahmi had lapsed into an infantile regressive coma from which she showed no sign of emerging, Truzenzuzex and Clarity had sedated her and secured her in an empty cabin. Performing the same service for the surviving but wounded members of the Order of Null, they then were able to join their companions in turning their full attention to Flinx.

Stripping him out of the survival suit, they carefully laid him out in the *Teacher*'s tiny, infrequently used dispensary and waited while the ship's instrumentation examined him. A pile of brightly colored iridescent blue and pink coils on a nearby folded towel, a twitching Pip was slowly returning to awareness.

Snuffling uncontrollably, Clarity peered down at the motionless figure on the padded table. Perched on her left shoulder, Scrap stretched out to lick tears from her master's cheeks. Flinx's eyes remained shut and his chest did not move.

"Is—is he dead?" She had to struggle to get her voice above a whisper.

"No." The *Teacher* responded calmly as attenuated probes and medical scanners mounted on the ends of flexible mechanical arms passed back and forth over the lean masculine shape.

Clarity sucked in air. "Then he's alive."

"No," the ship declared, repeating itself.

"Explain your diagnosis," Tse-Mallory demanded smartly.

The *Teacher* responded in the same unvarying tone it had employed since it had begun the examination. "He is barely taking in oxygen. Despite what you may see, his heart continues to beat, but at a rate slowed to five percent of normal. His pulse is present, but barely. Yet his brain exhibits functionality that is not merely normal but considerably heightened. Cerebral regions customarily quiescent in all humans are presently active."

"My head is killing me," a voice unexpectedly mumbled from the table, "but that's nothing new."

"*Flinx!*" Heedless of any effect it might have on him, Clarity threw herself at the table and did her best to wrap him in her arms.

Responding to the contact, his chest suddenly gave a great swell upward. His mammoth intake of breath could have been heard all the way to the front of the ship. As his lungs contracted, he coughed violently.

"As an aid to improved respiration," a startled but joyful Sylzenzuzex suggested as she looked on, "you might begin by removing a present impediment to his breathing."

"Oh, right. Sorry." Disengaging her mouth from Flinx's, an abashed Clarity stepped back. But she did not let go of his right hand, which continued to dangle over the side of the table. She wasn't sure she would ever let go of it again.

Placing a calloused palm beneath his young friend's back, Tse-Mallory helped Flinx to sit up. "How are you doing, m'boy?"

Flinx looked over at his mentor. "I'm not sure, but if my memory of recent events is valid, your 'boy' may just possibly have saved everything." Searching his immediate surroundings, he located Pip. Leaning toward her, he used both hands to pick up the limp pile of coils. The minidrag's wings drooped with exhaustion, but when he placed her in his lap her head came up almost immediately. Slitted pupils met round ones. It was enough to reassure them both.

"Then it worked, *zrin!!tt!*"

Standing at the foot of the table where he had been monitoring Flinx's sluggish recovery, Truzenzuzex broke into a little dance. Though he had known his mentor for a very long time, Flinx mused that he had never witnessed anything like the philosoph's current physical expression of sheer joy. Looking on, he marveled at the elderly thranx's ability to execute intricate steps and twirls without getting all those legs tangled up.

"I think it did," he affirmed. "I hope so. It felt—right. A great many things felt right." Sudden thoughts of what was right and what was not caused him to look around sharply. Pip looked up in alarm.

"Mahnahmi," Flinx said tightly.

Tse-Mallory met his concern as well as his gaze. "In a coma. Reverted to infancy, or a condition approximating it." He stared hard at his young friend. "Your doing?"

Reaching up, Flinx felt gingerly of the back of his head. To his great relief, it was still there. "I can't say for sure, but I think it might be. There was a lot happening all at the same time. I'm not definite on all the details of what took place or how. One thing I do know for certain: it wasn't all me. I had help."

Truzenzuzex eyed him quizzically. "Help? You were alone when we sent you out there. You were alone when we brought you back. Did someone or something come to you while you were locked inside the sphere?"

"Something like that," Flinx told him. "Old acquaintances, of a kind. Of several kinds, actually. It was all a dreaming, of course." He tapped his forehead with the middle and forefinger of his left hand. "All brought to fruition here. How it was realized I could not begin to tell you. That's how my life has been, Tru. Driven and governed and impelled forward by things I cannot begin to explain."

Tse-Mallory grunted softly. "While Flinx's testimony is encouraging, we still need to validate the effectiveness of his efforts through other sources. We can't do that until we return to a developed world where we can make use of advanced astronomical facilities." Reaching behind him, Tse-Mallory slipped his young friend's jumpsuit off a hanger and passed the bundle of fabric to its owner. "Until then, we will assume at least a modicum of success." He eyed his companions. "To do otherwise would be to capitulate to wretchedness and despair." A broad smile creased his deeply lined face as he turned back to Flinx.

"Now get dressed. Tru and I are anxious to hear in detail everything that happened to you while you were out of contact. Or at the very least, everything that you *think* happened to you."

"And I will make it my responsibility to check on our guests." Sylzenzuzex started out of the dispensary. "They will be very unhappy to learn that we believe that Flinx has, with the aid of the Xunca apparatus, eliminated the rationale for the continued existence of their disagreeable Order."

When the others had departed, Clarity once again moved close to Flinx, looking on as he slowly continued dressing. Utterly fatigued, Pip remained sprawled on the now empty table. Spreading his wings, an energetic Scrap glided down to join her.

"Is there anything, Flinx, I can get you? Anything I can do for you?"

Sealing the front of the jumpsuit, he smiled tenderly down at her. What this woman had been through because of him no human being ought to have had to endure, he thought. That she had done so, had done all of it, of her own free will and out of love for him did not to any degree mitigate the sacrifices she had made on his behalf.

It was a good thing he kept such musings to himself, because had he voiced them aloud she would have told him he was being seriously silly.

Putting her arms around him, she placed her head against his chest and squeezed tight. He hugged her gently and rested his head lightly on hers.

"You may have saved civilization," she murmured. "Time and time again you've risked your life to preserve it, and no one except those on board this ship will ever know what you've done." Leaning back slightly, she looked up to meet his gaze. "You're fated to be the Commonwealth's illustrious but anonymous savior, Philip Lynx."

He nodded slowly, thinking how utterly, supremely, incomparably beautiful she was.

"Clarity, that suits me just fine."

The physicians and the secure medical shell at the advanced long-term care-and-repair facility on Earth to whose guardianship they commended Mahnahmi accepted the unique case without too many questions. Preliminary diagnostics hinted at severe long-term paralysis of selected neural connections. There was a significant chance, Flinx and his companions were told, that even if repairs could be effected to the damaged areas, full recovery of memory and other functions was unlikely. The patient would live—after a fashion, and with her capacity for higher cognition much reduced.

Without suffering so much as a twinge of irony, Flinx made arrangements to pay for her extended treatment and care.

The downcast surviving members of the Order of Null were repatriated to their respective homeworlds and set free to spread the word that the whole foundation for their continuation as an organized society had vanished. The same surreptitious monitoring of sophisticated Commonwealth astronomical instrumentation that had originally established that phenomenon as a reality now confirmed its disappearance. Having nothing left to work toward, the Order's chapters disbanded one by one.

Despite that, lingering die-hard elements that either did not receive the word or chose to disbelieve it continued to pose a potential threat. Bearing that possibility in mind, it was decided not to return to New

Riviera/Nur. Having previously spent time on and caused a certain amount of trouble on Earth, Flinx felt that humankind's homeworld should also for the foreseeable future remain out of his purview. Booster was too remote and desolate to constitute a realistic refuge. Both he and Clarity had flawed memories of Longtunnel. Of the other worlds that he was familiar with, Jast was too unstable, Visaria down-right unpleasant, Repler pregnant with discomfiture, Gestalt too cold and full of meaning, and Midworld—as much a part of him as it had become, it was still not the kind of place where one would want to spend a honeymoon.

Honeymoon? Wasn't he getting a little ahead of himself?

Then he noticed Pip and her son, Scrap, writhing and play-striking at one another on the folded towel and he knew he had his answer.

It was, to say the least, an uncommon ceremony.

As just one example, few couples could boast of a full thranx Eint as the Conductor of Services. Though he had never before presided over such a rite, much less one involving humans, Truzenzuzex was fully qualified and considered it a privilege to do so. Tse-Mallory was equally tickled to be asked to give away the bride. And no one could recall when a thranx, not to mention a full padre in the Security Services of the United Church, had been asked to serve as a bridesmaid at the peculiarly human ritual. Though uncertain as to her exact role, Sylzen-zuzex was willing to be so conscripted.

Standing in a field of green surrounded by one of the many extensive stretches of rain forest on Alaspin, the early-morning wedding party was serenaded by a cacophonous assortment of indigenous life-forms that had not the slightest idea as to the nature of the strange exercise taking place in their midst. Tolerating occasional inspection from the occasional curious wild minidrag, Pip and Scrap looked on from a particularly well-sited tree.

It was left to the ring-bearer to fill out the multispecies character of the ceremony. Though its purpose was utterly unfamiliar to Kiijeem, Fourth-born of the Family AVM and present on Alaspin thanks to a special diplomatic dispensation arranged by Truzenzuzex and Tse-Mallory, the modus operandi was straightforward enough. Walk a few steps, maintain a serious mien, hand over a circlet of bright metal, and in the process try not to hit anyone with your tail. Having concluded this undertaking without inflicting any damage or outrage, the young AAnn noble was surprised at how relieved he felt when he was finally able to step clear of the others.

A few very close acquaintances of the group looked on from nearby. Among them was a short, gimlet-eyed, seriously antique woman who kept the integrated cooling setting on her clothing cranked as cold as possible while she waited impatiently for the seemingly interminable proceedings to end.

"Knew that boy would spend too much on frivolities. Damned unnecessary expensive get-together!" Brought from Moth, Mother Mastiff could hardly wait for it all to end so she could get back to Drallar. She did not trust the man she had left in charge of her shop. Though a lifelong friend, he would not have been offended by her assessment. Mother Mastiff trusted no one and nobody.

"At least," she muttered to herself as she used a handkerchief to mop dribs of the omnipresent heat and humidity from her forehead, "it looks like he found himself a nice girl. Maybe she'll be able to keep him from wasting his life."

An unpretentious reception followed the formal ceremony, after which the exceedingly dissimilar members of the party departed to diverse and sometimes distant regions of the Commonwealth and beyond. Tse-Mallory and Truzenzuzex to Hivehom, where closing studies of the Great Evil and its inexplicable disappearance were being hotly debated among those select scientists who had been aware of its existence. Kiijeem, Fourth-born of the Family AVM, having gained much status from his unprecedented excursion to and experience of a Commonwealth world previously unvisited by his kind, set out upon his long and carefully monitored journey homeward.

Sylzenzuzex returned to her work with United Church Security, vowing to stay in touch with her new friends as well as with her esteemed Eighth. At Alaspin's only large shuttleport, Mother Mastiff deigned to deposit a peck on Flinx's cheek and a slightly longer one on Clarity's prior to her departure for Moth.

"A strange boy, he is," she grumbled as she prepared to take her leave. "Always was. But he has a good heart. I was never able to keep him out of trouble. Maybe you'll have better luck." Before Clarity could offer a reply the old woman let out a disdainful snort and turned away, heading for the final boarding area as her last words lingered behind her. "But I doubt it."

Looking for a safe place to relax at last, the new couple chose to settle on Cachalot. It proved the perfect choice. The small human population was too busy to have time to pry into the lives of new arrivals. Flinx and Clarity could spend the majority of their time on an automated sailing ship out of sight and out of contact with the rest of the civilization he had saved, and whenever they found themselves isolated or in need of company there always seemed to be a chatty cetacean escort ready to accompany their rented craft. The climate was semitropical, the alien sea idyllic, and for the first time in memory Flinx was untroubled by his persistent headaches.

So it was that after several weeks Clarity was surprised to find him sitting one morning on the prow of their craft, staring out to sea and looking uncertain and depressed. Pip lay coiled sound asleep around his right arm and shoulder, her iridescent scales shimmering in the sun.

"Flinx?"

He looked back at her and mustered a halfhearted smile. She could not have surprised him, she knew. You couldn't surprise Philip Lynx, who felt your feelings coming. She sat down beside him, letting her bare legs dangle off the front of the boat. White spume gurgled merrily beneath the bow. Gliding skalats, the sunlight shining through their quadruple membranous wings, hovered off the starboard side, riding the same breeze that drove the boat forward.

"Is everything all right?" Sudden alarm shot through her. "The thing that was coming this way, the Great Evil—it *is* gone, isn't it? All of it?"

He nodded. "It's gone, Clarity. All of it."

"Then," she inquired uncertainly, "what's wrong?"

Turning away from her so she would not have to gaze upon his melancholy visage, he stared out to sea. The horizon was distant, flat, and calm. Only when after a while her hand came up to rest gently on his arm did he look back at her. Though she felt that by now she knew him as well as anyone possibly could, his expression at that moment was quite unreadable.

"Is it me?" she asked in a timid, apprehensive voice.

"No. Oh, no, Clarity!" The verve of his reaction reassured her, though it did nothing to reveal the source of his apparent discontent. "Nothing about you could *ever* disappoint me."

"Well then," she prodded him a little more forcefully, "what *is* it?"

He looked away again and it struck her then that he was not upset. It seemed, actually, that he might in fact be just a little embarrassed. He did not, could not, meet her eyes.

"I'm—bored."

About the Author

ALAN DEAN FOSTER has written more than a hundred books in a variety of genres, including hard science fiction, fantasy, horror, detective, western, historical, and contemporary fiction. He is the author of the *New York Times* bestseller *Star Wars: The Approaching Storm* and the popular Pip & Flinx novels, as well as novelizations of several films, including *Transformers, Star Wars,* the first three *Alien* films, and *Alien Nation.* His novel *Cyber Way* won the Southwest Book Award for Fiction in 1990, the first science fiction work ever to do so. Foster and his wife, JoAnn Oxley, live in Prescott, Arizona, in a house built of brick that was salvaged from an early-twentieth-century miners' brothel. He is currently at work on several new novels and media projects. For more about the author, go to www.alandeanfoster.com.

About the Type

This book was set in Times Roman, designed by Stanley Morrison specifically for *The Times* of London. The typeface was introduced in the newspaper in 1932. Times Roman had its greatest success in the United States as a book and commercial typeface, rather than one used in newspapers.